Praise for the novels of Naima Simone

"Simone balances crackling, electric love scenes with exquisitely rendered characters."
—*Entertainment Weekly*

"Passion, heat and deep emotion—Naima Simone is a gem!"
—*New York Times* bestselling author Maisey Yates

"Simone never falters in mining the complexity of two people who grow and heal and eventually love together."
—*New York Times* bestselling author Sarah MacLean

"Small-town charm, a colorful cast, and a hero to root for give this romance its legs as it moves toward a hard-earned happily ever after. [This] slow-burning romance is well worth the wait."
—*Publishers Weekly* on *The Road to Rose Bend*

"Simone masterfully balances heart and heat...building a convincing slow-burning romance."
—*Publishers Weekly* on *Christmas in Rose Bend*

"I am a huge Naima Simone fan. With her stories, she has the ability to transport you to places you can only dream of, with characters who have a realness to them."
—*Read Your Writes*

"[Naima Simone] excels at creating drama and emotional scenes as well as strong heroines who are resilient survivors."
—*Harlequin Junkie*

NAIMA SIMONE

The Single Dad Project

CANARY STREET PRESS

CANARY
STREET
PRESS™

Recycling programs
for this product may
not exist in your area.

ISBN-13: 978-1-335-44802-6

The Single Dad Project

Copyright © 2024 by Harlequin Enterprises ULC

The Single Dad Project
Copyright © 2024 by Naima Simone

The Husband Situation
Copyright © 2024 by Naima Simone

For questions and comments about the quality of this book,
please contact us at CustomerService@Harlequin.com.

TM is a trademark of Harlequin Enterprises ULC.

Canary Street Press
22 Adelaide St. West, 41st Floor
Toronto, Ontario M5H 4E3, Canada
CanaryStPress.com

Printed in U.S.A.

CONTENTS

THE SINGLE DAD PROJECT

To Gary. 143.

To Connie Marie Butts.
I'll miss you forever, and I'll love you longer than that.

CHAPTER ONE

A ONE-NIGHT STAND hadn't been on Florence "Flo" Dennison's bingo card, but who was she to argue when Fate wanted something for her?

And by *something* Flo meant big, bearded and sexy as get-on-your-knees-in-your-prayer-closet sin.

To think, she mused, lifting her Sam Adams to her mouth for a sip, she'd almost gone directly home on her return to Rose Bend, Massachusetts, after being away for two weeks instead of stopping by Road's End, the local—okay, the only—dive bar. Spending the past fifteen days in Thailand should've left her exhilarated. Tired from the travel but exhilarated. Instead, she was exhausted both physically and emotionally. And angry. So fucking angry.

She hadn't wanted to return to Kinsale Inn, the bed-and-breakfast her family owned as well as where they all lived, with this thick, dark tangle of…rage stuck to her ribs like glue. Her parents and whatever siblings were hanging around would take one look at her and deduce something was up. And then poke and prod until she either confessed or screamed. Or confessed *and* screamed. They were great and annoying like that.

But she didn't want either at the moment.

She just wanted to…wallow.

Wallow in her anger. Her hurt. At twenty-four, maybe that wasn't very adult of her, but there it was.

But now, looking at Big, Bearded and Sinful, she wanted something else.

To work it off.

And yes, if desperation threaded through that admission, well, again, there it was.

"Flo." Maddox Holt, owner of the bar, stopped in front of her, nodding at her with a smile. "You good? Need another beer?"

She shook her head, lowering the half-empty bottle to the bar top.

"No, I'm still working on this one. But—" she tipped the bottle toward the stranger at the other end of the bar "—you can refill whatever he's having. On me."

Maddox's dark auburn eyebrow arched high. Shaking his head, he rapped his knuckles on the wooden top, his smile widening into a grin. "I swear, you Dennison women never fail to make my evenings entertaining."

Since her sister Leo and sisters-in-law, Sydney and Nessa, regularly held their girls' nights here with their friends, Flo didn't doubt Maddox's words. They were all a handful when they got together. A hilarious, no-filter, show-tunes-when-drunk handful.

She smirked. "Well, I promise not to debut my rendition of 'I'll Always Love You' for all and sundry, if that makes you feel any better."

Leo couldn't say the same as she'd jumped up on the empty stage and belted out the Whitney Houston version of the hit during their last visit. And though Flo's older sister had been named after the famed opera singer Leontyne Price, her voice sounded more like cats battling it out in an alley. Yeah, not pretty at all.

Maddox winced before smiling again, wider this time. "It does. It definitely does."

She raised her bottle to her mouth again and studied the man at the end of the bar.

Even though Rose Bend was a small, postcard-pretty town dropped right in the middle of the Southern Berkshires, strangers weren't foreign to its borders. Not when nearly every season or holiday brought visitors far and wide for town-hosted festivals or carnivals or motorcycle rallies. Strangers weren't odd around here.

But the impact this one had on her was unusual.

Or rather, the heat this one stirred inside her, like a sauna switched on high, was unusual.

She studied the man, trying not to be too obvious. But hell, it was a Tuesday night and besides them, only about fifteen other people gathered at the tables, played pool or bellied up to the bar. She couldn't exactly hide her fascination.

And oh yes, she was indeed fascinated.

His high fade had her fingers tingling with the need to comb through that thick, textured hair. A neat, full mustache and beard framed a wide mouth, the sensual lips appearing almost too lush. Her belly pulled tight below her navel, the ache sweet and painful. The longer she stared at that mouth, the sharper the ache.

From this distance, she couldn't catch the color of his eyes, but the patrician slope of his nose with its round, flared nostrils, and the bold, clean lines of his face declared his stark beauty from across the bar.

Or maybe it was just her.

Maybe she was the only one captivated by broad shoulders that stretched the soft-looking black sweater to its limits. Mesmerized by the big, long-fingered hands wrapped around a short tumbler of amber alcohol. Enraptured by the seemingly endless denim-encased legs that stretched out on either side of the bar stool. Absurdly fascinated by the large feet planted on the dark tile floor.

He was so…huge.

A low, heated thrum buzzed under her skin at the thought of just how he would completely surround a person. Fill a person.

Okay, her. Surround *her*. Fill *her*.

She should really show some dignity and stop ogling him. It was rude at best, a little unnerving at worst. Any moment, she would stop staring. Honestly. Aaaany moment…

Maddox approached the man with another glass and set it on the bar in front of him. Leaning forward, the bar owner said something to Big, Bearded and Sinful, most likely passing along that she'd paid for that drink. And she braced herself as those wide shoulders tensed. Braced for the moment when he…

Damn.

Still couldn't see his eyes at this distance, with the bar's dim lighting, but the impact of his gaze slammed into her like a velvet sledgehammer. And no, she wasn't too proud to admit she might've gasped. Just a small one, though.

Because… Damn.

Yes, she'd said that already, but it bore repeating.

He cocked his head to the side and, *whew*. That little move was all kinds of sexy. Did he know it? Did he practice it in a mirror to achieve the perfect angle that said, "Have you gotten a good enough look at what you see?" but didn't veer into "I'm a conceited asshole" territory. It was a careful balance and he nailed it.

Turning back to Maddox, he replied to the bar owner then slid off the stool and walked toward her in what could only be described as a sensual display of power and beauty in motion. She tried to keep her gaze off the flex and stretch of all that muscle in his thick thighs. But good God. She was only human and those thighs, *thooo*…

Swallowing a sigh along with another gulp of beer, she resisted, pressing the cool bottle to her cheek. Not that it would do anything for the heat pooling between her legs. Seriously, he had to know what that body and sensual, confident stride did to a woman who hadn't had sex in, oh eight months, three weeks and four days.

But who's counting?

"I believe the bartender said this was courtesy of you?"

She should've expected it. Everything about him was big, almost an exaggeration of beautiful. From the thick, tight coils of his hair to his smooth, dark brown skin, to the broad, powerful frame… So yes, she should've expected his voice to be this deep, resonant timbre. It somehow agitated the ache he'd stirred while soothing… *something* inside her she couldn't identify.

Should've expected it? Still wasn't ready.

And even when he set the thick glass tumbler down on the bar top and settled on the stool next to her, she couldn't find her voice. It lodged in her throat, snared by surprise and lust.

So she nodded.

He glanced down at the drink then turned, fully facing her, and—she didn't sigh. Her whole fucking *being* did.

Hazel.

His eyes were hazel.

Although that name seemed so inadequate to describe the stunning blend of dark green and golden brown. God, she'd go back in time and return the past two weeks of travel and amazing shots just to have her camera in her hands so she could photograph him. Her fingers and palms itched to capture him in different light, with different expressions.

He made an utterly fascinating canvas.

"I appreciate the gesture but this—" he tipped the other glass he'd already been nursing toward her "—is my second drink and also my limit since I'm driving home. So I'm afraid I'll have to decline your offer. But it's appreciated."

Driving home?

As in Rose Bend?

Twenty-three of her twenty-four years had been spent in this town, except for the years she'd grudgingly spent in college. Newcomers traveled through the gossip vines faster than a sugar rush through a toddler. No way she would've missed it. And no way she would've missed *him*.

Maybe he'd stopped by while on his way to one of the neighboring towns or cities.

Which made her intentions for tonight even better.

Lifting a shoulder in a shrug, she picked up the glass and slung it back. Scotch. She didn't really like hard liquor, but she wasn't about to let it go to waste either. And besides, what was that about liquid courage? She could definitely use some right now. The alcohol burned its way over her tongue, hit her chest and mushroomed in a burst of heat toward her stomach.

Burned away the last vestiges of her reticence, too.

"You're welcome," she said, voice hoarse from the liquor and the sensual punch of him. "Thank you for coming over and softening the blow. You let me save face and the drink." Smiling, she held up the empty tumbler, dipping her chin toward him. "Which was pretty awful, by the way." She gave a shudder. It really did taste bad. "I think I'll stick to beer and the occasional Sex on the Beach."

Something flared in his eyes—something she didn't feel comfortable naming. No, no. Not true. And since she'd decided to be all big and bold tonight, she at least owed it to herself to be honest. Something she was *afraid* to name in case she was wrong.

In case she was disappointed.

"Occasional, huh?" He arched a dark, thick eyebrow, swirling the small amount of amber whiskey left in his glass. His green-and-gold gaze didn't move from her face and for the briefest of moments, she felt like a drowning victim, sinking for a final time. In over her head. "This place doesn't strike me as the kind to have Sex on the Beach, even the occasional one."

"Which place? The bar or Rose Bend?"

The corner of his mouth hitched in an almost smile. And against her will, curiosity tugged at her. She didn't need curiosity for her plans tonight. And yet, she couldn't stop her mind from wondering, *Why* almost? *Do you smile often? If not, why?*

Yeah, she had to stop this dicey spiral of thoughts before it got her in trouble.

And talked her right out of orgasms.

"Take your pick," he murmured. Or challenged.

It was low, couched in what could still be considered polite, harmless conversation, but oh yes, it was still a challenge. To see how far she was willing to push it.

Oh Mr. Big, Bearded and Sinful, I've had a shitty two weeks fending off a mentor-turned-octopus. I am angry, have whiskey lighting me up like a UFO sighting and left my last fuck back over the Massachusetts state line. I'm ready to, in the immortal words of Salt-N-Pepa, push it real good.

Not quite tipsy enough to say all that aloud, she finished off the rest of her beer and signaled Maddox for another one. In moments, he replaced her empty with a fresh bottle, his blue gaze running over her face, probably gauging her sobriety. Flo flashed him a smile, letting him know she was fine. Shaking his head, he gave her a small smirk in return then walked off.

"Well, Road's End is a dive bar, so you're pretty much going to get beer, local IPAs and some top-shelf liquor." She nodded toward his glass. "But if you know people—" she leaned toward him, lowering her voice "—and I know people, you can sometimes get away with fancier drinks." Another of those almost smiles, and it glimmered in his eyes. God, the sight of that wide, sensual mouth pulled into a full, genuine grin might be more than her poor heart could take.

For a brief moment she'd wanted to see the full Monty of that smile.

She'd changed her mind.

"Rose Bend seems like a small, innocent town, but don't let the church steeple fool you. There's Rose Bend After Dark if you know where to look. Or if you want to look."

A long, silent moment practically pulsed with heat between them. Now she waited to see how far he would push.

"So you're from here?" he asked.

Tilting her head, she lobbed back, "Are you?"

"No."

Relief streamed through her, and she lifted her beer for a sip to hide her smile. She must've done a terrible job of it, though, because he huffed out a soft chuckle.

"That seems to please you. Now my curiosity won't let me *not* ask why. Is being a resident of Rose Bend such a crime?"

"Of course not," she said, adding a shake of her head for emphasis. "This is a great town. Wonderful place to grow up. But small pool for what I want."

"And that is?"

Nerves tangled in her belly, and that steady, jeweled gaze didn't help. Quite the opposite. It further entangled the liquor-infused bravado. But it also ignited the need already simmering inside her. Stifling the urge to shift on the bar stool, to somehow alleviate the ache setting up a slow, insistent throb between her legs, she met that stare.

"One night. With you."

There. She put it out there. No taking it back. And though she'd murmured the words, they seemed to echo. She fought to maintain their visual connection when a part of her desired to duck her head or rescind that bold statement.

No, that was a lie.

Embarrassment over his potential rejection might stain her neck and chest, but she didn't want to take back the offer. She'd been honest. And hell, in the spirit of that honesty, she was a little desperate, too.

Being alone tonight… Yeah, avoiding the empty ache was worth the risk of some embarrassment.

"Why?"

She blinked. Slowly straightened and set her bottle on the bar top.

Okay. Hadn't been expecting that response. "I'm sorry. What do you mean, *why*?"

He set his glass on the bar, too, and his scrutiny seemed to narrow, intensify as it scanned her face, searching for… what? Confusion crowded out the mortification.

"I mean," he said, "why? Why me? Why do you want one night?"

The abrupt burst of laughter she released reflected the surprise swirling inside her. She tipped her head back, her locs tickling her lower back as she blankly studied the wood-beamed ceiling.

Leave it to her to approach the one man who wanted to discuss her feelings about a one-night stand. Dammit. Where was a fuck boy when you needed one?

"Look, if you're not interested—"

"Did I say that?" he interrupted. "Don't put words in my mouth."

"I'm trying to put other things in your mouth, but you don't seem in a rush for that," she muttered.

"Clever." That quirk at the corner of his mouth. Resentment filled her that she still wanted to kiss that lush curve. Bite it. "Are you going to answer?"

She swallowed a sigh and eyed her beer. She might need it for this conversation. Out of all the Dennisons, *she* was the one he wanted to go deeper with. It would be laughable if it wasn't so frustrating. She avoided *deep* like vampires dodged direct sunlight.

"Why you?" She addressed the easiest question first, hoping he'd leave the second one alone. She scoffed, waving a hand up and down, encompassing his big self. "Have you seen yourself? I don't think you need me to tell you how attractive women find your big, tall body. How it makes them want to climb it like a tree just to get to that beautiful mouth. Or grab ahold of that beard so they can run their fingers through it, see if it's soft and springy or coarse and thick. Imagine how it would feel over their bare skin. And then there's those eyes." Her breath hitched as they brightened. "I called you Big, Bearded and Sinful in my head before you even walked over here. But one glimpse of those stunning eyes and it confirmed that impression. That's what you are. So does that clear up the *why*? The *why you*?"

Her heart pounded after that little speech, and it left her mouth dry.

He didn't immediately answer. Or maybe he did. That

something flashed in his eyes again and he lifted his tumbler to his mouth, tossed back the rest of the whiskey, then slowly set the glass back on the bar. All while never releasing her from his stare.

Damn.

The flames in her veins evaporated all the air from her lungs. Until this moment, she hadn't believed in insta-lust. That was a vehicle rolled out to sell romance novels and movies, not real life. Had she been attracted to men and women before? Sure. But this demanding, clawing, hungry thing defied mere *attraction*.

But something this hot, this needy, couldn't last. It burned too hot. Still, she wanted to go up in its flames before it died.

"No," he finally said, sending a frisson of shock shivering through her. "You haven't finished answering. Why the one night?"

Her lips twisted. "Are we really discussing this?" She shrugged, throwing up her hands, palms up. "Why does anyone have a one-night stand? To get off? Because they're not looking for a relationship but a strings-free time?"

"Okay." He cocked his head. "Now that we've discussed *anyone's* reasons, let's talk about yours."

Embers of anger sizzled beneath the desire, and she lifted her beer to her mouth again, gulping down a mouthful, but the cold brew did nothing to douse her annoyance.

Discomfort.

"This is the funniest way of saying you'd rather not—"

"Still trying to put words in my mouth," he murmured. "Or are you trying to avoid the question?"

"Yes," she nearly snapped. "Either you want to fuck or opt out, but I don't want to have a therapy session about it."

Even in the noisy hum of the bar, silence beat between them.

It pounded with its own rhythm, holding her chained to her chair. And when he put an elbow on the edge of the bar and leaned closer to her, invading her personal space, she didn't move. Couldn't move. She inhaled his rich, woodsy scent that carried notes of a heady, earthen musk, sweet and light like milk chocolate and fruit and caramel from the whiskey. He was a veritable buffet of fragrance. And her mouth watered for a taste.

"Let's just get this out the way, queen. I might question why you want this, but not if I want *you*. Fucking you isn't the issue. If that was my only concern, we would already be outside in my truck and headed to the nearest flat surface. And even *flat surface* is negotiable. But I want to make sure you don't wake up tomorrow and I'm a regret you wish you'd given five more minutes to consider. I would hate to be that for you."

"Queen?" she whispered, surprise winging through her for the second time that night. Surprise and a flood of warmth she had no name for, but it made her...feel.

That alone should've had her backing away from him, from this. Should've had her changing her mind.

"I have to call you something since I don't know your name. And call it intuition, but I'm guessing if I asked, you're not going to give it to me." He paused, his gaze roaming her face as if on a treasure hunt. "Will you?"

"No."

He laughed, and the low, deep, *knowing* sound stroked over her skin. But then he sobered, and though he leaned back, the intensity didn't lessen.

"Are you ready to tell me why, then? Why the one night?"

She studied him, a stinging retort hot on her tongue.

But the unwavering, almost *gentle* look in his eyes stifled her reply.

Part of her melted.

Part of her battled the urge to run.

And yet, she stayed.

"I just returned home from a trip abroad," she murmured, then hiked her shoulders up before letting them
fall. "I have no idea why I'm telling you this," she admitted more to herself than to him.

"For the same reason you sent me that drink. You want
to. Where did you go?"

He sounded so damn reasonable. But it was his calm
that had her smoothing a hand over her locs, her fingers
bumping the bun on the top of her head before trailing
down to the strands falling over her shoulders.

"Thailand. Two weeks. I went for work, but they still
should've been two wonderful weeks doing something
I love in a gorgeous country I've always wanted to visit.
Instead..." Anger, bitterness and a marrow-deep grief
roiled inside her. "Instead, my visit turned into a nightmare where I not only lost my joy in a dream assignment,
but I also lost a mentor and friend—well, someone I believed was a friend. I thought he respected me, valued
my talent, and in the end, all I was to him was easy ass."

The words were almost flippant, but the emotions
were...anything but. She still raged. She still fumed.

She still hurt.

Paul Coolidge, her college professor-turned-mentor,
had betrayed her friendship, her trust. Had abused his
position of authority to make her feel small. Powerless.

And she hated that most of all.

She'd been there before. Understood more intimately
than most what it was to be rendered invisible and helpless by someone she trusted—someone she loved. It

made her sick that she found herself there again. And she wanted, *needed*, to purge the stench of it.

"I'm sorry, queen," he murmured. "You didn't deserve that."

"You know what was the worst part? Well, besides having to find ways not to bend over, kneel, lean forward or hell, fucking breathe, around this man? Because apparently *everything* I did sent him signals to touch me, groan as if I were a steak dinner being served up just for his pleasure, or proposition me." She snorted, her grip tightening around her beer bottle. The cold chilled her fingers, but she barely felt it, mired in the recent past. "The other people there with us saw what he was doing. Saw how uncomfortable he made me. A couple of them even overheard a few of his comments. But they did nothing. Said nothing. They acted like everything was normal. I felt invisible. Voiceless. Like I was screaming into this void for help, and no one heard me."

Betrayal, hurt and a powerless fury beat within her chest.

"What did you do?" he asked after a moment.

She released a caustic chuckle. "I started setting my phone up to secretly record anytime I had to interact with him. I caught him saying offensive shit to me and touching my ass 'by mistake.' I played it back for him and threatened that if he didn't stop, the videos would be on social media by that night. And I would be tagging his university. That got his notice, and he cut it out, but that last week in Bangkok was…horrible. And now I'm not sure if he will blackball me or start some kind of smear campaign against me."

She shook her head, loosing another sharp-edged laugh.

"I know for sure I lost a friend and that I can kiss any

work opportunities from his recommendation goodbye. At the end of the day, I'm still paying a high price and he gets off with a warning—literally."

Silence fell between them, and heat suffused her chest, neck and face. She hated appearing weak. Hated waving her vulnerability like a dirty rag. Most people didn't respect it, only viewed it as something to either scorn or abuse.

And here she was just handing over that emotional ammo to him.

This called for more beer.

She tipped the bottle up for a longer, deeper sip.

"I won't give you some trite cliché saying 'I know how you feel.' I can't. I've never been in a position where I've been sexually objectified or had my livelihood threatened because I wouldn't play 'the game.' Yes, I'm a Black man in America, and that's a whole different discussion, but not this one. And I won't insult you by co-opting your experience as a woman. A Black woman. So I'm just going to say I'm sorry. And you're right. In this situation, you'll pay the cost more than he will. If he does at all. But that doesn't make him innocent. He had a responsibility toward you, as your employer, mentor and friend. As a person. He violated those boundaries, not you. I hope you recognize that."

"Here." She tapped a fingertip to her temple. "I do recognize it. But here?" She lowered her arm, splaying her fingers wide over her chest. "Is a different story. I'm working on it, though."

"And working on it—or working *through* it—entails fucking me for the night?" he asked, almost nonchalantly.

The blunt, casual tone of *fucking me* set the lust that had been simmering inside her to flash fire level.

"Yes," she admitted, just as blunt but softer.

"Will it work?" He toyed with the tumbler, but that magnetic green-and-gold gaze fixed on her.

"I don't know… But it'll prevent me from obsessively thinking about it for the next few hours. It'll help me forget for a little while." It'd help her feel something other than anger, confusion and disillusionment. "For that, I'm willing to take a chance. Are you going to be my chance?"

He stared at her, and if her breath stilled in her lungs… if her whole body stilled in anticipation of his answer, well, she chalked it up to her sexual fast and the whole gluttonous meal of a man sitting next to her. Simple lust. Nothing more.

Although, while she didn't make a habit of one-night stands—how could she in her Your Business is My Business small town—she'd indulged occasionally before. And never, *never* had she felt the need to confess her inner thoughts as foreplay.

"Depends." He cocked his head. "What're you going to be for me?"

Whatever you need me to be, danced on her tongue, and she nearly uttered the flippant, and corny, response. But a closer look into his golden eyes stopped her. That shuttered expression compelled her to give more of the honesty she'd delivered tonight.

"I'll be the opposite of whatever drove you here to drink alone," she finally said, unsure if that was the correct answer.

But the flare of heat in his gaze assured her it was.

And yet, he didn't say anything. Pride kept her from asking him again.

Yet, even pride had its limits. Just one glance down—at his broad, solid chest, at those powerful thighs—and begging didn't seem all *that* bad. Not when she could have all of him pressed against her. Covering her.

She shivered.

God, she wanted him covering her. Filling her.

There had to be another time when she'd been this turned on. But for the life of her, she couldn't remember it in this moment.

"No regrets," he murmured.

"No regrets."

He nodded, and turning to face the bar, held up a hand, signaling for Maddox. Seconds later the bar owner approached them.

"What can I do for you?" Maddox asked.

"I need to pay my tab. And hers."

Flo shook her head. "That's not nece—"

"I know it's not. But I am," he quietly interrupted her, and her lips snapped shut around the rest of her protest.

That low, bourbon-and-bad-decisions voice brooked no argument. And though part of her balked at the dominance humming in his tone, a larger part damn near purred.

Purred.

Who did that?

Her, apparently.

Flo dipped her chin and finished off the rest of her beer while he handed Maddox several bills. From the look of it, more than enough to cover their drinks and a healthy tip.

So he wasn't stingy.

Hopefully, that translated to…other things.

Sex.

Other things were sex and the universe owed her a selfless, generous lover after her hellish past two weeks.

"Ready?" he asked, rising from the stool and holding out his hand to her.

For a moment, she stared at the wide palm and long, elegant fingers. And the urge to tell him this wasn't a hand-holding situation crowded into the back of her throat. But instead of letting it fly off her tongue, she swallowed it back down. Something told her this man didn't care about typical one-night stands or what was customary for everyone else—including her. A niggling intuition warned her nothing about this night would be usual. Starting with the man she'd chosen.

"You want my arm to fall off?" Humor laced the question, but she barely heard it.

A jolt of icy shock blasted through her, and she froze midclimb down from the bar stool. She blinked at him, a disorienting sense of…familiarity rippling through her. There was no way this man could know that Billy Dee Williams's quote from the classic movie *Lady Sings the Blues* was one of her favorites. Just as he couldn't know that the movie starring Billy Dee and Diana Ross had been her mother's favorite.

Not Lucille "Moe" Dennison, her adoptive mother who was probably just locking Kinsale Inn's doors and heading up to bed.

No, her biological mother. The one Flo barely remembered. The one she'd known only from old pictures, diaries and her parents' memories.

No, he couldn't possibly know that the only way she felt close to the mother whose memory was like a smudged fingerprint—tangible but with blurred details—was to become familiar with and love the things she'd loved.

But it didn't stop her from feeling like he in some way *did* know…

She shook her head, as if the abrupt motion could rid her of the fanciful thought. This was a one-night stand. A fuck-and-flee. There was nothing sentimental about this other than the tender feelings she would have toward her orgasms.

Another reason not to hold his hand—

She slid her palm across his.

Dammit. She must've left her sense of self-preservation at the Grand Palace and the Temple of the Emerald Buddha.

She smothered a sigh.

"Ready."

CHAPTER TWO

"THIS IS YOURS?"

Flo closed and locked the front door to the apartment behind her and turned to study the man whose tall frame seemed to shrink the living space to Lilliputian dimensions. Slipping her keys in the back pocket of her jeans, she surveyed the place, attempting to view it through his eyes.

A large living room/dining room with nearly floor-to-ceiling, front-facing windows. An eclectic hodgepodge of furniture filled the open space—the couches from the previous owners, tables donated by her parents from the inn, dining room set from the thrift store, armchairs a gift from her sister Leo. The only things not previously owned or gifted by someone were the photographs on the wall. Hers.

A small kitchen with a bar separating the rooms. A short hall leading to the bedroom and bathroom. The small apartment over her photography studio had come as part of the purchase, and though she spent half her time at the inn with her family—still had her room there—this place was her hideaway away from the…noise.

She said none of this to him; she'd confessed far too much personal information tonight. Even though he didn't know her name.

And she didn't know his. Still…

"I can't keep calling you Big, Bearded and Sinful. Want to give me a name?"

He turned, dark eyebrow arched.

"Mine or will any do?"

"Any will do."

No real names. She had no intention of sharing hers. It might seem silly that she planned to get naked with this man and allow him access to all of her body parts, but exchanging names? Too intimate. Whatever. Those were her rules. At least with *him*.

"You can call me Adam."

She squinted at him. "Is there something subliminal in that choice? Like you're trying to tell me you'll be the first man to rock my world?"

His eyes narrowed. "One, you should never say *rock my world* again. And two—" that quirk of a smile had her belly trembling "—I was actually thinking of Adam from *Buffy the Vampire Slayer*."

She scrunched her nose. "You mean the Frankenstein made from demon and vampire parts? That Adam?"

He shrugged a shoulder. "He was the first of his kind, too."

"Not really. Daryl Epps steals that honor. I mean, he was reverse engineered by two high school students instead of the military, but the science is the same."

"Science." He arched an eyebrow. "Daryl was a zombie not a totally new creation. Doesn't count."

Oh. Well. "Touché." She frowned although humor and heat swirled in her belly. Crossing her arms, she said, "I've never debated Buffy canon as foreplay but strangely—" she tilted her head, scrutinized him "—it's sexy. And I didn't believe it was possible, but you just got hotter."

He snorted. "Ditto. But you are giving me a couple of firsts tonight, and that alone makes you sexier. And too intriguing for comfort."

Now it was her turn to snort. "Are you trying to tell me you've never had a one-night stand before?" she challenged.

"I'm not telling you that." He paused, and his bright gaze grew hooded. That look punched her directly in the chest and spread into a glowing warmth as if she'd slung back another gulp of the scotch he'd been drinking earlier. "But I've never had a one-night stand with *you*."

Oh. He was good.

And damn, she might actually believe him.

Stop that. He's here for one reason. Sex. Hot, sweaty, mind-blanking sex. Remember your priorities.

"You haven't had one with me…yet. About that…" She waved a hand back and forth between them. "You think we can get started on that?"

"Queen." A shiver tangoed down her spine at both the name and the rough silk voice wrapped around it. "Come here."

For the second—or third?—time that evening, she tried to dredge up some sense of rebellion or affront at being ordered around. Seriously, *something.*

But instead, her feet—and vagina—snatched control, and she walked forward, crossing the small space separating them. She came to a halt in front of him, tipping her head back to meet his steady hazel gaze. This close, his earthy scent wrapped around her like an invisible embrace. It teased and taunted, and another quiver rippled through her. One born of anticipation, impatience. Need.

And when he lifted one of those thickly muscled arms and slid a hand around the nape of her neck to cup it, that need almost collapsed her legs from under her.

"I get you're trying to reduce me to a walking dick, so this—" he squeezed her nape "—isn't personal. But for me, there's nothing more *personal* than a woman allowing me inside her. Even if it's only for the next few hours. We're going to be intimate, and I won't let you use me any more than I'm going to be using you."

Panic spiked behind her sternum, and though logic reasoned she was being ridiculous, that admonishment didn't do shit for her racing pulse. No, this was supposed to be a straightforward fucking not, not…intimate. He had the wrong woman for that.

She raised her hands between them, flattened her palms on his chest, preparing to push him away. "Listen, I—"

"It's fascinating how that seems to scare you," he murmured, interrupting her. Bowing his head, he brushed his beautiful lips up her throat. "I see it in your eyes," he continued, and the timbre of that deep voice vibrated against her skin, causing a hitch in her breathing.

Well, that was if she'd been actually pushing air out of her lungs. That necessary function halted as soon as his mouth touched her for the first time.

"No, it doesn't," she rasped. And lied.

His low chuckle hummed over her throat, sending waves of sultry, damn near tropical warmth undulating through her.

"Little liar," he accused, voice rumbling with humor. And something else. Something darker, thicker. Hotter. "But I'll let you have it, queen." His teeth grazed where his lips had trailed, leaving a hint—a forewarning—of sharper edged desire in their wake. "But right here is where you need to make your decision."

He lifted his head, and the gleam in his eyes darkened the gold-and-green hues until they appeared a rich amber. "Are we going to give each other what we need, or are we over before we start?"

It was really unfair of him to ask her that question

while that beautiful, sinful mouth hovered only centimeters above hers. How could he expect her to concentrate when such extreme temptation distracted her? When she could practically taste the flavor of his kiss on the breath that brushed her lips?

His hand briefly tightened on her nape. "What's your answer?"

If that squeeze on her neck—and the corresponding exquisite ache in her sex—hadn't already tipped the scales to a resounding "yes" then that note of impatience that crept into his voice sent the scales toppling over.

Until this moment he'd been collected, almost unbothered while desire scratched at the underside of her skin. But that edginess… It, more than anything, placed them on even ground. He wanted her. Possibly as much as she wanted him.

She felt empowered by that knowledge.

"We're going to give each other what we need. For tonight," she tacked on, not just for his sake, but for hers. A strict reminder and definite time limit. She needed both. "What else—?"

His mouth and the hungry thrust and sweep of his tongue prevented her from finishing her question. Didn't matter. The words fled from her head, and a jagged moan replaced them.

If she'd harbored any doubt about his desire for her, the growl that rumbled up his chest and onto her tongue obliterated it. She accepted that sound as eagerly as she did the next stroke, the next lick, the next sweet suck.

His hand shifted upward, tangling in her locs, gripping them and tugging her head back. So he could dive deeper, harder. Take more. And God, she wanted him to take it all.

Sliding her hands from his chest and around his back,

she fisted his sweater—hanging on or pulling him closer? She couldn't answer that.

Didn't want to answer that.

No, she didn't want to do anything but feel. Just shut off her brain and allow herself to be swept away and hauled under by this carnal undertow. By him.

No.

The objection echoed so loud and adamant in her mind, she jerked her head back, breaking their kiss. Not by *him*. No matter what he said, tonight was not personal. She wanted sex. Not a connection.

"Queen." He pinched her chin between his thumb and forefinger, tipping her face up.

Just that. His nickname for her. But coupled with his piercing gaze, that one word said a wealth of things.

Your choice.

This stops here if that's what you want.

It's on you.

She inhaled a deep breath, her fingers flexing against the unyielding muscles of his back. A calm settled over her along with knowledge that he might be bigger, but he didn't hold the power here. At least, not all of it. And he proved that by reminding her of her choice.

After the past two weeks, that assurance—that comfort—was almost as sexy as the man staring down at her.

She didn't reply to Adam. Well, not verbally. But she did rise on her toes and press her mouth to his once more. This kiss was slower, lazier, more indulgent. He followed her lead, chasing the curl of her tongue, the rub of her lips, the nip of her teeth. It wasn't a clash of mouths like the first kiss, but the hard grip on her hair and the hot brand of his cock against her belly relayed that it affected him. *She* affected him.

The hand still gripping her chin lowered, skimming down the front of her throat, over her collarbone, trailing over the top of her breast. As if testing her or…asking permission. In answer, she arched into his chest, loosing a low moan. With a rumble of sound that had her nipples beading, he cupped her breast, his big hand lifting her, molding her, squeezing her. Tearing her mouth from his, she tipped her head back, and when he swept a caress over the aching tip, lightly pinching it, she emitted another groan.

His teeth grazed her jaw, soothing the slightly abrasive touch with a brush of those beautiful, lush lips.

"More," she murmured, and he didn't make her wait.

Within moments, he pulled her sweater up over her head and tossed it, leaving her clad only in a dark blue lace bra. His hands returned to her—and so did his mouth.

Oh God.

Lust twisted her belly, and she helplessly undulated against him, grinding against his cock as he closed his lips around her nipple and sucked. The erotic tug echoed in the wet flesh between her legs, and she gasped at the delicious and utterly wicked sensation. The contrast of the wet lace and his hot mouth… She whined. Honest to God *whined*.

And yet…not enough.

Impatience snaked through her, and she cradled his head, fingers threading through his coarse, thick hair. She pushed into his mouth, and he snagged the cup of her bra, jerking it down and then, *thank God*, her bare flesh was consumed by his heat. He seared her, and each hard suck and rough lick sent her careening closer to an impossible release. How? She shook her head. Her breasts had always been a sensitive part of her body, but orgasm from touch alone? She'd never thought it could happen, but damn, he was making a believer out of her.

As he switched breasts, giving the other the same carnal attention, she couldn't prevent the stream of cries escaping her. His mouth worked magic on her, transforming her into a hungry, insatiable creature solely bent on pursuing pleasure.

He released her nipple with a soft pop, and slowly sank to his knees. Her breath caught in her throat as he licked a path down the valley between her breasts, over her stomach and lower until his lips bumped the button of her jeans. Her breath blasted out of her lungs, and she struggled to control the twisting in her stomach. Not because she didn't want this. Quite the opposite.

Because she *did* want this.

Badly.

She wanted his mouth, his hands, on her. Wanted to see pleasure that she gave him darken his eyes. Wanted him to take her. In every way.

He tipped his head back, meeting her gaze as his fingers worked the button and dragged the zipper down. He didn't glance away—didn't release her from their visual connection. And part of her wanted to look anywhere but in his eyes. She was tempted to close hers and let herself be dragged further down into the sensations swamping her. But she couldn't. Couldn't look away. Couldn't shut out that beautiful face or stunning gaze.

Couldn't shut him out.

A whisper of awe tangled with the need grinding away at her, and she grazed her fingertips across his lips…then one slipped between them. His tongue curled around her, drawing hard. Hot pulses of pleasure throbbed in her sex, and she squeezed her thighs together to…alleviate it? To trap it inside her? She didn't know. Didn't care to analyze it. Not now with him circling her wrist and pulling her fingers free.

Not with him guiding her hand beneath the band of her panties.

Not with their intertwined fingers sliding through her wet, aching flesh.

A gasp escaped her, and she jerked under their combined touch. Groaned. Melted.

"Don't stop," he ordered in a low, dark tone that brooked no argument. Not that she intended to.

Sinking her teeth into her bottom lip, she obeyed, circling a fingertip over and around her clit even as he jerked her jeans down her hips and legs, pausing only to snatch off her boots before removing the denim. Before she could dwell on standing naked before him, he replaced her fingers with his mouth.

A cry erupted from her, and she tilted her head back and screamed toward the ceiling.

Oh. *God.*

The heat. The pleasure. They tore through her with the speed and power of an incoming storm, and like any good northeasterner, all she could do was batten down and brace herself for impact. But damn… There was no steadying herself for that skillful tongue that glided through her folds, curled around that nerve-packed button of flesh. No preparing herself for the nearly ravenous way he consumed her, licking, stroking, sucking. He *savored* her. Staring down at him, she couldn't describe it any other way. The lowered eyes. That smooth brown skin pulled taut over bold cheekbones. Those beautiful, ever-moving lips glistening with *her.*

Oh yes. He enjoyed her.

And when he cupped the back of her thigh and hefted it over his shoulder, opening her more, he solidified that opinion. Well, that and the deep, rumbling hum that vibrated over her sensitive flesh.

Sinking her teeth into her bottom lip, she tunneled her fingers through his thick hair, gripping the short strands, holding him to her. Silently demanding he stay right where he was as she rocked her hips to a rhythm he created with his mouth and the fingers that drew small circles around her entrance.

"Adam."

She gasped at the sudden and hot-as-fuck display of strength as he lifted her and moved her to the floor. In most cases, a man bodily shifting her from one place to the other would've elicited a response that had his ancestors cringing. But now, with the blunt tips of his fingers pressing inside her, he and his forefathers were safe. Just as long as he kept filling her. Kept fucking her with those long, beautiful fingers.

"Dammit," she breathed, her fingernails scratching his scalp, praying she didn't hurt him. Not having much air in her lungs to ask.

In the bar, she'd admired the length and width of his fingers, and now as they pushed inside her, she appreciated them on a whole new level. A whimper clawed its way free of her throat, and she undulated into his touch, his invasion, his possession.

As he slowly withdrew, she shook her head, mewling— yes, fucking *mewling*—a protest.

"No, please." She tugged on his hair, punching her hips into the air, chasing that wonderful, already addictive feeling.

"Shh," he softly admonished, placing a warm, firm kiss on her clit that had her jolting. "Can you take another one, queen? Another finger?"

Before he finished the question, she jerked her head in

a nod. "Yes, dammit. Yes. Give it to me." She was begging and didn't give the nearest damn.

"Of course you can," he praised, giving her sex another one of those hot kisses, this one on her folds. "Because you're a beautiful, fierce queen who doesn't back down, isn't that right?"

He didn't wait for her answer; hell, she didn't know if he expected one. Not that it mattered. Her reply would've been the one he wanted. The one they both did. A resounding "yes."

And when he gently but steadily thrust three fingers into her, she didn't retreat from that almost too-full sensation. Not from the slight burn. Not from the stretching.

No, she gloried in it. Delighted in it.

Ran toward it with the arch of her neck. The strain of her back. The needy twist of her hips.

The hungry clamp of sex.

"Goddamn, queen. You're so tight," he growled, and nipped her upper thigh. "I need you to come so I can feel this around my dick. Come on, baby. Give it to me." He issued that order and followed it with heavy, measured thrusts that bumped his knuckles against her sex.

Each stroke rippled through her, sending ecstasy jangling over nerve endings that felt exposed and overstimulated. Closing her eyes, she clenched her teeth against the electrified currents crackling through her. Each twist of his wrist and each curve of his fingers against a place high inside her shoved her closer to an orgasm that loomed like a bomb.

"Adam," she rasped, nails scrabbling at his shoulders now, desperate to find purchase, stability.

He answered by circling his tongue around her clit and sucking, drawing hard even as the pad of his fingers thrust and rubbed.

She was done. Gone.

Dimly, she heard the muted sounds of clothing moving over skin, of the same hitting the floor. And when she lifted her lashes, the sight of Adam removing a condom and ripping it open greeted her.

It should've been impossible. Seriously, remnants from a reality-bending orgasm lingered within her; lethargy weighted her limbs. And yet...watching him roll the protection down an impossibly long, wide and thick cock sent a hydraulic wave of lust through her, energizing her.

Clothed, Adam was a beautiful, imposing man.

Naked?

Breathtaking.

And not in the hyperbolic sense. He stole her breath. A broad chest sprinkled with curly hair that narrowed into a silky line down a compact, hard stomach. Not a ridged stomach curated in a gym with machines, but a solid one derived from hard, honest work. Powerful, muscled thighs and calves. If he'd seemed huge in his sweater and jeans, stripped of those civilized trappings, he was gigantic. Almost intimidating.

Good thing she liked that.

Flo stretched her arms toward him, welcoming him. Urging him to hurry. Yes, he'd given her more pleasure than even she'd imagined he could dole out when she'd approached him at the bar. But an emptiness still throbbed within her.

An emptiness she suspected only he could fill.

At least for tonight.

With his hooded gaze fixed on her, Adam smoothed the condom down his length then crawled his way up her body. Staring down at her, he settled his big palms on either side of her head, caging her. He didn't say a word, but that golden eagle stare studied her, and she sank her teeth into her bottom lip, imprisoning the urge to ask him, "What are you thinking?"

This wasn't the place for talking. Unless it was a command to go harder, deeper.

A spark of resentment flashed through her, and though it smacked too much of cowardice, she closed her eyes. She'd told him what she wanted from him. Sex. Fucking. Forgetfulness. Not intimacy. Not sharing. Even without words, he pushed her boundaries, and she hated him a little for it.

But with her sex wet and aching, apparently not enough to push him away and order him out of her apartment.

Her fucking vagina had no principles.

Gentle but implacable fingers pinched her chin, tilted her head back…and waited. Waited for her to open her eyes. For her to acknowledge him. And though she didn't know much beyond him other than he gave amazing orgasms, she sensed he possessed the patience of Job and the stubbornness of an ass. Meaning, he'd probably wait here all night for her to give in.

More resentment flickered inside her as she submitted first. And opened her eyes.

"What was that?" he asked, voice calm. As if the essence of her didn't still moisten his lips and beard, and his hard cock didn't brush her thigh.

"What was what?" she threw back at him, unable to quell the sharpness in her tone. "We're here to fuck. We should get on with that."

He didn't immediately respond to her words or react to the tone. Once more he considered her, and she forced herself to meet his gaze. And maybe he decided to get on with it because the blunt, wide tip of his cock nudged her entrance, then pressed, pushing forward. The air was expelled from her lungs on a long, low breath.

Be careful what you wish for.

Thank God he prepared me with three fingers.

The two thoughts warred in her head as he slowly, increasingly claimed her, not stopping until he fully seated himself inside her.

Damn. *Oh damn.*

Amazing, gorgeous pressure and pleasure edged in the thinnest rim of pain consumed her, surged and crackled through her. She blinked against the…enormity of the sensations filling her to capacity. Like the man.

Holy hell.

Adam.

She'd never been so…possessed. Not one iota of her sex remained unavailable to him. He stamped all of her— branded her. It was almost too much. Almost not enough.

Crazy.

How could both be true at the same time? And yet, they were. Tears burned her eyes, and she squeezed her lids closed against the sting. This was a mistake. Sex shouldn't feel like *this*. Not one-night-stand sex. Fun. Pleasurable. Sometimes regrettable. That was one-night-stand sex. But never *this*.

Never monumental.

Never *important*.

Panic scratched at her throat. No, fucking clawed. With tearing talons.

An embarrassing sound emanated from her—a sound like a wounded, scared animal—and she slapped at his shoulders. She couldn't utter words. Just those awful, humiliating sounds.

In a startling shift of movement, Adam twisted, and though they remained connected, she straddled him. And the air, the freedom—the hint of control—dulled the razor edges of panic.

"Open your eyes, queen." She opened her eyes, submitting to his order. And stared down into his bright, intense gaze. "Focus on me and only me."

She wasn't only helpless to obey; she *wanted* to obey.

Another thing that didn't make sense.

It'd been him—this night with him—that had hurled her into a panic attack, and yet, she clung to him like a shipwreck victim clinging to the only remaining piece of driftwood.

She did as he demanded and focused on him, on the beacon of his stare.

"Breathe with me," he murmured. "In. Out. In. Out. That's good, baby. In. Out."

She followed his instructions, not even aware, just falling into his rhythm, and slowly, oh so slowly, the panic released its talons. But not without leaving behind wounds. Humiliating, burning wounds.

"Don't do it." His fingers gripped her chin again, tipping it up. A frown arrowed his thick eyebrows down, and his eyes seemed to gleam brighter. "Don't you dare do it. Whatever just happened, it happened, and there's no shame. Not here. You need to fuck out what's going on here—" he tapped her temple "—and here—" he stroked a caress over her heart "—then do it. Forget what I said about using me. Use me and my dick to get it out, but never be embarrassed, queen. It doesn't sit well on you."

She closed her eyes, but only briefly. Long enough for those words to resonate through her. To...not heal but maybe soothe her. To cleanse some of the dirty mortification.

"You're still hard," she whispered, circling her hips, swallowing a gasp at the resurgence of pleasure.

"I'm inside you, aren't I?" He grunted, shaking his

head as if her observation was the most absurd thing he'd ever heard. "Ride me, queen. Fuck me."

With the dregs of emotion and confusion still eddying inside her alongside the rising tide of lust, she didn't need another invitation. Palming his wide shoulders, she ground her hips against his, dragging groans from them both. She tilted her head back, but a hand at the nape of her neck nudged her face up.

"Eyes on me," Adam mandated. "If you're going to use me, look at me."

With his cock pulsing inside her, and her flesh quivering around that thick length, she was too hungry, too desperate, to put up an argument. Not removing her gaze from his, she slid halfway up his dick, then dropped back down, slamming him deep. Again, their twin sounds—his low and graveled, hers higher and keening—punched the air.

"More," she breathed to herself. But Adam answered as if she spoke to him.

"Take it, queen. Take all you need," he encouraged, one big palm cupping her hip, the other covering her breast, his thumb flicking a nipple, sending a cascade of fire through her veins.

She lost herself.

With his permission and with total abandon, she threw herself into a wild ride that would've scared her at another time. Would probably terrify her in the morning. But now, with his cock granting her a physical and emotional outlet with every thrust, every piston, every dirty grind... She would gladly face the consequences.

True to his word, Adam let her dominate, use him, fuck him. Nothing was off-limits. Not when she climbed off him and put her mouth to him, condom and all. Not when she sank back onto him, facing his thick thighs. And when he surged up with a growl, his damp chest pressed to her spine, she curled an arm around his neck, welcoming the edge of his teeth to her shoulder.

"Please," she whispered, voice hoarse with need.

He didn't ask her to expound; he seemed to know for what she pleaded. And he gave it to her. Cradling one breast and pinching the diamond-hard nipple between his fingers, his other hand snaked down over her trembling belly and between her thighs. He circled her clit, rubbing it. Then pinched it just as he did the beaded tip of her breast.

She exploded.

Detonated with a cry that abraded her throat and a fear that shuddered through her soul.

Because even as he powered into her from below and followed her into orgasm, she couldn't shake the instinct from earlier.

This—Adam, the night with him, *sex* with him— might've been the biggest mistake she'd made.

CHAPTER THREE

"Baby, I promise I'll be back. You be a sweet boy for your daddy, okay? Listen to him and be good. I'll see you soon."

"No. Don't go." Adam clutched at his mother's arm, putting all his weight on her.

Desperately trying to keep her there, in the house. Even at seven years old he knew if she walked out that door, he wouldn't see her again. She wouldn't be there to meet him at the bus stop after school and take him home to share a snack she'd prepared as she questioned him about his day. Wouldn't be there to help him with his homework and never yell at him if he didn't get the answers right away. Wouldn't be there to read him his favorite bedtime story about the Wild Things and not get mean when he asked to leave the bathroom light on and the door cracked.

She just wouldn't...be there.

And he would be stuck with Daddy.

Adam tugged harder. "Please, Mommy. Please. Stay," he begged.

"Stop that fucking whining and get off of her," his father snapped.

A second later he yanked on Adam's arm. For a moment Adam's grasp tightened on his mother, but in the next, he stumbled backward, his hands grasping air.

Grasping for her. His back slapped his father's leg before he tripped and hit the wall of the foyer.

"Get out, bitch."

Adam knew his father wasn't talking to him because he hadn't said "lil' bitch" just "bitch." So he meant his mother.

"Maurice..." his mother whispered.

"You let another man get his dick wet in what's mine and think you're going to stay in my house?" he snarled. "Get the fuck out and don't come back. We don't exist for you anymore. None of us."

Adam didn't understand all of what his father said, but he more than got one part. Don't come back.

A wild grief and fear churned inside him, and that morning's Froot Loops pitched toward his throat. His mouth watered in the way it did just before he'd thrown up on Halloween after he'd eaten too much candy.

"Mommy, don't go," he pleaded, risking his father's anger turned on him. He didn't care. Just as long as she didn't leave. "Please."

"Shut up," his father barked, glaring down at him. Then he switched his narrowed gaze back to his mother. "Why are you still here? Get. Out. Before I put you out."

Adam went still, quiet. And his mother swallowed, releasing a soft sound that made his stomach hurt, his chest tight.

"I'll be back, baby," his mother said to him, and she smiled.

But the sight of the small, shaky curve of her lips only caused his belly to hurt worse. And tears burned his eyes. Even knowing his father would call him a bad name, he still couldn't hold them back.

His father snorted. "The hell you will. When you fucked another man, you gave up all your rights to this."

He slashed a hand in front of Adam. "Say goodbye, bitch. This is the last time you'll see him."

She stared into Adam's eyes, and even though tears blurred his vision, he stared at her, burning her face into his memory.

"I love you, Adam," she said as his father grabbed the knob and yanked the front door open. As he gripped her shoulder and shoved her toward it. "I love you. I'll see you soon..."

Adam jerked awake, chest heaving, breath shuddering out of his lungs. Sweat dampened his skin, and his heart beat against his rib cage like a drum. Just like seven-year-old him, sour swill roiled in his gut.

"Fuck." He scrubbed his fingers over his head, then down his face.

That dream hadn't visited him in a long time. It'd been years. Why now, dammit? Why had his subconscious decided to delight him with it now?

Rubbing the heel of his palm over his chest—directly over his still pounding heart—he sat up, staring at the dark TV screen across from him. He held his breath, then after several seconds, slowly, deliberately exhaled it. The sticky remnants of the dream started to loosen their grim hold, and he lowered his arms to his sides.

Just a dream. Just a fucked-up dream of a fucked-up time. But he was no longer that scared little boy crying for his mother. A mother who hadn't kept her promise. A mother who hadn't come back.

"Shit," he muttered, throwing back the covers that had warded off the early-spring chill.

He was too old for nightmares about his mommy, for God's sake. After pushing off the bed, he padded across the room, but before he could reach the hallway and the bathroom, his cell phone rang. The jangle of *Labyrinth*'s

"Magic Dance" filled the room, and a smile lifted a corner of his mouth. Retracing his footsteps, he picked up the cell, not needing the screen to identify the caller. He'd assigned only one person that song.

"Hey, Addie," he greeted his sister. Technically, half sister since they shared a father, but she would rip him a new asshole if she ever heard the *half* come out of his mouth. "Are you two almost here?"

Adele laughed, the warm sound infectious, and his own smile grew.

"What you mean is am I almost there with your precious Justine," she teased, and he shrugged even though she couldn't see the gesture.

"True."

Another chuckle, and he could imagine her shaking her head, her signature long ponytail swinging over her shoulder.

"Asshole," she said, humor lacing her voice. "I'm leaving Hartford Airport now and should be to you in about forty minutes, give or take."

"Good." He glanced behind him at the clock on the bedside table. Almost nine o'clock. Damn. He scrubbed a hand down his face again. He usually didn't sleep this late, especially with a five-year-old daughter. But that dream… He shook his head, refusing to acknowledge it could have that much power over him. "I still wish you would've let me meet you at the airport. You're being as difficult as you've always been. I swear, I should've taken you off in the woods and left you like I started to when you were ten."

Adele loosed a bark of laughter. "Please. You would've never got rid of me. Breadcrumbs, bruh. I'm always at the ready, messing around with you."

"They should've named your ass barnacle instead of Adele."

Another cackle. "You lucky I know talking shit is your love language."

"Hey," he admonished, fighting a grin. "My baby's in the car with you. If she comes home cursing, I'm blaming you."

"Well, let me just say 'my bad' in advance." She chuckled. "Seriously, though, thank you for letting me have Jussy for a couple of weeks. She's been an absolute angel, as usual. Obviously, she gets that from me."

"I'm going to let you have that one." He shook his head and continued toward the bathroom. "But thank *you* for keeping her while I got settled here." *Here* being Rose Bend, Massachusetts. "I've missed my baby girl, but I did manage to unpack and get the house straight."

And I managed to have a one-night stand with a woman who blew my mind.

He pinched the bridge of his nose, closing his eyes as he drew to a halt in front of the bathroom sink. But when he opened them and met his reflection, the same wince that had been crossing his face for the past three days lifted his lips and narrowed his eyes. Again.

And, just like he'd been telling himself for the past three days, this wasn't New York City or Boston where he could walk around for years and never meet the same person twice. No, this was small town, USA, and chances were he could run into "Queen" at any time. Hell, yesterday he'd surveyed the crowded Mimi's Café in search of that face of arresting angles, heavy-lidded eyes and lascivious curves.

He didn't know—or didn't want to acknowledge— if he was relieved or disappointed about not seeing her.

If he didn't dig too deep then he wouldn't analyze

why in the hell he'd given in to that one-night stand in the first place. It wasn't like that had been the first time he'd been hit on by a beautiful woman. Or man, for that matter. And it damn sure hadn't been the first time he'd been instantly attracted to a person.

But he'd promised himself years ago never to mix business with pleasure—even if that pleasure continued to haunt him days later. The first time he'd done it had ultimately ended in a broken marriage. And while the woman he'd met and spent the night with didn't work for him, she did live in the small town where he would live for a few short months. Just as long as it required him to complete the Victorian house renovation.

He didn't need any entanglements to distract him from his daughter, Justine, or the job.

"Adam?" Adele asked, voice softening. "You good?"

"Yeah." He gave his head an abrupt shake. "Yeah, I'm fine. Just can't wait to see you two. But don't hurry, take your time on the road. You have special cargo and I want you to get her here safely."

"Aww, thank you, punkin," she drawled. "I knew you cared."

"Now we both know I was referring to Jussy. Talk to you in a few," he said.

Adele snorted. "Bye. But I'm googling big brother outlets to see where I can trade one in. You suck at this."

Chuckling, he ended the call, and the heaviness that had dogged him since waking up shifted and started to lift. His little girl would be home in less than an hour. No nightmare compared to that.

"Daddy!"

Adam grinned as Justine flew out of the car's back seat as soon as Adele opened the door. A whirlwind in pink and purple hurled toward him. Before his daughter got halfway, he met her in the middle of the walk, swinging her up into his arms.

He closed his eyes as he inhaled her familiar scent of cocoa butter, bubble gum and that undefinable little-girl smell. It'd only been a couple of weeks—fifteen days, to be exact—but he'd missed the hell out of her.

"Hi, Daddy!" she yelled as if he were across the street instead of holding her in his arms. Clapping her hands on either side of his face, she smushed his cheeks and planted a loud, smacking kiss on his mouth. "I missed you!" she declared, again at a volume between loud and *I have no idea what an inside voice is.* "Kadie missed you, too!"

Justine thrust the teddy bear that she was never without in front of his face, and as expected, he gave Kadie a loud kiss on the nose. His little girl giggled and tucked the stuffed animal her mom had given her on her third birthday under her arm.

His chest tightened, but he inhaled a deep breath, then deliberately exhaled, attempting to douse the familiar burn of anger and frustration.

"I missed you, too, baby girl." Smiling, he squeezed her tight just so she could squeal and squirm. Unable to hold in his laughter at her antics, he kissed her cheek, then glanced over Justine's head at his sister. "Hey, Addie."

"I mean, I'm just standing here." His sister spread her arms wide, Justine's small unicorn book bag in one hand and a purse in the other. "Don't mind me. I just got her here safely."

"Jussy, do you hear anyone talking?"

"Nope." She shook her head so hard, her braided ponytails slapped her rounded cheeks. "I don't hear nuthin'," she said, giggling at their running joke.

"I see how you are, you little traitor," Adele grumbled, walking up to them. She slid the backpack strap over her shoulder and poked Justine in the side, making his daughter giggle harder. "You look good. Real good for someone who's been unpacking a house for the last few days."

He shook his head, turning to retrace his path back to the house.

"I'm an old pro at this by now." Sad but true.

His career often took him away from Chicago for months at a time, several times a year.

"Emphasis on *old*," she teased, and he arched an eyebrow.

"Really? Age jokes? That's not beneath you at your big age of thirty?"

"Not as long as you remain seven years older than me, no, not beneath me and it'll never grow old." She laughed, climbing the short flight of steps leading to the wide porch that bellied up to the rental home. "That's going to have to change in another year. Jussy's getting older and will be starting kindergarten this coming school year. Unless you plan on continuing to homeschool her?"

He didn't immediately answer, pulling open the storm door and holding it for Adele. Irritation tugged at him, and he deliberately smothered it.

Adele loved him, adored Justine. And he returned the sentiment, considering she was his only family— at least the only family he had a relationship with. Yet, sometimes he chafed at her mothering. He was the older brother, had taken care of her—damn near raised her— for most of their childhood. But being a natural nurturer, Adele seemed to have forgotten that lately. No, forget *lately*. In the past two years since his divorce. Only because her concern and nagging originated from a loving source had he kept his mouth shut.

And because his telling her to back off a little, that he wasn't the lost man he'd been after Jennifer walked out, would hurt Adele's feelings. *That* he tried to avoid at all costs. In the end, she was still his little sister, and he was still the protective big brother. Even if he needed to protect her from his mouth.

"I'm still thinking on it," he finally replied, setting Justine down in the tiny foyer. "Here you go, Jussy. Your room is the first one down there." He pointed toward the short hallway. "Want to go check it out?"

"Yeah!" She took off running, and when he reminded her of no running in the house, she slowed to a power walk.

Chuckling, Adele stepped inside, heading toward the living room. Once there, she dropped down on the couch with a sigh.

"So…" She squinted up at him. "This town. It's pretty, but I swear, I started to pull over and check my mouth for cavities. It's so—" she scrunched up her face "—sweet. There's an honest-to-God ice cream shop named Six Ways to Sundae. That's too fucking cute. Leaves me wondering what seedy underbelly this place is hiding."

Shaking his head, he headed for the kitchen.

"Watch out, Addie. Your cynicism is showing." He slid a pod and mug into the single-cup coffeemaker and in moments, the delicious fragrance of roasted beans permeated the room. Hell, he'd drink the air right now, that scent was so addicting.

"Tell me I'm wrong." He glanced over his shoulder to find his sister peering at him, eyebrows arched and folded arms propped on the back of the couch. "Tell me this place is too perfect and pretty not to have dirty secrets."

For some reason, an image of him pinning "Queen's"

hands above her head, those perfect, dark-tipped breasts pointing toward the ceiling, while he thrust into her over and over flashed in his mind. He didn't even need to concentrate hard to hear her jagged, soft cries in his ear or feel the clasp of her strong thighs around his hips.

His fingers tightened around the handle of the full coffee cup.

Dirty secrets. Yeah, they might be that to each other, and the flex of his dick behind his zipper telegraphed he had no problem with it.

"It's a beautiful town, but no different from others I've been in," he said, his tone carefully neutral, not betraying the pull in his gut or the slight elevation of his pulse at the intrusion of the other night's memory. Swiftly, he replaced the used pod with another and the full mug with an empty one. "And just like those, I'm sure a hub of Hydra isn't using it as a front for global destruction."

"How you know?" She stretched her hands out to him as he approached her with the coffee-filled cup. Nearly snatching it from him, she took a sip with an appreciative hum. "I mean, it's not like you'd know if their agents were up to no good until it was too late. One moment you're looking at crown molding and *bam*, the next you're kidnapped to construct a Victorian-style bunker for their next nefarious plot for world domination."

He poked her in the forehead, frowning.

"I know there's an off button somewhere…" he muttered, then grinned when Adele slapped his hand away. "I hope you don't get as creative with numbers at that CPA firm as you do with these tangents you go off on. Just say you're going to miss us and be done with it."

"Damn right I am," she grumbled, scowling at him over the cup's rim. "You keep taking these jobs in No-wheresville, USA, leaving me alone for months at a time with…" She didn't finish the sentence, but her sigh and eye roll completed the thought as if she'd yelled it through a megaphone.

"Right." His lips curled, but he knew it didn't resemble a smile. He hadn't smiled around his father for more years than he could remember. "How is Maurice?"

He hadn't been "Dad" in more years than he could remember, either.

"Dad is—" another sigh "—Dad. Difficult. Mad at the world. Always right."

Adam snorted. "And the new stepmother?" he asked, but more out of consideration for Adele, who actually seemed to care for their father.

Adam didn't really give a damn. After wife number four, he'd stopped learning their names. None of them ever stuck around for very long.

His father possessed the singular talent of running the women who loved him away. Sour acid swilled in his stomach. Like father, like son. Adam had inherited that "gift."

Turning on his heel, he headed back to the kitchen and the cup waiting for him. Anger and another emotion that trudged too close to fear trickled through him. The coffee wouldn't sit well right about now, but he needed something to do with his hands. And his face. Adele, who knew him better than any other person, would glimpse the emotion churning through him. And he damn sure didn't feel like having that conversation.

"Firmly entrenched in 'I'd love to heal the relationship between your dad and his kids' mode." Adele scoffed. "Why does every wife default to that? I had to tell her straight up that many women have tried and failed before her. She isn't listening, though. So if you get a call with a

312 area code, avoid it. Maybe she thinks because she's wife number seven, she's lucky or something."

Ahh. Number seven.

"She'll lose that optimism soon enough." Adam picked up his cup, and only when he felt like he'd wiped all emotion from his face did he turn around to meet his sister's steady gaze. "They always do."

"Speaking of wives…" Adele tipped her head to the side. And *oh shit*. He recognized the gleam in her eyes. "When was the last time you heard from Jennifer?"

Instinctively, he glanced toward the hallway, but only the sound of Justine's bright chatter reached him. From experience, he assumed she was "talking" to her dolls. Still, he crossed the room again, circling the couch to sit on the other end. Though his feelings about his ex-wife veered toward frustration, Justine adored her mother. Missed her, was confused about why she didn't live with them anymore, but still, adored her. He wouldn't do anything, including letting her overhear his comments, to change that.

"It's been a little over three months." He huffed out a short, bitter laugh. "She didn't even call on her birthday, Addie. Her daughter's birthday. When I *finally* got in touch with her three days later, do you know what her excuse was?"

"I'm afraid to ask," Adele murmured.

"She'd gone camping in Joshua Tree National Park so her cell reception was bad." Anger flashed inside him, and just as quickly, he snuffed it out. Being mad didn't serve a damn thing. Hadn't saved his marriage. Didn't make his ex want to be a better mother—hell, a present mother—to their daughter. Just…pointless. "What responsible mother thinks it's okay to not give their only daughter one call on her birthday? Hell, what mother thinks it's okay to go days without cell reception? What if something had happened to Jussy? What if she'd fallen sick? There would've been no way to get in touch with Jennifer because she was off on another of her 'I'm finding myself' expeditions. I don't fucking get it," he ground out.

Him, he didn't care about her walking away from. But Jussy? No matter which way he analyzed it, he couldn't understand that.

"What kind of mother thinks that's okay? One who doesn't deserve the name. If anyone knows that, you and I do."

He nodded, frowning down into his coffee cup as if the dark brew would dole up answers. But just as he hadn't comprehended how his mother could abandon him and never contact him again, he couldn't grasp his wife's behavior. And no amount of coffee would help him figure it out.

"There's something else I need to tell you," Adele quietly said, drawing his attention back to her. "Dad had a health scare about a month back. After a routine doctor's office visit, he ended up getting a biopsy done on a tumor in his neck."

"What?" he demanded. "I was in Chicago then. No one said anything to me about this."

She shrugged a shoulder, but didn't meet his eyes. "He ordered us…not to. He didn't want—"

"Please." He shot up a hand, halting the excuse about to come out of her mouth. "Don't bother making up an excuse for him. We're so far past that."

Her shoulders slumped as if a weight dropped down on them. "You're right. Still, I'm sorry," she whispered, finally looking at him. Regret swam in eyes the same color as his, both an inheritance from their father. "It was ultimately benign so everything's okay there, but I thought you should know. I mean, he's an ass most of the time but he's still our dad. You should've known weeks ago."

"Thanks for the heads-up."

She winced, pain flashing across her features. "Adam, don't say—"

"I'm good, Addie. And I mean that. Glad the results weren't worse."

He did mean it; he didn't hate Maurice. Definitely didn't wish any kind of illness on him. His father just didn't add to his life, nor did he take away from it. He was just a nonfactor.

Heaving a sigh, Adele nodded then, raising her cup to her mouth, slowly surveyed the living room, dining room and what was available of the kitchen.

"I have no shame in admitting I'm going to miss you two. I do every time you leave Chicago," she said. "You and Jussy, you're the only real family I have."

Like him, she didn't have a relationship with her mother, though she did possess a slightly better one with their father than he did. Still, from the time they were young until now, it had mostly been the two of them.

"I miss you, too. And any time you want to come visit us for however long, whether it's a couple of days or months until my job's done, there's an extra room for you."

"I know." She nodded. "And thank you. Just don't fall in love with this place, okay? No, don't shake your head at me," she ordered when he started to do just that. "This place has a certain charm. I peeped that as soon as I drove through downtown. So promise me you won't fall under the spell of it, decide to stay and not return home."

Even as he scoffed, an image of a certain woman with gorgeous, long locs, wide, dark brown eyes and a plush, worship-worthy mouth flickered across his mind's eye.

Heat circled his gut, but he ignored it as he smiled at his sister.

"I promise, Addie. I'm coming home when I'm finished here. Rose Bend is nothing but a job and a pretty town."

A more suspicious man would feel like those were famous last words.

Good thing he wasn't a suspicious man.

CHAPTER FOUR

"*VINTAGE RENOVATION?* SERIOUSLY? They're coming here?" Flo gaped at her brother, Coltrane "Cole" Dennison. Honest to God gaped, and she couldn't help herself.

Because *Vintage Renovation.* In *Rose Bend.* She *loved* that show. It was one of her favorites on cable's Home Improvement Channel.

"Yes, *Vintage Renovation: Queen Anne Edition*, to be exact. It's a new version of the series. A couple just bought the old Hudson place and hired an outside contractor to renovate it as well as restore it. And *Vintage Renovation* wants to feature the project," Cole explained.

"How amazing." Flo set the take-out container from the Sunnyside Grille, the local diner—the best diner in town—on top of his desk. "When does filming start?"

"Thank you for this," Cole said, sliding the container closer. He flicked the top open and grinned at the sight of the squash casserole, macaroni and cheese and meat loaf. The delicious aroma filled his office and elicited a grumble from her own stomach. "Where's yours? Because I'm not sharing."

She cocked her head, smirking. "Really? You're an ungrateful ass." Laughing, she waved a hand toward the meal. "I'm picking up my own lunch on the way back to the studio. I didn't want it to be cold since I have a client coming in at one-thirty." Copping a glance down at her watch, she noticed that was about an hour and a half from now. "When Sydney brought Patience in on Tuesday for pictures," she said, referring to his wife and five-year-old stepdaughter, "she mentioned how you barely left the office for lunch. So I thought I'd bring you some food so your wife wouldn't worry about you wasting away to nothing."

His grin softened into a smile, love lighting his eyes. Something tugged at her chest, twisting between her ribs as she glimpsed the emotion. *Something* because she refused to name it—was too ashamed to. It swerved too close to envy for her comfort. Which made zero sense because she didn't desire a relationship.

No, she wanted none of that.

But maybe, just maybe, she might wonder what it felt like to be so loved, so secure in that love, that your eyes lit up at just the thought of your person.

She was thrilled that Cole had that. Especially since before Sydney returned to Rose Bend six years ago, he'd suffered a tragedy no person should ever have to endure. He'd lost his first wife and baby in childbirth, and for a while Flo and the rest of the family believed they'd never see him smile again. But then Sydney had returned home, pregnant with Patience, and she'd given him back love and a family. Flo would always be grateful and adore Sydney for that.

Also helped that she was really cool people.

"Getting back to *Vintage Renovation*, it *is* amazing as you said," he said, scooping a forkful of mac 'n' cheese. "And not just for the new buyers of the Hudson house, but Rose Bend, too. This will bring the town national attention, and that converts into tourists and revenue."

"Always thinking about your constituents, huh?" she teased, smiling.

Cole was mayor of Rose Bend, this being his sixth

year. The townspeople kept reelecting him because he was one of those rare species of politicians who actually kept his promises. Not only had he expanded the annual motorcycle ride, brought more festivals and spearheaded the construction of new projects, including an elder and children's care center, but he also cared about this town and its citizens, as well as their concerns. The same couldn't be said for their previous mayor, Jasper Landon. To put it simply, he'd been a condescending jerk of a racist—and wasn't that kind of redundant? His daughter, Jenna, who'd been known as the town bitch for the longest time, was now family and could often be found at their dinner table on Sunday and at their regular girls' night.

Jenna's father was still a douche, though.

"If by constituents you mean my favorite little sister…" He jabbed his fork in her direction. "If you tell Leo, Sinead or Cher I said that, I'll deny, deny, deny."

Flo snickered. "Hell, you really *are* a politician."

Cole narrowed his eyes on her. "I'm reconsidering that favorite little sister part all of a sudden. And you really shouldn't be antagonizing the person who comes bearing gifts."

"Gifts?" Flo straightened in her chair, leaning forward. Curiosity sparked inside her, as did anticipation. "You should've led with that. What is it? What's the occasion?"

"You're so predictable, you know that?" Cole gave a huff of laughter. "Hold on a second. Let me explain."

Sliding one last helping of food between his lips, he set the container aside and focused all his attention on her. Looking every inch the mayor and attorney he was, he set his clasped hands on the desktop, shifting forward, his dark curls brushing his high cheekbones. Even after all these years, the sight of those curls set off a tight pinch in her sternum. Right after his first wife's death, Cole had cut off his hair, a show of mourning. Only after he'd married Sydney had he finally let his curls grow back. Everyone had welcomed them, had seen them as a sign of his healing.

She still did.

"Having *Vintage Renovation* here is a great prospect for Rose Bend. So with the new home buyers' permission, the town council brainstormed ways to capitalize on the filming, and we came up with something." He paused for effect, and when she rolled her eyes at his dramatics, twirling a hand for him to get on with it, Cole grinned. "A coffee-table book documenting the restoration project and the television show. We would sell it in the gift shop and pharmacy, and it would be the perfect tourist gift. Also, the production company has opted to purchase photos for their site and social media, as well. It would be a wonderful opportunity for the perfect photographer."

Flo's heart pounded in her chest, echoed in her eardrums. Swallowing, she could only stare at her brother, unable to gather enough moisture to wet her suddenly dry mouth. Working on the set of one of her favorite TV shows aside, she *needed* this. And not just for her limited résumé. But for *her*. Her self-confidence. Her self-esteem.

It'd been a week since she'd returned home from Thailand…a week since she'd spent that sizzling hot night with Adam to distract her from the bust that trip had been. But in the days that followed, the anger had fled, and the doubts and insecurities had crowded in, chipping away at her piece by piece. She recognized that it was negative, destructive thinking, tried to combat it with working, with doing the very thing that imbued her with joy and purpose.

But as grateful as she was for the studio, taking birthday and holiday pictures didn't encapsulate her dream.

Immortalizing the energy of the teeming, boat-filled Chao Phraya River in Bangkok did.

Capturing the passion, outrage and grief of a protest over police brutality on an urban city street.

Celebrating the love of a couple celebrating fifty years of marriage as they visited the Grand Canyon for the first time.

That was why she'd chosen photography.

To praise the intricacies of humans and their emotions. To stir conversations about the conditions of people's hearts. To reveal with her camera lens what could remain hidden to the naked eye.

That wasn't *Vintage Renovation*.

But it was a stepping stone toward exposure so she could have more projects like that.

"Are you saying I'm that perfect photographer?" she whispered, addressing his comment.

He cocked his head, studied her, the humor ebbing from his gaze to be replaced by something sharper and yet softer.

"*Are* you that perfect photographer, Flo?" he asked.

She didn't hesitate. "Yes. I'm her."

Cole smiled, and if she wasn't mistaken, a flash of pride glittered in his eyes.

"Good." He nodded. "Glad to know we're in agreement on that. Especially since I already proposed your name to the town council, and we voted on you taking the job. It would've been pretty embarrassing to have to go back and tell them you turned me down. Which—" he arched an eyebrow as he grabbed his take-out container and reopened the lid "—let's be clear, I wasn't doing. If I had to drag Moe into this, you were going to be on this project."

Flo groaned, but her grin probably ruined the effect. Billie Dennison—or Moe, as they all called her, including everyone in town—had a huge heart, but as she often told Flo and the rest of her children, "I may have only brought half of you in this world, but I'll take you all out." Now, Moe loved all of them too much to do them bodily harm, but still...Flo didn't try her.

Needless to say, Moe Dennison proved to be a suitable threat.

"Really?" Flo squinted at her brother. "You're a little too tall and old to be tattling to your mama."

He snorted. "Says who? Not if it works. Now, is it working?"

"You could've saved that one in your back pocket. I would've taken the job without it." She pushed up out of her seat and rounded the desk, smacking a loud kiss on her brother's cheek. "Thank you, Cole. Thank you for believing in me."

"Of course, Flo," he murmured. "I have so much confidence in you and your talent. What you can do with a camera..." He shook his head. "Yes, I'm excited about the TV show and the restoration. But I'm so damn excited about how you're going to shine. Because, little sister, you're going to rival the sun."

Love so bright, so hot, burst in her chest, she fought not to press the heel of her hand right over her heart. God, she loved her brother. Where one man had tried to strip her of her self-esteem, her strength, her voice, another man, *this* man, built her up, encouraged her, sought to empower her.

"You're my favorite big brother, Cole Dennison." She blinked against the sudden and unwanted burn of tears. Glancing away, she cleared her throat, taking a moment.

When she looked back at him, she grinned. "Don't tell Wolf or Sonny, though. That stays between you and me."

"Oh, of course." Cole slowly nodded. "But if I did happen to let it slip, I'm about eighty-six percent sure they would say you've told them the same thing."

She gasped, spreading her fingers wide over her chest. "Why, Cole. That hurts. It really does."

"And yet, I hear no denial." He snorted, then slowly, the humor evaporated from his face.

Her stomach flipped. "What's wrong?" she asked, stepping back. "Why're you looking like that?"

Cole sighed. "Damn photographers. You don't miss anything."

She shook her head. "Nothing to do with being a photographer. I'm your sister and I've known you almost all my life. Which means I recognize all your expressions. And this one clearly says, 'Oh shit. I'd rather be anywhere else but here.'"

"Okay, I stand corrected. Damn baby sisters. You don't miss anything." Releasing another sigh, he opened the desk drawer above his lap and withdrew a red envelope. The kind that accompanied greeting cards.

She froze, her gaze latching on to the piece of mail as if it contained a biological agent instead of a harmless card.

But it's not harmless, is it?

Flo tried to shush that know-it-all voice in her head, but her heart… Her heavily thumping heart couldn't ignore that sly question. Because it wasn't innocuous. Not to her peace of mind. Not to the carefully constructed guard erected around her past and all the shit that threatened to leak out every time she received one of these fucking cards.

"Thanks." She injected a careful calm into the word as she forced herself to accept the card from Cole.

She didn't need to peruse the return address to determine the identity of the sender. Didn't need to open the flap to discover a birthday card inside, although hers had been three weeks ago. No, she didn't need to do any of that. Because every birthday and Christmas the same mail arrived. Sometimes the frequency changed due to life's special occasions—like her high school and college graduation. But other than that, they were the same. And from the same person.

And like all the others that had come before this one, it would end up tossed in the same place.

A shoebox tucked on a shelf in the hall closet.

She hid them from sight, just as the first father she'd known hid her from his.

"Flo, I can just tell Dad I gave it to you," Cole said, reaching for the envelope. "He won't question me."

A flash of anger shimmered bright and hard in her chest before she doused it, weariness creeping into her bones, adding a heaviness to her body that she couldn't shake loose.

She tried so hard to pretend as if the biannual mail from Noah Dennison didn't affect her. As if she didn't walk around like a real life Pig-Pen, her emotions swarming around her in a dark, dusty cloud, dragging her every step. She acted like the cards were no big deal to protect her father, Ian Dennison.

After all, it wouldn't do for her father to know Flo resented everything about his brother.

Now it seemed her acting skills had gone to waste. If Cole sensed she didn't want the cards, who else knew? All her brothers and sisters? Moe?

She didn't want their concern.

Didn't need their pity.

Both made her feel like an ungrateful bitch. And a horrible daughter.

"Not necessary." She scrounged up a smile for Cole's sake, but when his eyes narrowed on her, she figured that effort had been an epic fail. So she shrugged a shoulder. "It's no big deal. Definitely not worth lying to Dad about. It's fine."

"I wouldn't be lying," he countered like the attorney he was. "I did give you the card. Doesn't mean I can't take it back."

That hauled a dry laugh out of her, and she moved closer to him. Leaning down, she kissed his cheek again. "Thank you for being willing to prevaricate on my behalf like any self-respecting big brother. But like I said, it's fine. *I'm* fine. Now," she said, arching an eyebrow, "back to why I'm here, besides making sure you don't starve yourself. *Vintage Renovation*. When do I start?"

After a pause where she could practically spy the war waging in his head over whether or not to push the subject of his uncle and her absentee father, he finally conceded. "In two days. Check your email later tonight."

"Great. And thanks again. This means the world."

"Uh-huh." He picked up his fork and dug into the mac 'n' cheese. "Just remember that the next time you talk to Wolf."

"Right."

She patted his shoulder and walked out of his office. Closing the door on her laughter, she maintained her grin until she stood alone in the hall. Then she searched for a calm that, from past experience, would be elusive for at least the next few days. If not the week.

After a moment, she headed toward the stairs, the envelope searing her hand, a corporal reminder that love could not only be selfish and self-satisfying but also disappointing.

Over and over again.

Good thing she didn't plan on falling for that trap.

FLO PULLED UP to the curb outside the Queen Anne Victorian and parked, staring up at the house that sat on top of the small rise like the royalty it was named after. When she'd left the studio this afternoon, she'd intended to head back to the inn for dinner with the family, but as hard as she tried, that damn card had her in her feelings. And none of them were good. Definitely not conducive to putting on a happy face for the way-too-perceptive Dennison clan.

Needing a distraction, she'd ended up here. This house where she would spend a good part of her time for the next few months when not in her photography studio.

As far back as she could remember, the huge white, blue and pastel green home with its turrets and pitched roofs had made her believe a real-life castle existed in Rose Bend's midst. Now, at twenty-four, she might not see Sleeping Beauty's home, but that grand wraparound porch with the peeling white columns still evoked dreams of late summer, lazy naps. The former owner had stopped maintaining the landscaping some time ago, but even the overgrown lawn and shrubbery couldn't detract from the once beautiful red-brick driveway or the steep, graceful walkway. Once restored, this majestic beauty would shine like it was meant to.

And she couldn't wait to document each and every step with her camera.

Pushing her door open, she exited her Jeep Renegade, gaze centered on the Victorian. In a matter of days, this area would be swarming with a television crew, contractors and repairmen, but right now only the distant cry of children's laughter and the call of adult voices peppered the air. Trees and big lots separated the nearest house. Which would be a blessing when the television crews arrived and the construction started.

Though the house had passed through several owners in the past few years, everyone in Rose Bend still referred to it as the Hudson House, named after the original homeowners from the late 1800s. Until the mid-1960s, one of their family members had lived there, but then it had been sold to a couple from New York, so the story went. To Flo, the history of the Victorian was as much a part of its beauty as the wide, dark green front door, the large bay windows and the battered but lovely gazebo around back.

She sighed, a sense of peace settling in her spirit, as she approached the porch steps. Her fingers tingled to have her Sony A7 III in her hands. With the sun inching toward the horizon, its rays hit the spires of the turrets like a halo, causing the roof, with some of its missing shingles, to appear like a great, slumbering dragon and its spiked tail. She glanced behind her toward her car, a slight frown creasing her brow. Her studio and apartment were about ten minutes away. By the time she made it there, picked up her camera and returned here, the light would probably be gone—

"Hi. Who are you?"

Flo stiffened at the sound of the sweet, high-pitched voice, surprise winging through her. Turning around, she frowned, only seeing the towering red maple trees that stood guard in front of the white wooden fence.

"I'm Jussy. Who're you?" the small voice spoke again, and Flo dropped her gaze, meeting a pair of curious dark brown eyes.

"Hi, Jussy." Smiling, Flo hunkered down on her heels, getting closer to the little girl's level. Petite, slender and adorable with almond skin, pretty eyes and puffy pigtails, she couldn't have been much more than six years old. Glancing around and spying just her, Flo returned her attention to the girl. "It's nice to meet you. I'm Florence Dennison. But everyone calls me Flo."

"Hi, Flo." Jussy waved the hand not clutched around a pink-and-yellow teddy bear that had seen better days. "Do you live here?"

"No, I don't. I'm just visiting." She shook her head then surveyed the quiet, deserted area again. "Jussy, are you here alone? Where are your parents?"

"My mommy's gone," she said simply, and Flo blinked.

Gone? As in died? *God.* The urge to gather the little girl close and hug her swelled inside Flo. She had been several years younger than this little girl when she'd lost her own mother. Though she'd been blessed to be raised by a wonderful, beautiful woman, there would always be a part of her that missed the mother she remembered only through faint impressions and pictures.

"My daddy's over there." Jussy twisted her upper body around, pointing toward the Victorian. "He's planning."

Planning? *O-kay.* Flo had zero idea what that meant.

"Planning, huh?" Palming her knees, Flo rose and stretched out a hand toward Jussy. "That sounds super important—" *not* "—but let's go find him so you're not here by yourself, okay?"

Slowly, Jussy shook her head and crossed her thin arms over her chest, strangling her teddy bear.

"I'm not supposed to go anywhere with strangers, Flo," Jussy informed her.

Flo swallowed a snort. *I'm sure you're not supposed to talk to them either, but that ship has sailed.*

"True, and that's really smart of you," Flo praised, reaching out and tugging on the stuffed animal's ear. "If you don't mind, though, I'll wait here with you until your dad is finished, um, planning, so you're not out here by yourself. I know you're a big girl, but is that okay with you?"

Jussy grinned, lowering her arms and enclosing her small, delicate fingers around Flo's.

"Okay, Flo. I am a big girl, too. I'm five. Do you have candy?" she asked, swinging their clasped hands back and forth.

She couldn't go anywhere with strangers, but didn't seem to have a problem taking candy from them. Flo fought back a chuckle only because she didn't want to hurt the girl's feelings, even unintentionally.

"Sorry, sweetheart, I don't have any."

"Gum?"

"Nope, don't have that, either."

Jussy sighed, sounding incredibly put out, and Flo bit the inside of her cheek, still managing to hold in her laughter. This one looked like she could be a handful. Tilting her head, Jussy peered up at her, lips twisted to the side as if deep in thought.

"You could go get some candy, and I'll wait here for you," she suggested.

This time Flo let her laughter fly. Jussy, probably thinking her hilarity meant capitulation, giggled with her.

"Jussy, I don't think—"

"Jussy! Justine, where are you?" A tall man stalked into view from around the side of the house, his steps hurried. Jussy's father? Good. She had some words for a man who let his daughter just roam around a dilapidated, empty property unsupervised. "Jus—" He bit off his daughter's name as he caught sight of them from a distance and slammed to a halt. But only for a moment. His body propelled forward, and his long legs, encased in black denim, swiftly carried him closer. "Who are you, and what are you doing with my daughter?" he growled. "What are you doing here— *You*."

"You."

Shock plowed into her, and she stumbled back a couple of steps, loosening her grip on Jussy's hand.

It was *him*. The man who was supposed to be a scalding-hot one-night stand, then a memory. The man who'd refused to be said memory and followed her into sleep to torture her with by-plays of those sex-filled hours.

Adam.

What? Why... *How?*

He'd said he wasn't from Rose Bend; she clearly remembered that. Because if he'd answered "yes," there was no way she would've asked him to come home with her.

No, no. She would've *remembered*. Especially since there was nothing about that night she'd forgotten. Nothing.

Oh God. Was *he* the new owner of the house? The disconcerting idea flashed through her mind, and right on the heels of it nipped horror. Was that the *planning* Jussy had been referring to? No, Fate couldn't be this cruel to her.

"Daddy, this is Flo," Jussy announced, grabbing Flo's hand again and holding her arm up as if her father hadn't seen her. "She's my new friend."

His stare dropped to their clasped hands and narrowed as if the sight of it offended him to his soul. And when that golden gaze lifted to hers, she convinced herself a shiver didn't work itself through her. And that a wake of heat didn't follow.

The last time she'd seen these hazel eyes, they'd been burning into hers as she shook and trembled in orgasm beneath him, her arms and legs squeezing him close. Her hand rose to her stomach and pressed to the slick tug just under her navel. It didn't take much effort on her part to feel the phantom thrust of his cock inside her, stretching her, possessing her...

She released a low, shaky breath.

"Your new friend," he repeated, and that low rumble of a voice rolled through her, reawakening nerve endings and stirring a desire that had never fully banked. "Flo, is it?"

For a moment her throat closed around the answer, a part of her still wary of giving him her name. But this wasn't a bar or her apartment above the studio. They were in the real world now. She could no longer hide behind anonymity.

"Florence Dennison." Though her naked body had been pressed to his only days ago, she still ground her teeth together, bracing herself as she extended her hand toward him. "Nice to meet you."

Oh yes. She was doing this. Playing the "I've never seen you before in my life, please play along" card. *Shit.* This was a new low for her. She usually didn't give a damn what people thought about her or her choices. But in her defense, she'd never been in this position before, either.

Never had to greet a man she'd taken home in front of his young child.

That made things...awkward.

"You can call her Flo," Jussy volunteered, wrapping Flo's arm around her shoulders and leaning into her thigh. "That's what everyone calls her."

"Is that right?" he murmured finally, as if in slow

motion, reaching out and enclosing her hand in his. His gaze moved over her face like a physical caress—*no*. No caressing. But even as she admonished herself, she couldn't stop hearing that same voice growl "queen" in her head. Or prevent the dull, nagging ache from throbbing between her legs. "It's a pleasure to meet you, Flo. Adam Reed."

Adam.

Immediately, every time she'd called his name—on a soft sigh of pleasure, on a sharp cry, on the edge of an orgasm so intense it toyed with pain—bombarded her. He hadn't played fair. She'd specifically requested no names. And he'd given her his.

Irrational anger simmered inside her. Realizing he still caught her hand in his, she jerked it free. Damn him for giving their…encounter another level of intimacy she hadn't asked for. On the contrary, she expressly *hadn't* asked for it.

But hadn't that been the theme of their evening? She'd wanted nothing more than a way to blow off steam, and at every turn, he'd pushed for deeper. For…more.

Damn. Him.

And damn her for surrendering to that weak need for *more*. That need was a careless, reckless step down a slippery, well-intentioned slope to pain, loneliness and abandonment. All she had to do was look at the base of that slope to see the debris of her past as a reminder.

"Not to be rude, Flo—" She choked back a snort. Because whenever someone started with that opener, chances were they'd be rude. "But what are you doing here?"

His gaze dropped to Jussy, who still stood next to Flo, and the *with my daughter* might've gone unspoken, but Flo heard it loud and clear.

"Stopping by for a visit," she said, purposefully keeping her answer vague. "But then I saw Jussy out here *by herself*—" she threw some grit behind those two words "—and decided to stick around a little while."

"You were planning, Daddy." Jussy's voice took on a bit of a whine, and call it intuition, but Flo had the sense the two of them might've had this conversation a time or two before. "And I wanted to see the 'sebo."

It took Flo several moments, but she translated *'sebo* to *gazebo* and glanced toward the run-down structure with its peeling white paint. The skin tightened across his cheekbones as his mouth flattened. Probably thinking the same thing as she was. While the gazebo stood, it wasn't very stable or safe.

"Jussy, what did we say about you walking away from me without letting me know where you're going? And doing this without asking for permission first?" he asked his daughter, his tone gentle but firm.

Hell, she wasn't even his child, and she wanted to apologize and confess all her sins.

Was that as dirty as it sounded in her head?

Damn this man and his lingering effect on her.

"Not to do it and to always ask you," Jussy mumbled, head bowed and little foot twisting in the scruffy grass. "I'm sorry."

"Jussy." He waited until she lifted her head, tilted it back and looked at him. "It's okay, baby girl. Just be more careful next time, all right?"

"Yes, Daddy." Her downtrodden expression immediately brightened with a wide grin that exposed the gap where her bottom front tooth had been. "I love you."

"I love you, too, baby girl." Adam—even *thinking* the name sent an unwanted and resented shiver coursing through her—returned his attention to Flo, and she steadily met it, hoping all those times Moe had made her attend Sunday school had copped her some points with God. If so, none of her thoughts about shivers, heat and naked, sweaty skin pressed against naked, sweaty skin would reflect on her face. "So why are you here again, Flo? Since the house has been vacant for at least the last four years, who exactly did you stop by to visit?"

So he wasn't allowing her to get away with her vague reply from earlier. Another thing she should've remembered from their night together. He pushed and pushed, not backing down until he was satisfied with an answer... or an orgasm.

Good Lord, she had to *stop*. There were kids—or *a* kid—present, for God's sake. Flo couldn't just be out here lusting after the child's daddy like she had zero home training. Though, to be fair, Moe's talks about sex had never covered *this* situation.

"Not *who*," Flo corrected, proud of her cool, even tone. "*What*. In a few days I'll be here working. So I decided to stop by and see the place."

"Working?" he asked, his big body stiffening and his chin snapping back toward his neck.

At the same time, Jussy bounced on her toes and clapped her hands.

"Daddy, too! He works here, too! Right, Daddy?" Not waiting for her father's reply, she grabbed Flo's hand again and swung it back and forth. "My friend works here!"

He works here, too.

Those words, yelled in such childlike exuberance, echoed in Flo's head like a death knell, deafening her to everything else Jussy said.

He works here, too.

Holy. *Shit.*

Had she said Fate couldn't be this cruel? Oh no. No, no, no. She severely underestimated the bitch. She wasn't only cruel.

She was downright vengeful.

"So." Flo paused, cleared her throat. Tried again. "So you're here for the renovation, as well? You're not the new owner?"

A tiny muscle ticked along the line of his jaw and, for a long moment, he just studied her. If that hard glint in his eyes was anything to go by, this news had thrown him as hard as it had her. Thrown, hell. Catapulted.

"No," he finally ground out. "The architect, not the homeowner.

Well…damn.

"The architect," she slowly repeated, a part of her insisting on clinging to denial. "Which means you're…"

"Heading this renovation, and you are?"

The last wispy remnants of that stubborn denial blew away like wind sweeping away the fog.

"The photographer," she murmured, her stomach bottoming out. "As of today."

It didn't seem possible, but that full, sensual mouth flattened even farther, and his nostrils flared with the audible breath he inhaled. Her skin flamed under the heat in his golden-brown gaze.

And not the consuming, lust-filled heat she'd been on the receiving end of for hours.

No, this was anger.

At her? Himself? The situation neither of them could've seen coming?

Oh shit. A new, humiliating and horrible thought crashed into her mind, and it refused to shake loose. Instead, spreading like poisonous, strangling vines.

Did he…? Did he think she'd deliberately approached

him and had sex with him for this job? That she'd lied about not knowing his identity? That she would somehow contact him and use their night against him to secure her spot on this televised project?

That's bullshit, her mind yelled in protest. She'd never use someone like that. Never put them in a "play ball" position similar to the one Paul had placed her in. That wasn't her.

But even as the objections resounded in her head like a screaming gale, the truth of the matter was he *didn't* know her. Until a few minutes ago, he hadn't even known her name.

Even though she didn't have anything to apologize for, she inexplicably still felt the need to explain.

"Listen, I didn't—"

"I'll see you on Thursday, then," he cut her off. "I'm looking forward to seeing your work." With a nod as terse as his voice, he switched his attention to his daughter. "I'm ready to go, baby girl. Time to head back and get some dinner."

"Okay, Daddy." Jussy moved forward, but then stopped short, tilting her head back to peer up at Flo. Through the embarrassment and shock continuing to swirl inside her, Flo rummaged up a smile for Jussy. She couldn't be faulted that her father was a lying, rude asshole. "Can Flo have dinner, too? She's my friend," she reminded her dad, jabbing a small finger at Flo. "Are you hungry, Flo?" Jussy asked, not waiting for her father's reply.

Wow. The strain melted from Flo's smile, and it warmed. This little girl should never learn the power of the cuteness she harnessed. She would be a terror. Bad enough Flo had to battle back the urge to capitulate, and all because she didn't want to see disappointment on the child's face. Damn, she was a sucker.

A sucker? Yes. A masochistic fool? No.

No way she could sit across from this big, brooding giant and share a meal as if she hadn't seen him naked. Especially with him glaring at her as if she'd personally offended him.

Nope. Not even for a five-year-old's smile that could rival the sun.

"Sweetie, I—" Flo began, intent on letting her down gently with an excuse. But she didn't get the chance.

"Another time, Jussy. I'm sure Flo already has plans."

The words might've been casual and directed at his daughter, but the tone and message were all for her. *Go away. You're not wanted here.*

She was damn near bilingual in the language of rejection.

Why it should have pain twinging in her chest— especially when she'd been about to turn down Jussy— she couldn't explain. And didn't care to analyze.

Swallowing the absurd hurt, she dragged her gaze from Adam and returned it to the little girl whose mouth had already started to curl down at the corners.

"Your dad's right, sweetie. I'm sorry, but I have dinner plans with my family tonight. I'm sure we'll see each other again. Friends, right?" Flo held up her pinkie finger, and after a moment Jussy's beautiful, gapped smile broke free on her face, and she hooked her finger around Flo's.

"Right!" the little girl cheered.

"All right, Jussy. Let's go back to the house for a minute. I need to lock up." Adam stretched his hand out toward his daughter, and she skipped to him.

"Okay, Daddy. You got to get your plans," she announced, slipping her hand in his, and Flo stared down at them—the tiny, fragile fingers disappearing in her father's bigger, stronger clasp—fascinated for a moment.

Flo's palms and fingers itched for her camera again. To capture the purity of this moment. This instance of... safety, security. Trust.

She snatched her gaze away from the sight, but she couldn't dismiss the oily glide of shame slicking its way to her stomach.

Because for a brief moment—long enough to be disgusted with herself—she was envious of little Jussy.

She looked at the child, with those small, dainty fingers resting in her father's hand. She possessed the confidence that came with a child who recognized she wasn't only loved, but also protected. That she would never wake up one day and find he'd disappeared, rocking the only world she knew. Even with her mother gone, Jussy still stood on the solid ground of her father's affection and dependability.

Flo shuffled back a step.

From the feeling that shamed her.

From the pair that stirred up old memories and unwanted thoughts.

"I should go," she whispered, and could do nothing about the hoarseness. Clearing her throat, she tried again. "You two have a great evening."

Not daring to meet those too intense, too piercing eyes, she kept her attention focused on Jussy as she forced a trembling smile and waved.

Spinning on her heel, Flo headed toward the walkway. And though Jussy called another cheerful goodbye, Flo didn't glance over her shoulder. Didn't look back.

Yes, she was running. She could admit that to herself.

But not from Adam and Jussy.

From herself.

CHAPTER FIVE

"THIS HOME IS GORGEOUS. The pictures didn't do it justice," the producer of *Vintage Renovation* murmured, strolling through the bare living room into the connected dining room.

The petite woman with her natural dark curls bound into a bun on top of her head glanced over her shoulder at Adam as she stroked a hand with short, pink nails over decorative scrollwork on one of the sliding doors that, once closed, separated the two rooms.

"It is lovely," Adam agreed, standing a little distance away, arms crossed over his chest. "And there are more than enough strong bones here for the house to be fully restored to its former state."

A low hum of anticipation buzzed beneath his skin as he surveyed the living room with its large bay windows and box storage seating that provided streams of light to the area. With the open floor plan, he could easily envision parties being held in this home, and guests flowing from the living room to the dining room. Or from the small vestibule area into the parlor and ballroom. Only the kitchen and bathroom were sectioned off and enclosed.

The rooms were airy with high ceilings, while the dark paneling prevented the space from being too cold or formal. Of course, how the homeowners decided to decorate this place could take these rooms from cozy and intimate to aloof and reserved. But that would be long after he finished his job. In the meantime, he would do his best to restore this home to its stately beauty while remaining as close to the original design and aesthetic as possible.

"Do you think you'll be able to salvage anything in here?" The producer—Mira, was her name?—was coming back through the wide doorway into the living room.

Sliding his hands into the pockets of his jeans, Adam cocked his head, taking in the finer details of the space, even though he could probably enumerate each feature in his head without looking. That was how often he'd been over the house.

"Definitely. Like I said, the structure is sound, and some of that elaborate crown molding—" he pointed to where the wall met the ceiling and around the door "—we're absolutely going to save. Our goal is to conserve as much as possible. But we'll end up having to replace some, of course. We've already gathered samples from throughout the house and sent them off to have them prefabricated to match. And at some point one of the owners replaced the fireplace with marble. We'll redesign it with Italian tile, like the original, and change it back to wood burning instead of gas. That's the theme of the renovation. Retaining as much of the original design as possible while keeping it modern and comfortable. The owner doesn't want a showplace, but a home."

"Please remember every bit of that for when we start filming. I will need you to repeat it," she directed, smiling. "I have to admit, I'm eager to see the transformation. How long do you think the whole reno will take? We've estimated about sixteen weeks."

Adam nodded. "That sounds about right. No longer than twenty, and that's if we run into some unforeseen complications."

He'd worked with a couple of home improvement TV shows before, and understood their production schedule, and how they preferred to keep it as tight as possible. But those prior projects hadn't been as extensive as this one, and most of his job had taken place off camera, prior to filming. This one was different.

First *Vintage Renovation* didn't shoot a renovation per episode. They dedicated an entire season to one rehab, each weekly installment focusing on one aspect of the reno. Or, as sometimes happened, an issue that cropped up during the reno.

So for the next four or five months, he would be surrounded by cameras as they followed the reformation from the beginning to when the homeowners arrived and set eyes on their fully restored home for the first time.

It had been a no-brainer to accept the job. It meant more exposure for him as viewers would see him weekly for months. And he couldn't pass up the financial compensation for a project this size, as well. Those two factors evened the scales against the aggravation of having a camera in his face for nine to ten hours a day.

But of course, when he'd accepted the contract, he hadn't calculated in the presence of a beautiful, distracting woman.

Shit. What were the odds?

He could count on one hand the number of women he'd been involved with since his divorce, and none of them had met Justine. How was it when he'd indulged in his first and probably only one-night stand, she had somehow ended up being his daughter's new best friend?

Like father, like daughter.

He mentally winced. How could he blame Justine for being drawn to Flo? Sure, it'd been for vastly different reasons, but hadn't he just as quickly been attracted to her? But unlike his daughter, he didn't want a friend. Didn't want any kind of...relationship. History had shown he was bad at them.

Like father, like son.

Only he wasn't in denial about it like his father. He didn't need to repeatedly go down that dead end to figure out a truth that blinked like a neon caution sign.

While he'd learned that lesson, Justine hadn't. But at five, how could he expect her to? Still, he worried about her becoming attached to women because of her mother's absence. Justine didn't ask about Jennifer much, but the way she latched on to the women in her life screamed volumes. Women like Addie were fine; his sister wasn't going anywhere.

But like Flo? Women who were transitory and would only disappear from Justine's life in a few short months? That presented a problem. Their absence would rip off a barely healed scab and leave his daughter hurt all over again.

And it scared the shit out of him wondering how often that particular wound would be inflicted before the damage to his daughter was irreparable.

Locking down a sigh behind clenched teeth, he redirected his attention to the room that would be the focus of the first couple of episodes and the woman currently walking a circuit of the space.

"I have a shooting schedule, but to make sure the renovation finishes on time, construction will continue even after filming has ended for the day," Mira said, stopping near the bank of bay windows.

"That's fine. I'll occasionally drop in during those hours to make sure everything is as it should be, though," he warned her.

She flashed him a smile over her shoulder. "I wouldn't

expect anything less." She turned and headed toward the foyer. "The rest of the crew is arriving along with a couple of visitors. The mayor of this town, if I'm not mistaken."

In moments she opened the front door and stepped out onto the porch. Adam moved across the floor to the window. Mira descended the steps, approaching a group of about twenty people carrying equipment in large cases as well as tripods, microphones and reflectors. And those were just the things he recognized.

Here we go.

Inhaling a breath, he held it, then deliberately exhaled. And followed in Mira's footsteps toward the home's entrance. Familiar nerves jumbled and snarled in his stomach. They visited him at the beginning of every project, and he welcomed them. What did his grandmother used to say?

If you're not nervous, you've lost your passion.

He never stopped trying to better himself; he was his own competition. And that meant doing the best for all his clients. *Being* the best for them…and for Justine.

This job wasn't his first restoration or his biggest. But it was his most important. This house in the small town of Rose Bend truly was the opportunity of a lifetime.

And he couldn't fuck it up.

As he stepped onto the porch, he spotted the person who could be a threat to that vow.

Florence Dennison.

Look away, goddammit. Look. Away.

The order from his brain ricocheted off his skull, but he couldn't cooperate. Couldn't snatch his gaze from the woman who already had his cock thickening beneath his zipper from just a glimpse of her.

One glimpse.

Damn. How was he going to survive several months working with her?

Because you will. Because you have no choice.

Because you have to keep your dick in your pants.

With this warning ringing in his head, he forced his attention away from her and concentrated on the crew gathered on the walkway and lawn. Yet, even as he went to meet them, he couldn't burn away the image of Flo Dennison from his mind's eye.

Hell, if he could do that, he would've accomplished that feat days ago.

But for now, he still saw those heavy-lidded brown eyes under dark brows. The long locs he'd smoothed with his fingers were gathered in a bun on top of her head, providing an unrestricted view of her elegant bone structure. The pouty mouth with its almost too full bottom lip. More than once during their night together, he'd sunk his teeth into that curve. A cropped denim jacket accentuated the thrust of her firm breasts and her tucked-in waist. Dark blue jeans conformed to the flare of her hips and the long length of her slender legs.

His hands itched with the sensory memories, with the knowledge of how those curves fit into his palms. Of the butter-soft texture of that beautiful brown skin.

No, he didn't need to be looking at her for her image to be imprinted on his brain. Didn't need to be standing right next to her to inhale that sweet, woodsy scent of jasmine and cedarwood and subtle notes that had no name. They were just...her.

"Mr. Reed."

Adam turned at the sound of his name and smiled as Cole Dennison approached him. He'd met Rose Bend's mayor during one of the meetings with the producers of *Vintage Renovation*, and had liked the other man, respected his vision for his town. Given Cole was about Adam's age and had accomplished so much impressed him, as well.

"Adam," he corrected, extending his hand toward Cole. "Please call me Adam. And it's good to see you again."

"You, too." Cole took his hand in a firm, friendly grip, briefly shaking it before releasing him. "I hope your move to Rose Bend has been smooth. In other words, I hope settling here hasn't felt like you've stepped into the Twilight Zone." He grinned. "It's different from Chicago."

"That it is," Adam agreed with a chuckle. "But no, it's been great. My daughter can't get enough of the playset in the backyard. And as long as she's happy, that's half the battle right there."

"Ah, the playset. Proof that God does love us." Cole barked out a laugh. "I don't know if I told you, but I have two daughters. One is five and the other just turned one. As long as everything is okay with them—and no one's screaming bloody murder—then all is right in the world." Cole shook his head, affection and humor lighting his voice and eyes. "If I remember right, your daughter is five, as well?" When Adam nodded, Cole held up his phone. "I have your cell number and I'll make sure you have mine. Let me know if you want to get together and have the kids meet. My family owns the local inn here, Kinsale Inn, and we are a huge clan with kids of all ages underfoot. We'd love to have you and your daughter over for dinner. That way, you get to know the people you'll be spending the next few months with, and your daughter has some kids she can call friends. One thing you'll discover about Rose Bend, the people will be here for you if you need them."

It sounded like something out of a Hallmark movie— too good to be true. And the cynical part of Adam probed his words, trying to find the catch. Maybe the skepticism could be attributed to living in a big city for most of his life, except for those pockets of time when his job carried him to different locations.

But he suspected his natural distrust was more a byproduct of how he grew up—or rather who he grew up with. Nothing in his family had been free. If his father doled out any kindness, it always carried a price tag.

Turning off the part of him that didn't trust easily would be akin to shutting down his lungs for breathing. Impossible.

"Thank you." Adam nodded. "I appreciate the invitation."

"You got it. Hey, you haven't met my sister yet." He shifted, glancing over his shoulder, and held up a hand. "Flo, can you come over here for a moment? I'd like to introduce you to the architect over the renovation."

Flo?

His sister?

No fucking way.

Frowning, Adam looked from Cole to Flo as she extricated herself from the TV crew and headed toward them. *Dennison.* Their shared last name had gone completely over his head; it was common enough. And studying her features, searching for the resemblance to the man in front of him, Adam still couldn't find it. The mayor appeared to be Latino, and Flo was a Black woman. Maybe they shared a parent...

Cole softly chuckled, drawing Adam's attention back to him.

"I recognize that expression." He wrapped an arm around Flo's shoulders as she came to stand by his side. "Flo, this is Adam Reed. I just mentioned you were my sister."

She snorted, a smile flirting with her full lips. He really shouldn't stare at those lips. Damn sure not right in front of the man she called *brother*.

"Just wait until he sees Wolf," Flo drawled.

And though Adam didn't get the joke, Cole grinned.

"If you accept that invitation to dinner, you will get to meet my brother Wolf as well as the rest of my family and see that we're kind of Rose Bend's clap back to *This is Us*."

Oh. Now it made sense. The famed TV show had featured a family with two white siblings and an adopted Black brother.

Adam jerked his chin up. "Good to know. Now when I eventually meet this Wolf, I'll make sure to mention the family resemblance."

Barking out a laugh, Cole's grin widened. "Please do. And feel free to drop in that I obviously got the lion's share of the looks and brains in the family."

"Uh, excuse you?" Flo arched an eyebrow. "I'm standing right here."

"Well, present company excepted, of course." He paused. "You're almost as pretty as me."

Flo elbowed him in the stomach, and Cole's chuckle ended in an *oof.*

"You're a little late, Cole. Mr. Reed and I have already met." Her brown eyes met his, and for a moment he got tangled in them, powerless to unravel himself from their snare even as a sliver of panic rippled through him. Surely, she wasn't about to tell her *brother* about their night... "I had the pleasure of meeting him and his little girl a couple of days ago when I stopped by here after work."

Relief smoothed out the jagged edges of alarm, and he caught the twitch at the corner of her mouth. Very funny.

"Yes, Justine is still talking about her friend Flo," he said, tone wry. "You made quite the impression."

"Same. She's adorable and funny. And to avoid her shade, I've now started carrying candy and gum on me at all times." In spite of the awkward situation, humor trickled through him. Jussy was a staunch advocate of treats. Flo shifted her attention away from him, and he vacillated between releasing a relieved sigh and demanding she fix that beautiful, soulful gaze back on him. "Is she here? I'd like to say hi."

"No, she's with her babysitter, but I'll let her know you said hello."

Cole smiled, dropping his arm from around Flo, stepping back. "Since I'm not needed here, I'll go meet the rest of the crew as the official Rose Bend welcome wagon." He pressed a kiss to the top of Flo's head, murmuring, "Knock 'em dead, lil' sis."

Giving a last wave, Cole turned and walked toward the crew, leaving his sister alone with Adam. If the other man suspected just how well he knew his baby sister, Adam doubted Cole would've been so magnanimous.

"You gave me your real name," she softly said. No, accused.

He stared down at her, momentarily taken aback. By both her blunt words and by the almost instinctive urge to give her an excuse.

But *I couldn't stand the thought of you calling anyone else's name but mine when you came* probably wouldn't go over well. It was the truth, but he doubted she would appreciate it. And he could barely admit that to himself much less to her. So he went with something less incendiary to his pride.

"You said any would do. And I chose to give you mine." Simple. And still honest.

Mostly.

Her eyes narrowed at his answer, and he would be

lying if he denied the spark of anticipation that glimmered inside him. *This* was what had drawn him to her that night at the bar. Yes, she was beautiful. But it'd been that barbed wit, the glints of vulnerability and the sensual charisma that had kept his ass on that stool. The desire to discover how that clever, sharp tongue and unexpected hints of softness would translate to sex...

Now he knew. And fuck his curiosity. Because now he couldn't forget. Even when he wanted to. When he needed to.

"Semantics seem to be your thing," she murmured, the bite in her tone unmistakable. He checked himself before he could lean in, feel the razor edge of it scrape over his senses, his skin. "First with your name and then about whether you were from here or not."

"I didn't lie." He hadn't given her all of the information. But he hadn't lied. "I'm from Chicago, not Rose Bend."

"You knew what I was asking," she bit out, glaring at him. "If I'd believed for one second that I would run into you again, there's no way in hell I would've..."

She trailed off, a frown creasing her forehead. Adam crossed his arms, cocking his head.

"I believe the words you're looking for are 'fucked you.' There's no way in hell you would've invited me home to fuck me," he calmly supplied. He huffed out a short, acerbic chuckle. "I'm having the damnedest time imagining you at a loss for words."

Especially when she'd been so bold about what she wanted that night.

"Well, when I'm just feet away from my brother and a whole crew of people with cameras and microphones, then yes, I'm at a loss for words. Particularly those," she snapped.

On reflex, he cast a look around them, scanning the front lawn to see if anyone had overheard.

"That's fair," he said, returning his attention to her. "But I did warn you about regret, didn't I?"

She didn't quite manage to conceal her flinch. And though it made zero fucking sense, a hole opened up behind his sternum. One that eddied with resentment and—God, help him—sadness that he'd become something she looked back on with remorse.

A one-night stand. That was all he was to her, and she to him. And after the lust cleared and reason returned, a lot of people probably regretted having them. This wasn't anything special. What they shared hadn't been unique.

Even in his head, the words fell flat.

"If it's any consolation, if I had known you would end up being the photographer on my next project, I would've made a different choice, too," he said. Because he didn't shit where he ate.

Ever.

He'd made that mistake with Jennifer and look how that had turned out. A miserable marriage that had ended in divorce, and a daughter with an absentee mother. Not that he regretted Justine. God, no. And he'd suffer through the hellscape of his marriage all over again just to have her. But would he have willingly chosen a mother who'd rather be on a plane to the next adventure—and by adventure, he meant party—than actually *mother*? No. No, he wouldn't have wanted that for Justine.

Flo glanced away from him, her hand lifting and hovering near her bound locs before her arm dropped back to her side.

"About that. I need to clear the air." When her gaze met his again, her frown hadn't completely faded, a small crease wrinkling the space above the bridge of her nose.

"I don't want you to think I lied in the bar. I had no clue you were the architect on this renovation. Hell, I didn't even know about the renovation or the show until days later when I spoke with Cole. I wouldn't have placed you, or myself for that matter, in this uncomfortable position. I just..." She did that almost-touch thing again with her hair. "I wouldn't have lied about that."

"I didn't believe you did," he said, and relief flashed in her eyes, and her shoulders loosened just a bit. Maybe no one else would've noticed those details, but he did.

Nothing much about her escaped him, dammit.

"Oh good. I didn't—"

"But if we're being honest, I have to admit I don't think you are the appropriate person for this job."

Her lips parted, and her slender frame stiffened again. Those brown eyes, more expressive than she probably wished, widened for a fraction of a second, betraying her shock and...and something else. The thick fringe of her lashes lowered too fast, hiding that *something else* from his view.

"Wow. That went right from awkward to super fucking awkward." She huffed out a chuckle that he didn't dare misinterpret as humorous. "How can you make that determination when you've known me for five minutes? And three of those were spent—" she cut off the rest of the sentence, her full lips momentarily flattening as she glanced behind her "—spent *not talking,*" she finished on a low growl. "That's pretty presumptuous and asshole-ish of you."

"Maybe," he said, cocking his head. "But this is a big project partnering with a major cable network. It needs a photographer with experience. Tell me, Flo—" he crossed his arms over his chest "—how many of these have you worked on? Or, since opportunities like working with a television show don't come by often, what about smaller jobs? Have you undertaken smaller, similar assignments? Because this—" he waved a hand toward the Victorian "—is different than taking travel pictures of an exotic location or babies on blankets."

Yes, he'd done a little bit of research on her since the evening they met right there at the house. At twenty-four, she was the proprietor of and sole photographer for Perfect Images, the local photography studio. While owning her own business at such a young age was impressive, it didn't mean she was ready or the best choice for a job of this magnitude.

Amazing sex and an unfortunate fascination with those sleek cheekbones, almond-shaped eyes and overtly carnal mouth didn't blind him to those facts.

"Are you listening to yourself? Are you even the least bit bothered by how condescending you sound?" she scoffed, waving a hand. "I think you're more bothered by the fact that you'll have to face me every day after seeing me naked."

Shit.

Unbidden, an image of her slender yet curvy body, beautiful brown skin damn near luminescent with perspiration, burst across the vivid, HD screen of his mind.

A growl threatened to rumble through him, that mental picture pumping arousal into his veins like a hydraulic engine. He clenched his jaw, imprisoning the betraying sound inside him.

"Oh, it definitely bothers me," he admitted, a hint of gravel roughening his voice. Uncrossing his arms, he stepped closer and lowered his head and voice so only she heard his next words. "That I'm standing right here with about thirty witnesses only feet away from us, and I know exactly how your breasts fill my hands and the precise shade of your nipples after they've been teased by my mouth. Or that those gorgeous, strong thighs tremble just before you come… Yeah, it bothers me, Flo. Because all my focus needs to be on this project and not on the beautiful flush that spreads over your skin when you're aroused." He ignored her sharp, soft inhale. But damn him, he couldn't pretend not to see the lust darkening her eyes. Those fucking eyes. "But what bothers me more?" he ground out. "That nepotism and favoritism got you this job and robbed it from someone else who has the experience to pull it off."

She blinked. Stared at him. Then shifted backward a step.

Had he thought her face, her eyes, too expressive?

He stood corrected. Her expression wiped completely clean, as if she took an eraser to it and swept every emotion away.

A curious twist screwed tight behind his chest bone, pulling taut. It didn't sit well within him that he couldn't read her, couldn't decipher the thoughts running through her head. He didn't like it…although he'd been the cause of it.

But he couldn't take back his words, because they were the truth. She was young—too young to have acquired the work experience a project like this required. But he couldn't do anything about it. The town council had hired her, and while he and *Vintage Renovation* would use some of her photos, the coffee-table book would belong to Rose Bend. He didn't hire her and couldn't fire her.

Still… He had to force his arm to remain by his side or he would rub that sore spot in the middle of his chest.

"Just because you've been inside me doesn't mean you know me," she quietly said, but the intensity behind the words razed his ears like a piercing scream. "And your opinion doesn't move me. It's a nonfactor since the people I respect, the people who are aware of my experience and talent, have already hired me for this job, and I will not walk away from it, whether you believe it's merited or not. So if me being here bothers you then you'll have to quit or deal with it. Because that's your issue, not mine. Now, if you'll excuse me." She moved again, inserting more space between them. "I'm going to meet more of my coworkers. But you have the day you deserve."

On the heels of that parting shot, she turned and strode away from him.

Have the day you deserve.

Damned if that wasn't the most polite "fuck you" he'd ever heard.

CHAPTER SIX

WHAT AN ASSHOLE.

Flo glared down into the pot of potatoes she'd mashed and whipped as if it'd tried to steal her prized, autographed Backstreet Boys' Millennium CD.

How dare he tell her *to her face* she didn't deserve to work on the renovation? Who made him the architect god that he could now deliver judgments like he descended a mountain with twin tablets?

Screw. Him.

No. Wait. She'd done that already and that was partly responsible for landing her in the position she found herself in.

Damn him. Adam Reed could go take a long walk off that short, dilapidated dock that butted up against the edge of the Hudson property.

But what bothers me more? That nepotism and favoritism got you this job and robbed it from someone else who has the experience to pull it off.

Grinding her jaw, she stirred harder.

All day she'd been trying to scrub those words from her head. And even now, hours later while she stood in her family inn's kitchen, they still gripped her like barnacles clinging to the side of a boat. They refused to be scraped off. She'd told him his opinion didn't mean shit to her. And it didn't. But...

But maybe if the same doubts hadn't floated through

her own mind… Maybe if she hadn't wondered the same thing… Then his accusation might not claim so much space in her head.

Damn him *twice*.

"I don't know what those potatoes could've possibly done to offend you, but I think they're ready to ask for forgiveness and mercy."

Flo didn't glance up at the sound of her sister Leo's voice, but continued to whip the potatoes into shape.

"They should've watched their damn mouths," Flo muttered.

And by *they* she meant Adam.

Leo laughed, and a glass of wine appeared on the kitchen island next to the pot. Her older sister understood her so well. Setting down the big serving spoon, Flo picked up the glass and downed a large sip, meeting Leo's blue-gray eyes. With her dark brown hair captured in a high ponytail and a lilac wrap dress adorning her svelte figure, she must've just wrapped up a meeting with a client.

Kinsale Inn often stayed fully booked no matter the season as it was a popular bed-and-breakfast. While Cole had his mayoral appointment and law firm, Wolf had his carpentry business, Sinead her own law career in Boston and Flo, her studio, Leo's passion was the family inn.

And she had increased its popularity by expanding its services to include outdoor weddings and receptions. Their sprawling back property included a pond, a thick throng of trees and a breathtaking view of Monument Mountain and Mount Everett. It was the perfect backdrop for engagements, ceremonies and parties. And under Leo's management, Kinsale Inn had become a premiere wedding venue.

"You look nice. Who'd you sucker into the dream of

happily-ever-after now?" Flo asked, arching an eyebrow as her sister settled onto the stool across from her.

"A very sweet couple out of Concord. Their daughter got married here last year, and they loved the inn so much they want to renew their vows here in the fall on their fiftieth anniversary." Leo picked up her own glass of wine and sipped, squinting at Flo over the rim. "And be careful. Don't want any of that bitterness spilling into the potatoes. Yech." She grimaced.

"I'd give you the finger, but that'd mean I'd have to put down my wine. Oh wait." Flo widened her eyes in mock surprise, waving her free hand in the air. "Would you look at that? I have another hand." And she flipped her sister off.

Cackling, Leo set down her glass and propped her folded arms on top of the wood island.

"Good one. I'm going to save that for later use." Grinning, she dipped her head toward the pot. "Seriously, though, what's wrong? And don't tell me nothing. Those soupy potatoes are proof that something's upset you. So spill. Owen doesn't get here with Bono for another hour. That gives me plenty of time to bug the hell out of you," she said, mentioning her husband and two year-old son.

Owen Strafford, Leo's husband and star quarterback for the Jersey Knights, had continued the Dennison family tradition of naming their children after musicians, much to Moe and Dad's delight. It was too soon to tell if the toddler would have the pipes and talent of his namesake, but he was beyond adorable.

Sighing, Flo debated whether or not to be completely honest. She loved her sister—all six of her brothers and sisters—dearly, but Leo wouldn't know how to mind her business even if she was given color-by-number instructions. None of them did. And she would prefer if none of them were privy to the details of her sex life. Especially Cole, given he and the town council had hired her without knowing she'd fucked the head architect.

She needed more potatoes to mash.

"Flo?" Leo pressed.

"All right, I'll talk," she muttered, lifting her glass to her lips. After a moment, and another long, deep sip, she lowered it and admitted, "In a roundabout way, I *might* have told the architect on the Hudson renovation to go fuck himself."

Leo blinked. Slowly straightened. Blinked again.

"You did what, now?"

Instead of answering, Flo took another big gulp of wine.

Her sister stared at her then burst out laughing, the sound filling the kitchen. Flo's lips twitched, and the longer Leo cackled, the bigger her smile grew until her chuckles joined her sister's.

"Whew." Leo held her fingers under her eyes, dabbing at them. "Holy crap. Wasn't today your first day? I mean, I'm assuming because the town is buzzing with news about the television crews arriving. So how did he get on your bad side so quickly?"

As Adam's words crept back into her head, her humor evaporated, and annoyance and hurt slunk in.

"Oh babe." Leo frowned. "What happened?"

It's fine sat on her tongue like a heavy stone, but she couldn't push it out. Couldn't lie. Because it wasn't fine. Nothing was fine.

"Adam Reed, the architect on the renovation, told me I only got the job because Cole's my brother. And that I took the job from someone else who deserves it. Someone with more experience and knowledge than me."

"Are you serious?" Leo snapped, her bright eyes shooting fire.

"Hey! Leo, did you wait for us?" Sydney, Flo's sister-in-law, barreled into the kitchen, their good friend Jenna Landon behind her. "I bet you started without us, you hussy."

Leo winced then reached over and lifted the bottle of wine she'd set to the side.

"I brought wine," she said in lieu of confessing she began what obviously seemed like a planned ambush without them.

"You're forgiven." Jenna crossed over to one of the cabinets and opened it, removing two more wineglasses.

"Really? We didn't even make her squirm," Sydney complained, scowling at Jenna.

But it was wasted on the tall redhead. She set the glasses on the island and curled her fingers in a "gimme" gesture toward the wine bottle.

"Yes, really. I just finished breastfeeding. Which means I have gone without a single sip of Riesling in fourteen months. If she committed acts against humanity, I'd probably let her off with a stern warning just as long as she offered up that wine. Now—" Jenna jabbed a finger toward the bowl of her glass "—pour."

"Yes, ma'am." With a snicker, Leo tipped the bottle until the alcohol filled half the glass.

"So are you going to tell them, or should I do the honors?" Sydney asked, sliding onto a stool next to Jenna. Nabbing the empty glass, she held it out to Leo, but her gaze remained on the redhead.

Jenna sighed, twirling a hand, gesturing for Sydney to go ahead while she sipped wine.

"On our way here, we received a phone call from

Remi," Sydney said, brushing her thick, natural curls off her shoulder. "Jasper Landon is at it again."

Flo frowned, flattening her palms on the island, and prepared herself for the bullshit undoubtedly coming her way. Whenever Jasper Landon, Jenna's father and Rose Bend's former mayor, was mentioned, bullshit most certainly followed. It had been years since Cole won the mayor's race that ended Jasper's long reign as the town's main politician, and yet, to this day, he remained bitter and tiresome. Like an irritating pebble in a shoe that rubbed the foot raw.

Jenna had a…complicated history with her parents. For the longest time she'd lived under their thumb and in her father's toxic shadow. That influence had affected not just her, but her relationships. About five years ago Jenna had finally come up from under that suffocating emotional control, found love and reunited with her two childhood best friends, Leo and Sydney. Now Jenna—who they'd also discovered was *New York Times* bestselling author Beck Dansing—was like family. Forget *like*. She *was* family. She, her husband, Isaac, and their six-month-old daughter, Grace—they were a part of the Dennison clan. Which explained her presence in the kitchen as Flo mashed potatoes for dinner.

"What did he do now?" Flo picked up the bottle and tipped just a bit more wine into Jenna's glass. With talk of her father, she would need it. Hell, they all would. "If you mentioned Remi," she continued, referring to the librarian at Rose Bend's public library, "I'm really hoping you're not about to say what I think you are definitely going to say."

Sydney's mouth twisted. "Oh, you know where this is going. He's started a petition to have certain books in the library banned. Claims they're not appropriate for children."

Even though Flo'd suspected the announcement would lead to just this, shock still rippled through her, and she stared at Sydney, then Jenna.

"Oh, it gets better," Jenna added, arching an eyebrow. "Every book in the Anakim Academy series is on the list."

"That fucker," Flo snapped. The Anakim Academy series was Jenna's, or Beck Dansing's, very popular paranormal young adult series. "He did that on purpose."

Jenna lifted a shoulder. "Probably… Okay, very likely. He is him, after all." A small smile ghosted across her lips, but her nonchalant tone belied the hurt dulling her bright blue eyes. "You'd think he and my mother would be proud of having a bestselling author as a daughter. But all these years later, they're still embarrassed and angry that I didn't tell them. As if I could." She huffed out a humorless chuckle. "They didn't make it possible for me to share the truth with them."

"Don't do that, Jenna." Leo moved around the island and curled an arm around her friend's shoulders as Sydney covered the hand not clasped around the wineglass. "You can't take on their issues. And no one—not here in this kitchen or in this town—will blame you for Jasper's asinine actions. You're. Not. Them."

Jenna's smile warmed a fraction, and it appeared more real.

"Thank you for that. I know what you're saying is true. It's just good to hear it from someone else every now and again."

"Anytime you need us to remind you, we got you covered," Sydney assured her.

Jenna smiled, then shook her head. "You know what's

the messed-up part about this? Well, one of them? Because it's censorship and book banning, there are a ton of messed-up parts," she wryly said. "The books they're demanding be removed? Not all of them are children's or young adult novels. And none of them have sex or gratuitous, graphic violence in them. But all either directly or indirectly touch on the topics of racism, misogyny, sexual identity, reproductive autonomy... In other words, the topics that would nurture free-thinking, tolerant and open-minded individuals."

"Assholes assholing. What's new about that?" Flo scoffed. God, if they could jettison all the bigoted idiots to a far-off island and let them Survivor it out among themselves, the world would be a much better place. "What did Remi say? What does the library plan on doing about this?"

Sydney snorted. "This is Remi Howard we're talking about. You know she's not caving to pressure. In her words, she refuses to allow a loudmouth, ignorant minority to determine the freedoms of the majority. Oh, and that they can go fuck themselves."

Flo barked out a laugh, because while the pretty, kind librarian was endlessly sweet, no one would dare call her a doormat. Particularly when it came to those she loved and her passion for books.

"We might be planning a rally against book banning with Israel and me attending," Jenna said, studying her nails with a satisfied smirk. Israel Ford, also known as number one *New York Times* bestselling romance author I.M. Kelly, also resided in Rose Bend, and Jenna counted him as a good friend. "Coincidentally, with a television crew already in town, it should be a real good time."

"I'm sure I'll be free whatever day that is to take pictures so they can magically appear on social media," Flo casually mentioned.

"And I'm sure I'll have no problem encouraging Cole to push a permit through for the rally. As a matter of fact, I'm positive he'll make it a priority once he finds out what Jasper's up to." Sydney held up a finger as if dotting an i.

"And I will personally contact local business owners to see if they're willing to support, from donations to food to posting flyers in their storefront windows," Leo volunteered. "Once I explain not only the importance of the cause, but also that any event including two internationally known bestselling authors will bring press and visitors to Rose Bend—which means possible revenue for their establishments—most of them will be on board."

"Is it me, or did we just prove in my mother's kitchen that women run this world?" Flo mused, tapping a bare fingernail against her bottom lip.

"Hell yeah, we did." Sydney crossed her arms over her chest and dipped her chin in the "Wakanda, Forever" salute. When Flo squinted at her, Sydney waved her off, picking up her wineglass. "What? It's never not appropriate." Her sister-in-law flicked a couple of fingers in her direction. "Now, back to the other important matter... Flo, your first day on the *Vintage Renovation* set. More specifically, your first day on the *Vintage Renovation* set with one gorgeous architect. Dish, baby sis-in-law. Is he as—"

"He's an ass," Leo snapped. "We don't like him."

Sydney blinked and Jenna glanced from Leo to Flo.

"We don't?" Jenna asked.

"No." Leo scowled. "Women solidarity."

"You know I'm down," Sydney said, moving around the island to where the delicious aroma of baked chicken emanated. "But just so I know why we're hating on him, what'd he do to earn ass status?"

"He told our Flo that she didn't deserve to be on the renovation."

Jenna arched a dark auburn eyebrow. "He actually let those words exit his mouth?"

Flo sighed, eyeing the mashed potatoes again. "Pretty much." Then she recounted for them her conversation with Adam.

Varying degrees of surprise and outrage crossed their expressions.

"Damn." Jenna shook her head. "And here I thought Isaac's days of working on his truck and blasting that godawful country music at the crack of dawn were behind me. Seems I'm going to have to get him out there again."

"You will not." Flo laughed. They'd all heard the story of how Jenna met her then neighbor and nemesis turned love of her life. And now, Adam rented Isaac's former house. "As much as Adam Reed can kick rocks with flip-flops, he has an adorable, sweet little girl. Otherwise, I'd say, add acid rock to the line-up."

The redhead heaved a loud, exaggerated sigh.

"Fine. But he says something slick to you again and it's neighborhood wars on our street."

"I'm here!" Nessa, Wolf's wife, burst into the kitchen, their four-year-old son riding her hip. "Whew. The clinic was super busy today," she complained, setting Everett down. Crossing the room to the island, she grabbed one of the cookies Moe always had available for the inn's guests and handed it to her son. "Sweetie, go on to the living room and play with your cousins while we finish up dinner, okay?"

Everett didn't need to be told twice. Chocolate chip

cookie in hand, he dashed out of the kitchen to find his cousins.

Nessa frowned, hands propped on her scrubs-covered hips.

"I should feel a little offended that he ran out of here so fast, right? I mean, I carried him for nine months and two weeks, his lil' rugrat cousins didn't."

"Hey!" Leo scowled.

"Hold up!" Sydney protested. "Yes, you should be offended because obviously he likes them more than you, but my daughters are among those rugrats."

"My son, too," Leo added.

"Uh-huh. Come at me after alcohol and food." Nessa waved away their objections, moving toward the wine. Jenna retrieved a glass from the cabinet and set it down in front of her. "Is dinner almost ready? I'm starved. I need to eat Moe's baked chicken and my feelings about Ivy being asked to the prom by some fast-ass football player. I know what a senior wants with my junior sister," she grumbled, double-palming her glass as Jenna poured the Riesling.

Leo laughed. "You sound like Moe. She's been in denial about Cher graduating this year, and prom is just a reminder she can't run away from. Hence—" she jabbed a finger toward the oven "—us having an impromptu family dinner on top of our usual Sunday one."

"I heard that, Leontyne Dennison Strafford." Moe stalked into the kitchen, scowling. "You might be another man's wife, but you will always be my daughter. And that means you'll never be too old for me to take my spoon to that ass."

Flo glanced toward the sink and the Spoon of Mass Destruction—it honest to God had that engraved in the handle since Wolf and Cole had it done for a Mother's

Day long ago—hanging on the hook. She'd threatened to smack them with it many times over the years. Moe had yet to follow through, but not one of her children was foolish enough to try her.

"You know, you're getting a tad more violent in your old age, woman," Flo drawled, moving the pot of mashed potatoes to the counter next to the stove. "First it was the knuckles, now it's the ass. I'm about to start worrying about my daddy."

Moe snorted. "Ask your father if he'd want to be in anyone else's hands but mine. Matter of fact, you should've asked him just this morning when—"

"Ew!" Leo clapped her hands over her ears. "Stop traumatizing me! I got here by stork, dammit, and I mean that." With ears still covered, she power walked for the kitchen door. "Hey, Bono! Mommy's coming!" she yelled, even though her son hadn't made a peep.

Flo chuckled at her sister's antics, while a smirk rode Moe's mouth. She grabbed a pair of oven mitts before turning and waving them in Sydney, Nessa and Jenna's direction.

"You three go and give me a minute with Flo," she ordered.

Nessa sighed. "Can I take the wine?" she asked, already reaching for the bottle and her glass.

"Yes, baby," Moe said, lips twitching. "But I don't want you face-planting in my squash casserole tonight."

"Of course not." Nessa grinned. "You wouldn't know it by looking at him, but your son is super fast. He'd catch me before I hit the plate."

"Get out of here." Moe snatched up a dish towel and mock snapped it after Nessa, who laughed, darting across the kitchen—but still holding on to the wine.

As soon as Sydney and Jenna followed her, and only

Flo remained with Moe, her mother turned to her, eyebrow risen.

"If my chicken is dry, I'm going to blame you since you appear to be the only one not on their way to tipsy," Moe said. Setting the towel on the island, she held her arms out toward Flo, who didn't hesitate to walk into her mother's embrace.

The familiar baby powder-and-lavender scent surrounded her, and for the first time since stepping onto the Hudson property, the tension in her muscles slowly released and she exhaled a full deep breath. Here, in Moe's arms, was her safety. Her place of refuge. The only other place she'd found this kind of peace was in her father's embrace. From the time she'd been a confused, hurting little girl who clung to her anchors in a chaotic storm after losing not just her mother but also the only father she'd known.

"Sonny and Cher might be my youngest, but you're my baby girl. You're the one I hold tightest to because in some ways you've always had one foot out the door." Flo parted her lips to object, but Moe shook her head, cupping Flo's cheeks. "No, I don't mean you're running away from us, Flo. But out of all my kids, you're the seeker. The one who's always searching. Whether it's a new place to visit and discover or take pictures of, or a truth to uncover. There's something inside of you that remains unsatisfied…seeking. And it's that something that makes me a little nervous and worried for you."

"Moe…" Flo lifted her hands, circling her mother's wrists as unease sliced through her. "What's wrong? Why are you saying this? There's no reason to be worried about me. I'm—"

"Fine," Moe finished. "That might work with other people, but not me. I haven't pushed it, waiting on you to come to me when you're ready, but something happened while you were in Thailand. Don't think just because you glossed over talking about it when you returned home that I didn't notice. And when you're finally prepared to confide in me, I'm here."

Moe dropped her hands, brushing them over Flo's shoulders and down her arms, then clasping her hands.

"Moe…" Her words stuttered and died on her tongue. Because she couldn't lie to her mother. So she deflected, avoided the subject. "What's going on? That can't be the only reason you wanted to talk to me."

Quietly studying her for several long moments, Moe released Flo and turned, retrieving her mitts and removing the baked chicken from the oven. Only once she set the dish on top of the stove and removed the gloves did she face her again.

"Cole told me he gave you the mail from Noah."

She hadn't said "her father," and for that, Flo appreciated her.

"He did," Flo said, spinning around to open the cabinet and stretch an arm, rise on her toes and grab a large bowl to transfer the potatoes from the pot.

"Flo," Moe murmured. "Please look at me, honey."

Setting the bowl down, she flattened her palms, staring at the white-and-gold dotted pattern on the counter. But even at her big age of twenty-four, she couldn't disobey her mother. Inhaling a deep breath, she turned, propping a hip against the counter, and faced Moe.

"Your father has—" Moe sighed, briefly closing her eyes "—complicated feelings about his brother reaching out to you. But he would never want to pressure you into replying to Noah or feeling obligated not to reach out because of loyalty to him. I haven't said anything before, but if this hurts you…" She trailed off. "I care about *you* and your feelings more than anything else. If you don't want to receive those cards any longer, I will personally intercept them and return each one to sender. Or hold on to them until you're ready to read the letters. Whatever *you* want."

A flash of pain skittered across Moe's face, and she glanced over her shoulder. But not as if she was looking for someone. No. More as if she couldn't bring herself to look at Flo. But when her gaze did meet Flo's again, the guilt swimming there only solidified that thought.

"I'm sorry I'm just saying this to you now. We should've had this conversation," she murmured.

"Moe, it's okay. *I'm* okay." Flo clasped her mother's hands, giving them a gentle shake.

Her throat tightened for a moment, emotion shoving into it. How many times had she wished Moe or Wolf or Cole had interceded on her behalf when those cards showed up, reminding her of who she wasn't?

Wanted. Needed.

Loved.

She'd desperately wanted someone to step in and tell her father, "Why don't we ask Flo if she wants those letters? Why don't we ask if it hurts her to even see them?"

But then again, why hadn't she said anything in all this time? Why hadn't she voiced her discomfort to her family? She trusted them, adored them, and yet...

You were afraid.

She smothered the soft yet smug voice whispering that know-it-all accusation, but not before it bounced off the walls of her skull a couple of times. And it required every scrap of control not to flinch because Moe, with her eagle eyes, would catch the telltale gesture.

So she covered it up. Hid in plain sight.

Like always.

"Now…" Flo squeezed her mother's hands and let them drop, returning her attention to the pot of mashed potatoes. "Let's get ready to feed the horde. I can hear the impatient rumblings all the way in here from the main room."

Moe's grin was genuine if a little strained as she crossed the kitchen to nab plates to set the dinner table.

"You're probably right. When I came in here, I swear Wolf was eyeing little Ryan like she'd transformed into a cartoon hot dog. If we don't get this food out, we might have a *Lord of the Flies* outbreak. And I will throw all of you in the path first to save my grandchildren."

Flo laughed, because, yeah, her mother wasn't lying. Moe would make them all fodder for her precious grand-kids.

"Let's do it, then."

CHAPTER SEVEN

"DADDY, CAN I have a milkshake?"

Adam shot a pointed look at his daughter's nearly full plate of spaghetti and meatballs. Justine followed his glance and scrunched up her face.

"I'm thirsty," she complained.

He arrowed another look toward her half-full glass of apple juice. This time a sheepish half smile lit her expression.

"I'm thirsty *and* hungry." She shrugged.

Swallowing down a chuckle, he cut into his steak, forking a piece to his mouth.

"No, baby girl, you can't have a milkshake," he said, softening his rejection with a smile. "Maybe next time." When her lips parted and her brow knotted, he arched an eyebrow. And she dug back into her spaghetti. But he knew his little girl. At some point before their dinner ended, she would round back to the milkshake argument. "So how was your day with Ms. Angela? Did you have fun with her?"

Finding a babysitter for Justine had been his first priority after settling on a place for them to live. And Angela Fischer had come highly recommended by the real estate agent who'd arranged the rental.

"She's fun." Justine twirled her fork in the pasta. "We went to the park and then we got hot chocolate. She's got a boyfriend." She dropped in that random bit of information as if asking him to add pepper to her spaghetti.

"She does, huh?" Amusement bubbled in him. *Nosy.* "How do you know that?"

Justine scratched the side of her nose, leaving a spot of marinara there.

"'Cause she's on the phone with him a lot. They miss each other and like to kiss."

The baked potato he'd been in the process of swallowing lodged in his throat, and he choked on it.

Holy shit.

Coughing until his eyes watered, he fumbled for his glass of water.

"You okay, Daddy?" Through misty eyes, he caught her frown and he managed to nod his head to reassure her, even as he desperately gulped down water. Just as he was starting to feel like he wasn't suffocating, her face brightened like the sun breaking through storm clouds. "Flo! Flo, over here!" She waved her arm just in case her yell didn't do the job of catching Flo's attention.

Clenching his teeth, he shifted in his seat and stared at Flo Dennison. At the sound of his little girl screaming her name, she turned away from the older lady behind the counter and grinned at Justine, the gesture reflected in her pretty brown eyes.

He'd just seen her a couple of hours ago when filming and construction for the day crew had wrapped, but she didn't look as if she'd just worked an entire day capturing image after image of an intensely paced renovation. Her locs hung, healthy and thick, around her shoulders and down her back. A formfitting gray cropped sweater and loose, wide-legged pants might have appeared like a bohemian mess on someone else, but on her? She could've walked a catwalk and orders would've poured in with demands for the outfit. Long, teardrop hoops brushed her slender shoulders as she crossed the diner toward them. Unbidden, his mind drifted to a memory of how a similar pair of earrings had looked grazing her bare shoulders with those beautiful locs spread across her pillow.

Maybe she felt his regard, because she flicked a cool gaze toward him. Yeah, Flo Dennison held one hell of a grudge. Today, Monday, marked the second full week of them working together, and he could count on one hand the number of times she'd had a conversation with him. And those had been perfunctory as hell. To everyone else, she was cordial and friendly, but him?

How do you say, "Get fucked" without saying "Get fucked"?

Ask Flo, because she'd perfected it.

"Hey, Jussy," Flo greeted, reaching their table. "How're you doing, sweetie? I haven't seen you in a while."

"Hi, Flo!" Justine beamed. "I've missed you! Why're you here?"

"Jussy, inside voice. Remember?" Adam softly reminded her.

He loved her—her and her bullhorn volume.

Amusement stained Flo's tone as she smiled at his daughter.

"I'm picking up dinner."

"Thank you for not telling her to mind her business," he drawled.

"Daddy!" Justine scowled at him.

He shrugged. "You're being nosy, baby girl."

"No, I'm not. I'm not, right, Flo?" She tipped her head back, poking her lip out and giving Flo the saddest look possible.

"Um…" Flo bit her bottom lip, shooting a look at Adam, and for once, humor gleamed there instead of the usual indifference or annoyance. "You are kinda up in my business, but the fact that you're adorable is working for you." She laughed, pulling on one of Justine's ponytails.

"Daddy says you won't know if you don't ask," Justine opined, and Adam silently groaned, because yeah, he had said that.

Nice time for her to become a parrot.

"Is that so?" Flo smirked, sliding him side-eye. "Well, there you go."

Justine smiled again, and it lit up her face. "You should eat with us," she announced, returning to shouting. "Can she, Daddy? Can Flo eat dinner with us?"

Well, shit.

He should've seen where this was headed. Justine possessed a fascination with Flo, and she'd only seen her a couple of times since they temporarily moved to Rose Bend. Although, he couldn't blame his daughter. Hell, he worked with Flo almost every day, and an attraction that should've dissipated with exposure seemed to grow every time she looked through him or gave him short, to-the-point answers that edged the line of rude.

And yet... Yet, he couldn't call a halt to this preoccupation with that sensually full mouth that sported a small silver hoop through the left corner of her bottom lip, drawing even more attention to the plump curve. Couldn't stop the fall into a borderline obsession with her delicate, almost elfin bone structure or the elegantly arched, dark brows over thickly lashed brown eyes.

Yeah, while his fascination might be covert and unwelcome, he still couldn't blame Justine for hers.

Didn't mean he wanted to sit down and break bread with Flo, either.

Only distance would cure this self-inflicted malady.

"I'm sure Flo is busy, bab—"

"Sure, I would, Jussy," Flo damn near purred, and when he slid a glance up at her, the smile she wore could've sliced him to pieces.

Sliding in next to Justine, Flo set down the shoulder bag she carried then carefully adjusted the booster seat, and whatever she whispered to his daughter had her giggling. He tried not to stare at them. Tried not to let his imagination wander to a place it didn't need to go. Tried not to allow his mind to create a longing that had nowhere to go.

"Hey, Grace," she called to the older Black woman behind the counter. "I'm going to change my order for here instead of to-go."

"You got it, honey," she said, not looking up from pouring coffee into a customer's waiting cup.

"So what've you been up to today, Jussy?" Flo asked, folding her arms on top of the diner table and giving his daughter all her attention.

"Ms. Angela cooked me French toast, and it was good. But my Daddy's is better. I didn't tell her because I didn't want to hurt her feelings," she confessed, her expression and tone solemn.

"That was really nice of you, sweetie," Flo praised in the same serious tone, even though he caught the twitch of her cheek that betrayed a smile. Adam bent his head to hide his, because damn. "Angela Fischer?" Flo hitched her chin, throwing the question at him, taking him off guard.

"Yes," he answered. "Gwendolyn Dansen, the real estate agent who helped me find our house, recommended her."

Flo nodded, then returned her attention to Justine.

"Pretty good French toast still sounds like a good start to a day. How'd the rest of it go?"

"I watched *Bluey* and Ms. Angela talked on the phone to her boyfriend. Aaron doesn't like her working so much," she informed Flo like a miniature TV reporter.

"Um, well, that's unfortunate," Flo said, laughter trembling in her voice.

"Uh-huh," Justine blithely continued. "And then we went to the park. I went on the swings and the slide. And Ms. Angela kissed her boyfriend on the phone. A lot. She likes to kiss."

Jesus.

Adam briefly closed his eyes, and when he opened them moments later, Flo looked at him, eyes wide, full lips pressed together in an attempt to trap the laughter that brimmed in her pretty eyes.

"Here you go, honey." Grace set a plate of hash browns, scrambled eggs, pancakes and sausage in front of Flo. "Let me go grab the syrup and ketchup for you."

"Thanks, Grace. This all looks delicious as always."

"You bet, honey."

Grace walked off, her stride quick and purposeful, easily belonging to a woman half her years.

"You two seem very familiar," Adam said.

"Grace and her husband, Ron, have owned and run Sunnyside Grille for longer than I can remember. They're a fixture here in Rose Bend. And they've seen me grow up, so yes, I guess you can say we're familiar." She shrugged a shoulder. "Small-town living."

He nodded. In Chicago, the owner of his favorite deli might know his usual lunch order, but they in no way shared the easy familiarity Flo did with Grace. And Mr. Donovan might be able to tell anyone Adam preferred light Thousand Island dressing on his Rueben, but he couldn't relay his family's names or any personal anecdotes. Well…not beyond that time Adam brought Justine into the deli for the first time when she was two, and she knocked down a display of olives and sun-dried tomatoes.

But Grace could probably run down Flo's family from oldest to youngest. Small-town living indeed.

"Daddy, can I go look at the music box?" Justine bounced in her booster seat. "Please?"

Adam glanced toward the jukebox several booths away, tucked in the rear corner of the diner. LED lights surrounded the face and brightened the inside so patrons could watch their choice of "record" being chosen and played, although the BTS track currently playing obviously wasn't on a 45.

God, he could identify a BTS song. *And* knew the hook. Who had he become?

"Yes, baby girl. But be sure to stand where I can see you. And no touching, okay?" He slid out of the booth, waiting for Flo to slide out and stand.

Surprise whispered through him when she turned to Justine and gently helped her free of the booster and guided her out of the seat. So small a thing. But it'd been so long since he'd had anyone's help with the daily *small* things that he stared, bemused, at the sight of Flo with her hands under Justine's arms, lifting her then settling the little girl on the floor. And how Justine tilted her head back and grinned at Flo…

A tangled ball of emotion snarled around his rib cage—appreciation, affection, sadness…resentment. The first three? He understood those. Other than his sister, his baby girl had been without a woman's sole attention since her mother left, and he would have to be blind or neglectful not to notice it. Justine reminded him of the sunflowers Addie couldn't go a week without buying for her apartment in Chicago. How they turned their brown faces to the sun from their perch on the windowsill. Justine soaked up affection and kindness from a woman like those flowers basked in the sun's rays. It hurt him to see a need in her that he couldn't exactly fill, no matter how much love and attention he showered on her.

And that was where his resentment came in, he mused, watching as Flo playfully tugged on his daughter's ponytail. Her mother should be here, helping her out of the booth, smiling down at her, teasing her. Not this woman she barely knew who could break her heart so easily if Justine became attached. Because they weren't staying. And Flo would soon be another ephemeral presence in Justine's life.

Like her mother.

"Come on, Jussy. Let me walk you over," he said, holding his hand out to his daughter.

She and Flo glanced up at him, and he mentally winced as he caught the slightly brusque note in his voice. *Shit.* He'd never been the kind of person to inflict his own mood on others, especially those who couldn't do a damn thing about it. Like Justine.

"Let's go, Daddy." She tugged on his hand, already skipping ahead.

He easily kept stride with her to the jukebox, and once there, helped her find a song she liked and slid a dollar into the feeder. In seconds the latest Taylor Swift song streamed out of the speakers, and he strolled back over to his booth, leaving Justine to wiggle her body and wave her arms to the music. Taylor. Beyoncé. Lizzo. His daughter loved them all, and whenever they came on the internet radio stations Adam set for Justine, she could entertain herself for a while dancing and singing along to the lyrics.

"Oh my God, she's adorable." Flo shook her head, a smile curving her lips.

For the first time since their night together, humor and delight washed away her guarded expression, and he dragged his gaze from that full, sensual mouth that he knew all too well.

"I have a Swiftie under my roof. I've come to terms with it," he muttered.

She snorted. "Could be worse. I mean, she could be over there singing about a wet ass—"

"Stop," he growled, snapping up a hand. "I don't even want to think about that. Ever. And besides, I seriously doubt Grace has Cardi B in her jukebox."

"You don't know what Grace and Ron get up to after hours. Including putting on some Cardi and doing what grown folks do."

"You got that right, honey," Grace chimed in, appearing beside their table with a plastic carafe of water and the promised syrup. She set the syrup in front of Flo then leaned forward and topped off his and Justine's glasses. Afterward, she straightened with a wink in his direction. "You're not married for as long as me and my Ron and not learn a few things to keep it fresh."

"Um..." He had nothing.

"I think you broke him, Grace," Flo said, unrestrained glee coloring her tone.

"Come around here some more. You'll get used to it," the diner owner assured him with a pat to his upper arm. "Now, I'm about to go over there and feed another dollar into that box so your cute lil' girl can keep doing her thing. Folks didn't know they would get dinner *and* a show this evening. She's great for business."

Grace headed toward Justine, and when she reached her, she knelt next to her.

"Do you mind?" Flo's soft question distracted him, and she removed a camera, different than the one she used on the reno set, from the bag on the booth seat. Lifting it and an eyebrow, she said, "I don't like to take photos of children without their parents' permission. And if she seems uncomfortable with it, I'll stop."

If it'd been anyone else, he might have politely but firmly turned them down. But not her. Not Flo. He couldn't explain the "why" of it, but he'd witnessed her work ethic these past two weeks. Seen some of the digital downloads of the photos himself. There was a quiet... joy in her work. And while he still harbored some doubts about her résumé for the renovation, he couldn't deny her talent or the care she took. Plus, her asking his permission proved that. And had him inching down the extremely high protective hedge he'd built around his family of two.

He nodded, and with a smile, Flo shifted past him, raising the camera to her face as she moved.

Graceful.

Though she commanded his attention as she neared his daughter and the older woman, she remained unintrusive, letting their interaction play out. Catching the laughter and grins on their faces—one rounded and so painfully innocent in youth, and the other leaner, creased with lines from life and experience in her maturity—Flo deftly moved from one position to the next, the succession of muted clicks whirring away.

Justine caught sight of Flo as the next song by Beyoncé filled the diner, and his daughter waved hard, then being the little performer she was, started to dance and twirl, putting on more of a show for Grace and Flo. And when the older woman joined in, Justine's light, high-pitched laughter was infectious.

He glanced around, ready to call a halt to their shenanigans if the other diners appeared disturbed, but the patrons at the counter and in the booths laughed and some even sang along.

What was this place? When had he stumbled onto the set of a Disney TV show, and better question: Why wasn't he charging toward the exit? He shook his head as Flo returned, her focus on the tiny screen on the back of her camera.

"I got some really wonderful shots," she said, that unguarded smile still claiming her mouth. "I'll make sure to send them over to you."

"Thank you. I really appreciate it."

"No problem." She carefully replaced her equipment in its carrying case and zipped it closed. Standing next to him, she crossed her arms and leaned against the edge of the booth. "She's a natural."

"If by *natural* you mean a ham, then yes, she is," he replied, tone wry. "She doesn't get it from me."

Flo tipped her head to the side, her eyes widened and her lips parted on an exaggerated gasp.

"No! You don't say!" At his grunt, she chuckled and shifted her gaze back to Justine. "I don't mean to pry—"

"Which just means that's exactly what you're about to do," he drawled, sensing where this was headed.

"True," she conceded with a huff of laughter. "But I'm also prefacing it with please feel free to tell me to mind my own business." She paused, but when he didn't say anything, she said with a hint of hesitation, "Where is Justine's mother?"

He'd been correct. Inhaling a breath, he held it then slowly released it after a couple of long moments. But the tightness in his frame didn't abate. When the topic of Jennifer came up, this seemed to be his body's default reaction.

"I get I'm virtually a stranger," Flo murmured, filling

in his silence with a rush of words. "And like I said, tell me to get out of your private business. It's just that..." She trailed off and though he could only see her profile, he didn't miss the slight flex of muscle along her jaw, as if she were physically imprisoning words that warred to get out. He rubbed the pad of his thumb against his forefinger, attempting to erase the urge to brush that delicate jaw. Ease whatever caused that telltale sign. "It's just that I know what it is to not have your mom there for the everyday things, to wonder why and not really understand the answers."

His attention sharpened to a laser focus on her, on the note of...wistfulness and pain in her words. Now he was the one wanting to pose questions, to press for information.

"Justine's mother and I divorced, with me having primary physical custody. Jennifer, her mother, moved so Jussy doesn't get to see her as often as she'd like," he explained, offering Flo the more sanitized version of the truth.

"Oh, I'm sorry. That can't have been easy for her. Or you," she said, some of the stiffness evaporating from her slim frame.

He shrugged, sliding his hands into the front pockets of his pants. "Divorce happens." If anyone knew that, he did. Jerking his chin in Justine's direction, he continued, "She misses her mom. Sometimes she can get... attached quickly."

"Are you warning me, Adam?" she murmured, sliding him a glance. "Again?"

A pause, sticky with memories, descended between them, ensnaring them. Memories of another time when he'd cautioned her, but then it'd been about him. And look how that had turned out.

"She's a great little girl, with the kind of personality that would make friends out of any stranger she meets. But I hear you." Flo nodded. "Speaking of getting attached, how is she doing with Angela? They're doing okay together?"

Mimicking her pose, Adam crossed his arms and, in his head, imagined how they appeared. Two people standing side by side but in defensive postures, like two retired boxers unwilling to lay down their grudges after numerous bouts in the ring. That was them. A short but hot, tangled history and neither one willing to wave the white flag and call a cease-fire.

"Aside from the seeming obsession with kissing?" he asked wryly. "They get along fine. I am a little concerned about the amount of time she might be spending on the phone, though. And what Jussy's overhearing."

"I know Angela. She's a couple of years younger than me and is the oldest of five." She nodded when his eyebrows rose high. "I have that in common with her, too. I'm one of seven. But needless to say, she has a ton of experience with younger children. Not to mention she's made a career out of babysitting since she was about fourteen. She's also been with her boyfriend, Aaron Karr, since high school. They just got engaged about a month ago, so that might explain the extra, uh, PDA. Just talk to her about cutting back on the phone time," Flo suggested. "Angela's cool. She won't be hurt or offended."

Honestly, Angela was a nice young woman, but her hurt feelings hadn't even occurred to him when it came to the quality of his daughter's care.

"Will do."

Applause broke out around them, and Adam looked toward the jukebox. Justine ran full speed toward him, arms widespread as if playing an old-fashioned game of airplane. He moved forward, meeting her halfway and scooping her up and holding her close.

"Daddy, did you see me dance?" She grinned, and he couldn't help but smile back. His little girl's joy was infectious. "Me and Ms. Grace danced, and I can come back and do it again. She said so!"

Grace winced as she approached them, a hand pressed to her hip. "Whew. In my mind, I'm twenty-five, but my hips are shouting you're—well, not twenty-five," the older woman muttered on a chuckle. "If it's okay with you, Adam, I have a slice of million-dollar pie up there with Justine's name on it. I promise to give her milk so it's healthier."

Justine sucked in a breath and held it, giving him eyes that would've had a puppy signing up to take a master class in begging. His firm ground over the milkshake gave way to pie thanks to a pleading look from his daughter and slick maneuvering from a diner owner.

He knew when he was beat.

"One slice. With milk." As if it mattered.

"Of course," Grace said, and as he set Justine down, the older woman grasped her hand and led his daughter to a free stool at the counter.

"You didn't stand a chance, you know that, right?" Flo smirked, sliding back into the booth. Shaking his head, he followed suit, settling in across from her. But his gaze kept skirting over to Justine, who chatted away with Grace and a customer sitting next to her. "She's fine."

Flo's low murmur drew his attention, and she picked up her fork to dive back into her dinner.

"She's fine," Flo repeated. "Grace will keep an eagle eye on her and, I can promise you, Justine couldn't be in safer hands."

He lifted his refilled glass of water and sipped from it.

Shaking his head, he tossed her a rueful smile. "You're probably thinking I'm being overprotective and ridiculous. I mean, she's only several feet away from me."

Since the divorce and Jennifer's absence, he'd become damn near obsessed with ensuring Justine had a semblance of stability in her everyday life. And that need didn't stem from trying to fill the space vacated by her mother. Or rather, it didn't *just* stem from that.

He had endured the abandonment of one parent and the emotional neglect of another. Had been fucking shaped by the hollowness left behind after the grief, anger and confusion extinguished themselves. And as a child, those emotions had seemed overwhelming and incomprehensible. The powerlessness, the pain of loss—some adults couldn't handle it, but he'd been expected to accept it and move forward as a child.

He'd do anything, sacrifice anything, for Justine not to feel that chaotic emotional earthquake that could permanently alter her world.

"I don't think that at all." Some emotion moved over Flo's face. He couldn't pinpoint it as the expression was there and gone. If pressed to label it, he'd call that flash sadness, but more complicated and...darker. "You should never apologize or second-guess your need to protect her. Five feet or five hundred miles. Distance doesn't matter. A father's love is a shield and safety net that every daughter, every child, should have." She blinked, and clearing her throat, forked up more food. "Now, she might not feel that way at sixteen," she said, attempting to inject a levity that wasn't reflected in her brown eyes. "But at five, I promise you, she just feels secure and loved."

"You sound like you speak from experience," he said.

Again, that flicker, but she smiled, and this time it did reach her eyes. "I have a wonderful father. He might not be my biological father, but he's been in my life longer than I can remember. My parents officially adopted me when I was four, but they've cared for me, accepted me, before then. Ian Dennison doesn't have adopted and biological children—he just has children. He's never differentiated between any of us, and even at twenty-four, I can say with certainty that my father would go scorched earth if anyone hurt me."

Then why the sadness? Why the darkness he'd glimpsed in her expression? The more he uncovered about Flo Dennison, the more he craved to peel back the next layer. And this woman was created of *layers*. That presented a clear and present danger to him. He feared he wouldn't want to—wouldn't be able to—stop once he started.

"The little girl who could get up there in front of a diner full of people and sing and dance…the girl who's over there chatting up a stranger like he's her long-lost best friend is someone who possesses a confidence that is nurtured. She doesn't fear rejection because, even with her mother not physically with her every day, she knows she's loved. That says a lot about you as a father, Adam."

A fist-size ball of emotion—too thick to parse through—lodged in the base of his throat.

He'd needed to hear that. God, he hadn't even known how much he'd needed it until now.

Until she'd said it in her low, husky voice.

He raised his glass for another sip of water, but maybe she recognized he needed a moment because she returned her focus to her plate and resumed eating.

"What about you? You mentioned being one of seven children. Where do you fall in?" he asked, switching the subject away from him.

Strictly self-preservation and *not* a need to hear her talk or learn more about her.

Funny how denial sounded a hell of a lot like lying. "I'm fifth."

"And how many of your brothers and sisters are…"

He didn't know why he hesitated over "adopted." Not like it was a curse. But probably because of how she'd described her father's view of his children, it seemed… wrong to segregate them.

"Adopted," she said with a half smile. "You can say it. We don't consider it a dirty word in our house. It's just how we came to be family. It doesn't determine how much family we are." While she lifted a glass of orange juice to her mouth, he let that sink in. And tightened his grip around his own glass to prevent himself from rubbing a fist over his chest where those unexpected words had taken a direct hit. "There are four of us. Cole, me, Sonny and Cher are adopted, and Wolf, Leo and Sinead are my parents' biological children."

"Wait." He frowned, holding up a hand. Did she just…? No way. "Did you just say Sonny and Cher?"

She grinned, and he blinked, briefly stunned at that unfettered, free and gorgeous smile.

Damn.

It dawned on him in that moment that Flo had never truly *smiled* at him until right now. He'd received a smirk, a soft half smile, even a teasing grin, but never…*this*, where her entire face brightened as if with an inner light. She appeared younger, and God, she was just twenty-four. And yet, a twenty-four-year-old who carried a weight that lent her brown eyes more wisdom than someone her age should possess.

But not here. Not now.

He already hungered to see this special side of her again. He wanted more.

"You heard right." She laughed. "My parents named all their kids after musicians and composers."

"So your brother and sister, Sonny and Cher— No," he said, staring at her. *Gaping* at her. Because *no*.

She snickered. "Oh yes. Story for another time, but Cole was already named after John Coltrane from birth. But me and the twins, we had the choice of keeping our birth names or legally changing them when we reached an appropriate age. For some reason—to this day, none of us have ever figured out how they even discovered who they were—they were adamant about being called Sonny and Cher. Sometimes, I don't know what my parents were thinking not using their veto power on that one." She shook her head, that beautiful smile still lighting her face.

He loosed a bark of laughter, leaning against the back of the booth.

"So Wolf would be…" He narrowed his eyes. "Wolfgang? As in Amadeus?"

"Yep. And you want to see a grown man cry? Call him that in mixed company."

Still trying to wrap his mind around her family's unique situation, he cocked his head, considering her.

"And you? Florence?" he asked.

When he'd initially discovered her full name, he'd been a little surprised. It was pretty, yes, if a little old-fashioned. But after watching her the past two weeks, it fit her. Elegant, reserved, beautiful. He knew what lay underneath that reserve, though. How hot she could burn.

Focus, dammit. Don't even go there.

"Florence Ballard from the Supremes."

"Ah. Of course." He nodded. "Can I ask why you chose her? Don't get me wrong, Florence Ballard was an amazing talent with a beautiful voice. But why her?"

Flo set her fork down and folded her arms on top of

the table. For a long moment she stared down at her plate of half-eaten food, and he leaned forward, prepared to tell her never mind. But then she lifted her gaze to his, and the words froze on his tongue.

Besides, he wanted to hear her story. More than he should admit.

"My biological mom had a thing for music from the '60s and '70s," she murmured. "Especially Motown. The Jackson 5. The Miracles. Marvin Gaye. The Temptations. And most definitely, the Supremes. And it's funny, I almost chose Diana—my mom adored her. Had all of her music and movies. But I don't know." She shrugged a shoulder. "I was just eight or nine when I decided on Florence, though the legal name change didn't come until a couple of years later. Still, way too early to truly grasp everything she endured, such as alcoholism, but I still had an affinity toward her. Back then she seemed like the quiet one. The beautiful, amazing and overshadowed singer."

"Is that how you felt in your family? Overshadowed?" he asked even as he questioned how that could even be possible.

A tiny frown wrinkled her brow, and Flo lifted a hand, absently rubbing the backs of her fingers along her jaw.

"No, not overshadowed, exactly. Moe and Dad—"

"Moe?" he interrupted. "Is that your mother?"

"Yes." She nodded. Another smile. "We blame Cole for that. The story goes that when he was a baby, he called her Moe instead of mom or mother, and it stuck. Not just for all of us, but for most everyone here in town, too." Waving a hand, she continued, "So Moe and Dad were too—" her frown deepened "—intentional for us to feel overshadowed. Yes, they had a lot of children, but they also made time and space for each of us. Gave each of us room to grow in our own identities and they nurtured them, never stifled us or tried to conform us to an ideal of what the perfect family should be. And that was especially important for me, Cole and the twins since we're not white. They made sure—" She abruptly broke off, a wry quirk to the corner of her mouth. "Am I protesting too much?"

He hiked a shoulder. "Little bit."

But her love for them—her parents, her family— radiated from her.

She huffed a short breath, shaking her head. "I guess I just wanted to make it clear that my parents created a safe space for all of us."

"I get that." He leaned back against the booth again, crossing his arms. "Now just say what you're trying really hard not to."

She blinked, appearing momentarily surprised. Then she loosed a short, breathy chuckle that contained more deprecation than humor. "I'd almost forgotten how jarring that straightforward manner can be. Jarring and irritating."

Not the first time he'd heard that, so he didn't contradict her.

"If you don't want to say it aloud, that's your choice, Flo. I get we're not exactly…friends," he murmured.

"No." She straightened, flattening her hands on either side of her plate. "Maybe because we're not *friends* it's a little easier." Yet, it was another long beat of silence before she continued. "When you're the quiet child in a house full of extroverts, you can kind of…not get lost, but melt into the background. And sometimes you start to believe your needs or wants aren't as important as someone else's. If you want a new SD card for your camera, but someone else needs money for a college application, you don't speak up, because obviously college is more important. It doesn't occur to you at the time that both would be equally important to your parents, and they'd make a way for their child who's passionate about photography to have her memory card and for the other to get their needs met, too."

Their childhoods had been different. While both had lost their biological mothers, she'd been blessed enough to grow up in a loving home while he'd had a father who married and discarded women with the ease of switching out household furniture. He and Addie had been pawns in relationship battles when Maurice remembered them, and ghosts in their own home when he didn't.

Yet...

Yet, despite their childhoods and the age difference separating him and Flo, they shared that sense of disappearing, of becoming invisible in a family.

"I get that," he said, and though it went against the grain for him to reveal personal information about himself, particularly to someone who'd so recently called him an asshole, he offered her a little of what she'd given him. "I only have one sister—younger than me—but I essentially cared for her. In our family it was a toss-up whether being noticed was better than being ignored. Not that my father was necessarily abusive. He was just shitty. So whenever we did have to ask for something, I put her needs before mine. I could get by—I could take care of myself—but she couldn't. I think no matter what age, we find reasons to justify why our needs aren't as important."

Especially when that was the message a kid received from his only "present" parent.

"And now? Do you still find those reasons?" Flo asked, her gaze searching his, and for an absurd moment he had the impulse to swipe a hand down his face to make sure none of his thoughts leaked out into his expression. Like he said, absurd. And yet, he dug his fingers into his arms to keep them in place. "At your big age of, what?" She squinted. "Exactly how old are you?"

"You're asking that now?" He snorted. "I'm thirty-seven. Thirteen years older than you. Thirteen years that might as well be three hundred," he softly said.

"And here we are again," she said, voice light, but no way he could miss that mocking lilt. "Somehow, we find ourselves back to the subject of experience. I'm not just lacking it on the job but in life, too, is that it?"

"And let me guess, I'm back to being the presumptuous asshole."

"We meet again." She tilted her head, the taunting tone making its way to her mouth in a smirk. "And yet you didn't seem to give a damn about my *inexperience* the night we met."

"I was wondering if you would eventually get around to throwing that out there."

"Glad I didn't disappoint."

Tension—rife with anger and, fuck if he could deny it, lust—vibrated between them, seemed to wrap around them like electrified barbed wire. And here they were, the temporary cease-fire dissipated.

"Daddy, I'm finished!" Justine appeared at his elbow, startling him.

Shit. He'd been so caught up in his verbal sparring with Flo—so caught up in *Flo*—that he hadn't even noticed his daughter crossing the diner to him.

"Hey, baby girl," he said, nabbing his napkin and wiping away her milk mustache. He chose to ignore the graveled texture to his voice. Chose to ignore the source of it. Despite the source sitting right across from him. "Did you tell Ms. Grace thank you for the pie?"

"Yep! She got you a piece, too," Justine announced. "It's at our house."

He frowned, but Flo drew his gaze with her low, amused chuckle. She didn't look at him, but at Justine, and that derisive smirk she seemed to save just for him had abandoned her face. Instead, she warmly smiled at his daughter.

"Did Ms. Grace say, *on the house*, Jussy?" she asked.

"Uh-huh. At our house." Justine nodded.

Adam swallowed a laugh. "That's nice of her. I'll pick it up in a few minutes. But we need to go. It's getting late." He slid from the booth, removing his wallet from his back pocket. "Tell Flo good night."

"'Night, Flo." Justine clambered up onto the booth seat and threw her arms around Flo's neck, squeezing tight. "Can I see my pictures?"

"I'll send them to your dad so you can have them, okay?" Flo returned her hug.

"Okay, don't forget!"

Chuckling, Flo held up a pinkie. "I won't. Pinkie swear."

Justine hooked her finger around Flo's and Flo pumped their arms up and down then kissed her fist. His daughter laughed and demanded Flo "do it again." After a couple more run-throughs of the "handshake," Adam intervened, or they would never get out of the diner.

"All right, baby girl, we'll practice it at home." He held his hand out to her.

Justine inched out of the booth and slid her hand into his, and that familiar awe and love filled him.

"Bye, Flo," Justine called, waving.

And as his little girl sang out a similar goodbye to Grace, Adam glanced at Flo, who met his gaze with a steady but shuttered stare.

"See you tomorrow, Adam."

"'Night, Flo," he murmured, ushering Justine toward the diner exit.

As he walked out, his daughter's chatter dancing on the spring night air, he silently answered Flo's question.

More than ever, he had reasons why his needs had to come second. No, not reasons, plural. Just one.

And he held her hand in his.

CHAPTER EIGHT

FLO STOOD ON the scarred wood floor of the tower room of the Hudson home, staring at the gorgeous circle of stained glass high on the wall. Though the rest of the house was currently in various stages of repair—and disrepair—this ornamental piece had survived all its owners intact. Early-afternoon sunlight streamed through like a portal, scattering the beams like fragments of colored crystal.

Raising her Sony A7 III to her eye, she focused the lens and moved back until she captured several shots. She couldn't help comparing it to a church as she studied the images. The same sense of reverence and stillness. Beautiful.

The crew was filming below in the kitchen today, and she'd head back down there in a few minutes, but with all the noise and so many people, she'd taken a few minutes to herself. And up here in this circular room under the castle-like turret, she easily remembered herself as a little girl staring up at the tower from outside. Wondering if a princess lived here.

Huffing out a soft laugh at her past whimsical self, she tilted her head, studying the stained glass again. It might have survived the test of time, but it wasn't perfect. It had a few cracks the owners might find tired instead of charming.

"Who am I kidding? They'll replace it," she murmured. "No, they won't."

Her heart thudded against her sternum, her pulse an insistent drum in her veins. Since her back was to Adam, she surrendered to the need to close her eyes and savor that deep, smooth timbre.

God, that voice did things to her.

Things that his hands and mouth had already done to her.

"How do you know?" she asked, still gazing at the stained glass.

His footsteps fell heavy on the floor as he neared her. She forced her body to remain relaxed, but awareness had her strung tight.

"Because I recommended that it stay put," he said. "Although to be fair, I don't think the new owners intended to replace it. They want to preserve as much of the original structure as possible. What we'll do—" he moved so he stood next to her and pointed toward the window "—is remove the glass and clean it, of course. Then we'll double pane it for energy efficiency."

He turned slightly, lowering his arm and tucking his hand into the front pocket of his dark gray pants.

"I believe the owners appreciate what they have here. They don't want a showpiece. Yes, they bought a beautiful historic home, but that's just what they want—a home. They do want to tailor the house to be theirs, and that's understandable and completely their right. But still, it isn't their intention to disturb the architectural and historical integrity."

A shimmer of guilt rippled through her, and she lifted her camera, focused on a small crack that resembled the state of California and fired off a shot.

"I'm being a little selfish," she confessed.

"About?"

She sighed. Why did she possess this urge to *talk* to

him? Hadn't it just been last night when he'd called her inexperienced and implied she was too young *again*? Whenever she allowed her guard down around this man it somehow ended up backfiring on her.

Yet...

Glancing at him, she found herself captured by his hazel gaze, and the pounding in her pulse intensified. It resonated between her legs in a hot, aching pulse. Only he could create this curious phenomenon where he irritated her, got under her skin like an itch. And at the same time he set her on fire with one look.

Forcing her feet forward, she strode toward the other bank of windows and peered out to the lawn below. At some point the grass had been mowed. Probably one of the neighbors as the TV crew wouldn't have considered it a priority now since the landscaping wasn't scheduled to be worked on for several weeks.

"Flo? Selfish about?" Adam pressed.

She stared down at the sidewalk, and as if an apparition of her former self shimmered and appeared, she could easily envision the girl she'd been, standing next to her pink-and-white bike.

"I used to ride past this house all the time when I was younger. I'd sit on my bike and stare up at it, imagining I lived here, and my room was right here. I wasn't ever the princess type, but the stained glass, the resemblance to a castle, the colors... It seemed like a fairy tale sitting right here in the middle of Rose Bend. And who doesn't want to live in a fairy tale? Even if I'd rather have been the knight than the comatose heroine." She snorted. "Anyway, my disposable camera—and eventually first digital camera—contained many images of this house."

"You've come full circle, then."

"Yes," she whispered. "I guess I have."

Shaking her head and feeling a little silly for admitting her childish fantasies to him of all people, she turned around and faced him. And tried not to notice that the tower room seemed smaller with his huge, wide-shouldered frame inside it.

"Is that the reason you took this job? Nostalgia?" he asked, and her shoulders stiffened.

"What was that? Ten minutes? That might be a personal best." Narrowing her eyes, she scoffed. "Is it really so difficult to believe that I took this job not out of nepotism or on a lark, but because I truly believe I'm the best person for it? That no one could capture not just the process of the renovation but the heart of the house like I can?"

"Flo."

"No." Anger crackled through her, and she slapped a hand up in the air. "You're entitled to your opinion, but I'm entitled to not have to hear it again. So if you don't mi—"

"Be. Quiet." His low but steely voice cut through her irritation as well as her tirade.

Her chin snapped back as shock knocked the rest of the words out of her mind. She quieted. Then she frowned. Oh, wait just a minute. Who the hell...?

Matter of fact, she should ask him.

"Are you serious?" she snapped. "Who the—"

"Can I see your camera?" he interrupted again, and surprising her, *again*.

"I'm sorry?" On reflex, she held her camera close to her chest.

He arched an eyebrow. "Are you afraid I'll eat it like the ogre you've made me out to be?"

"I don't know." Flo sniffed, a trace of humor whispering through her annoyance. "Appetite proclivities aside, those ham-size hands look a little too clumsy to handle my equipment."

As soon as she said it, she heard it.

And he did, too. She could tell by the flash of heat in his golden eyes and the taut pull at the corners of his mouth.

God knew there was nothing clumsy about the way he handled anything on her. He'd proven that several times in the one night they'd been together. A flippant comment rode the tip of her tongue, but in the warmth of that bright gaze, it evaporated.

"Can I see?" he asked again.

Instead of giving him a reply, she walked over to him, camera outstretched.

He accepted it and pressed the arrow buttons next to the viewfinder, silently scanning through the pictures. Not just the stained glass but the ones from earlier—of the now finished living room from different angles and in different lighting. At the time, she'd been proud of how... romantic they'd turned out, as if caught between this century and a past one. Now, though, with Adam peering at them, she felt kind of silly. As if they would confirm his belief she was too immature for this job.

When he finished he remained silent, and she hated the anxiety that amped up inside her. Hated that she cared what he thought.

But damn, it was just rude that he didn't say *any*-thing—

"These are stunning," he murmured.

Not looking up from the camera, he scrolled through the shots again, and once he made it to the end, he finally glanced up and met her eyes.

"I mean it, Flo. They are truly beautiful." He passed the camera back to her, but didn't let go when she grasped it. "When we finished that living room, I saw refurbished and new crown molding. A replaced fireplace, new hardwood flooring and insulated bay windows. Sound structuring. I see a job well done and a vision completed. But there—" he dipped his chin "—I just saw art. You took what we did and created beauty and inspiration. You are incredibly talented and gifted. I was wrong, Flo."

He released his hold on the camera, and she grabbed it, abruptly thankful for something to do with her hands. Because then she wouldn't press a fist to the fluttering in her stomach.

"I take back what I said about you not deserving this job. From those pictures, the town council hired the perfect person, and that's you."

She shouldn't be affected by his apology or his praise; she hadn't asked for either. But she would be a liar if she denied the pleasure unfurling in her chest. She didn't want his validation.

No, she didn't *want* to want it.

And God, did that make her sad.

"Thank you. I appreciate that." Clearing her throat, she slipped the camera strap over her head. "We should probably—" A loud creak groaned in the room, and they looked at each other. Her eyes widened, and shock laced with unease had her blood pumping. Only the two of them occupied the room, and no wind blew on this cloudless afternoon, so...what the hell? "What was that?"

He surveyed the area, and when their gazes met again, a hint of a smile flirted with his full, sensual mouth.

"You mean you've never heard of the Hudson Bride?" he asked.

The Hudson Bride? What was he talking about? The questions flitted through her head even as she peered into the rounded shadows of the tower room as if she would discover answers there. Or, God forbid, a bride.

"I'll take that confused look as a no." He chuckled, pivoting on his heel and scanning the room along with her. "I'm not surprised. I found the story in the old papers from the first two owners and sellers of the house. Apparently, Mr. Theodore Hudson, the original owner of this home, had a sister, Catherine, who lived with him, his wife and two small children when they moved here from New York back in 1885. This was her room."

Flo tried not to gape. Tried, and failed. A ghost story. Was he really about to relate a ghost story? A delicious shiver tripped down her spine. As one who attended ghost tours in every city she visited, it baffled her that she'd never heard one connected to this house—in her very own hometown.

"According to the papers, Catherine was engaged to be married to one Mark Chandler, the son of a very wealthy and prestigious banker in New York. The Hudsons were a family of means as well, but not on the level of the Chandlers, and Mark's parents weren't happy about the engagement. So when Catherine moved to Massachusetts with her brother, his parents used the time and distance to pressure their son into meeting another woman of their choice. Mark evidently caved and married this other woman. But he neglected to tell Catherine. The entire time, she believed they were still set to be married, and she didn't find out about the end of their relationship until friends visited Theodore and his wife and brought news of Mark's marriage."

So caught up in the tale, Flo gasped, her stomach bottoming out for poor Catherine.

"What a piece of shit coward," she said, voice hushed, but anger on behalf of the long-dead jilted woman swirling inside her.

Adam nodded. "He was that. And Catherine was understandably devastated. She tried to reach out to him, but he refused all contact. Heartbroken, she retired to this room, and it's said she spent most of her time here until she died sometime in the 1930s. She only left the house to go down to the gazebo or the stream, which was a river back then. And she hardly ever went into town, which explains why most people don't remember her. But…" Adam paused, pretty dramatically, Flo mused, and she didn't miss the gleam in his bright eyes. "On dark, moonless nights, past owners have reported hearing a creaking in this room as if someone was walking the floorboards. Pacing back and forth. Longing for a love that will never come."

Flo stared at him, at the twitching of his lips as he tried not to smile.

"You obviously missed your calling," she drawled. "But they have storytelling hour at the library for the kids. You would be a massive hit."

"What?" He laughed, cocking his head. "You don't believe in the story or the possibility of a ghost?"

"You have the papers," she said, letting that be her answer. But curiosity niggled at her, and she crossed her arms. "Do you? Believe in the ghost story, I mean?"

"Not everything can be explained by what we see with our eyes or our limited reason. If that was the case, why would we need faith? Or…" He shrugged, then that faint smile grew, and he flashed his pretty white teeth. And damn if she didn't feel the phantom graze of those same teeth down the side of her throat and over her shoulder.

Walking over to the far wall, he stood directly beneath the stained-glass window, planted his foot on a board right in front of the baseboard and eased his weight on it.

A creak echoed in the room again.

"Or it could be this right here."

A chuckle bubbled up inside her at his unexpected and—screw it, yes—charming display of whimsy. But she swallowed it down, narrowing her eyes.

"Did you just *Mystic Pizza* me? I can't really tell because the other older guy's endgame was to fuck, and we've already done that."

He blinked, and after a long moment, he barked out a sharp crack of laughter, shaking his head. "You can say the weirdest shit and I have no idea what to do with that."

But he didn't deny knowing the old '80s movie, or her reference of trying to seduce a younger woman with a ghost story, pizza and a rainy night.

And didn't that just make him even more attractive? *Damn it*.

"Seriously, though, I'd like to include that story in the coffee book. I've never heard of it, and I bet most people around here haven't, either. If they had, there definitely would've been more teenagers trying to sneak in here on dark, moonless nights to catch a glimpse of a ghost." She snickered, imagining she would've been one of those teenagers, especially around Halloween. "Maybe I can take pictures of the documents with the stories and include pictures of this room from old records and today. It would make a wonderful piece of lore."

Adam nodded. "I'll gather the documents I have and make them available to you."

"That would be amazing. Thank y—" Her cell rang, and the peal of Sister Sledge's *We are Family* relayed that a member of her family called. "Excuse me a minute," she said, reaching for the phone in her back pocket.

"Sure." Adam dipped his chin.

Swiping her thumb across the screen, she answered the call and pressed the cell to her ear.

"Hey, Cole," she greeted with a smile. "What's up?"

"Flo." The grim note flattening his usually warm voice had a seed of disquiet lodging between her ribs. "Are you at the reno site or your studio?"

"The Hudson house," she quietly said, attempting to remain calm, but that question did shit all to help the nerves already knotting her belly. "Cole, what's wrong?"

"Listen, I hate to do this, but do you think you could meet me at the inn?"

Disquiet mushroomed into full panic, and her knees trembled, causing her to sway. Her heart shot for her throat and wedged there, beating so hard it constricted her breath. She didn't hear Adam move across the room, but suddenly his arm grasped her elbow and his other hand spread across her back, steadying her.

"Why?" she rasped, her fingers clutching the cell so tightly the blunt edges bit into her skin. "Why, Cole? Did something happen to...?"

She couldn't voice a name. Couldn't because that might bring her biggest fear into fruition.

Not again.

Though her mother had died when Flo was barely two, the hole she'd left behind had haunted Flo far into her adulthood. As did the absence of the man who'd been her original father figure. And then, when Cole had lost his first wife and son in childbirth a little over seven years ago, the pain had cut so deep Flo had sometimes doubted any of them would heal. She didn't think she could bear that agony again. Especially if it were her parents or brothers and sisters...

"*No.* God, no, Flo," Cole nearly shouted in her ear.

And she nearly wilted in relief as it surged through her like a swollen flood. Adam's hold on her tightened, and he shifted closer, his body bracing her. And she leaned on that strength. Took advantage of that strength in this moment, when her greatest fear had been alleviated, but she still trembled with the remnants of it.

"I'm sorry, Flo. I didn't mean to scare you like that. Everyone is okay and safe, I promise," Cole said, an urgency in his tone. "But if you can, I do still need you at the inn. Do you think you can get here soon?"

"Yes," she rasped, then clearing her throat, repeated, "Yes, I can. I'm leaving now. I'll see you in about fifteen minutes."

"Good. Drive safe. I'll be waiting for you."

She ended the call, tucking the cell back into her pocket with shaky fingers, her mind whirling with the cryptic conversation.

"Is everything okay?" Adam asked, his chest still pressed against the back of her shoulder and his big body still bracing her.

"I'm sorry. I have to go."

Because she had to—because she needed to—she stepped away from him, turned and headed toward the door. The urgency in Cole's voice had taken up root inside her, propelling her forward even though she didn't understand the why or what. But if he needed her, she had to get to the inn.

"Flo, wait." A hand grasped her wrist, and she halted, but impatience hummed through her. Adam moved in front of her. "Take a beat, please, and tell me what's going on. Is everything okay? Are *you* okay?"

She shook her head, tugging lightly against his hold, and he released her, though he didn't shift out of her way.

"I don't know anything yet. Cole asked me to come home, and he wouldn't do that while I was working unless it was important. I'm sorry to leave, and it might be unprofessional, but I have to go."

"Forget about all that." He sliced a hand between them

as if cutting off her explanation. "It's not unprofessional. You need time for a family emergency, and family always comes first. Besides, technically, you work for Cole and the town council, not me or *Vintage Renovation*. But I will let anyone know just in case they ask." He shifted backward out of her space, and an irrational part of her wanted to grab him back to her. Because of that need, she, too, shifted away a step, inserting more space between them. "Go ahead," he continued. "And be careful driving."

She nodded then continued down the hall and stairs. People from the crew called out to her, and she waved but didn't stop to talk, hurrying out of the house and across the lawn to her car. Now that her primary fear had been allayed, a myriad of other possibilities crowded into her head.

Cole's solemn tone crossed out the possibility of the news being positive or happy. So what could it be? Something with the twins at school? Did something happen with Sinead in Boston? Flo had talked to her sister a couple of days earlier, and she hadn't mentioned anything out of the ordinary. And Flo couldn't imagine one of her siblings' marriages being in trouble...

Stop. Just stop it.

She could teach a master class in borrowing trouble. But once it turned on, she couldn't twist it off. And the barrage of thoughts blitzed her until she was on the road leading to Kinsale Inn. As soon as her family's business and her childhood home came into view, she exhaled a heavy breath that sounded more like a low groan in the confines of the car.

The white bed-and-breakfast had a wide porch encircling the whole building. A short set of stairs led up to the red boards of a front door with pretty glass panes along the top. The two lower levels boasted banks of glistening green shuttered windows, and the third, smaller story, a quaint dormer window. A slanted red roof capped it all. It'd been a lovely place to grow up, and though she spent most of her time at her apartment over the photography studio in town, Flo loved coming home. It was her safe haven.

Even with her belly churning and nerves jangling like a live wire.

Pulling her car to a stop in the circular driveway, she swallowed to moisten her abruptly dry mouth as Cole and Wolf rose from leaning on the porch railings and descended the front steps. They waited, and though they didn't resemble each other in appearance, their tall, wide builds and identical serious expression denoted them as brothers.

Her pulse clanged in her ears as she pushed her driver's door open and climbed out of the vehicle.

"It takes both of you to meet me," she said, arching her eyebrow. "You're not doing much for my anxiety."

"Flo." Wolf tugged her into a hug, squeezing her. His scent of cedar reminded her of the wood he worked with as a carpenter. It enveloped her, and she breathed him in, taking comfort in the familiarity of her big brother. He pulled back, his hands cupping her shoulders, and his green eyes swept over her. "You good?"

"No." She loosed a nervous chuckle. "Didn't you just hear what I said? What's going on, Wolf?" Glancing at Cole, she said, "I've made up every scenario in my head. Put me out of my misery."

"Jesus," Wolf muttered, thrusting a hand through his long dark brown hair. "I hate this."

Cole stroked a hand down her back, his gaze sympathetic.

"Flo, we wanted to get to you first. Try to make this a little easier—"

"Deandrea?"

Ice slicked through her as she heard her birth name called in a deep, familiar voice. She stared into Wolf's green gaze and Cole's amber one, unable to move. Her chest barely rose and fell on her shallow breaths, but in her head, it sounded like a wind tunnel. Cold sweat dripped down her spine.

"Deandrea?" he repeated.

"Flo?"

She closed her eyes, squeezed them shut.

Wolf cupped the back of her neck and Cole slid his arm around her shoulders. And only with the strength of her brothers to lean on did she finally turn around.

Turn around and face Noah Dennison.

Her father.

CHAPTER NINE

IT'D BEEN WEEKS since Adam had been to this brick build-ing off Main Street, but he remembered the sturdy iron staircase that led to the apartment above Perfect Images. Of course, the last time he'd been here, he hadn't known Flo owned the studio below.

Of course, last time, he hadn't known Flo's name.

Climbing the stairs, he silently cursed himself for being here at eight o'clock at night instead of home with his lit-tle girl. Cursed himself for not letting it go when it came to Florence Dennison.

Common sense insisted he keep this...thing, whatever it was between them, professional. It couldn't go any-where. He had a job to do here in Rose Bend and as soon as it ended, he and Justine would be returning to Chicago. Not to mention, Flo was thirteen years his junior. A life-time of experiences and differences.

And yet, recognizing all of that, here he stood. Ready to be...involved.

Raising his arm, he knocked his fist against the apart-ment door. Moments later the lock twisted and the door opened. He studied that crack as it creaked wider and wider, waiting for his first glimpse of her.

Flo had claimed space in his head since rushing out of the Hudson house earlier today, refusing to be evicted. He couldn't get the image of her stricken expression out of his mind. Her body had trembled against his, and she'd allowed him to support her. While that had sent a bolt of fierce protectiveness through him, it'd also ratcheted up his worry. Because he might've only known Flo for a few short weeks, but he was certain she would've only allowed him to hold her up if she was scared or ill.

Flo stood in the doorway, and he ran his gaze over her, taking in her locs pulled into a ponytail at the back of her head, the black tank top molding to her slim frame and firm breasts, down to her loose dark red pants. When he met her dark brown eyes again, he caught the surprise flickering there.

"You made it home in one piece. That's a plus," he said in lieu of a greeting.

"Adam." She grasped the doorjamb. "What're you doing here?"

"I apologize for showing up unannounced, Flo, but after earlier, I just wanted to check on you."

I wanted to make sure you were okay. Make sure you weren't still wearing that shattered expression that damn near stopped my heart.

Flo shuffled back a step, opening the door wider. He took that as her invitation to come in. And he accepted.

Moving forward, he entered her apartment, and déjà vu slammed into him. That evening, admittedly never far from his memory, shimmered in front of him like some kind of desert-induced mirage. The living/dining room combo decorated with tall windows facing the quiet street and its interesting collection of mismatched furniture that somehow seemed to, well…match. The small kitchen to his left separated by a bar and stool. What he remembered most, though?

The gorgeous framed photographs on the walls.

Vivid, lush images of beautiful landscapes, even more beautiful people. He didn't need to be told it was her work.

Not after today. Not after seeing the absolute magic she could wield with a camera. He could identify her pieces in an array of others.

"Where's Jussy?" she asked, heading for the kitchen, disappearing around the short wall.

"My neighbor offered to watch her for a little while. They're nice, with a small child of their own, and Justine's played with their niece and nephew a couple of times. You might know them. Isaac and Jenna Hunter?"

She strode back into the living room with two water bottles in hand, extending one toward him.

Huffing out a small laugh, she twisted the cap off. "A little familiar with them seeing as how I sat across from both of them at dinner last Sunday." She took a sip. "Jenna is my older sister and sister-in-law's best friend. She and Isaac are great."

"That makes me feel even better, thank you. For that and this." He held up the bottle though he didn't open it. "How are you, Flo?"

Her jaw worked, her lips tightening before she lifted her bottle for another sip.

"Fine," she finally said.

Yeah, that wasn't going to work for him. He crossed the small space separating them, lifted his hand and pinched her chin. Her water bottle, halfway to her mouth again, stopped. She stared at him, and that flicker of surprise flashed in her eyes once more. He much preferred it over the careful blankness that had been in her voice.

"Still a little liar, I see," he murmured, drawing them both back to the night they met. The night they ended up right here in her apartment. "I have eyes, Flo. And you're anything but fine."

"We're not friends," she stated, but without heat.

More like…desperation. He'd visited that place called

desperation. Knew it intimately enough to identify it when he heard it.

"As you pointed out the other day. And what did you tell me then? That fact makes talking to me easier," he continued, not granting her a chance to answer. "I'm here again. Don't think. Don't censor. Just let go."

He cupped her jaw. His thumb brushed over her cheekbone. Back and forth. Back and forth. And he waited—studied her and waited.

Finally, she shuddered out a shaky breath and, after turning her face into his palm for a brief moment, she stepped back, and he dropped his arm to his side.

Setting the water bottle down on the coffee table with more care than it warranted, she paced away from him, arms crossed tightly over her chest. To warn off others—others being him—or to keep the pieces of herself together? Something whispered that it was more the latter. Because she seemed...on edge. Restless.

"I am a liar," she softly admitted, though there was nothing "soft" about the confession. "Omission. Smoke and screens. Evasion. When it all comes down to it, they're still lies. And that's what I've been doing with my family for a long time." She walked back toward him, sinking to the middle of her couch. Staring down at her flattened hands on top of her thighs, she murmured, "Those fucking letters. Every one of them have been tearing out a strip of my soul, but I say nothing. Just accept them and say nothing. Saying you're fine when you're not. Pretending you're complete when you're not. But to admit it would be worse. It would be ungrateful, mean. No, it would be damaging. Not just to me, but to my family who have done nothing but love me, and I would never want them to feel as if they weren't enough."

Adam followed very little of what Flo said. Letters?

Damaging? He understood none of that, but he did get hurt and guilt when he heard it. And in her jumbled words existed a wealth of both.

Crossing the short distance to her, he lowered himself to the heavy wood coffee table in front of the sofa. His spread legs bracketed hers, and he propped his elbows just above his knees.

"Start from the beginning, queen," he gently urged, using the moniker he hadn't used since their night together. He hadn't meant to use it now, except it slipped from his lips without his permission. Flo jerked the faintest bit, her lips parting. But no sound emerged. "Go on. Let it go," he encouraged again.

Her eyes closed, and she dipped her head, and the need to stroke his palm over those thick, beautiful locs, to rub her scalp, screamed through him so loud, so fierce, he clutched his fingers tighter together.

Touching her wasn't why he'd come here this evening. Touching was so far off the table, it hadn't been invited to the fucking party.

"My father's back."

Well...damn.

Whatever he'd been expecting her to say, that—the arrival of a parent—hadn't been it.

Adam stiffened, confusion rolling through his head as he flipped back through all their conversations. All the information about her family that she'd sparingly doled out.

Hadn't she said Ian Dennison was her father? That she'd been adopted by him and Moe Dennison as a baby? And as far as Adam knew—thanks in part to Flo and the other part to helpful, chatty gossips in town—Ian had been in Rose Bend all along, running Kinsale Inn.

So what did Flo mean by her father was back?

"Flo," he said, reaching behind him, nabbing her water bottle and pressing it into her hand, "start at the beginning."

"Right. Sometimes I forget you're not from here so wouldn't know the story like everyone else." Her fingers curled around the bottle, but she didn't drink from it. A sad smile ghosted across her lips. His chest constricted, and this time he did grant himself permission to rub the taut spot in the middle of his breastbone. "Originally, I'm not from Rose Bend, either. My biological parents met after my father returned home on leave from Iraq. He was in the army, and it was his first night back in New York. He went out to a bar, saw my mom and fell. Apparently, it was a whirlwind romance. They married, she became pregnant, but he had to return overseas. And that was the last time she saw him. And I never knew him."

Sympathy for the young military wife swept through him. Left alone and pregnant, their life together over before it even really began had to be devastating. But…

Then how did he return here to Rose Bend if he died?

The question ping-ponged against his skull, but he let her continue.

"A year after my biological father died, my mother worked as a receptionist in a legal office, and Noah Dennison walked in for an appointment. I wasn't even a year old when they started dating, and eventually my mom fell hard for him, and he fell in return. For both her and me. They eventually married. He was an attorney as well, and when a career opportunity opened up for him to move to Rose Bend where his brother and his family lived, he took it. And my mother and I went with him. I was about eighteen months old then, and the Dennison family accepted us like we were their own. Noah opened his law offices, and they were happy. We were happy. It was a good time."

"How do you know all of this?" Adam asked, swept up in her tale.

Fascinated by the glimpse she afforded him into her past, into the events that shaped her into the woman who'd been bold enough to ask for and claim her own sexuality but feared and avoided intimacy.

She didn't immediately reply; instead, she lifted the bottle to her lips for a deep sip then set the plastic container on the floor. The sadness in her voice shadowed her eyes, and he wanted to brush the tender skin under them as if that caress could so easily sweep away her pain.

"She left a diary." Flo loosed a breathy, heavy chuckle. "Isn't that crazy? I mean, how many adopted children would give anything for that window into their biological mother? To know her thoughts and discover who she was instead of just a name on a birth certificate? I had that. Aisha Lock Dennison gifted me with that by maintaining diaries she started just after my biological father deployed, after they married."

"That's a gift," Adam murmured, stunned.

And God, it disgusted him, but he was envious.

Flo was right; he would've sacrificed anything for so much as a letter or text from his mother, much less a diary packed with her thoughts, impressions, feelings... Insight into how she felt about him.

Why she'd left him and never returned.

Did she ever think about him...?

"It was...is," she amended. "I still read them. They're my most prized possessions. Especially since they're all I have of her. Because not long after I turned two, she died. Undiagnosed heart condition. One morning she just didn't wake up. And though I was very young, I still have faint memories, or more like impressions, of feeling lost. Of a terrible grief that wasn't just mine but Noah's.

At that time Noah was the only father I'd known. He'd tucked me in at night, read bedtime stories to me, made me laugh. And from what Moe and Dad tell me, I clung to him after my mother's death. Literally, clung. As if I was afraid he would disappear like my mother."

"God, Flo." Adam reached for her, surrendering to the need to touch her, comfort her.

Before, he'd resisted. But with this cloying grief thickening her voice, drenching her eyes until they appeared nearly black, he couldn't *not* touch her. Shifting forward, he slid his hand under her hair and cradled the nape of her neck. A shiver coursed through her, and she didn't try to evade him. On the contrary, she leaned toward him, and he met her halfway, pressing his forehead to hers.

Her vulnerability tore at him with great, greedy handfuls. He harbored zero doubt she would regret this slip in the morning—hell, later tonight. But right now he took her defenselessness and covered it, protected it.

"It's silly for me to feel so fucking *much* nearly twenty-two years later, right? It's not like I *remember*, remember her. Not like I had a lot of time with her—"

"Don't do that," he growled, then softening his tone, repeated, "Don't do that, queen. You lost your mother. It wouldn't matter if it happened while you were a day old, it's a loss of the woman who gave you life. A loss that deserves to be grieved."

She shook her head, her forehead rolling against his.

"But," she objected, "it's not like I didn't have parents. Parents who loved, adored and raised me—"

He squeezed her neck, cutting her off.

"It doesn't mean the life you lost with your biological mother can't be mourned. Having a great life doesn't make less valuable the one you could've had if she'd lived. And there's no guilt in thinking about what-ifs.

Or in wishing things could have been different. She was your mother. Of course, you wish she could've lived to raise you, to teach you, to love you. I'd think even your parents would tell you that."

Inhaling a shaky breath, Flo leaned back, dislodging his hand. Eyes closed, she ran her hands over the top of her head, smoothing one down her ponytail. She exhaled on a sigh and lifted her lashes, meeting his gaze.

"Go on with your story, Flo. You're not finished," he quietly urged.

"No, I wish it was, but it's not."

Falling against the back of the couch, she spread her fingers across her thighs and peered down at them as if they would somehow supply answers she sought. But he'd be the first to tell her, they wouldn't. If they could, he'd have materialized his own answers a long time ago.

"After my mother died, Noah didn't handle her death well. At all. My parents told me he deteriorated quickly into a spiral of grief and alcohol. I ended up spending more time with them at the inn because he just…crumbled. I had to practically drag it out of Moe, but the last straw for them was when they visited Noah's house and he didn't answer. They used their key to enter and found him passed out on the living room floor and me playing with his empty liquor bottles next to him. That night I returned to the inn with them, and they forced him into rehab. Only thing is…he didn't return. Noah left rehab and didn't come back to Rose Bend for me. He wrote a letter to Moe and Dad explaining how I was better off with them because he wasn't in a place to care for me. In the letter were papers he'd had drawn up terminating his parental rights and granting Moe and Dad guardianship over me."

He'd abandoned her. Her first father figure had abandoned her after she'd already lost her mother. Jesus. They had more in common than he'd believed. He remembered the pain and betrayal that seeped into his bones. And he suspected she felt the same. Knew the taste of that particular bitterness.

"I'm sorry, Flo. I'm so damn sorry." He shook his head, the words sounding inadequate even as he voiced them. "I take it he's back?" he murmured.

"Yes," she whispered. "After all these years, he shows up. And calling me Deandrea."

"Deandrea?"

She nodded. "That's my birth name. Now it's my middle name—Florence Deandrea Dennison." Her fingers fisted on her thighs. "After years of just cards on my birthday and Christmas, he suddenly shows up out of the blue, calling me *that*. As if I'm the same little girl he claimed to love as his own and then walked away from without a backward glance," she snapped.

But as quick as that glint of temper flashed, it was doused, and she along with it.

"Okay, queen, okay. Good, baby." He cupped her knee, rubbed his thumb over the skin above it. "Do you have anything stronger than water in there?" he asked, standing up from the table, jerking his chin in the direction of the kitchen.

"Wine. In the refrigerator."

"Okay, good. Be right back."

He strode toward her kitchen and retrieved the nearly full bottle of Moscato. Within moments he returned to her with a glass and took his seat on the coffee table. He clasped her hand and pressed the wine into it. Then waited for her to sip.

"One more," he urged when she lowered the glass.

When she obeyed, he took the wine, turned the flute so

his mouth fit over the same place and drank, as well. Why he did that—such a small but intimate act—he couldn't explain to himself, so he didn't even try.

"You good?" he asked.

"Yes. No." On a short laugh, she scrubbed her palms down her face.

"What did he have to say?" He didn't want to press, but like a festering wound that needed to be lanced, he pushed her to get the last little bit out.

"I don't know." Another of those humorless, sharp-edged chuckles. "I left. After he called my name and started down the steps toward me, I got in my car and left. Like a coward. Or like the girl you're always calling me."

"I have never called you a girl. And I've never thought of you that way. If I did, we would have bigger issues here," he said, setting the glass behind him. She snorted, but her dark brown eyes didn't lose those haunted shadows. "Let's get this clear between us. I've said you were inexperienced when it came to the project you were hired for. And on paper, it's true. But anyone looking at your work wouldn't deny your talent. Even though I told myself and you that I didn't allow our night together to cloud my judgment, I did. And I apologize for it."

"What was in that wine?" she murmured. "That might be the first time I've heard you apologize. And to me, no less. Either you're drunk or I am."

"Smart-ass." He tilted his head. "Now, let's get back to this bullshit about you being a coward." Her eyebrows jacked up at his wording, but he leaned forward again, pushing into her personal space. "Bullshit, queen. Because that's what it is. Cowards don't stand up to sexual harassment even when they're the only person willing to do it. Cowards don't take on a business in their early twenties. Cowards don't protect the feelings of those they love at the expense of their own. You're not a coward or a liar. You're a queen." He paused, his gaze running over her face. "Queen."

Slowly, she eased off the couch and got into his space. He inhaled her breath, tasting the sweetness of the Moscato and her. He remembered that unique flavor of *her*, and it teased him. Had been teasing him—no, haunting him—for weeks. His study dropped to her mouth, to the temptation of those lush, nearly too full lips.

And as he'd been doing all night, he surrendered to it.

All the reasons why he shouldn't touch her, especially with his mouth, evacuated his head and conscience, and he closed the last few inches separating them and took that tease of a mouth.

She parted for him, and he sank inside, his tongue seeking out and tangling with hers. They didn't need a reintroduction; their mouths met, parted, met again. He groaned as she flicked the tip of her tongue over the roof of his mouth, and he sucked that tongue, earning an answering moan from her.

Angling his head, he dove deeper. Took more. Drew harder. The hardest task he assigned himself was keeping his hands on his knees, not pushing a thumb against her bottom lip and opening her wider for him. Not pressing his palm to the front of her throat, savoring that racing pulse against his skin. No, he did none of that because if he did... If he did, he might not walk out her apartment door. Not until tomorrow morning after they had thoroughly used each other.

He needed to end this, but then she nipped his bottom lip and slicked her tongue across it. But that didn't soothe the sting. It tossed kindling on the fire already licking at him, demanding he take them further, give her another night of forgetfulness. And him? Give himself hours of oblivion.

With a will that belied how he hungrily thrust between her lips, he dragged his mouth away and pressed his cheek to hers. Her fast, warm pants bathed his ear and neck, twisting the screw in his gut tighter. Hardening his cock even further.

Just a little shift… One little shift and he could be kneeling between her legs, hands beneath that tank top, covering her small and utterly perfect breasts…

Shit.

"I should go," he said, and not waiting for her agreement, or God help both of them, her objection, he shot to his feet and headed for the front door.

But halfway there, he halted. Turned. And glanced back at Flo, who remained sitting where he'd left her.

Don't you fucking do it. Don't do i—

"Goddamn," he growled, sharply pivoting and striding back over to her. Bending down, he grasped her hand and gently yet firmly tugged her up.

Then he pulled her into his arms and held her.

Held her until her body relaxed against him and her sigh whispered across his chest. Slipping his fingers through her locs, he cradled her head, tipping it back.

"I can stay if you need me," he quietly offered.

And he meant it. He'd either have to ask the Hunters if they would mind keeping Justine or bring her over here, but he'd stay. He wouldn't be another person to walk away from her, to leave her.

"No." She shook her head, her lashes lowering. "You're right. You should go and get home to Jussy. I'm fine." He didn't say anything, and also didn't move. And she huffed out a short chuckle, meeting his gaze again. "Okay, I will be fine. But go."

Stepping back and out of his arms, she dipped her chin toward the front door. Part of him wanted to gather her close again and ignore her assertions of being *fine*. But the other part... The part that understood she was saving them both from bad decisions, took her at her word and moved for the door.

"Adam?"

He halted, his hand on the doorknob. Looking over his shoulder, he saw, again, she stood where he'd left her.

"Thank you," she whispered.

He didn't ask for what; he nodded, opened the door and left her apartment. On the postage-stamp-size stoop, he paused and inhaled a breath that didn't contain the sweet notes of jasmine and woodsy scents of cedarwood.

Shaking his head, he descended the staircase and tried to convince himself his errand was completed, time to head home and put this behind him. He and Flo had cleared the air, too, so they could continue as coworkers without any lingering awkwardness.

Well, damn.

Turned out he was a pretty good liar.

CHAPTER TEN

"I CAN'T BELIEVE the town is throwing us a picnic," Mira mused, holding a hand to her forehead and shading her eyes. The producer laughed. "Just when I start to think this town can't get any more perfect." Dropping her arm, she squinted at Flo. "Go ahead, you can tell me. What's the seedy underbelly of Rose Bend? Spill."

Grinning, Flo steadied her camera on the tripod and shot Mira side-eye. She and the producer had become friendly over the last few weeks of filming. Mira and some of the crew had even joined Flo at Road's End a couple of times.

"If I can trust you," she said, lowering her voice and crooking a finger at the woman, beckoning her closer. Mira's eyes widened, sparkling with humor and probably the anticipation of some tea. "You didn't hear it from me, but you know Mrs. Roman over at The Cat and Chew?"

"The owner of that cat tea shop? Yes, sweet lady. I mean, I'm not one for sitting down and eating while a bunch of cats stare me down like they're plotting my death, but—" she shrugged, adjusting her headset "—cute place and cuter lady."

The Cat and Chew, the cat café Mrs. Anna Roman had opened a couple of years ago, had become one of the most popular places in town. But Flo was a fish person. Not that she had any, but still... Flo was firmly on the same page as Mira.

"Well, Mrs. Roman moved into town, and she might be this sophisticated, elegant businesswoman by day, but once night falls..." Flo trailed off dramatically.

"Yeah?" Mira breathed, leaning closer.

"She locks herself in that store and..."

"What?" Mira pressed, impatience lining the other woman's voice.

"Bathes herself in the blood of virgins so she maintains that porcelain smooth complexion. Now the town council is set to discuss an ordinance limiting people to one virgin sacrifice per quarter. Bad for the tourism."

Mira blinked. Then a loud crack of laughter burst from her, and she pointed at Flo.

"Okay, good one. Just remember payback is a bitch and I have a television crew at my disposal."

Flo winced. "See, you're not playing fair." Turning back to her camera, she fired off a couple shots of the surrounding trees, gazebo and creek in the distance. "I love my hometown, and though I love to travel, I also love returning home. But it's not perfect. We have our issues, too, like bigger cities, just not on as large a scale. Still, we're not exempt from society's problems."

"Name one," Mira challenged.

Flo straightened, arching an eyebrow. "Okay. As we speak the local librarian is organizing a rally to protest the banning of books by a small but virulent group who want to remove 'inappropriate' material from the library. In other words, the books are too Black, too gay, too trans, too other."

"Get out." Interest gleamed in Mira's eyes as she crossed her arms. "When is the rally supposed to be taking place?"

"In a week or two."

"And can anyone join? Including, say, a producer and

a film crew who are off the clock and might be walking near the library with their cameras?"

Flo laughed. "That's very specific. And yes, anyone can join. The more people show up, the better. Including said producer, film crew and cameras. I think Remi—the head librarian—would love that. Beck Dansing and I.M. Kelly have already agreed to participate, which, hopefully, will bring even more people out. But I'll get you firmer details as soon as I have them."

"Great." Mira grinned. "If you could also give me the contact info for the librarian, I would be more than happy to pass it along to a friend of mine. She's a field reporter out of a station in Albany. I can't guarantee anything, but I think she would love this kind of community interest story. Especially with this book-banning bullshit happening all over the country. And throw in two very popular *New York Times* bestselling authors? Oh yeah, like I said, I can't promise, but I see this grabbing her interest."

"That would be amazing. I'll send you Remi's info now." Excitement and delight sparked inside Flo as she whipped out her cell, pulled up the librarian's contacts and texted them to the producer. "And you wonder why the town wants to throw you a picnic," Flo teased, returning her phone to her back pocket.

"Whatever." Mira snorted. "Let me get inside. We're still filming in the kitchen—good morning, Adam," she broke off, turning to wave to the man who might've left Flo's apartment last night, but not her thoughts or dreams. "And who's this little sweetheart?"

Flo spun around, her gaze crashing into Adam's bright one before falling to his daughter, who grinned widely.

"Hi, Flo!" Justine yelled.

"Hey, Jussy," Flo greeted at a lower volume and walked over to them.

What was going on? He'd never brought Justine to work with him before.

"Morning, Mira," he said to the producer with a dip of his head. "This is my daughter, Justine. She'll be visiting with me today."

The innocuous words somehow didn't match up with the vein of steel threading through his voice. Flo frowned, briefly studying his impassive expression, then she shifted her attention back to Justine.

"Hi, Justine, it's nice to meet you." Mira squatted down and stretched out her hand. "A pretty name for a very pretty girl. My name's Mira, and I work with your dad and Flo."

"Hi," Justine said, and in an uncharacteristic show of shyness—well, as long as Flo had known her—the little girl crowded closer to her father's leg.

"Jussy, how cool you get to spend the day at your daddy's job," Flo said, smiling down at the five-year-old. "I guess that officially makes you a big girl."

"I am." The bout of shyness gone, Justine puffed out her small chest. "Ms. Angela flaked on me, so I'm here."

Uh-oh.

"Justine," Adam called her name, the warning unmistakable.

"That's what you said, Daddy." She tilted her head back, nose wrinkled. "You said she—"

Flo moved forward, hopefully cutting off what was sure to be more of her father's opinion on the absentee Angela.

"Hey, Jussy. What do you think about hanging with me today while I take pictures? I even have a camera for you, and you can show your dad all your pictures when he's finished working," Flo suggested, glancing up at Adam.

Technically, she should've asked him for permission

first, to watch Justine. There was a difference between letting Flo eat dinner with them at a diner and letting her babysit his daughter by herself, even if he would be near.

But to be honest, she hadn't expected the proposition to fly out of her mouth. The same surprise that flickered through his golden eyes shimmered inside her. But now that the offer sat between them, waiting to be accepted or rejected, she hoped he said yes. And not just because she liked Justine and hanging with her would be like spending the day with her younger nieces and nephews.

But also because... Well, she wanted to help him.

As he'd shown up for her last night.

Except she wouldn't be kissing the ever loving hell out of him in front of God and television crew.

Staring into his eyes, she almost lifted her fingertips to her lips as if she could still feel the hungry and insistent molding of his mouth over hers. With a will constructed of scotch tape and tissue paper, she managed to keep her arm by her side, but a slight narrowing of his eyes had her wondering if the same thoughts of that incendiary kiss filtered through his mind, too.

Why did you kiss me? Did you mean to take my mouth like you've been starved for me? Why did you come back and hold me...offer to stay?

The questions flew through her mind at warp speed.

Nope. Nopenopenope. Not going there. Anything having to do with Adam's body parts meeting—or being inside of—hers was off-limits.

"Yay!" Justine bounced on her feet, practically vibrating with excitement, and Flo smiled at her enthusiasm. "Daddy, can I play with Flo today? *Please?*"

"Are you sure?" Adam quietly asked, and Flo nodded. Relief eased some of the stiffness from his expression, and he exhaled a low breath. "Thank you, Flo." Looking down at his daughter, he arched an eyebrow. "Be a good girl for Flo, okay? And listen to everything she says."

"Okay, Daddy!" Justine boomed, back to bouncing and throwing in a wiggle. God, she was cute. Flo smothered a snicker and held her hand out to Justine. Immediately, she released her father and clasped onto Flo. "I can still take pictures?" she asked.

"You sure can," Flo assured her. "You can be my assistant today. How's that sound?"

"Daddy," Justine excitedly called out to her father as if he wasn't standing right there. "I'm going to be Flo's 'stant."

"I heard, baby girl."

Mira laughed. "Welcome to the crew, Justine." Giving them a wave, she climbed the porch steps and disappeared inside the house.

"Come on, Jussy. I have a camera just for you in my car. We'll go get it and start our workday."

With the child's hand still clasped in hers, Flo started for the curb and succession of parked cars.

"Flo." Her name in Adam's deep rumble of a voice halted her midstep.

And before she turned around, she schooled her features so he couldn't see the effect it had on her. His gaze roamed over her face, and though it made her sound like a heroine in those romance books Sinead devoured, she swore that gaze swept over her skin like a physical caress. Warm, heavy, yet gentle.

Yeah, enough of that.

"Yes?" she asked, notching her chin up.

For a moment he remained silent, but then he glanced down at Justine.

"You carry extra cameras in your car?"

She mentally stumbled, not expecting that question—

there had been…more in his eyes. Something more intimate there.

But she replied anyway.

"Disposable cameras, yes. I have nieces and nephews who like to take pictures, so I started keeping them on hand."

He nodded, a ghost of a smile flirting with his full lips.

"C'mon, Flo!" Justine tugged on her hand. "Bye, Daddy! Have a good day! We have to work!"

That faint smile grew into a full, genuine one that damn near knocked the air out of her lungs.

Time for her to get to work like Justine said.

Past time for Flo to stop dwelling on Adam.

"Look, Flo!" Justine ran over as she zoomed her lens in on the sparkle of the creek just through a break in the thick copse of trees.

Capturing the image quickly, Flo lowered her camera and smiled as Justine skidded to a stop in front of her, waving the disposable camera. They'd spent the past two and a half hours together, and Flo had enjoyed herself. The little girl's exuberance in taking pictures, and her endless questions about Flo's work, had been an absolute joy. And besides, how could anyone not enjoy Justine? Her delight in even the smallest things—from the little bench in the time-warped gazebo to a ladybug crawling along a leaf—was infectious.

Wisps of anger and hurt undulated through Flo.

Every woman had the right to choose whether or not they wanted to become a mother. There was no shame in deciding for themselves that birthing and raising children weren't for them—because being a mother wasn't every woman's chosen path or destiny.

But Justine's mother *had* decided on that path. She

had decided to bring this precious baby into the world, and for the life of Flo, she couldn't understand how the other woman could walk away. If Flo had her standing in front of her right now, she'd shake the hell out of her, remind her that Justine didn't ask to be here. Remind her that the moment she decided to have the little girl, her priority became her baby, protecting her and nurturing her. She didn't have the fucking right to abandon her.

Shoving down the emotion brimming inside her, Flo knelt down so she was eye level with Justine.

"What do you have?" Flo asked the beaming child.

"I finished this camera," Justine announced. "Can I have another one?"

It was a good thing Flo had grabbed a few of the disposable cameras; Justine had gone through two already.

Still smiling, Flo nodded and swapped out the cameras.

"Here you go."

"Thank you, Flo." Justine hugged it to her chest, her torso swaying back and forth. "Are you going to babysit me tomorrow, too? Can we take more pictures?"

"I don't know about tomorrow, Jussy. Ms. Angela might be back so you would be with her again," Flo said, but the little girl shook her head, a mutinous expression crossing her face.

"I don't want her. I want you." Then a look that seemed far too anxious for a girl her age replaced the stubborn one. "We're friends, Flo. You like me?"

"Of course, sweetie," Flo rushed to reassure her, alarmed that she would possess even one second of doubt about that. "You and me, we're best friends. Pinkie swear." She held up her smallest finger.

A huge smile brightened the little girl's face again, ushering away the shadows that had darkened it. Justine hooked her finger through Flo's, and they completed their handshake ritual.

"Pinkie swear!" Justine yelled.

Flo laughed, but let her humor ebb as she cupped the girl's shoulder. She murmured, "Jussy, you do know we all like you very much, right? I can't imagine anyone not loving you as soon as they meet you."

Instead of giving Flo her trademark open, unguarded grin, Jussy wrinkled her nose, frowning.

"Mommy, too?"

Holy shit.

"Sweetie," Flo breathed, her fingers lightly squeezing Justine's shoulder. "Of course she does—"

"Lunch."

Flo didn't jolt at the sound of the deep voice behind her. Relief and hurt swirled inside her. Relief because this conversation was now averted. How did she explain a mother's decisions to a five-year-old when Flo didn't understand them herself? And hurt because eventually someone would need to have this conversation with Justine. It wasn't fair. It wasn't right.

And at this moment she couldn't be more thankful for the interruption Adam presented. Rising, she turned around.

Adam glanced down at Justine before returning his gaze to hers. "Everything okay?" he asked.

"Yes." She pinned a smile on her lips. But she also gave him a tiny shake of her head to relay they would talk later. Without an avid audience. "Did you say something about lunch?"

He studied her for a long moment then slowly nodded and held up a couple of paper bags.

"Daddy!" Justine flew to her father, arms outstretched, and he swooped her up into his arms, hugging her.

"Hey, Jussy. You been having fun?" he asked, and she nodded so hard, Flo inwardly winced in sympathy.

"Uh-huh," the little girl said and thrust out the new camera Flo had given her. "I have lots of pictures!"

"Good job, baby girl," he praised, kissing her cheek. "Ready to eat lunch?"

"Yes!"

He set her down and pulled a sandwich, chips and juice box free from his bag.

"Here you go. Take this over to the bench and don't wander, okay?"

Justine nodded, and clasping her lunch to her chest, ran over to the little black bench at the side of the house.

"She doesn't ever walk anywhere, does she?" Flo asked, chuckling.

"No." Adam shook his head, a smile playing about his lips. "She has two speeds. Stop and Mach 10." He dipped into the brown paper bag once more, retrieved another sandwich and chips and extended them to her. "Lunch?"

"What? I don't get a juice box?" Grinning, she accepted the meal and dipped her chin toward the gazebo. "Are you taking a break and eating, too?"

"Sure."

She led the way toward the gazebo and settled down on the bench inside, glancing over to make sure Justine remained in view. Opening the wrap around her sandwich, she bit into it and hummed in appreciation.

"Thank you." She held up the sandwich, swallowing the bite of tuna fish. "This is good."

"It's Jussy's favorite," he said, sitting down next to her and pulling his own meal free of the sack. They spent the next several minutes in silence, eating their lunch.

Once she finished her sandwich, he softly said, "So the conversation I walked up on…"

Damn. She'd hoped he would let that go.

Shaking her head, she picked up one of the bottles of water he'd set between them.

"I think she just misses her mother," she murmured.

Sighing, Adam rubbed a hand over his head. "She's so upbeat and happy, I sometimes convince myself our divorce and her mother's absence doesn't affect her. Maybe I *want* to believe that, but I, more than anyone, know it's not true. Children can find ways to blame themselves for almost everything."

So true. For the longest time Flo had blamed herself for Noah's leaving. Blamed herself that her adopted father's brother stayed away because he couldn't bear looking at her and seeing her biological mother, the love of his life. Blamed herself for not being enough to make Noah stay or return.

As she grew older, she acknowledged the truth—that all of Noah's choices were on him, not her. But emotionally?

Emotionally, she couldn't completely eradicate the footprints of that guilt.

"Just from the amount of time I've spent around Jussy, she *is* a happy, upbeat little girl. You've done a remarkable job with her. But it's tough for a five-year-old to understand what most adults don't."

"Yeah, I get that." He nodded. "It's just…" He didn't finish the thought, trailing off and shaking his head. "Never mind."

"You said, *more than anyone* you could relate to what Justine is going through." She paused, fearing she was treading where she had no right. But curiosity and an inexplicable desire to know everything about this man propelled her. "Did you lose a parent, too?"

A heartbeat of silence passed, and she almost rescinded her question, almost told him to forget answering. But then he nodded, rubbing a hand over his bearded jaw.

"My parents separated when I was seven, and I haven't seen my mother since. I guess I should be thankful that Jennifer at least calls Jussy. Because I didn't get even that."

Unable to stop herself, Flo scooted closer to him, laying a hand on his hard thigh. Muscles flexed beneath her palm, almost distracting her. Almost.

"I'm sorry, Adam."

He flicked a hand, as if brushing away her sentiment. "It was a long time ago."

Right. Her mother had died decades ago, and her first father figure had walked away from her not long after that. And yet, she still bore the scars. Would Adam really be any different? From his reaction, she didn't think so.

"So your father raised you by himself?"

He snorted, picking up his bottle of water and taking a long sip.

"Well, he provided food and shelter. But much more than that is debatable." He loosed a low, dry laugh, twisting the cap of the bottle back on. "I learned a lot about fatherhood from him. Mostly what *not* to do with my own child. Having Jussy, being her parent... It's like redemption."

Flo tilted her head, studied him. "Redemption implies being absolved of a wrong, a sin. And I thought we just agreed you couldn't possibly be at fault for something that happened to you as a child."

A rueful smile twisted his mouth. "Right. We did agree on that." He sighed, the smile growing tight. "Anyway, how did Jussy do today?"

A part of her was tempted to refuse the switch in subject. But a bigger, admittedly more cowardly part of her decided to let him have it. Because she still felt a little raw from the night he showed up at her apartment, when she'd been at her most vulnerable. He'd witnessed a side of her she allowed very few to see… She couldn't give him more. *More* terrified her.

"She did great. I enjoy hanging with her." A warmth unfurled inside her, easing the tension that had crept in. "And it's fun watching her excitement over taking pictures. I love photography—it's my passion—but it's also my job. Seeing it through her eyes reminds me of my own joy when I first discovered it." She huffed out a laugh. "Even the pictures with my finger in them were amazing."

His low chuckle joined hers. "I'm pretty sure there are going to be plenty of those."

"Oh, most definitely." Twisting the water bottle back and forth between her palms, she glanced toward the bench where Justine still sat, sipping on her juice box. "Have you heard anything else from Angela?"

His irritated sigh punctuated the air between them.

"No, nothing. I'm guessing she's too busy celebrating her elopement." He frowned. "I placed a call to my real estate agent who originally recommended Angela to see if she knows anyone else, but no luck so far."

Even as she silently warned herself against getting any further involved with Adam and his daughter, Flo heard herself saying, "I don't mind keeping her with me."

Huge. Ass. Sigh.

But she didn't take the offer back. The sense of… rightness settling in her chest informed her it was the right thing to do.

And if she was honest with herself, she wanted to do it.

Adam's frown deepened. "I can't ask you to do that."

"You're not asking me. I'm offering." The more she talked, the more certain she became. "She can hang with me while I work. If you don't mind her going to the studio with me for the appointments I have, then she can come and be my assistant. I can bring her back here to meet you or I can take her to your house and wait for you there, whichever is easiest for you." When he remained silent, his eyebrows still drawn down in a vee, she settled a hand over his knee. "Honestly, Adam. I don't mind. She won't be a bother."

After a long moment, he gave a slow nod.

"Okay, if you're sure."

"I am." Realizing she still cupped his knee, and his skin seemed to warm hers through his jeans, she jerked her arm back, pressing her hand to the cool water bottle. Not that it did anything to relieve or erase the imprint of him on her palm. She felt branded. "I have another couple of hours here, then I have to run by the studio and set up for a shoot first thing in the morning. After that I'll take Justine to the pharmacy and get her pictures developed. Would you prefer I drop her off here or bring her home?"

"Home." Standing, he slid a hand into his pocket, emerging a second later with a key ring. He wrestled a silver one off and handed it to her. "I'll have one made for you, but could you take her home? I'll bring pizza."

"Is that your way of inviting me to stay for dinner?" She accepted the key, closing her fingers around it.

The light note in her voice belied the burst of flutters in her belly, and damn if that didn't disgust her a little. She was twenty-four, not fourteen. *Get your shit together, woman.*

"The very least I can do for you helping us out is feed you."

She shouldn't.

Between working and watching Justine, she was already in his sphere more than she should be. More than was wise.

So no, she absolutely should *not* accept this dinner invitation...

"Sure, I'll stay for dinner."

Somebody shoot me and just put me out of my misery.

"Good." A beat of silence, and his gaze dipped to her mouth, lingered there. Her breath stalled in her throat. "Last night..."

"Was a mistake," she rushed to complete his sentence. "Emotions were running high and—"

"I wanted to know if you were okay," he interrupted.

Well...damn.

It was still a mistake. He thought so, right? He had to because she couldn't be the strong one when it came to keeping things platonic between them. Just sitting this close to him with that earthy and sweet scent teasing her nose had heat stirring low in her belly and between her thighs.

He's leaving.

You don't do commitments.

And if you did, he's all wrong for you.

His dick isn't.

Shit.

She was doing so well.

"I'm doing fine, thanks," she said, ducking her head on the pretense of picking up the discarded paper bag and stuffing the remnants of their lunch inside. "Nothing that a good night's rest couldn't fix."

A good night's rest and Marty McFly's DeLorean time machine, but whatever.

He stared at her, and it required every bit of her self-control to meet that golden scrutiny. At one point in her life, all she'd desired was to feel seen.

Now, under his intense gaze, that need was severely overrated.

"Good," he finally said.

She did not need a second job as a mentalist to determine he didn't believe her.

Funny.

She'd been good at hiding the truth all her life, and one sexy single father torpedoed that record to hell.

"Well…" She stood, grabbing the brown bag. "We should get back to it. Justine and I have more photos to take."

He nodded, extending his hand for the trash. "Thank you again, Flo. I'll see you later at the house for dinner."

Handing over the bag, she nodded. "I'll text you when we get to each of our stops and give you an update."

"I appreciate that." A smile lit his face, slowly spreading as Justine glanced up, caught sight of them and raced across the lawn. He knelt, opening his arms, and his daughter flew into them, embracing him as if they'd last seen each other a day ago instead of a half hour. It was both corny and immensely…heartwarming. "I'm headed back to work, Jussy. Keep being good for Flo, okay?"

"Yes, Daddy." She looked up and grinned at Flo. "I've been good, right, Flo?"

"The best, Jussy," Flo agreed. "Ready to go get some more pictures?"

"Yep!" She smacked a kiss on Adam's cheek then skipped back over to the tripod and camera bags. "C'mon, Flo!"

"I'm being summoned," Flo drawled.

"You better get to it, then," Adam said, standing. "Thanks again, Flo."

"You're welcome, Adam."

With another long look that had her fighting back a

rush of heat to her face and other body parts farther south, he turned and walked back toward the house. Leaving her to wonder if she had done a good thing by helping out.

Or if she'd made the biggest mistake outside of taking Adam Reed home.

Either way, she was in too deep.

"I SEE YOU'VE already learned one of our secret treasures here in Rose Bend." Flo picked up her plate and followed Adam into the kitchen, setting the dish in the sink as he threw the grease-spotted empty pizza box in the trash.

He smirked, a flash of surprise flickering through him as she twisted the faucets, running water in the sink. It'd been years since someone else washed dishes in his house—even before Jennifer left. Domestic duties fell on him, and to watch someone else take them up, particularly without him asking, took him aback for a second.

"You mean Morelli's Pizzeria?" He snorted. "I don't think you can call it a secret if half the town was crowded in there, waiting on their order."

"It's not a secret to us here in Rose Bend," she pointed out, shooting him a look over her shoulder. "But to the rest of you outside of our town limits, well..."

The corner of her mouth twitched with an almost smile, and he dragged his gaze up from that too-tempting enticement back to her eyes.

"Do I need to sign a pact in blood that this all remains hush-hush?"

She shrugged a shoulder. "I mean, I'm not *not* saying you shouldn't..."

Chuckling, he walked over to the sink, gently bumping her shoulder. Flo shifted over, reaching for the dish detergent and squeezing the liquid into the water. They worked in silent and surprisingly comfortable tandem, washing up the few dishes the three of them had used for dinner. On the counter's corner a baby monitor emitted the sounds from Justine's room as she sang to herself and played with her toys.

It should worry him how happy his little girl had been tonight with Flo in their home. Justine had always seemed well-adjusted—maybe a little too well-adjusted to the circumstances of the divorce and her mother's leaving, if he was honest—but this evening, snuggled right up against Flo's side as she ate pizza and chattered away, it was the most relaxed and…contented he'd seen her in a long while.

Yeah, it should worry him… And later, it probably would. But right now, with his baby girl's carefree singing echoing in the kitchen and the suspected source of that contentment drying dishes next to him, he couldn't bring himself to question it.

"You have plans for the rest of your evening?" he asked as she passed him the last plate and he moved to put it up in the cabinet.

"Editing some pictures," she said, wiping her hands on a dish towel.

"Jussy and I usually watch a movie a couple of days a week after dinner. Fair warning, it's her choice so that could be anything from *The Princess and the Frog* to *The Wiz*."

"*The Wiz*, huh?" Flo arched an eyebrow. "That's an oldie."

"What can I say? My daughter is a lover of the classics." He snorted. "And Michael Jackson as the Scarecrow doesn't hurt, either."

"I don't know." Flo scrunched up her nose, propping a hip against the edge of the counter and crossing her arms. "Unpopular opinion ahead, but the Wicked Witch was always my favorite character. I mean, nobody would dare bring that woman bad news. That's some serious influence right there."

"Hell yeah, that's an unpopular opinion. She tried to kill Dorothy."

"Meh." Flo twisted her hand back and forth. "She was just a little misunderstood. Powerful women always are."

Adam paused, stared at her. "Has anyone ever used the term 'morally gray' to describe you?"

She snickered. "You flatterer, you." Pushing off the counter, she stepped forward. "If that's an offer—or a warning—to stay and watch a movie with you, then I accept. And I'm really pulling for Diana Ross and Michael Jackson."

The warmth that bloomed in his chest had a shade of unease skittering down his spine like a drunk spider. But denial had apparently become a part of his daily repertoire and once again, he shoved the feeling aside, focusing on the here and now. And in the here and now, he couldn't come up with a reason why he shouldn't grab a couple more hours watching his daughter smile and hearing her unfettered laughter.

Or an excuse not to sit there for a couple more hours and pretend that Flo's scent, just the sight of her, didn't affect him.

"Let me go get Jussy, and you prepare to grovel." He dipped his chin toward the kitchen entrance and the direction of the living room. "Good part is I think you have more of an in with her than I do. So your chances of Team No Bad News look good."

Flo grinned, and the blood in his veins transformed to molten lava.

Shit.

He might have to let her and Justine have the couch

and make sure he sat in the armchair upwind of her. Hell, even catching a hint of that jasmine-and-cedarwood fragrance would have his control threatening to unravel.

Goddamn. Bricking up while in the same room with his daughter was *not* a shining example of fatherhood.

"You have chips or ice cream?" Flo asked. "I get the feeling she's susceptible to bribery—"

His cell phone vibrated, and he paused, removing it from his pocket. It was almost seven, too late for anyone to be calling him. Unless it was Addie. A sliver of disquiet crept through him. Had something else happened with their father—

He lifted the cell, peering down at the screen. And from one second to the next, trepidation switched to annoyance.

Jennifer.

His jaw clenched, and anger flared hot and bright in his chest before he quickly doused it. But he couldn't deny its existence. One day, just the glimpse of his ex-wife's name on a caller ID would only stir apathy. Today wasn't that day.

Then again, there might come a time when his ex would adhere to the court-ordered visitation and call schedule and not completely eschew it in favor of whatever camping trip, man or moon cycle caught her fancy.

But also, today wasn't that day.

Guilt swarmed low in his gut like a hive of angry bees. Jennifer was Justine's mother. No matter his personal feelings about her neglectful and selfish behavior, that fact always had to come first. Justine hadn't asked to be brought into this world…hadn't gotten a chance to choose her parents. So their responsibility was to make this transition into co-parenting as seamless and painless as possible.

Repeating that over and over to himself like a mantra, Adam pressed the screen, answering the call.

"Jennifer," he greeted his ex-wife, his tone even, almost flat.

Movement in his peripheral vision snagged his attention, and he glanced toward the kitchen entrance. Dammit. The unexpected call had distracted him, momentarily making him forget Flo hadn't completely left the room.

If guilt churned in his stomach, shame congealed the ugly mess. Logically, it didn't make sense. His absentee ex-wife wasn't his fault; he couldn't make her be there for her daughter. But a small, secret part of him blamed himself. Because *he'd* chosen Jennifer. *He'd* married her. *He'd* failed in keeping his family happy—in keeping them together.

"Hey, Adam," Jennifer chirped. "How're you?"

The lighthearted tone, as if it hadn't been *months* since they'd last heard from her, grated on his nerves, and he ground his teeth together to imprison the caustic response that seemed to burn a hole on his tongue.

"Fine. Let me get Jussy. I'm sure she'll be glad to talk to you."

At least he hoped that was the case. Sometimes he wondered if his ex-wife would one day become a non-factor in their daughter's everyday life, and the heaviness of that possibility weighed on him.

"Thanks. I can't wait to speak to my baby," Jennifer said.

Jesus. By the time he finished trapping everything he wanted to say, he might not have any enamel left.

Lowering the phone, he tightened his grip on it, taking a moment to inhale a deep breath. He couldn't go into

Justine's room looking like rage personified. Fuck if her mother knew, but no way in hell would he scare Justine.

Sliding Flo a glance, he took in her impassive expression and for a second, he paused, wondering what she had gleaned from the abbreviated side of his conversation? Did she judge him?

Hell, why not? He did.

Like father, like son. Like father, like son.

The indictment scrolled through his head, a sly taunt that followed him like a group of bullying kids as he nodded at Flo and moved past her, heading down the hall to Justine's room.

Briefly closing his eyes, he flattened his palm on the cracked bedroom door, schooling his features into what he prayed was a pleasant expression that didn't betray his turbulent roil of emotions.

He pushed the door open and stepped into the room, spotting Justine on her bed, reading one of her books aloud. His smile came a little easier at the sight of her, that clenching around his chest loosened just a fraction. She looked up, and a wide grin spread across her face, and he couldn't help but return it. God, she was pure, infectious joy, and a fierce surge of protectiveness swelled within him. At all costs, he had to guard and shelter that innocent joy. Even if it was from her mother.

On that thought, he held out the phone to Justine.

"Here, baby girl. It's your mom on the phone. She wants to talk to you."

Her grin remained, and Justine hopped off the bed, running the few feet separating them.

"Mommy? Yay!" She held up her arms, and he handed her the cell. Palpable excitement hummed in her voice as she pressed the phone to her ear and exclaimed, "Hi, Mommy!"

Adam didn't leave the room. Hell, if he'd thought about it, he would've put the phone on speaker to cut off the conversation if Jennifer uttered anything upsetting. His ex-wife had a bad habit of asking their daughter to understand why she couldn't come see her or handing out half-ass excuses about why she hadn't called and placing the blame everywhere but on herself. At five, Justine couldn't possibly grasp why a party in Los Angeles with her latest "friend" was more important than spending time with her daughter.

Hell, at thirty-seven, he didn't get it, either.

But it never occurred to Jennifer to ask that same question.

He crossed his arms over his chest and propped a shoulder against the wall as he eavesdropped on Justine's very animated exchange with her mother. She chattered away about Rose Bend, her new room, her new friends, especially Flo.

Flo gave me a camera.

Flo let me take pictures.

Flo and me got hot chocolate.

Flo. Flo. Flo. The other woman's name peppered Justine's conversation.

After another ten minutes, Justine told her mother goodbye and extended the phone to Adam. Accepting it with one hand, he laid the other on the top of her head.

"We're getting ready to watch a movie, okay? Go on out there with Flo and pick one for us."

Justine's eyes brightened and, cheering, she dashed out of her bedroom, calling Flo's name. Waiting until he was certain she no longer remained in earshot, he lifted the cell to his ear.

"If that's it, Jenni—"

"So she's there right now? This *Flo*," Jennifer said,

voice clipped and carrying more than a trace of irritation. "Don't try and deny it. I overheard you."

He swallowed a sigh, pinching the bridge of his nose.

"Why would I deny it? She's a friend and is helping me out with Justine. Why wouldn't she visit us?"

"It's after seven there," she pointed out, that same razor edge to her tone. "Isn't it almost Jussy's bedtime? You're there so what exactly is she *helping out* with? Can't you handle putting our daughter to bed by yourself?"

Anger sizzled beneath his sternum. Did she even hear the words that came out of her mouth? Resentment loosened the bands on his tongue.

"Yes, I can and have been handling Jussy's bedtime by myself. Bedtime. Breakfast time. Lunchtime. Every time in between. I've been doing it by myself for two years now," he ground out. "Do you really want to get on this subject?"

She sucked her teeth, the immaturity and petulance of the sound setting him further on edge. "Please, Adam. Always the martyr. Don't you ever get tired of being the victim?"

"The only one hurting in this situation is Jussy. We might be divorced but neither of us divorced *her*. And yet, this is the first time you've spoken to your daughter in over three months, and I can't even tell you the last time you laid eyes on her. So don't come at me about how I'm raising her when I'm the only one actually doing it."

He tried to remain calm, to keep the bite out of his voice. But last time he checked, the only perfect person had walked the earth two thousand years ago. Perfection was above his pay grade.

"No one can replace me as her mother, Adam," she snapped. "So don't you dare try and do it."

"Mother is a verb, Jennifer, not a noun. Not a title you

can trot out and dangle like a shiny thing on a special occasion. It's being there to celebrate with her when she reads a whole sentence by herself. It's being there when she's sick and waking up in the middle of night to creep into her room and just listen to her breathe. It's enjoying every smile and bearing through every whine. It's all the little and big things, Jennifer. And you've missed damn near all of them in the last couple of years. Because you're. Not. Here."

"That's not true—" she hotly objected.

"Her birthday, Jenn," he interrupted, voice quiet. "Her birthday. You didn't even call her or show up for her on her *birthday*. You're right about one thing—no one could ever replace her mother. And Justine's starved for her mother's attention. But don't be surprised or mad at anyone but yourself when she finds that attention somewhere else. You only have yourself to blame."

A cold silence shivered down their connection. He wouldn't be surprised if his ear came away frostbitten.

"I need to go," she said, ice clinging to every word.

"You can be as pissed off at me as you want to be, Jennifer. Frankly, I'm used to it," he added, his grip tightening around the phone. "But don't take it out on Jussy. For her sake—and yours—keep to the visitation and calling schedule. Don't start again only to disappear and disappoint her."

"Bye, Adam."

The call ended before he could reply, and he lowered the cell, staring at the screen for several long moments. Anger pitched inside him, swirling in his chest. But he couldn't find the strength to hold on to it. Thinning his lips, he dragged a hand over his head. He was just so fucking tired.

Tired of holding it together.

Tired of feeling guilty for being tired.

Tired of failing.

Inhaling a deep breath, he dropped his arm and stared blindly at the cracked bedroom door. The lightheartedness that had been so much a part of the evening dissipated, leaving him hollow, weighed down and a little defeated.

In a way, he should be grateful for Jennifer's call, he mused, moving toward the door. It'd served as the sharpest of reminders that the ability to sustain successful, healthy relationships wasn't wired into his DNA. All he had to do was look at his father. And at the wreckage of his own marriage that still littered his life.

No, his sole focus needed to be his daughter, her security and welfare.

A father, first.

He didn't have room for anything—or anyone—else.

CHAPTER ELEVEN

"Ooh, it's a dollhouse," Justine breathed, the wonder in the little girl's voice clear from the back seat of Flo's car.

Flo grinned as she slowed to a stop in front of Kinsale Inn. She could see it. Tilting her head, she studied her family's bed-and-breakfast and her childhood home. With the pitched roofs, colorful doors and shutters, she could definitely imagine how it would appear like the perfect dollhouse to a child.

I was blessed to grow up here.

The thought flittered through her head, and she glanced in her rearview mirror at the wide-eyed girl in her booster seat. At Justine's age, Flo had lost her biological parents and a father figure. But she'd also gained the loving and supportive family that had circled around her, protecting and nurturing her. Including a mother and father who had been there for every scrape, every heartbreak, every discovery, every celebration. Justine had Adam, and his love for her sometimes snatched the breath from Flo's lungs when she observed them together. But still... The girl's family was fractured, her mother absent.

Flo cleared her throat, dislodging the sudden thickness gathered there. She'd been fortunate to have the parents, the family, she'd been given. And as she slid the car into Park, opened her door and stepped out, she admonished herself to remember that more often.

"My mom and dad are excited to meet you, Jussy,"

Flo said, helping Justine out of her booster seat. "I've told them about you."

"This is your house?" she asked, her usually on-ten volume cranked down to about a three. Awe colored her words, and Flo held back a chuckle.

"It's where I grew up. I lived here when I was a girl, like you. But I always come back here to eat and see my parents and brothers and sisters. You might get to meet some of them, too."

"Cool." Justine grinned and wrapped her fingers around Flo's, her gaze fixed on the inn.

"Let's go." Leading her up the stairs and across the porch, Flo approached the front door and opened it, stepping into the wide foyer. Immediately, she noticed Leo behind the small desk tucked next to the curving wooden staircase that led to the upper levels and the family wing of the building. Smiling, Flo led Justine forward. "Hey, Leo, I have someone special for you to meet."

Her sister's blue-gray eyes brightened, a big smile curving her mouth as she moved out from behind the check-in desk.

"Let me guess." Twisting her lips to the side, she squinted and tapped a finger to the corner of her mouth. "Beyoncé. Nope, nope," she said over Justine's giggles.

"I'm not Beyoncé," Justine objected.

"Don't tell me, don't tell me. I got this." Leo waved a hand, shushing the little girl, and Flo snickered. "I got it." Her sister snapped her fingers. "Taylor Swift."

"Nooo!" Justine shook her head, her delighted laughter filling the lobby. "I'm Jussy!"

Leo heaved a loud, exaggerated sigh, throwing her hands in the air. "I told you not to tell me." Grinning, her sister hunkered down, putting herself on eye level with Jussy. "But of course, you're Jussy. Flo told me all about you, and I'd recognize you anywhere." Offering the little girl her hand, she said, "Hi, Jussy, I'm Leo, Flo's sister."

"Hi!" She loosened her grip on Flo's hand and took Leo's. "You're pretty."

"Thank you, sweetie. So are you." Rising, Leo arched an eyebrow at Flo. "I was going to give you one more day before I came looking for you," she murmured. "How're you doing?"

Flo didn't need to ask to what her sister referred. Guilt sidled through her, leaving a grimy path in its wake. Since Noah's arrival several days ago, she'd avoided all calls from her family, not ready to talk about their uncle and her stepfather's sudden appearance. She still wasn't. But cutting off her family was like amputating a limb, and the phantom ache of it, even for just a few days, throbbed.

"I figured," Flo quietly said with a nod. "That's part of the reason I came for a visit while I had some time in between the Hudson project and the studio."

"If you hadn't shown up for Saturday dinner, Moe would've driven to your apartment and raised he—" a quick glance down at Justine "—Hades herself. And I would've ridden shotgun. No one keeps you from family. Not even you."

Again, Flo nodded, a rueful smile twisting her lips even as her sister's fierceness and love wrapped around her like a warm blanket on a cold, bitter night.

"I figured that, too." Sighing, she rubbed a palm down the front of her jeans. "I wanted Jussy to meet Mom and Dad. Where are they?" she asked, switching the subject.

"Mom's back in the kitchen, getting ready to prepare dinner. And Dad went into town—with Uncle Noah." Leo cocked her head, her eyes softening as she added, "So the coast is clear. But it won't be forever, Flo."

"Thanks." Flo hitched her chin in the direction of the hall that led to the kitchen. "Would you mind taking Jussy to meet Moe? I'm going to grab my old camera from my room and be right down."

She'd promised Justine she'd loan her an old digital camera since she'd really taken to photography. The Nikon D7000 had been her first camera and was outdated but still in good condition.

"Of course I wouldn't mind." Leo edged closer, lowering her voice to a pitch that didn't reach Justine. "Dad still an asshole?"

"No." Flo shook her head, smirking. "His a-hole status has been temporarily revoked. But he's still on probation just in case he decides to act up."

"Duly noted." Leo shifted her attention back to Justine, grinning wide. "Want to meet our mom and get a cup of hot chocolate?"

"Oh yes," Justine agreed, bouncing up and down. "Hot chocolate is yummy!"

"And our mom's is the best," Flo said. "I'll be right back, okay?"

"Okay, Flo."

She grabbed Leo's hand again and allowed Flo's sister to lead her down the hall. Flo watched them for another moment then turned around and climbed the stairs. About ten minutes later she bounded back down, the camera and its small insulated bag in hand. She could practically hear Justine's squeal of happiness, see her wide grin. She was going to love having her own "grown-up" camera.

The front door opened, and her dad stepped inside. Noah stood behind him.

Flo froze on the third step from the bottom.

Her pulse thudded in her ears, her heart a mad drummer using her ribs as its kit.

Say something. Do something. She tried to obey that voice inside her head, but she couldn't move. Shock reverberated through her, and it was a wonder she didn't shake with it.

Silly that betrayal tightened her belly. Silly that a bone-deep hurt rattled within her at the sight of her dad with Noah. After all, he'd been Noah's brother longer than he'd been her father. Of course, he would be happy to see him again. To have him home again. His joy in Noah's reappearance didn't mean a deficit in his love for her.

She really did believe that. At least in her head. But her heart… Her heart railed at her father to *choose her, pick her,* first. God, couldn't that be the motto of her life?

"Flo." Her father smiled, and it reflected in the same blue-gray eyes he shared with his brother. "Hey, sweetheart. I didn't know you were stopping by today."

"Yeah, I came by to pick this up—" she silently ordered her arm to lift and show him the camera, but it wasn't obeying her command "—for a new friend of mine and bring her by to meet Moe."

His smile dimmed just a bit, and she couldn't miss the glint of sadness that crept into his gaze.

"Well, whatever brought you here, I'm just glad to see you. How're you doing?" he gently asked.

She glanced at Noah, who remained silent, his scrutiny not moving from her. It was amazing how much Noah and her dad resembled each other. They both shared the big, powerful build her father had bequeathed to Wolf, and Ian stood only a couple inches taller than Noah. But with their strong facial features, identical eyes and frames, they wouldn't be mistaken for anything but family.

"Fine, Dad. Good."

Against her will, she slid another look at Noah. To

glimpse his reaction at her calling another man—his brother—*Dad*? To detect any emotion at all?

Nothing. His impassive expression revealed nothing of his thoughts. And considering his decades-long silence only occasionally broken by birthdays and holidays revolving around Jesus, she shouldn't have expected more.

Fuck her glutton-for-punishment heart, but she did.

The manners her parents had force-fed her kicked in, and she nodded at him.

"Noah."

Even that felt strange, odd. He'd been the very first man she'd called Daddy; she remembered that much. But he'd long since stopped being *Daddy* in her head and heart—about a year after he left, when she realized he wouldn't be returning. Ian Dennison was her father, had been for so long that even thinking about his brother in that capacity felt blasphemous. But as the past couldn't be changed, neither could the facts.

Noah Dennison had been married to her mother. She'd chosen him as not just her husband, but a parent for Flo. Noah had been the first father figure in Flo's life.

Noah had abandoned her.

"Hi, Flo. It's good to see you again," Noah said, and the careful politeness of this exchange raked over her nerves.

Gripping the banister tighter, she nodded again. Silence seemed the best alternative to lying and reciprocating his words.

"I sent Justine in the kitchen with Leo to meet Moe. I should probably get in there…" She descended the last couple of stairs, but drew to an abrupt halt, nearly stumbling, when Noah shifted forward, his hand outstretched toward her.

"I'm sorry." He tunneled fingers through his hair, drawing the gray-streaked brown strands off his forehead. "I, uh…" Dropping his arm, he held up a hand, palm out. "Could I speak to you for a few minutes, Flo?" He lowered his arm, his palm rubbing down the side of his thigh. "Please?"

No. No way in hell.

The shout bounced off the walls of her head, and she parted her lips to deliver a flat *no*, but she made the mistake of glancing at her father. Of glimpsing the glint of pleading in his eyes. Pleading and something else. There and gone in an instant, Flo couldn't decipher what that *something else* was. Pleading from a man who'd done nothing but given to her over and over, asking for nothing in return—she couldn't say no.

Damn.

"Okay," she finally said, and though she caught the relief in her father's gaze, that didn't lessen the pressure constricting her ribs. "We can speak out on the porch."

The inn had too many ears, too many eyes. And the beautiful, open common room, the sizable foyer and the kitchen—rooms she'd always been perfectly comfortable in before—suddenly felt too small, too crowded and lacking efficient air. Even as she skirted around her father and Noah, she struggled to inhale a deep breath. One that didn't contain the fragrant aroma of the coffee Moe kept brewed for the inn's guests, the faint lemon-and-cedar scent used to clean and vacuum the rooms, or the stink of her own resentment and nerves.

Reaching the front door, she yanked it open with more force than necessary, pushed past the storm door and stepped out on the porch. Immediately, she moved to one of the posts, leaning a shoulder against it and crossing her arms. Moments later Noah followed, shutting the door behind him. Wisely, he didn't cross the space she'd created between them.

It'd been literal decades since she'd last seen him in Rose Bend. And the occasional cards and old pictures of him and her mother hadn't prepared her for this moment. This older, grizzled version of the man she faintly remembered superimposed itself over the younger, leaner version, and it left her unsteady as she tried to grasp the fact that he was here, in front of her, and not stuck in the nebulous, hazy recesses of her memories.

"Thank you for giving me a moment to talk with you, Flo," Noah said, mimicking her pose on the opposite post. "I have to imagine that wasn't easy for you." When she didn't agree or disagree, he dipped his chin, staring at his feet. "I'm sorry for just…showing up without any warning. Honestly, I wasn't sure I would return until my car hit the town limits. And even then…" He shook his head. "I guess I didn't want to give advance warning just in case someone told me not to bother."

Did he expect sympathy from her? Well, he would have a long-ass wait.

"Dad is happy you're here. And I'm sure Moe is, too," she murmured.

"Yeah, it's been awesome seeing them again. Although they're old now." He chuffed out soft laughter. "We all are. I think, in my mind, they still looked as they did while in their thirties. Which is ridiculous since I look in the mirror every morning and see my own gray." He swept a hand over his peppered strands again.

He was babbling.

Nerves? She stifled the pang in her chest at the thought of him being anxious just from talking to her.

He damn well should be. What do you say to the little

girl you promised to love and protect as your own then walked away from? *Sorry 'bout that* didn't exactly cut it.

Not that he'd said even that.

"We're all older," she said and fell quiet again.

She didn't miss his subtle wince.

"Yes, we are," he softly said. Uncrossing his arms and sliding his hands into the front pockets of his jeans, he cocked his head, studying her. "I couldn't believe when I first saw you. My mind knows, accepts, that you're twenty-four, an adult. And yet—" he shook his head "—not seeing that adorable little girl with a big laugh and even bigger personality shocked me. But I still recognized you. The eyes." He waved a hand in front of his. "They're all your mother. I don't know if Ian and Moe have shown you pictures of her, but you look like Aisha did at your age." He smiled and it held more than a trace of wistfulness and sadness. "She would be so proud of the woman you've become. And knowing her, she would get such a kick out of you resembling her so much."

"I have pictures," Flo said, deliberately flattening her tone. But it belied the tangled emotions twisting inside her. Concealed the gnawing need to lash out. "Moe and Dad made sure I received them and all her other things that were left behind."

Okay, yes, that was a jab and from the slight ducking of his head as he looked away from her, it landed. She expected satisfaction to bloom in her chest, but…it didn't. Shame plummeted like a heavy boulder to the pit of her stomach. She'd been raised better, been taught better than to deliberately hurt people. Even if they deserved it.

And Noah more than deserved it.

"Good," he murmured. "You were very young when we—" he paused, and his mouth firmed "—lost her, so your memories are probably not as strong or reliable as mine. I would hate for you to not have anything of her, anything to know her by."

I could've had you instead of a box of records, books and pictures to tell me about her, to ensure my memories didn't fade and to give me new ones.

The accusation damn near hummed on her tongue, eager to be lobbed at him. But she restrained herself. Instead, she pushed off the post and paced farther away from him, needing the space. This anger, confusion and...*grief* wrestling inside her was altering her into a person she didn't know, didn't like. A bitter, resentful person who needed to swipe at this man and deliver tiny barbs that would leave him in the same kind of pain he'd inflicted on her.

Hurt people...hurt people.

How many times had she heard that saying? How many times had she nodded in agreement? But only now, in this moment, did she truly grasp the full weight of the meaning.

Inhaling a deep, cleansing breath, she briefly closed her eyes and released the air from her lungs. Slowly, she turned back around to face Noah.

"You said you need to speak with me. What about?" she asked.

He nodded, clearing his throat. His unease skated across his expression, and the slight hunch of his shoulders telegraphed his awkwardness.

"I'm sorry. I'm rambling." He shook his head, his mouth twisting into a rueful smile. "I'm nervous seeing you again after so long. In my head, I imagined how this would go. Had my whole speech planned out and even your reaction to it. But now?" Shaking his head again, he lifted his shoulders in a shrug. "Reality is nothing like your dreams."

She was a living witness to the truth in that statement.

Blowing out a breath, he continued, "A million different times I've wanted to call you, reach out—"

"But you sent cards instead. I'm guessing wherever you've been all these years, phones don't work."

"I didn't think you would want to hear from me," he explained. Made excuses. "And after so much time passed, I believed inserting myself into your life would only be confusing for you."

"Bullshit." The curse exploded from her, but not on a shout. Still, the word echoed between them as if she had screamed it. "Those are nothing but excuses. When I was ten, fifteen, even eighteen, they might've worked. But not now. So please don't insult me with them."

She thought of Jussy. Remembered the pieces of the phone conversation she'd overheard between Adam and his ex-wife as she'd passed by on her way to the bathroom. Of Adam begging her to be a parent, to be present for her daughter. Anger had ignited behind her sternum and wasn't snuffed out by the time she returned to the living room or when Adam joined her and Jussy. Flo had been Jussy. And now, standing here across from Noah, she and Jussy could be twins. Connected by a selfish, neglectful parent full of bullshit excuses.

"I don't mean to make excuses, Flo, and I'm sorry if it came off that way. But I honestly didn't think you wanted me to be a bigger part in your life after a while. Yes, I didn't call you, but I also didn't hear from you, either. You never responded to my cards, so neither of us reached out—"

"Are you kidding me?" she snapped. "Now I'm partly to blame for you disappearing for twenty years? I didn't keep up my end?" With a laugh that abraded her throat, she flicked a hand toward her chest. "*I* was the child, *you* were the adult. No, not just any adult. My father. It wasn't on me to stick around. It wasn't on me to parent. It wasn't on me to keep the lines of communication open past the biannual card. Hell, Hallmark did more talking to me than you did."

"Flo," he said, holding a hand out, and though she noted the regret and sadness in his gaze, *too much* bubbled inside her.

Too much of her own hurt, grief and acidic anger.

"No." She backed away from the threat of that hand. It stirred twin yet warring urges inside her. Avoid it at all costs. Clasp it close and try to glean a connection to her biological mother. Try to recapture a time when she'd…belonged.

You do *belong. You're a Dennison, dammit. Loved, accepted and valued.*

If she knew it wouldn't make her look as if she was losing all control, Flo would've clapped her palms over her ears to trap that assurance in her head. To block out the doubt that this man's appearance agitated.

"No," she repeated, softer this time, but no less forceful. Giving him a wide berth, she edged toward the front door. "I can't do this. Not now."

"Flo, please give me a minute to explain." He scrubbed a hand down his weathered face. "To start over again and try not to make a damn mess of…"

But she shook her head, cutting him off.

"This is too much right now. I need space. And I know you can give me that. You've been a pro at it over the years."

Jerking open the screen door, she shoved back inside the inn and strode for the kitchen. Even the notes of Justine's high, happy voice alongside Moe's lower, more soothing one couldn't sweep away the noxious mix shoving against her chest with brutal fists.

She'd opened this old wound herself. And she couldn't place the blame on wanting to make her father happy. No, a part of her—that part of her who'd stood at windows every evening hoping Noah would return—needed to hear what he had to say. Yearned to hear a reason that would justify him leaving and not returning until now. That part had desperately longed for it so she could... She shut the thought down before it could fully form.

But it was too late. The rest of it shimmered in her head.

...desperately longed for it so she could know once and for all that she was lovable. Worthy.

Something inside her shrank at that humiliating admission. But she couldn't run away from her mind, from herself.

She slowed to a halt on the threshold of the kitchen, briefly closing her eyes. Walking in there at this moment would invite an inquisition from Moe. Inhaling a deep breath, Flo fixed her expression into a smile, and prayed it would pass muster under her mother's all-seeing, all-knowing eye. Confessing to her mother that she had to leave the house that had always been a safe space for her didn't sit well.

But she couldn't deny the truth.

She didn't feel comfortable here. And until Noah left, she didn't know when she would return.

Now it was her turn to run, to disappear.

And the irony didn't escape her.

CHAPTER TWELVE

Adam sighed as he turned the key in the lock of his temporary home, opened the front door and stepped inside. Immediately, a delicious scent had his stomach rumbling. Closing the door behind him, he paused, momentarily closing his eyes and inhaling the aroma that contained more than notes of food—was that gravy and chicken? Anyway, the scents also held a warm welcome that soothed the nerves that had been pulled tight all the way here from the renovation site.

Due to the production schedule for *Vintage Renovation*, a night crew continued to work on construction after filming ended for the day. Usually, Adam didn't have to be there, but because of issues with one of the bathrooms, he'd stayed late tonight to oversee installation of a clawfoot porcelain bathtub. It'd been a little after eight when he'd left, and he'd been tired as he'd walked up to the house. But now, standing inside the small foyer, the aroma of home-cooked food permeating the air, weariness eased out of his body along with any lingering tension.

Not by any means was he one of those men who expected his food, slippers and silence waiting on him when he arrived home from work. Even when he was married, more often than not, he'd helped with dinner and the house chores, though Jennifer stayed at home. And he hadn't minded. Hell, caring for their daughter had been a more important job than his. Since the divorce, 90 percent of the day-to-day care of the home and Justine had been on him. Except for those times Addie had stepped in, the bulk of childcare, chores, shopping, dinner was his responsibility. And he didn't mind.

Still… This was…nice.

To have help was a relief and a weight lifted that he hadn't realized he'd needed—or wanted.

Removing his wallet, he dropped it on the small table in the entryway and headed toward the living room where the canned laughter from the television echoed along with Justine's chatter and Flo's melodic voice. Like a magnet, the sounds drew him, and he decided not to dwell on the anticipation that rose within him as he neared the room. While he was at it, he'd ignore the bloom of warmth that smacked too close to satisfaction. And maybe delight.

Walking into the living room, he paused for a second, taking in the unexpectedly sweet picture before him.

Flo sat on the couch, and Justine perched on a stack of pillows between her knees. His daughter giggled at the sitcom playing—looked like one of the Disney Channel shows she loved—as Flo braided her hair. That bloom of warmth mushroomed until it threatened to cave in his chest. Since Jennifer left, his go-to hairstyle was variations of ponytails; they were easy and about all his limited repertoire could manage even with the help of several YouTube videos. He'd held his own, but he knew his little girl missed this with her mother. In Justine's bedroom, after her bath… That had been Jennifer and Jussy's time while her mom brushed and styled her hair and they chattered away. He should know. He'd stood outside the door often enough, smiling and listening to the two people he loved most in the world.

He shook his head, dislodging the memory, and moved farther into the room as Justine turned her head and noticed him. A wide grin broke across her face, and his heart gave that familiar leap it gave whenever he saw his daughter.

"Daddy!" she greeted at her usual *outside voice* volume.

Flo looked up from her task. Her smile wasn't as big as Justine's, but it still ignited a low burn deep in his gut for very different reasons.

"Hi, Adam."

"Hey." He dipped his chin. "Thank you for bringing her home and staying so late. I won't make a habit of this."

She shrugged a shoulder. "It's no problem at all. We've had a full and fun day."

"Yeah, we had fun, Daddy," Justine chimed in. "We went to Flo's 'tography studio. I saw her mom and sister in the dollhouse. She let me help cook dinner and Flo's doing my hair like hers," she finished, running out of breath.

"I hope it's okay," Flo quietly said. "She asked me if I could do her hair like mine. I explained mine took years to grow, so I did the closest I could for her with some two-strand twists."

"I understood nothing about what you just said," he dryly admitted. "But what you're doing is much prettier than my ponytails. So thank you."

She smiled. "You're welcome. I'll show you and Jussy how to tie her hair up at night and they should last a couple of weeks."

"Then you'll do it again?" Justine asked, twisting around and dislodging Flo's hands from her hair. "I want my hair to be long like yours."

"Yours is already long, sweetie." Flo slipped a twist over Justine's shoulder, and it brushed her collarbone. "You have such beautiful, thick hair. And it's like yours, not mine. That makes it extra special and pretty."

Justine beamed up at her, and Flo returned the smile. Watching the two of them, the little girl so enamored with the woman, a knot of emotion twisted around his throat.

And that scared the shit out of him.

Gently turning Justine back around, Flo resumed twisting his daughter's hair and shot him a look.

"We already ate, but I left a plate for you in the microwave," she informed him.

"Thank you," he said again.

He had the feeling those two words would become a habit with her. It was funny how life worked. He'd gone to that dive bar over a month ago, looking for a drink or two and a couple hours to relax before heading back to the house for the night. A one-night stand with a gorgeous woman hadn't been his plan. Having that same gorgeous woman show up at his job and then slowly become a part of his and his daughter's daily lives… No, it was almost surreal.

And it unnerved him that if he could press Rewind on these past weeks and have the choice of going forward, of going to that bar and meeting Flo, he wouldn't change one moment.

Unnerved him… Hell, it terrified him. Had him reeling.

Hadn't he learned anything from being with a woman who didn't have family, commitment and stability as her priorities? Didn't he and Justine still bear the scars, still endure the repercussions?

Flo was young—over a decade younger than him—and was just coming into her own in her career. When they'd met, she'd just returned from a weeks-long trip abroad. As a parent, he couldn't just up and leave. He had more than himself to consider. Flo wasn't ready for that kind of responsibility; she didn't want that kind of responsibility. Not right now.

At twenty-four, she didn't have enough life experience under her belt, and it would be the height of selfishness to expect her to sacrifice what most people had at her age to take on an instant family. Babysitting was one thing; parenting was another. And in the long run, it would be Justine who was hurt.

And you.

He shoved that ridiculous thought aside. He was too old to confuse lust with anything deeper, more permanent. The time had come and gone when his dick did his thinking for him.

Yet, as he retrieved his dinner plate, heated it and brought it back to the living room to sit with Flo and Justine, a calm settled over him. A peace. He'd missed this. Missed the simplicity of evenings with laughter, easy conversation. Of family.

No, Flo wasn't his and Justine's family, but maybe he could allow himself to pretend just for a little while. What was the harm in it if he kept it to himself and understood it was just…pretend?

No harm.

As he leaned against the back of the couch, cold beer bottle in hand, listening to Flo and Justine as she helped the little girl get ready for bed—Justine begged him to let Flo do the nightly duty—he let himself believe just a little bit longer.

Just for tonight.

"For my own information," Flo said, entering the living room and sinking down on the other end of the sofa, "how many bedtime stories do you usually read her?"

"One. But she can sometimes weasel two out of me," he admitted.

Flo narrowed her eyes. "She said you read her four stories."

He snorted. "Tell me you didn't fall for that."

Wrinkling her nose, she leaned forward and nabbed his beer. She took a deep sip, and it had his cock twitching. The sight of those full, sensual lips covering the opening of the bottle where his own mouth had just been… Did she taste him and the alcohol?

He fought not to shift on the couch cushion and betray the heat pumping through his veins. Why that should be so hot, he couldn't even begin to explain. But fuck if it wasn't.

"No, I didn't fall for it," she said, lowering the bottle. *Thank God.* "I read three."

He barked out a laugh. "Sucker."

Sighing, she offered his drink back to him. "Don't I know it. She got me."

His fingers grazed hers as he took the bottle, and he stiffened, unable to prevent the reaction. Her gaze dropped to where they touched before lifting to him. In her eyes, he glimpsed apprehension, a hint of confusion and, *damn*, heat. So much heat.

Flo Dennison was dangerous.

To his resolve. To his best intentions. To his—

"Don't beat yourself up," he said, shifting his attention to the television and the baseball game that played on the screen. Lifting his bottle, he downed a long, desperate sip, and only when he was certain he had his face under control did he look at her again. He reached deep for the casual humor they'd shared and grasped it like a drowning man about to go under. "She's a pro, and well, you're—" he arched an eyebrow "—an amateur."

She scowled. "I would take offense to that if it wasn't true. So I can't."

Chuckling, he leaned forward and set the nearly empty beer bottle on the coffee table.

"Thanks again for tonight. For staying late with her, cooking dinner, doing her hair, bedtime…" He loosed a puff of breath. "You went over and beyond what you signed up for in helping me out."

"I didn't mind—don't mind. Honestly," she said, waving off his words. "I had fun with her today. I know I've told you this before, but she's a wonderful little girl. Funny. Well behaved. Curious. And so damn smart." She shook her head, smiling. "You're doing an amazing job with her, Adam."

"Yeah, you've said it before, but I'm not too proud to admit that it feels good hearing it. I…worry if I'm giving her enough. Enough time, attention, of what she needs. Like you doing her hair, for example." He flipped his hands, staring down at his palms. "My skills and catalog of styles are very limited. They begin and end at ponytails." Another chuckle, but this one rueful and full of the things he couldn't say.

Like, how he tried to compensate for Jennifer's being absent. But in some areas, he just made do, and Justine was the one shortchanged.

"I think you should cut yourself some slack," Flo murmured. "Even in households where both parents are present, every day, everything isn't perfect. My sister-in-law grew up in a home with a mother and a father, and because of circumstances there, felt emotionally neglected and unloved. They're okay now, but it required healing and a slow rebuilding of their relationship years after the fact. Jussy might be a child of divorced parents, but she's not being raised in an environment that's devoid of love, encouragement and acceptance. I'm not saying not having her mother here doesn't affect her. But I am saying she wouldn't be such a confident, inquisitive child if she wasn't secure in your love and knew it's her safety net."

He had to glance away from the sincerity gleaming in those beautiful eyes. From the lips that spoke assurances that soothed his heart and hardened his cock.

God, he could use another beer. He picked up the bottle again, just giving his hands something to hold so they wouldn't grab her.

"That's one of my main worries," he confessed in a low, hoarse voice that rubbed like grit over his throat. "Are we—my ex-wife and I—fucking her up? Because of our selfishness…because we couldn't get it together… are we messing this up for her? What kind of father am I when I can't protect my baby from hurt? A hurt we're responsible for."

"I'm sorry, why didn't you tell me you were bitten by a radioactive spider? That seems like something that should have been disclosed before I offered to babysit for you."

He stared at her, equal parts perplexed and irritated. Then he noted her small smile, and though the puzzlement remained, the irritation faded.

"I never claimed to be Spider-Man or any superhero."

"You sure?" She tilted her head. "Because the way you were talking about protecting her from everything that could hurt her, I wasn't sure. Of course, I've never been a parent, but even I know that's an impossibility. You can do your absolute best, and you'll still never be able to keep her from all harm. And thank goodness, right? I'm no masochist, but it's the hurts, the disappointments and the failures that shape us as much as the joys, victories and wonderful times in our lives. She'll never know she's capable of being strong or independent if she doesn't experience one right alongside the other.

"You're not perfect. You won't always be there to

shield or defend her. But then again, she'd never grow in her own power and voice if you were." She snagged his beer, tipped it to her mouth and disappeared the little bit left in there. Lowering it, she rubbed a thumb over her bottom lip and pointed the bottle at him. "And whether you can fashion the perfect ponytail has nothing to do with how much she loves you or measures your love for her. Believe me. While I might not be a parent, I was in her place before, and I'm speaking from experience."

So many things crowded toward the base of his throat, shoving and vying to be the first to escape.

Thank you for that.

Are you sure?

I need you.

That last one he couldn't afford to loose. It revealed too much. Because as much as he longed to deny it, he didn't only need her in the physical sense.

So he said nothing, except… "Another beer?"

Understanding flickered in her eyes, but she didn't call him on his sudden shift in subject.

"No, thanks," she said.

With a nod, he rose, went to the kitchen and returned moments later with a fresh bottle, the cap twisted off. He briefly considered moving to the adjacent armchair, but at the last moment, changed his mind. That veered too close to cowardice. And while he considered it self-preservation, he feared how revealing it would appear to Flo.

"You mentioned speaking from experience. What do you mean?" he asked.

He just wanted to hear her speak. Wanted to know more about her. And not just in the capacity of his daughter's temporary nanny. He wanted—needed—to learn more about the woman, the artist. He was damn near voracious for more.

Flo rubbed her fingertips over her thigh, head bowed. After a moment, she lifted her chin, meeting his gaze, and he gripped his bottle tighter, the cold condensation grounding him. Reminding him that he couldn't reach for her, touch her.

She smiled, but something lingered in her eyes. And it was that *something* he wanted to both decipher and erase.

"I've told you a little about my family. We're blended, with four of us being adopted. And I was the first Black child—and a Black girl at that. I always roll my eyes a little when people say really nice-sounding but misinformed things like, 'Color doesn't matter. Children are children.'" She huffed out a small chuckle. "As if we're not individuals. As if our cultures, ethnic makeups and history don't contribute to our identities, how we see ourselves, how we stand in this world. And that doesn't just somehow start when we hit adulthood. It begins when we're children."

She fell silent for a moment, her expression clouded. But then she blinked, her eyes focusing back on him.

"One of my earliest memories is of Moe brushing and styling Leo's and Sinead's hair. She would sit them between her legs or on her lap, get the brush and comb, and they'd talk and laugh while she put their hair up in soft, silky ponytails or let it hang all long and straight down their backs. And then there was me. Moe tried. I'll give her that. But because she had no experience with Black hair, mine started to shed then break off from washing it every day like my sisters. My hair was thick, coarse, so very different from Leo's and Sinead's. She usually went with a ball or puff. But Moe being Moe, she understood how important a girl's hair is to her. Especially a

Black girl's hair. So she started making appointments at the local Black-owned hair salon as well as having Ms. Eva, a friend of the family, come in to braid my hair when we couldn't make it to the shop."

Adam nodded, understanding everything Flo said. Justine was only five. And though Adam made it a point to instill in her that being kind, considerate and unselfish were more important than being *pretty*, he still understood his little girl needed to hear she was just that—pretty. She needed to feel confident about her appearance, and that included her hair. Especially her hair. Because for the Black culture, it represented identity, creativity, expression…freedom.

And yet, he also empathized with Flo's adopted mother because he was that parent of a Black girl with no idea what to do with her hair. Afraid he would damage not just it, but her self-esteem. Being a parent wasn't easy. Matter of fact, it was the hardest damn job ever created.

And the best.

"It sounds like your Moe understood one of her children had different needs and did everything in her power to make sure you were good," he said.

"Oh, definitely." She nodded her head. "Moe didn't rely on others. She learned how to do some things, too. And, as an adult looking back, it only makes me appreciate and love her more. But four-, five-year-old me? All I knew back then was my mother couldn't do my hair like my sisters'. They had that special bond with her, that quality time that I didn't. They didn't need strangers to take care of them. It made me feel different. I already looked different from the rest of my family, and this small thing—which wasn't so small, really—solidified that feeling. So when Jussy asked me to do her hair, I didn't hesitate. It's about more than the hair and feeling pretty. It's about that time, that attention and affirmation."

"She misses it," Adam murmured. "I know she misses it."

"There's nothing wrong with asking for help or accepting it," she quietly said. "It's not a weakness or a commentary on you as a parent." A smile curved her lips. "One of the things I realized when I was older? Moe could've easily rejected any help for her child who was a different race than her. Could've ignored that she didn't have certain knowledge when it came to aspects of my care. But she didn't. Her reaching out and ensuring she and I had another community of friends that included people— women—who looked like me, who could talk to me about being a Black girl and later a Black woman in this world, was another display of her deep love for me. And that's one thing that wasn't in short supply in our home. Love. And it's the same with Justine. There's no need to feel guilt over what you can't give her. Not when what you are giving her far outweighs it. Stop keeping a running tally of the losses and celebrate the wins."

He remained silent, letting her words sink in, allowing them to fall into his heart and hopefully take root and grow.

Huffing out a short laugh, he lifted the beer to his lips again, downing a sip. "You're too young to be so wise," he said, lowering the bottle.

Arching an eyebrow, she snorted. "That didn't sound condescending at all." She paused, tilted her head, then quietly said, "Did you need that reminder of how old I am for me or for you?"

"Both of us."

The answer broke free of him before he could censor it.

And as it sat between them, it seemed to echo in the space, the meaning behind it both a revelation and a warning.

"Why do you need it? The reminder?" she pressed, and damn, why didn't she just leave it alone?

Why didn't he?

If he used the intelligence he'd been blessed with, he wouldn't answer her question; he'd deflect and dodge like a pro ball player. But from the moment he'd met this woman, he'd played with his boundaries, flirted with self-preservation. She threatened them all.

And this moment wasn't any different.

"Do you really need me to answer that?" He rubbed a hand down his beard. When she didn't reply, he met her steady gaze without flinching. "I need that reminder so I'll remember the real-life repercussions of making the wrong decision."

"And I'm the wrong decision?"

She didn't sound offended, just…curious.

"For me? For Jussy? Yes, you are."

Unfortunately, it was debatable whether that knowledge would be enough for him to maintain his distance. To keep his hands all the way to himself.

That, she didn't have to know.

If he hadn't been watching her so closely, he might've missed the nearly imperceptible flinch. But he studied her like a final exam loomed in his future and he planned on acing the test. He almost rescinded the words, or at least softened them. In the end, though, he remained quiet. Because as blunt and maybe hurtful as he'd been, it was still the unvarnished truth.

"I'm not your wife," she finally said, her voice low, but like a shout in his ears. "And last time I checked, Jesus went to the cross for someone else's sins. I'm not Him or your ex-wife. I don't want to pay for anyone's crimes but my own."

Damn, she had a way with words.

"Jennifer was only five years younger than me," he said. "We met when she was finishing up her Masters at the University of Chicago and I had already been with my old architectural firm for four years. Jennifer didn't have much of a childhood or young adulthood, for that matter. She'd grown up with a single mother who worked two jobs, and as the oldest child, much of the parenting of her two youngest siblings fell on her. And even when she left for college, she didn't live in the dorms, but remained living at home in that role, caring for her brother and sister."

"I can only imagine the weight of that responsibility on her at such a young age. Even though she was helping her mother, that would've still been a lot," Flo murmured.

"From what she told me, Jenn loved her sister and brother—and her mom. But because she'd been pushed into a role she didn't ask for, she became estranged from her mother. And her siblings were so used to viewing her as the gatekeeper and disciplinarian rather than just their older sister, their relationship was forever changed, too. The beginning of our relationship was—" he waved the beer bottle in front of him as if it were a wand capable of conjuring the explanation he sought "—freedom, in a way. Because by the time we met, her siblings were older, and she'd just moved into an apartment of her own. But that sense of freedom didn't last long."

Lifting his beer once more, he sipped the alcohol and glanced over the couch back toward the hall. Justine should be asleep by now, but he was always cautious when talking about her mother. He didn't want to badmouth his ex, his child's mother, poisoning Justine's mind against her.

"She became pregnant with Justine," Flo said, drawing his attention back to her. Surprise rippled through him, and she shrugged a shoulder. "I can add. Or subtract."

He nodded. "Yeah, she became pregnant. And we got married."

"Would you have, if the circumstances had been different?"

How many times had he asked himself that same question? Thousands. Tens of thousands over the years. Sighing, he pinched the bridge of his nose.

"I don't know. Maybe. In time, eventually." Obviously, even after the number of times he'd posed this question to himself, he *still* didn't know the answer. "Doesn't matter now. We made our choices, and we have to live with them. And maybe I would've done some things differently, but having Justine isn't one of them."

"Of course not," Flo whispered.

"For a while, we were good. But by the time Jussy turned two, I could see Jennifer getting restless. It was little things at first. We would argue over the smallest topics. She claimed to be bored, and then she said more pointed things, like she'd already been a parent, that this wasn't the life she'd imagined for herself. Long lunches with friends would turn into nights out. And then she occasionally stayed out all night. Said she'd gotten tipsy and slept over at a friend's house."

"She cheated on you?" Flo frowned, shifting and tucking her foot underneath a thigh.

Her voice held a note of disbelief, and in spite of the subject, a ghost of humor flickered inside him. She actually sounded offended on his behalf.

"No, she didn't," he said, but then amended, "Well,

I don't think so because I never did have proof of any infidelity. Your wife stays out all night, yeah, that's the first place your mind goes. But I don't know. And by the time we separated and then divorced, I didn't care. Because maybe we could've worked past that issue. But feeling too tied down, needing the space to discover who she was and live the life she never had the opportunity to experience because of her childhood? *That* we couldn't get over. Because Justine deserves more than a part-time parent who calls off work more than she shows up. I understood Jenn's needs—that's why I didn't fight her on the divorce—but not being there for our daughter?" He shook his head. "That I'll never understand."

A thick silence descended between them. It was weighted with emotion, words said and unsaid. And underneath, the simmering tension that never fully dissipated whenever they were within breathing distance of each other. Even as he relayed the biggest failure in his life, his cock pulsed with need.

And wasn't that the fucked-up part of it all? Why he'd issued that warning? Because no matter that he knew she had yet to experience more of life, he wanted her. Wanted her so badly he could still taste her, feel her hands stroke over his skin…feel the tight, silken clasp of her sex.

"I'm sorry, Adam. I've never been married so I've never suffered the pain and grief of a divorce. I can only imagine it's like a form of death. Not just the marriage and relationship, but a dream, too. That idea of what your future looked like for you and Jussy," she said, and in those pretty brown eyes, he glimpsed sympathy, not pity. His chest loosened a fraction. "But again, I'm not your wife," she added, as if plucking his thoughts right out of his head. "And it isn't fair to paint me with her brush. You don't know enough about me to assume that just because I'm younger I don't know my own mind."

"That's not how I see you," he countered. At this point he should shut down this conversation—a conversation he'd initiated—before it verged into territory neither one of them was ready to trek. So yes, he should shut up. But the hurt shimmering underneath the matter-of-fact tone of her voice wouldn't allow it. "There's nothing indecisive about you. On the contrary, Flo. You're driven, ambitious, focused. You're just twenty-four and you already have your own business. You're gifted and not just good at your job. It's your passion. Which is why you'd spend two weeks in another country pursuing that passion and learning from others to improve your craft. While you love your studio, there's a fire inside you, an almost restless need that won't permit you to be satisfied with just taking pictures for holidays, christenings and graduations. You want more. And there's nothing wrong with that."

But it was that *more* that made him nervous. Made him want to erect a hedge of protection around Justine's heart. Because one woman who needed *more* had already walked away from her. From them. He couldn't allow Flo to be another one.

He couldn't let himself forget the potential cost of becoming involved with Flo, of falling for her. The price would be too high, and it wouldn't only be him paying it.

"Then why does it still sound like an indictment?" she murmured.

"Not an indictment, just the truth," he returned in that same low voice. "You should want all of that. You should live it, experience it. That's your right, and nothing, or no one, should hold you back from it. That's all I'm saying, Flo."

A beat of silence pounded between them, and he ex-

pected her to look away from him, to change the subject.
To let it go. But this was Flo. And maybe, eventually, he
would learn to stop underestimating her. Apparently, tonight wasn't it.

"And you would hold me back from it?" she pressed,
exposing his explanation to the light of truth.

A truth he could choose to either back away from or
confront head-on.

"You've told me about your family, but I haven't been
honest about mine," he said. This was...odd for him. He
didn't talk about his past, his father. Hell, he didn't even
like *thinking* about the old man, much less discussing
him. Part of him felt like the man was part Candyman.
Say his name too many times, and he just might show
up. Best to keep Maurice Reed out his mouth. Silently
sighing, he scrubbed a hand over his head. "My parents
divorced when I was seven. Well, that's not entirely accu-
rate. My father kicked my mother out of our house when
I was seven. According to him, my mother cheated on
him and forfeited her rights to our family. That's who he
was—is—the kind of man who would use his child as a
pawn to hurt someone else. He was domineering, cold,
what we would call verbally abusive now. And selfish. I
don't know what he had on my mother to keep her away
from me, but he kept his promise that day she left. He
told her she'd never see me again, and she didn't."

But had his mother tried harder to go up against his
father and sued for custody? Even today, thirty years
later, he didn't have the answer to that. He couldn't trust
the truth to come out of Maurice Reed's mouth if it was
pried with the jaws of life. And his mother...

"I'm so sorry, Adam," Flo whispered.

He shrugged a shoulder and, *It is what it is* hovered
on his tongue. But at the last moment, he didn't say it.

Because if the delusion of his parents' marriage and the subsequent absence of his mother wasn't that big of a deal, he wouldn't still dream about it. Wouldn't still nurse an emotional wound that affected the man and parent he'd become.

Wouldn't still have fear trickling in his veins at even the thought of a relationship.

He nodded. "I didn't have my mother, but I had several mother figures—several stepmothers. See, my father had a thing for relationships, for falling in 'love.' Except he had no idea how to stay in love. Inevitably, the nitpicking would start. 'Why does this house look like this?' 'Is it too much to ask to have dinner on the table when I get home?' 'What kind of woman can't control her kid?' Then the name-calling. Bitch. Lazy ass. Whore. Then the threats. 'You think I can't find another woman? Fix your shit or you're out of here.'"

Though Adam repeated the vitriol he'd heard so often throughout his childhood, his father's voice rattled in his head like angry ghosts.

"None of my father's relationships lasted past the five-year mark. My mother was probably the exception. It seemed like he was incapable of being in a healthy union, and that bled over to me. Yes, I always had a roof over my head, clothes on my back. And never did I go to bed hungry. But he was a bully with exacting and unobtainable standards. God help anyone who didn't meet them. That's the thing, though—no one ever could. All I saw growing up was this toxic cycle, and though it takes two to make a relationship successful, my father was the common denominator. And when I left for college, I never returned home to stay. I visited because my sister remained with him and whatever girlfriend or wife he had at the time. She was only eleven when I went to school, and I tried to protect her as best as I could from the chaos in our house. But some things…" He shook his head. "Some things you can't outrun, you just have to outlive. Like your past. Like generational scars."

"Generational scars or curses—they don't define us or set us on a path like some divining rod. One can be healed and the other broken. Is that what you're trying to tell me, Adam?" she asked. "That you're destined to be your father? Because that's bullshit, as you once so eloquently put it to me. We're not our parents or their parents, and so on down the line. We take our history, glean from it the information we need to stay the course or change it. Every day we wake up, we have the opportunity to choose to be different, to behave different. We are not prisoners to our family tree or DNA."

Logically, he agreed with her. Things like being a bad, selfish partner didn't pass down through genetics like eye color or body frame.

But he also knew that nurture and nature were just two sides of the same coin. He'd strived all his life to be as unlike his father as possible—levelheaded, not jealous, open-minded—but none of that seemed to matter. He'd still run off his partner. He'd still failed at marriage and keeping his wife happy and contented—at keeping his family together.

No matter what he told himself in the light of day, he couldn't escape the shadows of his heart.

"You're not a bad bet, Adam," she softly added.

"I'm not a safe one, either."

She stared at him, then slowly stood from the couch. And straddled his lap.

Surprise whipped through him and he blinked, unmoving. Well, most of him was unmoving. As she settled on top of him, pressing her hot center over his cock, it stirred, thickened. Neither it nor he had forgotten the sweet oblivion they'd found inside her, the tight, wet clasp of her. After all, how did a person possibly not remember the single most erotic experience of his life?

And here she was, sitting on top of him, only a couple layers of clothes preventing him from sliding inside her again.

"Flo," he murmured, his hands rising to cradle her hips.

He should lift her up and off. Place much needed space between them. But instead, his fingers tightened their grip, holding her to him.

"Sometimes safe is overrated," she whispered, sliding her hands up his chest to hook behind his neck.

The softness of her touch, the sensuality of it, burned away the reasons why this was such a bad idea, and they drifted away like steam. And when she lowered her head, he didn't evade her. No, he tipped his head back and met her halfway. Their mouths barely connected before he thrust his tongue between her lips, greedy for the taste of her that had been haunting him for… God, it seemed like forever.

Or maybe he was just that addicted to her.

He shoved that too-dangerous thought aside, and dove deeper into her mouth, sucked her tongue harder, groaned louder. Drowning himself in the flavor and scent—the *feel* of her under his palms—distracting himself from the very real fear trickling into his veins.

The thing about addiction?

It wasn't just physical. The mind, the brain, cried out for that next hit just as much as the body.

Everything in him craved Flo's taste, the feel of her smooth, soft skin under his palms. The thrill of that sleek body and those subtle curves moving against him. The sweet oblivion found in burying himself inside her.

Yeah, addiction was a hazardous pitfall.

And yet, he stroked a hand up her slim back and tunneled his fingers through her hair, gripping the locs to hold her head still as he took her mouth harder, with a need that made him less gentle. But she didn't seem to mind. No, if the jerking of her hips and stroking of her sex over his cock were any indications, she didn't mind at all. Good. Because with this hunger roaring through him, he couldn't stop, couldn't slow down.

In just a matter of weeks, he'd become insatiable for her.

And though that sent another streak of unease racing through him, he couldn't stop. Couldn't stop himself from plunging repeatedly between her lips for another lick, another suck. Couldn't stop grinding against her with every rock of her hips. Couldn't stop from lifting his other hand to cup a firm breast, pinch the beaded tip.

Just. Couldn't. Stop.

She arched into his touch, one of her hands lowering to cover his. But not to remove it; she squeezed his fingers, silently encouraging him to handle her harder. He plumped the flesh, molding and tweaking the tip through her shirt. He raked his teeth and lips down the elegant line of her throat, nipping the sensitive base. A shiver rippled through her, vibrating against him, through him. The reaction tossed kindling on an already roaring flame, and he drew her skin between his teeth, sucking on it, hoping like hell he bruised her. He'd reverted to a teenage boy who wanted to leave his mark so any and everyone could see he'd had the pleasure, the honor of touching her, kissing her. That for even this short amount of time, she was his to brand.

Yeah. Teenage boy *and* caveman.

Fisting her locs again, he tugged her head back up and pressed a hard kiss to the corner of her mouth.

"Look at me, queen," he ordered, his voice sounding rough, ragged to his own ears.

She lifted her lashes, and in her eyes, he glimpsed the lust swamping him in greedy, potent waves. It was intoxicating, and the surge of power that pulsed inside him damn near eclipsed the pleasure. This beautiful, gifted woman granted *him* the permission to put his mouth and hands on her, and *he* caused those gorgeous eyes to go dark. *He* caused her to tremble. He was the reason those slim, toned thighs quivered around his legs. He vacillated between awe and hunger.

"Show me where you need me." Splaying his fingers wide between her breasts, he waited, the pounding of her heart under his palm echoing the beat in his own chest. "What do you want from me?"

He was courting danger, poking it like a relentless child; he acknowledged this. But could he stop? No. They were too far past the time for caution. At least that was what his throbbing pulse and aching dick told him.

Not breaking their visual connection, Flo circled his wrist and pulled his hand away—then slid it down her torso, over her abdomen and navel, not stopping until his fingertips grazed her zipper.

"Here?" He traced the metallic teeth, his touch light. A breath shuddered out from between her lips. "Or...here." Without preamble, he cupped her sex, grinding the heel of his palm over her clit.

Her soft cry was a thing of beauty, and he instantly wanted more of it. In that second it became his mission in life to hear it over and over.

"Tell me, queen," he insisted, pressing his fingers

against the seam of her jeans, right up against the entrance to her body. "Here?"

"Yes, Adam." She gasped, fisting the front of his shirt. "Yes."

The need saturating her voice had him jerking open the button at the top of her jeans, hauling the zipper down, and he thrust his hand between her body and denim. Groans escaped both of them as he slid his fingers through drenched, soft flesh. The side of his finger skimmed that nub at the top of her mound, and her hips jerked, punching forward. He didn't stop until his fingers pressed to the mouth of her sex.

Cupping her ass, he urged her up to her knees, granting him more access.

"Fuck," he growled as he sank inside her, those slick muscled walls closing around him. Liquid heat coated his skin, and he couldn't stop himself from dragging his hand free and lifting it to his mouth, sucking all that wet from his fingers. Her flavor exploded on his tongue—a delicious blend of sweet and tart—and his stomach damn near cramped with the greed for more. "How the hell do you taste this good, baby?"

She stared down at him, her brown eyes almost black with lust. Cradling his face between her hands, she lowered her head and crushed her mouth to his. Savoring herself on his tongue? The thought sent another spiral of heat twisting through him.

Uttering a harsh curse against her lips, he dove back inside her jeans, agitating her clit with firm, tight circles. Her hips worked against his fingers, imploring, demanding, in a sensual dance. Flo whimpered into his mouth, and that coaxed a growl from him. An insatiable need to be inside her pounded within him, hardening his cock.

All it would take was one brush over his length, and he would blow. That was how on edge she had him.

"Adam," she panted, "please."

Tightening his grip on her ass, he held her restless movement still and plunged his fingers back into her tight, hot channel. He withdrew until only the tips remained then buried them back inside. Over and over, he fucked her, drawing a fierce satisfaction from every cry, every tremble of her body, every spasm of her sex. Her nails scratched his scalp, and that bite rippled down his spine, adding another layer to the lust tearing through him.

"C'mon, queen." He thrust harder into her, twisting his wrist and stroking high and deep. "Give it to me. Let go," he demanded, grinding the heel of his palm against the top of her sex.

He didn't know if it was his command, the press of hand against her clit or that final stroke of his fingers or a combination of all three—not that it mattered. He only knew the damn near bruising grip of her flesh, the milking embrace and her muted, throaty scream that he swallowed. He continued to work her body, fighting the squeeze and clasp of her channel to give her every measure of the orgasm.

She jerked her mouth from his and buried her face against his throat. And as the last shudder left her, she sagged against him. Reluctantly slipping his fingers free of her body, he wrapped his arms around her, holding her until their breathing evened out. His dick railed at him, demanding it enjoy the same erotic embrace his fingers had enjoyed. Lust still streamed through his veins, hot and alive, and *God*, he wanted inside her.

Moments later, she leaned back, meeting his gaze. Though she'd just come, her brown eyes glittered with the same desire that had its claws dug into him. Something unspoken but loud as a shout passed between them. Cupping her ass in both his hands, he rose from the couch, and she wrapped her arms and legs around his neck and waist. He strode around the end of the sofa, heading toward the hallway, anticipation and lust propelling him—

His cell phone vibrated on the coffee table, and the buzz of it halted him midstride. He frowned, fighting through the lust that clouded his mind. Who the hell would be calling at nine o'clock? Giving his head a small shake, he moved forward again…and it rang again. And then again.

Shit.

"You should get that," Flo murmured, loosening her arms, and he took the hint, slowly lowering her to the floor. His arms momentarily tightened around her, loath to release her, but she briefly squeezed the back of his neck. "It could be important. Especially if someone's calling late at night."

Frustrated—and more than a little irritated at the interruption—he swallowed the growl that rumbled up his chest. Flo was right, but the throbbing in his cock couldn't give a damn at this second. But it could be Adele trying to contact him about something back at home. Maybe…their father. What if he'd had another health scare?

Disquiet tripped down his spine as he turned around and retraced his steps to the couch and the table in front of it. Were he and his father close? No. Not like a dad and son should be. But if something happened to him….

He bent down and reached for his phone, expecting to see his sister's name on the screen. When he spotted his ex-wife's instead, his fingers hovered above the cell then curled into a fist.

The hell?

Unease transformed into anger, and it swirled behind his ribs. Why would Jennifer be calling *now*? What could she possibly want?

Bullshit, a voice in his head supplied.

And even as he jabbed the screen, answering the phone, he silently agreed. But he couldn't afford not to at least find out the purpose behind this call. On the off chance it was an emergency.

She's Justine's mother. She's Justine's mother.

He repeated the mantra to himself as he lifted the cell to his ear.

"Jenn," he said, and yeah, his tone sounded abrupt and sharp, but with need still simmering under his skin, it would require an act of God to make him sound friendlier.

"Hey, Adam," his ex chirped as if it were nine in the morning rather than in the evening. "How're you doing?"

"Jenn," he repeated her name through clenched teeth. Inhaling a deep breath, he deliberately relaxed his jaw and tried again. "It's a little late to be calling. Is everything okay?"

"You're such a worrier. I see some things never change." Her light laughter echoed in his ear, and he scrubbed his fingers through his hair, stopping short of fisting it. "Everything's fine. I'm just calling to talk to my daughter. Can you put Jussy on the phone?"

"Are you kidding me?" he bit out. The last of the lust that had been humming in his veins dissipated under his anger. Closing his eyes, he pinched the bridge of his nose and paused. Regardless of the example he'd had growing up, he'd never purposefully disrespect a woman— especially the mother of his child. But goddamn, Jennifer tested him. He exhaled, dropped his arm and sightlessly stared ahead at the far wall. "Jenn," he said, attempting to inject calm into his voice. "Do you realize what time it is? After nine. Jussy is in bed, asleep."

A pause, then a soft gasp. "Oh God, I didn't even realize. It's just six here," Jennifer replied with a slight groan. "I don't— Hold on a second." In the background, he caught the muffled sounds of laughter, and wait…was that the splash of water? Jennifer shouted to someone, telling them she would be right there. Was she at a party? A damn pool party? He swallowed the bitter words that rappelled up his throat and clambered onto his tongue. By sheer force of will, he didn't let the words loose. "Sorry about that," Jennifer said with a soft chuckle. "I completely forgot about the time zone difference. But can I talk to Jussy anyway? I'm sure she'd love to talk to me."

"She is asleep, Jenn. Has been for a while now. Her bedtime is at eight like it's always been. I'm not going to wake her up."

"What? Adam, are you serious?" she demanded, incredulity coloring her tone. Moments later the noise in the background faded, and he assumed she must've moved to a different room or area. "I'm calling to speak with *my* daughter. You have no right to keep me from her."

"Jennifer," he ground out, and now he couldn't keep his anger and frustration from seeping into his words. "Don't pull that BS with me." A hand settled on his upper arm, giving his biceps a gentle squeeze. He jerked his chin down and met Flo's gaze. The concern and warmth there calmed him, centered him. And later, he would probably be terrified about that, but now he just clung to the life raft she tossed him.

Closing his eyes again, he shook his head and dragged in a cleansing breath. "I would never keep you from Jussy—I never have. You are free to talk to her or see her whenever you want. But she's been asleep for going on an hour now. I will not go in there and disturb her. This isn't about you. It's about her. After that five-minute call, you'll return to your party or whatever the hell you're doing, but it will be me who has to settle a cranky and tired child and hope she gets back to sleep before ten. No, I won't do it," he firmly said. "Set an alarm, write it down. If talking to your daughter is a priority, then you'll do whatever it takes to call and talk to her when she's awake, no matter the time difference."

"There you go again," she snapped. "I don't need you to tell me how to mother my child. You're so self-righteous. So fucking perfect, aren't you?"

Shaking off Flo's hand, he stalked forward, across the living room, heading for the front door. He didn't stop until he yanked it open and moved out onto the porch. The chilled spring air teased his skin, but he didn't heed it. His only goal? Take this conversation as far from Justine's hearing as possible. Didn't matter that she was asleep. He couldn't chance her waking up and possibly overhearing her parents arguing. All too well he remembered how the sound of raised voices and the anger thrumming through those voices scared him. He refused to do that to Justine.

"You've never made a mistake, have you? Oh no, not Saint Adam," Jennifer continued her diatribe. "You're not going to let me forget that you're there every day, the perfect parent. That doesn't make you her *only* parent, Adam. I love her and she loves me, and the only one you're hurting right now is Jus—"

"Don't. You. Dare." Adam curled his fingers around the porch railing, rocking on the balls of his feet as if her accusation was a physical blow. "Don't you dare lecture me on hurting Justine. My sole concern is her, her feelings, her well-being. Even though I've been forced to have conversations with her about why her mom was supposed to visit but didn't show. Why she was supposed to phone and didn't. I've made excuses for you time and time again, Jenn, and you won't even make the effort to call while she's awake. Forget coming to see her for your scheduled days and holidays. Forget paying child support. Forget all of that. A. Phone. Call. I'm not hurting our daughter. I'm here. I'm present. But you can't say the same, and I won't let you try and make me feel guilty for being her only plugged-in parent. One of us has to be."

Silence crackled on the April night and hummed across their connection. As his harsh words echoed on the evening air, the urge to apologize rose up from his gut, crowding into his chest.

Dammit.

Not only did he want to protect Justine, but he hated hurting Jennifer. She'd been his wife, his partner; he'd loved her once. And though she'd made choices—continued to make selfish choices—that had broken their family and confused their daughter, he still desired to shield her.

Savior complex. Jennifer had lobbed that at him during one of their many arguments when they were married. And maybe she was right. But she certainly wouldn't say that tonight.

And he couldn't bring himself to take back his words.

"Screw you, Adam," she quietly said and hung up.

He lowered the phone and stared at the screen, a heaviness taking up residence in his gut. Frustration, anger, sadness—they all mingled and eddied, until he couldn't separate one emotion from the other.

After sliding the cell into his back pocket, he gripped

the railing with both hands and leaned all his weight on them, his head bowed.

There are none so blind as those who will not see.

A small part of him would always love Jennifer, simply because of the years they'd shared, the family they created. And because she wasn't a bad person. Self-absorbed maybe, but not bad. Yet, when would she take the *me, me, me!* blinders off and see that she was hurting Justine? It aggravated and saddened him that he couldn't make Jennifer *see*. He felt helpless.

He felt like he was failing all of them.

The front door opened behind him, but he didn't turn around at the sound or at the soft tread of footfalls on the porch. He didn't look up when Flo came to stand beside him, and her body heat reached out to him despite the space separating them.

"Do you need me to stay?" she asked on a near whisper.

Yes. Please don't go.

The answer immediately leaped into his head, and it boomed like an internal megaphone. And the desperation, the need that rose within him... He might've swayed under that need if he hadn't been clutching the railing like it was his last lifeline.

And it was the power of that hunger to beg her to stay that had a layer of ice coating his chest, numbing him.

"No," he said, voice flat. "Thank you, but you should go. I'll see you in the morning."

For a long moment she didn't move. He still stared down at the railing, not looking at her. He couldn't; he was too afraid that if he glimpsed sympathy or, worse, remnants of their shared desire in her eyes, he would sink to his knees, wrap his arms around her and plead with her to come to his bed and not let him be alone tonight.

"Okay, Adam." She paused. "Good night."

"Good night, Flo."

She moved away from him, and though he told himself not to give in, he couldn't stop from lifting his head and watching her descend the porch steps and stride down the walkway to her car. Couldn't prevent himself from visually tracing the slim, proud line of her back.

He waited until she climbed into her car and drove away. And only then did he return inside his house.

Alone.

CHAPTER THIRTEEN

"IF I WASN'T such a Broadway and pizza whore, I might actually consider moving to Rose Bend." Mira shook her head, her large cup of lemonade in her hand.

With wide eyes, she surveyed The Glen where barrel grills, wooden tables, bouncy castles and an assortment of games now occupied the wide meadow at the end of Main Street. The town council and an army of volunteers had transformed the field into a huge picnic area, complete with fairy lights, balloons and music. A festive atmosphere claimed the place, and the bright chatter and laughter from the thick crowds of Rose Bend's residents only added to it. Their town didn't really need a reason to throw a party or festival, so celebrating the *Vintage Renovation* crew? They were in their element.

As the producer of the TV show was discovering, Flo mused with a smile.

"We have pizza here, you know," Flo pointed out with an arched eyebrow.

Mira snorted. "Stop playing. There's nothing that compares to *real* New York pizza. And as charming and amazing as this town and the people are, I can't give that up."

"Or *Hamilton*," Flo added.

"Or *Hamilton*," Mira agreed. "But I hope you realize and appreciate how blessed you are having a community like this. I've traveled all over the country, and out of it, but there's something special about your hometown.

And it's not just the coffee or the addictive donuts in that café." She rolled her eyes and groaned, hugging her lemonade tight to her chest as if she could taste the baked goods offered at Mimi's Café even now. "If anything had a chance of persuading me to give up New York pizza, it would be those donuts."

Flo laughed. "We've heard that before. We're all a little convinced the DEA might have some interest in what she puts in them."

"Ain't that the truth!" Mira grinned, then turning, appraised the packed meadow once more. "Thanks for all of this. I can honestly say out of all the places we've visited, not one has ever thrown a picnic in our honor. All of us really appreciate the effort."

"I can only imagine it's tough being away from home for months at a time," Flo said.

As thrilling and exciting as leaving on the occasional trip was for her, she wouldn't want to be away from her family for weeks on end. She would miss them like an amputated limb. They were that much a part of her.

Mira shrugged. "Sometimes I just miss being on familiar territory and in my own space, you know? My parents live in Florida now—they definitely don't miss the New York winters—and I don't have children, which is my own choice, and I don't regret it. I love what I do. I haven't met a man or woman yet that can compete with the satisfaction of seeing a project come together." She grinned. "But I'm always willing to give that person a try, to see if they can."

Chuckling, Flo nodded. "Amen to that."

Mira raised her cup of lemonade, sipping while eyeing Flo over the rim. Yeah, she didn't like the speculative gleam in the other woman's gaze. And Flo fought not to fidget.

"What?" she asked, unable to contain the question any longer.

A corner of Mira's mouth quirked. "Nothing," she said, tone nonchalant as she took another sip. Then the producer squinted at her. "I just could've sworn that maybe you did find that person in the form of one big, broody architect."

Well, damn.

Flo blinked. Then tried to control her face from revealing her surprise. "I, uh…" She blinked again. "I'm not sure what you mean."

"Uh-huh. Okay, we'll go with that." Mira smirked. "If that's the story you want to go with."

"I'm thinking it is." Flo paused, narrowed her eyes on the producer. "What do you know?"

"Nothing, I swear." With an unconvincing cackle, Mira held up her hands, palms out. "But God, girl. The sexual tension between you two." She mimed hacking at the air with a knife. "Thick and delicious."

Flo groaned, squeezing her eyes shut, while the other woman loosed another loud crack of laughter. Heat sailed up from her chest, shooting straight for her face, and it burned in mortification.

"Oh, stop that." Mira slid an arm around Flo's shoulders, giving her a little shake. "I'm just teasing you. Not about the sexual tension," she added. "It's hot. But what's the problem? There are worse things in life than being attracted to a gorgeous, intense man like Adam Reed. And having him lusting after you."

"First, it's unprofessional as hell—" Flo began, only to be cut off when Mira scoffed, flicking her fingers.

"Meh. We're together over ten hours a day for months on end. Shit happens. And yes, I've noticed the chemistry between the two of you, but neither you nor Adam have been anything less than professional. Now, if you want me to tell you about that time we were renovating a farmhouse and my *former* assistant got into a screaming match with the homeowner because he'd caught her with the— Ah well, never mind." She waved a hand again as if trying to shoo away the memory. She jabbed a finger at Flo. "Now *that* was unprofessional. And traumatizing."

"Wow." Flo stared at her. "So now I really want to know who he caught her with and what else went down."

Mira winced. "No, you really don't. I had to write a report for exactly why I was firing him and ended up with waaay more details than I ever wanted. Some things you can't unhear. Or unimagine." She grimaced again. "But yeah, this is nothing like *that*. So what's your other objection?"

"Well, the obvious one of him and Justine only staying in Rose Bend for as long as it takes this project to wrap up. He's leaving for Chicago, and I live here," Flo said.

"Yeah, that's a bit more of a hurdle," Mira conceded with a nod. "But not insurmountable. While this might not be the best place for me, who's to say it isn't for a single father raising a young daughter? Have you asked him about that possibility? Have you even had the conversation?"

Flo shook her head, admittedly a little forcefully. But panic flared in her chest, bright and scalding.

"No." This time she held up her hands, warding Mira off. "We are not even close to having *that* talk. Hell, I don't even know what we are…"

Coworkers? Single dad and nanny? Onetime fuck buddies?

They were a complicated, tangled mess of all three and none of it was neat or clear. None of it simple. And nowhere near ready for a "where are we going with this?" conversation.

"Got it." Taking another sip from her cup, Mira tilted her head, studying Flo with a scrutiny that had Flo itching to shield her face. Or just run. "Okay, so what's the less obvious objection?"

"Sorry?" Flo frowned, confused.

Mira shook the cup, ice cubes clinking. Then she took another long sip of the dregs of the lemonade. "Damn, that's good," she muttered, and squinted at Flo. "You said the obvious objection was his imminent departure from Rose Bend. What's the less obvious one?"

Flo heaved a sigh, smoothing a hand over her locs that were twisted into a bun on top of her head. Though being vulnerable was the thing for certain members of her family, it'd never been easy for her.

Except with Adam.

She mentally mean-mugged that know-it-all voice in her head. But she couldn't deny the veracity of the taunt. Even though she'd known Adam for a handful of weeks, she'd shared more with him than she had anyone else— including her family. Maybe it was his calm, stalwart demeanor or the quiet strength he exuded... Maybe it was the fact that he'd already seen her at her most exposed and hadn't judged her...

She couldn't pinpoint the exact reason. Hell, it could be all of them.

He was just...Adam.

And that in itself seemed like enough.

Not that he was entirely safe. Hadn't he said just that to her several nights ago? Hadn't he warned her he wasn't a safe bet? She'd contradicted him, but should she have?

Nothing about how he'd left her reeling on that porch had felt *safe*. Not after his big, calloused hands on her. Not after that mind-melting orgasm.

Not after that call from his ex and his pushing her away.

Even now the hurt from his sudden coldness, his rejection, shimmered through her. It was enough to capsize the desire that flickered to life at just the memory of how passionately he'd kissed her, touched her. The two emotions rivaled each other for dominance.

"All teasing aside, you don't have to talk to me about it if you're not comfortable," Mira said, breaking into Flo's unsettling thoughts.

"No, no. It's okay," Flo reassured the woman she considered a friend. "He has...baggage."

"You mean his daughter?"

"God, no." Flo shook her head, hard. "Jussy is an amazing little girl. I mean emotional baggage—and I do, too, for that matter. Between that and the age difference, which is more of an issue for him than me, I don't think it's a smart move to get too fully invested in anything but the here and now."

"Huh."

"I'm almost afraid to ask what that means." Flo paused, scowled at Mira. "Okay, what does *huh* mean?"

"Nothing, except..." She smiled, and to Flo, it held a rueful, perhaps even wistful, tint. "You know the thing about baggage, right?" Mira asked, and before Flo could replay, she said, "You can choose to check that shit anytime you decide to."

"I don't—"

"Hey, Flo! We've been looking everywhere for you," Leo called out as she approached them, Sydney by her side.

"Translation," Sydney said, tone dry. "She's been all over this picnic trying to keep away from Owen."

Flo arched an eyebrow, glancing at her sister. "Why are you avoiding my brother-in-law?"

Leo heaved an exaggerated and much aggrieved sigh.

"Because we're supposed to take shifts at those bouncy things with Bono. My turn miiiight've started—" she flipped her wrist and peered down at the slender gold watch there "—an hour ago."

Mira snickered, and Leo grinned and extended her hand toward the producer.

"I'm so rude. Hi, I'm Leontyne, Flo's sister. But you can call me Leo." As Mira shook her hand, her sister dipped her chin toward Sydney. "This is our sister-in-law, Sydney."

"It's nice to meet you." Mira clasped Sydney's hand next. "I'm Mira Heron, producer of *Vintage Renovation*."

"I love your show, by the way," Sydney said. "It's amazing what you guys do with those houses! And I'm always so jealous of the people who get to live in them."

"Same," Mira admitted with a chuckle. "And thank you. I never get tired of hearing how much people enjoy the show." Glancing at Flo then back at Sydney and Leo, she added, "If you will excuse me. I'm going to fix myself a plate before the savages I work with destroy everything."

She strolled off with a wave goodbye and made her way through the crowd. Flo chuckled as she was waylaid by their unofficial town matriarch, Eva Wright.

"How much you want to bet your producer friend will find herself volunteering for some kind of fundraiser while she's here?" Sydney drawled.

Flo snorted. "I don't take fools' bets. Mira will be volunteering, *and* members of the TV crew will end up filming it. For free."

The three of them burst out laughing because Eva was that persuasive and commanding. Not many people could withstand the efforts of the older woman. And

those on that short list included Superman and Thurgood
Marshall—one wasn't human and the other dead.

"Hey, seriously, though, I have been looking for you,"
Leo said, turning to Flo, and the abrupt switch in her sister's demeanor set off frissons of alarm.

"Why? What's wrong? What happened?"

"Nothing's wrong," Leo quickly assured her. "I just
wanted to give you a heads-up. Dad and Moe are here."
She paused, and before she even finished, Flo knew what
would follow. The constricting around her chest clued
her in. "So is Noah."

That band squeezed tighter.

She hadn't been back to the inn since that last conversation with Noah. Yes, she'd called and spoken with her
parents—had even met up with Moe at the studio and
took her over to the renovation where she hung out with
Flo and Jussy for a couple of hours. But no, she'd been
avoiding her childhood home. And Noah was the reason.

Now he was here, and The Glen that had seemed so
huge just a second ago shrank to the size of a postage
stamp. And though she didn't suffer from claustrophobia,
grasping fingers of panic scraped at her throat.

No. She wasn't ready to see him again. Wasn't ready
to confront the murky, convoluted snarl of emotion he
evoked. Not yet.

"Hey." Sydney reached out, gripped Flo's hand. "If
you want us to run interference, just say the word. We
got you."

"Absolutely," Leo agreed. "Haven't I proven today just
how amazing I am at subterfuge?"

Despite the anxiety clawing at her, she chuckled.
"Yeah, you're a regular 007."

"Please." Flo sneered. "Since Idris was nixed for Bond,
I'm boycotting. Nope, call me Evelyn Salt."

Sydney frowned. "Uh, wasn't she a double agent?"

Leo popped up a finger. "A *badass* double agent. Aaand, Angelina Jolie."

"That's fair."

Flo shook her head at their customary byplay, not distracted from the news Leo dropped, but thankful she had these two women at her back. But she wasn't a young girl needing her big sister to shield her. She had to fight her own battles. Still, she appreciated and loved Leo and Sydney for standing by her.

"Thanks for the heads-up. And—" she arched an eyebrow at Leo "—if I need you to stop, drop and roll, I'll let you know."

"That's fire safety, but whatever," her sister muttered.

Shaking her head, Flo grinned and her gaze landed on the one person *she'd* been trying to avoid all day.

Adam Reed.

Tall and just…big, he stood out among this crowd. Or maybe she just had a built-in radar that zeroed in on him no matter his location. God, she hated that might be true.

She also hated that she couldn't stop staring at him.

In deference to the perfect spring day, he wore a light blue button-down shirt that stretched over his wide shoulders and chest like a shameless hussy. Rolled-up sleeves revealed muscled forearms, and damn, the sight of them shouldn't have a ball of heat lodging beneath her navel. Nor should his powerful thighs pressed against slim-fitting khaki pants have the breath stuttering in her lungs.

But here she was. Heat lodging, breath stuttering.

She curled her fingers into her palms, nails denting the skin, but that tiny flare of pain did nothing to erase the tactile memory of his thick, coarse hair under her hands. Or eradicate the delicious stretch in her thighs as she straddled his.

With a will she didn't believe herself possible of possessing, she snatched her gaze away from him...it crashed into Leo's and Sydney's.

"Oh girl," Sydney breathed, shaking her head.

Flo grimaced as Leo said, "You got it bad, don't you?"

The *I don't know what you're talking about* leaped to her tongue, but as she met her sisters' way-too-perceptive eyes, she couldn't push out the lie.

But she also couldn't affirm what all three of them knew. Yes, she did have it bad. The man was an itch under her skin that, no matter how much she scratched, refused to go away. And she wanted to scratch it...a lot.

Voicing it aloud, though? No. That made it too real. Made it fact.

"His little girl is adorable and so sweet," Leo said, her tone gentle—careful.

"Don't, Leo," Flo warned. "A TV crew might be here, but this isn't going to be a thirty-minute sitcom where everyone ends up together in their happily-ever-after to a laugh track." When Leo's lips parted, Flo held up her hand. "I'm not going to deny there's...something between me and Adam. But he has a little girl to raise and protect. That and their life together are his first priorities. And his life is back in Chicago, not here in Rose Bend."

"When Owen came here, he intended his stay to be for a short time, too," Leo pointed out. "And he changed his mind. We made it work."

"Yes, but Owen didn't have a daughter to raise, who depends almost solely on him. Not everyone can have the fairy tale, Leo."

"But you want it," Sydney murmured. "The fairy tale."

Flo didn't immediately answer, and, against her will, her regard trailed to Adam again. As if he sensed her attention, he looked up from the older couple talking to him and their gazes met. Held.

The distance prevented her from reading what that golden stare contained, and still, shivers danced over her skin. Since that night on his couch, they hadn't talked about anything that didn't have to do with Justine. And as much as it terrified her, she missed him. Because if an emptiness sat in her stomach like a boulder now, when he was still near, still in Rose Bend, that barren hollowness just might swallow her whole when he left.

Dragging her gaze from him again, she refocused on Sydney and smiled. And prayed her sadness wasn't reflected in that gesture.

"Doesn't everybody?" she replied to her sister-in-law's question. "But that won't look the same for everyone." She shrugged and ordered herself not to glance in Adam's direction again. "And that's okay. *I'm* okay. So both of you can get that 'oh shit!' look off your faces," she teased.

"All right, we'll let it go. For now," Leo conceded, then hooked an arm through Flo's and tugged on her. "Let's go get some of Marion's lemonade," she said, mentioning Cole's secretary. "I heard she has a special stash with her." Leo tried to wriggle her eyebrows and, yeah, epic fail. She just looked maniacal.

"Ooh, I've had that special lemonade." Sydney smacked her lips and claimed Flo's other arm, steering them toward the small beverage booth. "Do you think anyone has dared to call Marion a moonshiner to her face?"

"Not if they wanted to walk away with it." Leo snickered.

Flo chuckled as she let herself be led away. Spiked lemonade wouldn't solve any of her problems, but it damn sure wouldn't hurt.

"THAT LITTLE GIRL adores you."

Flo smiled, both at the words and her mother slipping an arm around her waist and hugging her. She wrapped her own arm around Moe's shoulders and planted a kiss on Moe's smooth cheek.

"The feeling is completely mutual," Flo said, waving at Justine as she slid down the slide on the bouncy castle.

As soon as her little feet hit the ground, she darted off, running for the ball pit where Patience, Everett, Bella and the rest of the kids from their family jumped and played. Justine had met all of them that day she'd gone to Kinsale Inn, as well as the several times Flo had arranged playdates with them. They'd all gotten along and included Justine among their ranks as if she was another cousin.

"I've missed you," her mother said, squeezing her waist. "The inn isn't the same without you visiting. I've accepted you've moved out, and I had to come to terms with that. But not seeing you except for when I come into town? That's not doing it for me."

"I know." Flo leaned her head against Moe's. "I've just been busy with the renovation, the studio and babysitting Jussy. I promise to do better."

Moe turned and cradled Flo's face between her palms, tilting her head down so she could meet her blue, steady gaze.

"Don't isolate yourself from us, Florence. Please," she softly pleaded. "We can handle and overcome anything as a family. *Anything*. But being alone allows doubts, insecurities and fears to creep in. And they might convince you that your family isn't behind you, loving you." Moe shook her head, her long, brown-and-silver-streaked braid falling behind her shoulder. "And nothing could be further from the truth. You know that, right?"

"Of course I do," Flo assured her, covering Moe's hands with her own.

She did. It was just that the heaviness of their expectations—especially her father's—weighed her down, filled her with guilt. And she feared disappointing them, *him*. Feared hurting him.

Feared his rejection.

Briefly closing her eyes, she hugged Moe. Because in this moment, she needed the security of her mother's arms around her. And to avoid that all-knowing, all-seeing gaze.

"Now I'm jealous," her father announced from behind her. "Why does Moe get all the hugs?"

Joy at her father's voice mingled with resentment and sorrow. God, she hated that her usual happiness and love had been polluted with those darker emotions. They had no place inside her—not when it came to Ian. But since Noah's return, they'd taken root and their poisonous vines had grown, spread.

"Hey, Dad," she greeted, turning to Ian with a wide smile that belied the turmoil roiling inside her. "Now, you know there's no need to be jealous. Not when you're my favorite."

"Disrespectful child," Moe grumbled as Ian laughed.

A warmth bloomed behind Flo's breastbone at the loud, rumbling sound of her father's hilarity. Since she'd been a little girl, his laughter had always delighted her. Moe might be the gregarious and outgoing half of their pair, while he was a calming presence in the storm of his wife's personality, but he possessed a booming laugh that turned heads.

And she loved it.

Loved him.

Ian gathered her into his arms, and for a moment all

her worries and tensions tumbled away as if they never existed. She inhaled his familiar soap-and-crisp-fresh-air scent and pressed her cheek to his wide chest. Yes, she was a daddy's girl—that could possibly be attributed to her first father figure so abruptly leaving. As a result, she'd attached to Ian.

Or it could be that Ian Seamus Dennison was just an amazing man and dad.

Her deep love for him only made the anger that simmered within her more painful.

"I thought we agreed not to say that in front of your mother," Ian admonished with a chuckle.

"Oops."

Planting a kiss on her forehead, Ian released her, stepping back. "It's good to see you, Flo."

"You, too, Dad."

"Hi, Flo."

She stiffened. And her father, with his arm still around her shoulders, felt her reaction because his half embrace tightened. Her belly did the same thing, twisting until it ached.

"Hi… Noah."

She still stumbled over what to call him. He wasn't her uncle; she could never think of him that way like her brothers and sisters. Not when he'd been the first father she'd known. But she couldn't call him by the same name she called Ian either. Ian had raised her, nurtured her, corrected her when she needed it and, most importantly, he'd stayed. So no, Noah didn't get Dad or Daddy, either.

So she settled on Noah, even though it felt odd on her tongue. Because it felt too impersonal, like addressing a stranger. And though he was a stranger…he also wasn't.

Which perhaps explained why she drank in the weathered lines on his face, the gray peppering in his dark hair and the familiar blue-gray eyes.

God, no wonder confusion whirled inside her.

An awkward, stilted silence descended over the four of them, and it remained like an unwanted intruder.

"Moe told me how great you're doing with that renovation project," Noah finally said, breaking the pained quiet.

"Yes, it's coming along," Flo said, voice even, not betraying the childish impulse to ask her mother why she was discussing her with *him* in the first place.

Yes, she had suddenly reverted to a six-year-old.

Noah smiled, and he looked so much like her father it almost hurt to look at him.

"I find it amazing that you're a photographer. There's probably no way you remember this, but your mom, she was so creative and talented. She could draw just about anything. I bet you have that same eye."

A cavernous yearning yawned wide in her chest— a yearning for more information about her mother. A yearning to be close to her even if it was through someone else's memories.

Yet, anger threaded through that longing. Because she hadn't known that about her mother. Flo had always wondered if either of her biological parents had possessed an interest in photography or any of the arts, or if it was something she'd discovered on her own. And if Noah had stuck around, hadn't abandoned her, or hell, had just been more involved in her life past greeting cards, she wouldn't have wondered. She would've had the answers.

But now, here he was, doling them out like she should be happy, grateful.

And that only made her resent him more.

"No, I didn't know that," she said, struggling to maintain an even tone for her parents' sakes.

"Oh yeah," Noah continued, his smile widening. So completely oblivious. "She used to carry either a notebook or a sketching pad with her everywhere she went. I can't tell you how many times I'd find her either behind the inn or on our front porch drawing. And you would be sitting right there beside her with your paper and crayons. I'm sure I have some of those drawings around. I can find them for you, if you'd like to see them."

Yes.

The answer burned her tongue, but she didn't say it, couldn't bring herself to ask him. Pride was a terrible thing.

"We made sure she received Aisha's things," her father said when Flo didn't reply. "But if you have more, I know Flo would love them."

I don't need you to speak for me. Don't need you to make him feel better, she silently snapped. But she still remained silent, locking that down, too.

"No problem. I'll find them for you." Noah nodded as if it were Flo who had spoken instead of his brother. "If it's okay, Flo, I can bring them by your studio or apartment. Ian showed me where you live, and—"

"If you guys will excuse me," she interrupted, stepping forward and out from under her father's arm. The urge to *get away* shoved at her. Her breath echoed in her head, and she heeded the primal need to put space between her and the source of her pain. And right now that included her parents. "I'll find you later," she promised to Moe and her father, her gaze skating over Noah.

And though it was rude, and Moe and Ian had raised her better, she walked off.

No, she escaped.

She blindly pushed through the crowd, no specific destination in mind, just heeding the need for distance. Both physically and emotionally.

"Flo." The low, deep timbre wrapped around her name had her feet halting midstep, and when a large hand encircled her upper arm, she nearly sagged in relief.

She didn't need to look behind her to identify the person holding her. Even if she didn't recognize the voice, then her body's haywire reaction to his touch would've informed her of Adam's presence.

And God, she had every reason to avoid him—he was a heartache on two legs—yet she turned toward him, leaned into him. Her pulse raced and the skin under his hand heated as if he branded her through her thin sweater. She wanted that heat all over her, swamping her...claiming her.

She needed him. And it terrified her.

Yet... Yet, she tipped her head back, met his gaze. And whatever he saw there—the need, the desperation, the hurt—had him sliding his hand down her arm to clasp her fingers in his.

"Dance with me." He didn't wait for her answer, but led her toward the area designated in front of the band and makeshift stage.

Couples already crowded the temporary dance floor. Adam maneuvered them to the far corner. Once there, he pulled her close, one big hand cupping her nape and the other settling on the small of her back.

He didn't question her, didn't nudge her to talk. And leaning her forehead against his broad, solid shoulder, she was grateful for it. Her mind whirled, and the emotion herding into her chest and up toward her throat didn't allow her words. Not right now.

In this moment she just wanted, *needed*, this. To be held. To be understood.

Sliding her arms around him, she flattened her palms on his back and let him lead, following the gentle sway of his big body.

One song flowed into two, and with each passing minute, more of the tension seeped from her body. He sheltered her against his chest, and she willingly took the comfort he silently offered.

"You good?" he murmured near her ear.

Flo nodded, the gesture instinctive—concealing how she felt. Concealing the truth.

Adam stopped moving and slid his hand between her and his chest, pinching her chin and tilting her head back. She couldn't avoid that bright gaze, and…she didn't want to. Maybe because in this moment, with his arms around her, she felt safe. Like nothing could touch her as long as she stood in the shadow of his big frame.

"Now," he said in that same low voice, "let's try that again with you looking me in the eyes. You good?"

She nodded once more. "No."

He dipped his own chin in acknowledgment and released her. Returning his hand to her nape, he said, "When or if you're ready, I'm here."

If. He was granting her a choice, and who knew that could feel so precious, so sweet? Especially when it seemed like others in her life, regardless of their intention and motivation, wanted to take that from her.

"Noah's here," she admitted.

His gaze flicked across the dance floor.

"He was one of the three people you were just talking to?"

"Yes." She inhaled a deep breath, held it for several seconds, and when she loosed it, her eyes briefly closed. "Earlier, my sister and sister-in-law had warned me he'd come with my parents, but… I don't know." She shrugged.

"I still wasn't prepared to face him, speak with him since the last time. I've been kind of avoiding the inn for that reason. He wants to talk to me, spend time with me—and I can tell my parents want the same thing—but I'm just not ready. And I don't know when or if I will be."

Adam didn't immediately reply, but his hold on her neck firmed, his thumb stroking her skin. No doubt he meant the soothing caress to calm her. And it did… But it also stirred the embers of desire she was coming to discover only Adam could stoke.

"Why not? What are you scared of, Flo?"

"I'm not—" The lie stuck in her throat, and she sank her teeth into her bottom lip as if trapping it inside. She glanced away from him, from those golden eyes. "Shit," she whispered. "I really don't like you right now."

"I can take that, queen. I can take anything you say." His long fingers squeezed her nape, and obeying his unspoken command, she returned her regard to him. "What are you scared of?"

"I—" She stared up at him, the words lodged in her throat. But like a lock had been wrenched open, they tumbled out of her. "He left me."

She knew that didn't make much sense, that she hadn't really answered his question, but for her, those three words explained so much. That was where her story began.

"You're wrong," Adam said, a flinty note in his tone startling her.

Then she blinked in surprise, because it hit her that she must've spoken her thoughts aloud.

"Your story began long before Noah walked away. He didn't determine who you were, who you would be. You arrived here with purpose and destiny, with the potential to be the gifted, brilliant woman you are. And just as he didn't write that on the slate of who you are, he couldn't do anything to erase it. I don't ever want to hear you say that again, queen."

Okay.

Okay.

"Flo?" he asked, his hand pressing harder into her back.

"Yes," she breathed, and because astonishment still tripped through her at his impassioned admonishment, that hint of anger *on her behalf*, she said again, louder, "Yes."

"Good." He curved his hand back around her neck, tunneling his fingers into her locs.

He cradled her head in his big palm, and she could just imagine how they appeared to everyone around them. Intimate. Like lovers. Part of her wanted to shy away from the eyes she could practically feel. She hated being the center of attention; it was why she preferred being behind the camera and not in front of it.

But another part... God help her, but that part preened under that same regard. Was delighted Adam didn't seem to care if others suspected they were more than coworkers. That she was more important to him than just being his daughter's nanny.

That part didn't care that tomorrow they would be the newest item on the Rose Bend gossip grapevine.

And it was this same side that would lead her down a path that only held heartbreak and disappointment.

"You ready to go on?" he asked, fingers massaging her scalp.

Don't you dare fucking purr, she ordered herself.

Not yet trusting herself, she nodded. Then after several long moments of silence where that bright gaze studied her and he patiently waited, she released a breath and started again.

"Noah left me," she repeated. "And he never came back. Other than random cards through the years, he walked away and went on with his life. Without me. And he did it so easily. Yes, I get he was grieving, but I needed him. And he abandoned me."

It was an old hurt, but with Noah's reappearance, the scab had been ripped off, and it throbbed like a fresh wound.

"I felt like this changeling in my own family. I wasn't a biological child, but I was also different from the adopted kids. Cole's and the twins' parents died. Their parents didn't leave them by choice. But my legal guardian, the man I considered my father, has always been out there in the world. He just didn't want me anymore." Her voice lowered, dropped, as she aired the fear that had been eating away at her soul and confidence like a cancer. "My parents—especially, Dad—want me to welcome him back. Let him get to know me. Noah does, too. And I can't lie, there's a part of me that wants to do just that. Noah knew my mother better than Moe and Dad. He lived with her, loved her. He could share details about her with me that I can't get from a box of mementos. Details only Noah, as her husband, could give me. Like what was her favorite food? What made her laugh…cry? What was her favorite color? I look like her—so people keep telling me—but I don't know if she preferred purple to blue. I even want to learn about Noah, discover why she fell in love with him."

She heaved out a breath, and it scraped her throat.

"But if I give in—if I let Noah in—what's to stop him from up and leaving me again? If he did it so easily before, why wouldn't he do it again? I can't trust him not to. More importantly, though, I don't trust myself not to get attached to him. Because I did it before, too."

"You're not that little girl anymore, Flo," he murmured.

"Aren't I?" she countered. "Yes, I'm an adult, but that small, confused child who sat at the window of the inn and watched the road for her father to show up... She didn't just disappear."

"True, but that little girl also isn't in control. The grown woman is. *You* are. And yes, you might have history that you can't forget, but you've also gained wisdom, good judgment and perception. There's no reason you can't trust yourself to do what's best for not just you, but your family, as well."

Wasn't there a reason? Did she have wisdom and good judgment?

Because if she did, Adam would've remained off-limits after their night together. She would've heeded all the very valid reasons why she shouldn't have become involved with him and fallen for Justine. She would've protected herself...her heart.

But she hadn't. Worse. She still didn't.

He released her hair and lowered his hand to circle her neck, his thumb under her chin and nudging it up. Even if she wanted to avoid his gaze, she couldn't.

But who was she kidding? She didn't want to.

God. Most definitely headed for heartbreak.

And he said she had wisdom? If that was true, she would veer off this road, hit Reverse and drive away without a backward glance.

Instead, she hit the fucking accelerator to her ruin.

Wise, indeed.

"You don't give yourself, your strength, enough credit, queen. But at some point, you're going to have to stop running and face Noah and your father. Trying to wait out Noah won't give you the closure you need, and it won't save your father from hurt feelings."

Her head jerked back, but the reflexive action didn't dislodge Adam's hand.

"What? I don't—" When he arched an eyebrow, the rest of the objection, *the lie*, died a swift death. "I didn't say anything about hurting my dad," she settled on.

"You didn't have to. Anyone with eyes or ears would see or hear how much you love him. And isn't it only natural for a daughter to want to protect their father? He raised you, loved you, was always there for you. Of course you wouldn't want him to feel slighted because you might want to get to know Noah."

"It feels like a betrayal," she whispered, her lashes lowering. How had he explained with unerring insight the guilt swimming inside her? "He stayed. He deserves my loyalty. He and Moe gave me everything—not just a home, but a safe space. That I have this sense of, of missing something or someone isn't fair. It's not right. Especially when that someone voluntarily left me and then chose to remain out of my life."

Adam sighed and pulled her closer, both arms around her, and panic flared in her chest. This felt too right, too…necessary. When had that happened?

She pressed her cheek to his chest and inhaled a breath, taking his heady scent into her lungs. It didn't make sense that his now-familiar fragrance pushed back the serrated edges of the panic. Not when he was the source of that almost paralyzing fear.

"When my father started dating my sister's mother, and then married her, I didn't want to like her. But I couldn't help but fall in love with her. For the years she was with my father, she mothered me. Gave me the affection and emotional support that my father is incapable of offering. At nine, ten years old, the guilt ate me alive. Yes, I was angry with my mother for not coming back for me, for just disappearing out of my life. But I missed her. I still do. That's human, isn't it? *You're* human. Still loving Noah for the person he was in your life—and maybe the person he could be in your life—doesn't diminish your love for your father in any way. Honestly? It just says a lot about who you are. That in a world that seems to delight in hate and greed, your heart is capable of so much love, selflessness and forgiveness. It makes you even more special."

Tears stung her eyes, and *dammit*, she detested crying. Hadn't she been vulnerable enough around this man?

"Have you ever tried to find your mom? To find out what happened and get your own closure?" she asked, desperate to turn the conversation away from her. Even if for a few seconds.

The long pause had her belly plummeting, and before he answered, she already knew what he would say.

"She died. After I graduated college, I searched for her. Hired someone to locate her. It took almost a year, but when I finally did, she'd been dead for six months. Car accident."

She gasped. "Oh my God, Adam," she breathed. "I'm so sorry. I didn't mean... I—"

"Shh." He squeezed her back, and her clumsy effort at an apology halted. "It's okay. For a long time it bothered me that I just missed seeing her, talking to her again. But I've made my peace with it. But you have the chance I didn't, queen. Understand me, though. It doesn't mean you have to forge a relationship with Noah or even invite him to be a part of your life, if that ends up being something you don't want. It's about getting answers for yourself. It's about closing out a chapter so you're not left with that feeling of something missing."

A pang still throbbed in her chest for him and his

mother. For the missed opportunity for reconciliation or perhaps, just answers.

Her own arms tightened around him, and as if he understood what she tried to convey, he brushed his lips across her forehead.

"Daddy! Flo!"

Flo lifted her head, her body bracing just seconds before Justine's little frame barreled into both her and Adam. Her arms locked around their thighs, and she tipped her head back, grinning up at them.

A wave of relief washed over Flo like an ice-cold deluge.

She'd been falling deeper into Adam, a connection she hadn't expected or desired, weaving around them on this dance floor. Any longer and she might start wondering, wishing, for the impossible...

Glancing away from him, she focused on Justine with a grim determination as if she were a lifeline thrown to Flo to keep her from drowning.

"Hey, baby girl," Adam said, loosening his arms from around Flo and turning to his daughter. "You didn't come over here by yourself, did you?"

"Uh-uh." Justine whipped around and pointed toward the edge of the dance area. "Nessie walked with me."

Flo looked in the direction Justine indicated, and Nessa waved at them, her other hand clasping Everett's, her and Wolf's son. From the short distance separating them, Flo caught the speculative glance from her to Adam.

Great. Flo silently groaned. There would no doubt be an inquisition later.

"Okay, good. Remember, no going off by yourself," Adam reminded Justine, who nodded so hard, her twists swung around her face.

"I 'member, Daddy." She grinned again, and it lit up

her face. Throwing her arms wide, she spun in a circle. In spite of the confusion still swarming inside her, Flo smiled at the little girl's antics. Damn, she was so cute. "I played in the castle and went on the slide and played with Ev'rett and Bella and 'Tience." Justine twirled again while Flo ran the stream of words through her head, making sense of it. *Oh.* 'Tience must be Patience. She swallowed a snicker. "I'm hungry, Daddy," Justine bluntly announced, switching gears. "Nessie said I can eat with them. Can I?"

Because she was, no doubt, shamelessly eavesdropping, Nessa waved at them again.

"I don't mind," she called out. "Really. What's one more plate? Or kid?"

Adam smiled at her. "Thank you, but I'm coming. And thank you for bringing her over."

"Sure thing." Nessa and Everett waved goodbye to Justine and walked off.

"Daddy, I love it here," Justine declared, flinging her arms around his legs once more. "I have friends and I don't want to leave! Can we live here now?"

Why Justine's question slammed into Flo's chest like a Thor-size fist, she didn't care to analyze. Not here. Not with Adam's gaze shuttered and unreadable.

"Jussy, we're just visiting here for my job. Like the other places we've been. But home is in Chicago, with Auntie Addie. And you have friends there, too, that you would miss."

"How come Auntie Addie can't come here?" Justine insisted, a frown clouding her small face. "I love it here."

Whoa boy.

In the time she'd known Justine, Flo had never seen the girl throw a tantrum, but it seemed like one might be looming.

"Hey, Jussy," Flo said, deliberately keeping her voice calm. And when the little girl looked at her, that frown still in place, Flo tugged on one of her twists. "You still have plenty of time here in Rose Bend. And I know Bella, Patience and Everett would love to play with you some more. How about we go eat with them now? Then I can talk to Nessie about having them over to your house for a playdate? We can do ice cream and movies," she suggested.

Jussy's face cleared like the sun breaking through storm clouds. She brightened with another grin, and twisting her body in a too-adorable dance, she yelled, "Yeah! Can we watch *The Little Mermaid*?"

Flo scoffed. "Of course!" Holding up her hand, palm out, she waited for Justine to give her a high five. "Now, let's go eat."

"Okay!" She skipped the couple of steps to stand between Flo and Adam and grabbed both of their hands, swinging them. "Let's go!"

Not being given much of a choice, they walked off the dance floor while Justine continued to skip and chatter away.

"Thank you for that," Adam murmured low enough that his daughter didn't overhear.

Flo forced a smile, and damn if it didn't feel strained. And damn if his suddenly sharp and narrowed gaze didn't catch it.

"You're welcome," she said, ignoring the question in those hazel eyes. "I guess I should've asked you first if a playdate with the other kids is okay. I mean, bringing them all over to your place."

"It's fine. She'll enjoy it," he replied. Even though she purposefully stared ahead on the pretense of scanning the throngs of people, his scrutiny seemed to scorch her skin.

"I'm hungry," Justine announced again, louder this time, tugging on their hands and shifting her father's attention away from Flo.

Saved by the child.

Again.

But why did this only feel like a reprieve?

CHAPTER FOURTEEN

ADAM SIGHED AS he pulled the door to Justine's bedroom closed, leaving it open just a crack.

Finally.

After the full day at the town picnic, she should've been knocked out as soon as her head hit the pillow. But no. All the fun and excitement of the day seemed to have worked like a sugar high, and it'd taken three stories and a firm warning before she eventually fell asleep. Now that she was, though, it would require an earthquake to wake her. And only if it was about an eight on the Richter scale.

He paused outside her bedroom, his hand still gripping the doorknob.

I don't want to leave! Can we live here now?

Unbidden, Justine's words from earlier echoed in his head. And like then, unease rippled through him like a crack spiderwebbing across a windshield. Why did it affect him so much? Rose Bend wasn't the first town his daughter had liked. Wasn't even the first one she'd declared their new home.

But it was the first one that had ever tempted him to want the same thing.

Even as the words entered his mind, he flung them out, shaking his head as if that would make sure the traitorous, ridiculous thought wouldn't dare return.

Yes, this place had its charm, but just like when every

job ended, he and Justine would leave and return home.
To Chicago.

"Shit," he murmured, scrubbing a hand down his face
then over his head.

At the picnic, Flo had diverted Justine's potential tantrum like a pro. Like everything she did with his daughter. There was no denying the connection they shared;
Justine adored Flo, and from what he could see, the feeling was more than mutual.

When it came time to leave, that close relationship
would only make it harder to go.

Not just for Justine.

No, he couldn't deny that, either. It wouldn't only be
his daughter who would find it difficult not to look back.
But that didn't change the future. Didn't change the reasons why they wouldn't work in the long-term. He and
Flo might burn like fire together, but that wasn't a foun-
dation for a solid, lasting relationship or conducive to
providing a secure, nurturing environment for Justine.

Keep telling yourself that.

Damn, it was time to go to bed. Maybe his brain would
shut the hell up once he was asleep.

Striding down the hall, he returned to the living room,
turning off the lights for the night. As he flipped the
switch in the kitchen, a knock sounded on the front door.
Frowning, he paused, his hand still on the wall.

It was a little after nine. Who could be on his doorstep? And why? Everyone with the renovation and TV
crew had been at the picnic, so this couldn't be a work
emergency. He moved forward, the questions whirling
in his head.

Because you could take the man out of Chicago, but
not Chicago out of the man, he paused at the front door,
hand on the doorknob and peered through the peephole.

Shock rocked through him, and for a long moment, he stood there, staring at his side of the door. Blinking, he shook his head and quickly opened it.

"Flo," he greeted, unable to keep his surprise from his voice. "Is everything okay?"

"Yes." Pause. "No."

He arched an eyebrow and scanned her. Still dressed in the dark green, long-sleeved shirt and wide-legged jeans she'd worn at the picnic earlier, he didn't notice any obvious signs of injury or hurt. But when he raised his gaze back to hers, he caught a glimpse of what might have brought her to his doorstep tonight.

"You want to come in?" he asked, and the need reflected in her eyes churned inside him. Roughened his voice.

She stared at him, hesitated. Then...

"Yes," she whispered.

He shifted back a step, silently inviting her in. And she didn't hesitate to enter.

For a moment he closed his eyes, her jasmine-and-cedarwood fragrance teasing him, tempting him. Slowly, he shut the door, acknowledging that he was probably making his biggest mistake yet by letting her into the house.

Letting her into the house when just the sight and scent of her had his cock hardening and his heart pounding.

Nothing good could come from this visit. Nothing.

And yet, he followed her into the living room, studying the elegant line of her back, the flare of her hips, that proud, sensual stride. On that dance floor he'd felt branded by her tight, curvy body pressed to his. Even now his palms tingled with the sensory memory of touching her.

Flo paused next to the couch, her fingers trailing along

the arm. Was she thinking about what happened the last time they were together on that couch? Because hell, he couldn't walk past his living room without picturing it, feeling it.

"Thank you," she murmured.

He didn't need to ask what she thanked him for; because of that connection he didn't want to reflect on, he understood.

The dance. Listening to her. The conversation.

Jesus, Flo had been seconds from breaking him.

This beautiful, strong woman had allowed him to see her at her most vulnerable. Had clung to him. She'd allowed him to comfort her.

And *she* thanked *him*?

No, it should be the other way around. She'd blessed him with a gift.

"Is everything okay?" he asked again. "Did something happen with your family?"

"No." She huffed out a short chuckle. "You don't have to worry. There haven't been any more meltdowns."

"Is that why you're here?" he pressed, stepping forward. Damn, he hadn't intended to. He'd ordered himself to maintain distance, because that lowered the possibility of him getting his hands on her. But everything in him called to her, craved to be close because Florence Dennison fascinated him as much as she made his dick ache. It triggered his flight-or-fight response. And God help them both, he wasn't running. "Are you looking for a father figure in me?" He moved closer. "Because your gratitude isn't something I want."

She studied him, not responding to his this-side-of-rude jab. Staring down into those dark brown eyes, he suspected she deciphered the verbal swipe for what it was—self-preservation. A defense.

This time she took the step forward. And another. And another.

And didn't stop until her toes nudged his. Until their thighs and chests nearly brushed.

Until his cock nearly grazed her belly.

"I don't have daddy issues. I have two fathers, actually, and I don't need another one." She tilted her head. "I came here because I was lying in my bed, and it was too big, too empty. And here with you, it's not empty… I'm not alone."

Dammit. He locked down a growl that worked its way up his chest.

"What's not empty, queen?" he pushed.

"Your bed." She lifted a hand and clasped his, placing it low on her belly. "Me."

He crushed his mouth to hers. Her lips immediately parted under his thrusting tongue, and he dove deeper for more. Always more. God, she was…fucking phenomenal. He didn't have another word to effectively define the headiness of each thrust, lick, moan…

Lifting his hand to her locs, he threaded his fingers through them, dragging his nails over her scalp, cupping her head. She tilted, her lips parting wider, granting him deeper access. And he took full advantage, each stroke and suck granting her a preview of how he intended to fuck her.

Wild, hard and with complete possession.

Belatedly remembering he had a sleeping child under his roof, he reluctantly stepped back, but only to grab her hand in his and tug her down the hall to his bedroom. Once behind the closed door, he didn't waste time stripping her of her clothes. Yes, he'd seen her naked before, but goddamn, his memory must've faded over time because her beauty struck him in the chest as if it was the first time he was seeing her.

Gorgeous.

Glorious.

She was pure beauty wrapped in skin and bone. Created for the sole purpose of him worshipping her. And yeah, that sounded narcissistic, but he couldn't erase the thought. Couldn't evict the overpowering need to kneel before her and take what was his. At least his for tonight. Or however long she allowed.

He dipped his head, sucking her breast into his mouth, worrying the nipple with his teeth. She gasped above him, her groans driving him on, and he gave her a moan in return, continuing to flick and lick the beaded tip.

Impatient, he switched to the other tip, sweeping the flat of his tongue over her flesh, treating it to the same devotion he'd lavished on its twin. She trembled against him, her hands gripping his hair, yanking and sending sparks of pain and pleasure cascading down his spine, converging in his throbbing cock, tingling in his balls. Just her hands in his hair and her nipple in his mouth, and he veered too fucking close to coming.

And he was nowhere near ready for this to end.

With one last, slow sweep over the tight tip, he lowered himself. Down her chest, over her belly... But before he could reach his destination, she shoved against his shoulders, stepping back.

"Wait," she gasped. "My turn."

Before he could stop her, she dropped to her knees and had the button and zipper of his jeans open.

His heart damn near stopped before it thudded in triple time.

"Queen." He covered her hand with his, squeezing even

as lust burned a pathway through him, straight to where her mouth hovered above. "You don't have to do this."

But she shook her head.

"I know it. I don't have to do anything. I want it. I want you in my mouth, down my throat."

A shudder quaked through him, and his hand fell to his side, signaling she could have her way. Because, God, he wanted her to. *Needed* her to.

The hushed echo of his zipper lowering reverberated in the room. His chest rose and fell on harsh inhales, and his hand tunneled through her hair. And he stilled as she reached inside his jeans and boxer briefs, freeing his cock.

He glanced down, unable to *not* look at his erection appearing almost brutal in her small hand. And there was no way in hell he could look away as she arrowed him toward her waiting mouth.

Goddamn.

Fierce primal lust slammed into him as he sank into her warm, wet, willing mouth. His hunger for her surpassed anything as ephemeral as food. This was deeper, rawer.

She gripped him, pumping the lower half of his rigid flesh. His hips bucked and she hummed, the sound a mind-bending vibration up his cock, to his nuts and sizzling down his legs to the soles of his feet.

"Oh *damn*." He groaned, his grip on her locs tightening, and he pulled her closer, silently ordering her to take more, suck more. Fucking devastate him.

With a whimper, she set about doing just that. She bobbed her head over him, mouth bumping her fist before she withdrew, the drag of her tongue the loveliest and most insane pleasure. She traced the vein running along the length, circling the hood before teasing the tender spot tucked beneath.

Adam cursed again, and as if his reaction spurred her on, she swallowed more of him. The head nudged the narrow opening of her throat, and she gagged a little, pulling back before returning for another try. She relaxed the muscles in her throat and exhaled through her nose. And he slid back in until the tip slipped into the tight channel.

"That's so good," he praised, voice thick, rough. He grunted, repeating the stroke, going deeper. Losing some of his sanity along with his control.

She grabbed his hips, and he let go, fucking her mouth, trying to be gentle, but feared he wasn't. Not that she seemed to mind. No, she simply held and let him work out his lust on her. And when pleasure crackled and snapped down his spine, he jerked free, his breath loud bursts of air in the otherwise quiet room. He curved his hands underneath her arms and tugged her to her feet, ignoring her mewl of protest.

"I want inside you, queen. It's been too long. And I need to remind myself that reality is much better than fantasy."

He covered her mouth once more and walked her backward to the bed. When the backs of her legs hit the mattress, he bent and rearranged her on top of the covers. Then tore his clothes from his body, anxious to feel her smooth skin next to his. Feel that slim, curvy body pressed to his.

Be buried inside that hot, tight flesh between her thighs.

He climbed onto the bed, in between her spread thighs. Glistening, swollen flesh greeted him, and he couldn't resist dipping between her folds, gathering the evidence of her desire on his finger. Her soft gasp punctuated the silence, and he slid his finger between his lips, savoring the taste of her.

She stared at him as he sucked her clean from his skin, eyes glazed, lips swollen from not just his kiss but his cock. Brutal desire lanced him, and he slapped his hands on either side of her head. And with his gaze locked with hers, he slid deep inside her.

Twin groans rose from both of them.

She curled her arms around his neck, clinging to him, her smaller frame shivering beneath him, her pussy spasming around his cock. He fought the urge to thrust inside her like a wild thing. Grinding his teeth, he held still, letting her become accustomed to his possession. Again.

It was torture. And the utmost pleasure. She branded him. Claimed him. And in this moment, he felt…complete.

"Let me know when you're ready, queen." He continued to hold still above her and vowed to stay right there. Even if the effort, the ecstasy of being buried inside her, killed him.

And hell, it just might.

Bending his head, he took her mouth, kissed her for several long moments. Her slick feminine muscles rippled around his length, and soon she shifted restlessly beneath him, silently pleading for him to move.

Then she whispered, "Move."

Groaning with a wealth of gratitude and relief, he withdrew until only the tip of him remained inside then thrust, burying his entire length. She cried out, lifting her legs and locking them around his waist, her feet riding just above his ass. He rode her hard, and the erotic sounds of skin slapping against skin filled the room. His moans and her soft whimpers provided the accompanying soundtrack.

A cry tore from her, and he slammed his mouth over

hers once more to stifle the sound. Her sex clamped down on him, milking his cock, hauling him to the precipice to fall after her. Gritting his teeth, he continued to stroke and thrust through her orgasm, grinding the base of his dick against her clit. Before he gave in to this pleasure that clawed at him, he'd make sure she claimed every second of hers.

Only when the shudders wracking her body started to subside did he let go. He pistoned into her again and again. But on that fourth stroke, he came, release slamming into him like a sledgehammer. Ecstasy tore through him, robbing him of breath, and he gave her his muted roar. She took his as he'd taken her scream.

And as he completely surrendered to the pleasure, to *her*, he couldn't find room for regret.

Maybe tomorrow.

But not now in her arms and body.

"I SHOULD'VE LEFT last night or early this morning," Flo muttered.

Adam flipped the pancakes before glancing over his shoulder at her and smiling at her disgruntled expression. Her slight frown and pout didn't conceal the discomfort in her eyes, though.

Aside from the puffiness of her mouth and the faint smudges under her eyes from a night spent with more sex than sleep, she looked fine. Mostly *not* like she'd spent most of the night having more sex than sleep.

And that was her worry.

"C'mere." He beckoned her close with a curl of his fingers, and given this was Flo, there stood a chance she would resist purely on the basis of being ordered. But it just showed the level of her nerves that she crossed the kitchen and approached him. Twisting the flames off from under the pan, he reached for her. "It's fine. *You're* fine," he murmured against the top of her head, wrapping an arm around her shoulders.

"I just don't want Jussy to be confused or uncomfortable in her own house. I mean, I don't know how she would take me..." She waved her fingers back and forth between them. "Staying over," she finished softly.

That her first concern was his daughter's comfort and welfare squeezed the hell out of his chest, almost to the point of pain. He pulled her closer, tighter, and just held her. And locked his jaw, forcibly trapping the words that wanted to tumble free.

You're so fucking special.

Stay.

And not just for Jussy, but for me.

"Jussy will just assume you arrived this morning like you do when we have to work. Hell, she's happier to see you than me." He leaned back, cupping her face. "Stay for breakfast, Flo," he murmured and pressed a kiss to her lips. "Stay."

A breath shuddered out, whispering across his mouth.

"Okay. I'll stay."

"Pancakes!" Just as Justine darted down the hall in her pajamas and skidded into the kitchen, Flo stepped back, inserting space between them. "Flo!" Justine yelled and then launched herself at, apparently, her favorite person in the room. "Pancakes and Flo!"

Adam chuckled, turning back to the pan and moving the perfectly round—if he said so himself—pancakes onto the platter with the growing stack.

"Do I get one of those hugs?" he teased his daughter. "I am the one cooking breakfast."

"Hi, Daddy!" Justine released Flo and skipped to him. Adam stepped forward so she wasn't near the hot stove, and he scooped her up in his arms, hugging her until she squealed with laughter.

Then he smacked a kiss on her cheek and set her back down on her feet.

"Ready to eat?"

Justine yelled—as usual—her agreement, and Flo helped her sit in a chair at the small dining table while he carried platters of pancakes, bacon and scrambled eggs.

"This looks delicious," Flo said, smiling at him as she served up food on Justine's plate. "Thank you."

"You're welcome." He pulled his chair out, but just as he sat down, the doorbell rang.

He glanced toward the living room and in the direction of the front door with a frown. Two visitors in the matter of twelve hours. Flo had been a pleasant and welcome surprise. But who else would drop by unannounced? And early on a Sunday morning, too?

"Be right back," he said, sliding his chair back under the table and heading for the door.

Behind him, Justine and Flo kept up a running conversation, and he couldn't help but smile at his daughter's lighter chatter and Flo's lower, huskier tone. Justine was a cheerful child, but hearing her laughter... There wasn't a more beautiful sound for a father to hear.

And Flo's sultrier chuckle? There wasn't a more beautiful sound for a man to hear.

Maybe because his attention was back at the dining table with Flo and Justine, he didn't check the peephole. Maybe because the two people who should be in his house were there, and he wasn't much concerned about who stood on the porch, he didn't bother carrying out his usual precautionary peek.

Either way, he'd never forget again.

Not when he pulled open the door and the very last person he expected to see stood on his doorstep wearing a carefree grin.

"Hi, Adam. Surprise," his ex-wife greeted.

Fuck.

CHAPTER FIFTEEN

FLO RAISED HER CAMERA, focused the lens and captured the beauty of the morning sun streaming through the large bay windows of the cavernous rustic kitchen. It hit the brick-and-stone wall with its arch over a brand-new stainless steel stove; the forest green cabinetry with their glass fronts; the gleaming wood countertops and the brown tile flooring. A matching island sat in the middle of the floor.

It was a gorgeous room, she thought, snapping picture after picture—from the recessed ceiling with its hanging domed light fixtures to the farmhouse sink and shale countertops. It was hard to believe that just two weeks earlier, this space had been completely gutted with wiring hanging from the ceiling and walls. The before and after images were going to be stunning side by side.

She lowered her camera, scrolling through the digital pictures she'd taken in the last half hour. Without any effort, she could easily imagine what the room would look like with a small table and chairs tucked in the breakfast nook, copper pans and pots hanging on iron hooks… She'd adored this house for years, but now she was downright in love with it.

"This might be my favorite room."

She stiffened, her pulse echoing in her ears. But she didn't turn around. "Mine, too," she said, proud that her voice was level, even pleasant.

Some would say *unbothered*. But God, she was so *bothered*.

Adam's footsteps fell against the tile floor, and she still didn't turn around, though the urge rode her hard. Adam walking, moving, was all sensual grace. A symphony, melody in motion. She held firm, but when he stopped behind her, his body heat damn near scalded her.

Okay, so that was her imagination, but she had an active one. And it provided her with every detail of his stunning face with its bold angles, carnal curves and golden eyes. Of his wide shoulders, broad chest and powerful, thick thighs.

God, even her hurt and confusion couldn't compete against the desire he never ceased to stir. She was as predictable as the sun rising in the east. If Adam was within five feet of her, her body heated like a furnace.

Dammit.

"Flo," Adam said, that whiskey-and-midnight voice a caress over her skin. "You didn't come by the house this morning."

Was he kidding? He *had* to be.

The last time she'd been at his home, it'd been the most awkward "morning after" in history as his ex-wife sailed inside like she rented the place with him. Like she belonged there. And maybe she did. More than Flo, that was certain. Adam, Justine—they were her family, not Flo's. And the delighted squeal of "Mommy!" as Justine leaped down from her chair, raced across the room and threw herself into her mother's outstretched arms solidified that.

Of course the little girl would be thrilled to see the mother she hadn't been with in so long. And God, what did it say about Flo that jealousy had wormed its way through her? That she'd been hurt? Maybe she was as immature as he'd once called her.

This was why she didn't get attached, didn't get invested.

Emotions were messy and ugly.

And she sucked at them.

"Justine's mom is here. I didn't want to intrude on their time together." Didn't want to appear like the desperate… whatever she and Adam were, who didn't know where she stood with him or his daughter.

She kept her attention focused on the digital screen. Scrolling, scrolling. But not really seeing anything. Avoiding looking at him, so he didn't see the doubts that had been crawling through her since yesterday morning.

It'd been hell.

Hell, knowing he was alone with the woman he had so much history with.

Hell, knowing she could do nothing if the old chemistry that had brought them together—and kept them together for years—sparked again.

Hell, knowing her relationship with Justine might have come to an abrupt end.

Hell, knowing her heartache could have arrived much sooner than she believed.

"Flo," he murmured. "Will you look at me?"

No. Don't ask that of me.

God, she didn't want to, but she finally lifted her head and met his gaze. And prayed that the chaotic storm inside her wasn't reflected in her expression. He studied her, his scrutiny roaming over her face as if searching for…for what?

"I'm sorry," he said.

She shook her head. "There's nothing for you to apologize for, Adam."

"Yes, there is," he countered. "Yesterday did not go—" he paused, his full lips momentarily flattening "—anything like how I planned or imagined. And I feel like I put you in a very—" another pause, another grim firming of his mouth "—uncomfortable position. For that, I'm sorry."

"It's fine," she said, flicking her fingers and waving off his apology. "The most important thing is that Justine has time with her mother. She's really missed her."

"Yeah." That piercing gaze didn't move from her, and the plea for him to look away, to leave her some pride, some privacy, scrambled to her tongue. "She's happy her mom is here. It's good that Jennifer came to see her."

"Definitely."

God, this was awkward. And painful.

"Flo," Adam rumbled.

"I need to get some more pictures in here then move on to the parlor. You probably need to get to work, too." She stepped forward. Away from him. "We'll ta—"

"She isn't staying at the house with me, Flo. I took her to your parents' inn after you left."

A weight lifted from her chest—one that had been pressing on her lungs since the day before. She inhaled and a tremble shook her. Relief. A cool, almost drunken sensation shuddered through her, damn near weakening her knees. And then instantly she felt bad and petty for it.

Adam wasn't hers to claim; they'd never discussed being that to each other. On the contrary, he'd told her she wasn't good partner material. Too young. Too ambitious. Too inexperienced. And yet... Yet, her mind, her body, her...heart weren't on the same page. It would cost her. She understood that. When he left, not looking back in just a few weeks, it would absolutely cost her.

"Thank you for telling me that," she murmured.

He nodded, and after a long moment where things unspoken hummed between them in a thick silence, he lifted a hand and brushed her locs back over her shoulder. That simple, small gesture slammed into her sternum like a hammer. Because it seemed as if he just *had* to touch her. She ducked her head, returning her gaze to her camera, otherwise he might glimpse just how much that caress affected her.

"How is Jussy doing?" Flo asked, missing her little partner in crime.

By now, ordinarily, they would be leaving the rental house, headed over to the renovation where she would take pictures along with Flo. In such a short time, Jussy had become a part of Flo's daily routine, and not having Jussy there only served as a harsh reminder that she needed to adjust. Whether it was now with Jennifer in town or when Adam and Jussy eventually left for Chicago, Flo would be without her.

"Fine. Good," he amended, sliding his hands into his front pants pockets. "I dropped her off at the inn to be with Jennifer today. They're supposed to do some shopping." He exhaled, dragging his fingers over his head. "Flo, I—"

Someone called for him from deeper in the house and a small growl rumbled out of him.

"Listen, I have to go see what's going on upstairs, but don't leave today without finding me, okay?"

"Sure," she agreed, about 73 percent certain she'd follow through on that promise.

Maybe he suspected, because his eyes narrowed on her, but he finally nodded, turned and left the kitchen.

And she breathed again.

"Hey, baby sister." Cole grinned at Flo as he climbed the front walk, and Flo shook her head, returning his smile.

Setting her camera on a tripod, she met him as he neared the porch steps, and her brother pulled her into a hug, smacking a kiss on the top of her head. For a moment she closed her eyes, leaning on his familiar strength, savoring the safety and comfort in her older brother's embrace.

"Hey, hey." Cole leaned back, cupping her upper arms. "I just came over to check out the progress of the renovation, but it looks like you need me more than that TV crew." He smiled, but his dark brown eyes flitted over her face as if seeking out answers she hadn't divulged. "What's wrong, Flo?"

A thick knot of emotion tightened around her throat, and she swallowed past it.

"Nothing. I'm good."

He arched an eyebrow. "Sure you are. C'mon." He slipped his arm around her shoulders, waiting until she grabbed her camera, and led her to the side of the house, away from the clatter and voices emanating from inside the Victorian. Once they stood some distance away, he removed his arm and faced her. "Now, tell me what's wrong. You've known me almost all your life, and you should know by now that I'm not going anywhere until you spill. And since I have to pick up your niece from school in about, oh—" he flipped his wrist up and peered down at his watch "—one hour, you should start talking or you'll have to face Sydney's wrath for leaving her daughter on the curb. And nobody wants that."

As he probably intended, she huffed out a laugh.

"No, we definitely don't want that," she agreed. Sydney could be feral about her kids and her husband. The word *honey badger* came to mind.

Slipping the camera strap around her head, Flo sighed and swept her palms over her hair. Now that she thought about it, who better to talk to about how she was feeling? And not just because he was her brother, a person who loved her and would never judge her. But because he married a woman who carried her ex-husband's baby. And they'd all found a way to coexist and co-parent in a healthy, supportive manner for Patience.

"I'm going to guess me telling you that I'm…involved with Adam Reed isn't a surprise to you." When his expression didn't change, she shook her head, loosing another chuckle. Finding a new portal to Narnia would be easier than keeping a secret in the Dennison family. "He's a single dad, and I've become close to his daughter, Justine."

Cole nodded. "Yeah, Moe mentioned you were watching over her as a favor for Adam. And I saw you two together at the picnic. She seems to really like you."

"I love her, Cole. At first, she was just the cutest and funniest kid. But soon, she captured my heart, and I…" She trailed off, clearing her throat. "Anyway, Adam and his ex-wife divorced two years ago, and for the most part, she hasn't been present in Jussy's daily life. But she showed up at his house yesterday morning."

"And you were there?" Cole asked, both eyebrows arched now.

She grimaced. "Yes."

"Whew. Awkwaaard," he sang. When she winced again, Cole snorted. "But you don't need me to tell you that."

"I don't. Now, let's move along," she said. "I…care for Adam—"

"Uh-huh." Cole shook his head. "Care for him? Oh,

you're definitely my sister. The denial is strong in this family."

Ignoring him because she was not ready to even get near that comment or the connotation behind it, she continued, "I know he's leaving once this TV show wraps and the house is done. I have no claim on him, no rights to him, but…"

"But you would like to wrap that little girl up in your arms and yell, 'Mine. Stay away.'"

She blinked at her brother, then she gave him a small smile, rueful. "Damn. Am I that transparent? Or pathetic? Probably both, right?"

"No." He shrugged a shoulder and returned her smile. "None of that. I've just been exactly where you are, and you know that. Which is why I think you're talking to me instead of say, Leo, who would go scorched earth that her little sister's feelings are hurt, or Sinead, who would most likely give you her legal opinion—then offer ways around it. And of course, Wolf, who would just hug you."

Despite the subject matter—and the guilt clawing a hole in her chest—she laughed, and the loud crack of it echoed between them. This. This was why she loved her family, cherished them.

"Facts." She grinned. "All facts."

Smiling, he tipped his head back, squinting up at the sky before lowering his chin and looking at her again.

"One thing you should never apologize for is loving that little girl. No child can ever have too much love. Never." He cocked his head. "When Sydney and I married, I didn't expect to bond with Patience. I still grieved for Tonia and Matteo, and I didn't want to love her baby because one, it felt like a betrayal to the wife and son I'd lost. And second, I refused to get attached to another child because the pain of losing my own almost broke me."

Flo had been younger when Sydney first returned to town and she and Cole got together, but she remembered the grieving, lost man he'd been. And how he'd emotionally shut a part of himself down. She also recalled how the town's rebel and her baby girl had brought him back.

"But I came to love Patience like my own. She *is* my own. That's my little girl. There's no *step*daughter when it comes to her. She's just my daughter. But she had a biological father who not only wanted to be in the picture, but desired an active role in her life. Though I was married to Sydney, though I was there every day, and I knew Sydney loved me, I felt threatened." His gaze unfocused as if he stared back into the years when his marriage and fatherhood had been new. "What if Patience loved Daniel more? What if she didn't need me? What if Sydney saw him and realized that being with Patience's biological father would be best for all of them? Didn't matter that Daniel was married as well, I was scared of losing the joy and happiness that I'd found."

"I didn't know any of this," Flo whispered.

"It was tough to admit it to myself much less Sydney. I felt small, petty. I mean, who begrudges their child a relationship with their father? And yet, I wanted to be Daddy. I wanted to be the one she ran to, shouting my name when I came home from work. I wanted to be her superhero. And I didn't want to share that special place with anyone."

God, he nailed exactly how she felt. And it didn't matter that she'd only known Justine for weeks. The little girl had burrowed inside her heart, and there was no excavating her out.

"What did you do? How did you get over it?"

Cole huffed out a chuckle and raked his fingers through his dark curls.

"I can't lie, it wasn't easy at first. But Flo, children have the most amazing capacity to love. It's awe-inspiring. And we can learn so much from them—it's also why we have to protect them. They don't understand the concept of compartmentalizing affection. They just give and give. Patience loved me just as much as Daniel. Just as much as Sydney. For her, it was the more, the merrier." He softly laughed. "Daniel's Dad, and I'm Daddy. And I'm betting Justine is the same. Your relationship with her is newer, but in her childlike heart, loving her mother doesn't subtract from her affection for you. That heart just expands to include all of you. Now, as far as you and Adam…"

Cole studied her for several long moments, and he reached out, clasped her hand in his and squeezed.

"Flo, you can't let your fear be greater than your hope. Hope propels you forward even when your situation looks to be at its worst. It won't let you quit or give up on your dreams, your aspirations. Hope will let you love. But fear will hold you prisoner, won't let you trust. Fear is a cage and love picks the lock. Don't be afraid to love, little sister. It will set you free to truly live."

Don't be afraid to love.

So simple yet such a huge ask. But… An image that she hadn't allowed herself to picture wavered across her mind. Hope—that hope Cole spoke of—whispered through her like dandelion seeds floating on a summer wind. Scattered, delicate, but undeniable.

"Flo!" The high-pitched and happy yell echoed across the front lawn, reaching her and Cole.

And hearing it, Flo couldn't contain the smile that curved her mouth or the delight that bloomed behind her breastbone.

"Oh yeah. You're in love," Cole murmured, turning as Justine raced up the hill, her little legs and arms pumping as she ran toward them.

Flo knelt, arms open, and caught Justine when she crashed into her, thin arms wrapping around Flo's neck. Laughing, Flo hugged her, that little-girl scent of hers another embrace.

"Hey, Jussy," Flo greeted her.

"Hi, Flo! I missed you!" Justine palmed Flo's face on either side and smooshed her lips together. "You didn't come see me today."

Laughing, Flo squished Justine's face, too. The little girl giggled then gave Flo another hug, setting her head on Flo's shoulder. Love swelled in her chest, and she tightened her own arms around Justine.

"I'm sorry, sweetie. You know I love hanging out with you. But I wanted to give you and your mom special time together. I missed you." Flo tickled her belly, and that bright laughter broke through Flo's saddest, loneliest thoughts like dawn cresting for a new day.

"The famous Flo. Again."

Flo slightly stiffened at the new voice. True, she'd only heard it once before, but it was emblazoned on her memory. She didn't see Cole behind her, but she felt him move closer.

Slowly rising, Flo faced Adam's ex-wife, Jennifer.

She was a beautiful woman. Tall, curvy, with thick, natural curls, Flo could easily envision her and Adam together. Justine had her beautiful dark brown, thickly lashed eyes and her fine bone structure. Though Jennifer wore a polite smile, it didn't reach her eyes. They were hard, wary.

Jennifer Reed was not here to make nice.

"Hi, Jennifer. It's nice to see you again," Flo said,

keeping her voice even, pleasant. "This is my brother, Cole Dennison. Cole, this is Justine's mother, Jennifer."

A gleam entered Jennifer's gaze when she turned to Cole, the hard brown softening to a warm chocolate.

Sorry, sis. He's taken and his wife don't play about that one.

"It's a pleasure to meet you." Cole stretched his hand toward her, briefly shaking it then extricating his fingers from hers.

"Cole, is it?" Jennifer said with a bigger smile. "The pleasure is all mine."

He shifted, turning to Flo with the corner of his mouth twitching.

"I'm going to head inside and check out the progress. I'll talk to you later, okay?"

"Okay, thanks for…everything," she murmured as he pulled her in for a quick hug.

"You got it. Anytime. And I mean that." Releasing her, he looked down at Justine and grinned. "Hey, Jussy. Do you want to come with me and see your dad?"

He held his hand out and Justine immediately slipped hers into his.

"Yeah," she crowed. "I want to tell Daddy about my ice cream and my new shoes…"

She continued reciting the list of her new purchases as Cole led her toward the house, leaving Flo alone with Jennifer. When she looked at the other woman again, that overly polite smile had reappeared, as did the flint in her eyes.

"I have to thank your brother," Jennifer said. "I was hoping to have some time alone to speak with you. Jussy talks about you so much. On the phone and today. Flo, this. Flo, that. I was beginning to think you were a myth."

"No, flesh and blood." Flo itched to cross her arms,

but she forced them down by her sides, not wanting to appear defensive. But the ice in the other woman's stare definitely gave her a chill. "We've been spending a lot of time together since Adam's childcare fell through. I offered to watch over her."

God, why did she now sound like she was making excuses for her relationship with Justine? She didn't have anything to be apologetic about, especially with Jennifer.

"That was sweet of you." Jennifer's gaze dropped to the camera in Flo's hands. "Jussy mentioned something about pictures. I thought you were a photographer, not a nanny."

You can't curse out Justine's mother. You can't curse out Justine's mother.

"One doesn't prevent me from doing the other." She deserved a medal for how calm she sounded. And a place in heaven for not snapping.

"Hmm." Jennifer glanced toward the Victorian then, moments later, shifted her attention back to Flo. "It's a beautiful house. But Adam was always the best at his work. All that traveling, though. Here, in one place for a couple of months, then it's somewhere else for another few weeks…"

Okay, she'd never been one for games, and this was getting on her nerves. She'd tried to be polite; she really had. But Jennifer obviously had an agenda showing up not just in Rose Bend but here, at Adam and Flo's job. Maybe she needed help getting to the point.

Flo had always believed in helping others.

"Jennifer, I don't know you, but I sense there's a reason you wanted to talk to me. It would save us both a lot of time and uncomfortable small talk if you just came out and aired what you need to say."

Surprise flashed in the other woman's eyes, and her

chin jerked the smallest amount. But then, she recovered and tilted her head, considering Flo.

"That's fair, and you're right. I don't really care what you're doing with Adam or who you are to him. A warning from one woman to another, though? He doesn't stay so don't pin your hopes on having anything past the length of time it takes for him to put up the last sheet of drywall." Her smile vanished. "My concern is my daughter. She already likes you, and from what I saw yesterday, you've graduated to overnights. It's cruel to let her get attached when we both know she'll be crushed when she and Adam leave. Maybe it would be best for her if you stopped coming around so much. It would definitely be kinder."

"You mean best for you," Flo quietly said.

Again, Jennifer's head jerked, and she snapped, "Excuse me?"

"I said, you mean what would be best for you," Flo reiterated.

"I don't believe this." Jennifer huffed out an incredulous chuckle, crossing her arms. "You don't know me or my family."

Flo shook her head. "Like you said, that's fair. But I don't need to be friends with you to understand that you'd rather I spend less time with Jussy because it would make you feel more secure." Which was completely ironic since not moments ago, she'd had the same conversation with Cole. Huh. Turned out she and Jennifer had more in common than she thought. "And I get it. But I'm not going to abandon her so you can feel better."

"Who do you think you're talking to? I'm that girl's mother," Jennifer snarled, jabbing a finger in her own chest.

"Then act like it," Flo snapped, losing her temper.

"I'm not her mother, and I would never want to take your place."

"You couldn't ever take my place—"

"And I don't want to. She loves her mother—loves you so much. But she's not a toy you can just take down off the shelf, play with, then drop and forget about it. Am I her mother? No," Flo ground out, taking a step closer to Jennifer, invading her personal space and not giving one damn if it came off as aggressive. Hell, she burned with *aggression*. "But I know what it is to be motherless. To have the parent you adore, the rock that's your port in a confusing and chaotic world, disappear. Your daughter has her father, but she needs you. There's nothing like a mother's hug. A mother telling you how pretty you are, how smart you are. There's nothing like your mother's lap to crawl up on and curl against her chest. There's nothing like your mother's scent that you will know even when she's gone…"

Air heaved in and out of her lungs, and unexpected tears stung her eyes. Memories—both real and imagined—from her mother and Moe bombarded her, washed over her, but not dragging her under. Buoying her up. For too long she'd carried anger and loss when she thought of her biological mother. But she'd never stopped to think about what she *gave* her.

She brought her to Rose Bend.

Gifted her with a family that welcomed her and eventually raised her.

Gifted her with parents who loved her as much as she did, as she would've if she'd lived.

Gifted her with a…father who gave her a community, a family, parents…

Her mother had never left her. She lived on through the beauty she'd brought to Flo's life.

Flo inhaled a breath, and though it was fanciful and illogical, it felt like the first one she'd drawn in years. More years than she could count.

"Justine needs that. She deserves that. She deserves *you*," she finished, voice hoarse with newfound revelations and emotions rioting inside her.

Silence.

Then, "Are you okay?" Jennifer softly asked, the edge gone from her voice.

Flo shook her head and said, "Yes."

A wry smile quirked Jennifer's mouth. "You just shook your head no while saying yes. I believe Iyanla would call that leakage."

Clearing her throat, Flo gave the other woman a small smile in return.

"You watch Iyanla Vazant? Don't tell me we have something in common."

"Girl, you have no idea how many times I've come close to calling and asking her to *Fix My Life*."

Flo snorted, then laughed. And miracle of miracles, Jennifer joined her, and the two of them just stood there on the side lawn of the Queen Anne…cackling together until they both gasped for breath. At some point the hilarity wasn't about Iyanla's intervention in their potential fucked-upness, but about release. Maybe even…healing.

When their howls of laughter finally waned to low, quiet chuckles and cautious but genuine smiles, Jennifer reached out, took Flo's hand in hers.

"Flo, I'm sorry for your loss," she murmured, squeezing her fingers before releasing her. Then she laughed again, this one holding a note of self-deprecation. "You must think I'm the worst mother ever."

Flo frowned. "The worst? God, no. There's Cersei

Lannister. And then, y'know, the quokka. I mean, that animal throws its young at predators so it can escape."

Jennifer blinked. Blinked again. Then her loud bark of hilarity echoed on the air.

"Oh my God." She shook her head, still snickering. "You know, I came here to this town expecting to dislike you. I really hate that I don't."

Flo grinned. "Ditto."

Jennifer's gaze shifted to behind Flo, and her own smile grew, dark eyes gleaming.

"Uh-oh. Overprotective male at nine o'clock."

Flo turned around to see Adam headed toward them from the back of the house. His long legs ate up the distance, and damn, he was a sight. Like some avenging angel swooping down on them. A really powerful, sexy avenging angel. And yes, that sounded just slightly blasphemous.

Jennifer held up her hand, palm out, as Adam neared them. Though his expression remained calm, composed, tension radiated from him in pulsing waves.

"Hold up there, T'Challa," she drawled, and Flo coughed back a chuckle. Adam's gaze flicked toward her before returning to his ex-wife. "No need to come bearing down on us. Your girl and I were just having a friendly chat. Right, Flo?"

"Absolutely."

"It seems you're not only a great father but a good judge of character, too. She's a good one." Jennifer arched an eyebrow. "Don't fuck up and let her go." Adam's big frame slightly stiffened, and Flo decided to ignore the telltale sign. Jennifer wiggled her fingers at Flo and smiled. "See you later, Flo."

"Definitely." And on an impulse that she might or might not regret later, she added, "Since you're already staying at the inn, you should join me, my mom, sisters and friends for a girls' night. Great drinks, better food and the best gossip."

Jennifer slowly nodded, her eyes thoughtful.

"You know what? I just might. Thank you."

Then, with a final wave, she turned and strode toward the house. Quiet fell between Flo and Adam as they watched her climb the steps and disappear inside.

"What the hell just happened?" Adam asked, still staring at the house. "Did she just call me a great father? And did you two just make a date?"

"Yup. I believe that did just happen."

"Flo," he said, turning back to look at her. "I repeat, what the hell just happened?"

She shrugged. "Your ex-wife and I just either formed a truce or we're now besties."

Another beat of silence, then Adam exhaled a long, audible breath. "I think you might be a miracle worker."

"Meh." She waved her hand at him, dismissing his compliment. "I've already walked on water this morning. This was nothing."

"Funny." He grunted. Then, in the next instant, she was yanked into his arms and pressed against him. Held tight. "Thank you," he rasped in her ear after several moments. "Thank you, Flo."

She closed her eyes, inhaled his earth-and-wood scent, committed the tactile sensation of his big frame pressed against hers to memory. Savored the feel of his embrace, his voice vibrating against her chest, his thighs bracketing hers.

Treasured *him*.

Because while she loved being in the shelter of his

body—loved…him—she couldn't shake the ominous tick of the clock in her head.

His time here in Rose Bend was coming to an end.

And so were they.

CHAPTER SIXTEEN

FLO CLIMBED THE porch of Kinsale Inn, and for the first time in weeks, dread didn't permeate her lungs, heart, body. And she welcomed the relief that flowed through her like a cooling balm. This place that had been her home for so many years shouldn't stir unease and trepidation. That had been anathema to her.

But now, as she opened the front door and entered, the familiar and delicious aromas of fresh brewing coffee, even in the afternoon, whatever baked goods Moe had whipped up for the day and *home* greeted her. She smiled as Moe came bustling down the hallway from the direction of the kitchen, balancing a tray of muffins and cookies. Her mother drew up short on seeing Flo, a grin blooming across her lovely face, surprise tingeing her blue eyes.

"Well, this is a wonderful surprise. And gift," Moe said, then narrowed her eyes. "I'm going to ignore the coincidence of you showing up right about the time I'm setting out food."

"Purely a coincidence. But a good one." Flo moved forward and removed the platter from Moe, giving her a kiss on the cheek. Already knowing where the afternoon snacks went, she placed them on the banquet table running along the back of the common room.

"Thanks, sweetheart," Moe said. "What brings you by? Not that I'm complaining."

Flo turned, sliding her hands into the back pockets of her jeans. "I came to see…Noah." Eventually, she would stop pausing before saying his name.

"Oh." Moe went still, her eyes searching her face. "Okay." She crossed the space separating them and took both of Flo's hands in hers. "Sweetheart, are you sure? You don't have to do anything…"

Flo shook her head. "No, I want to, Moe. I think it's past time. And I can't keep running from it."

Her gaze roamed Flo's face again, and whatever she saw there must've reassured her because she nodded and squeezed her hands one last time before letting them go.

"If you need me, I'll be right here, okay?"

"I always know that," Flo said.

Moe cupped her cheek, then pulled her into a quick embrace. And Flo clung to her, absorbing some of that beautiful, dependable strength.

When she stepped back, Moe said, "Last time I saw Noah, he was out on the back porch reading."

"Thanks, Moe."

Before she could change her mind, she made her way down the hall, through the kitchen and mudroom and out onto the back porch. She paused in the doorway and studied the man who had been her first father figure and her first heartbreak. He sat in one of the rocking chairs, head bent, completely engrossed in his book.

"Hi, Noah," she said, stepping out onto the deck.

He looked up, his surprise morphing into a smile, albeit a hesitant one, as he rose to his feet.

"Flo?" He took a step toward her, then stopped. "Hi. I didn't expect to see you."

He ran a hand over his short hair, and she recognized the telltale gesture for what it was. Noah was unsure, nervous.

Well, that made two of them.

"Do you want to have a seat?" He waved the book he still held toward the second rocking chair right next to the one he'd just occupied. "Or were you looking for Ian? You probably are." He cleared his throat, rubbed a hand over his hair again. "He's out in the workshop with Wolf—"

"Actually, I was looking for you. To talk, if you have a moment?"

A smile brightened his face and eyes. "Of course, yes. I would love to." He moved to the adjacent chair and waved to the one he'd vacated. "Please, sit."

Flo lowered to the rocker, and for the space of several heartbeats, neither spoke, just gazed at each other.

"I'm so glad you—"

"I wanted to talk to you—"

They both abruptly cut off, stared at each other then smiled. Was hers as nervous as his appeared? She wouldn't be surprised if it was, given the swarm of butterflies in her belly and chest.

"Sorry." He dipped his chin. "You go first."

"I—" God, why was this so hard? She folded her hands in her lap, her spine so stiff it didn't even meet the back of the rocker. Realizing how ridiculous she must look, she loosed a self-deprecating chuckle. "This seemed so much easier in my head. I had everything I wanted to say planned out. Now…" She flattened her hands on her thighs, aware she was fidgeting. *Stop that.* "Now it's just a jumbled mess."

"Just go with your gut and be honest," Noah quietly advised. "It doesn't have to be pretty, only the truth."

Flo nodded, but it still took her a few seconds before she could begin to articulate the thoughts crowded into her head like an old storage unit. Hell, most of the stuff there had been cooped up for years and needed to be unpacked.

Or thrown away.

"I was talking to Cole earlier," she began, first haltingly, then, after a deep breath, the words started to emerge in an undammed rush. "And he mentioned something that stuck with me. He spoke about his grief after his wife and son died. Of course I knew what he experienced—we all went through it with him, but until today, I never did connect that with…you. Maybe I wasn't ready to hear it, or it could be my heart just wasn't open and prepared to receive it until now, but I started thinking about you, and how losing my mother must've devastated you. Just like it did Cole."

Noah didn't reply, but he swallowed hard. And he closed his eyes for a long second, and when he reopened them, a sheen glistened in the blue-gray depths. That was all the answer she needed.

"Here—" she tapped her temple "—I understood you grieved her. From all the stories Moe and Dad have told me, you were very much in love, and that went both ways. But here?" She splayed her fingers over her chest, directly over her heart. "I was too angry, too hurt, to completely grasp just how much that loss would level you. I know how much it has affected me, and I only have vague memories and some boxes of her things to connect me to her. You had all of her, and your memories are probably as bright and vivid today as they were twenty years ago."

"She was a uniquely amazing woman. I knew from the moment I first laid eyes on her, she would be my wife." He smiled, and it contained so much love, so much pain that it was almost hard to view. Even after all these years, he still mourned her. "Now, your mom, not so much. I had to do some major wooing. But it made sense. She didn't just have her to worry about, but you. And you were always her first concern and priority. And both of you were worth the time and effort."

She'd assumed that, from the stories about her biological mother, but hearing it from Noah, who'd been her husband, love and friend? It hit different and deep. And she appreciated him sharing that with her.

"I've been…angry with you for a long time," she softly admitted. "And I…" She trailed off, oddly not wanting to hurt his feelings, but needing to be honest.

"I know you are, Flo," he said just as softly—gently. "And it's okay to tell me that. I deserve your anger and your truth."

She nodded. Yet, a couple of moments passed before she continued.

"You left me. Even though you gave me the best family and parents in the world, you were the one who married my mother, became my father and promised to love and protect me just as you made the same vow to her. And then you were just gone. It's bothered me all these years that I was so easy for you to walk away from, so easy to abandon. And it made me question if there was something about me that wasn't good enough to make you stay. To make you fight for me."

When his lips parted, probably to object or try and explain, she held up a hand, halting him.

"I don't need you to apologize, Noah. Or feel bad. I needed to tell you so I could get to why I'm here."

A flicker of stubbornness crossed his expression, and obviously, he still wanted to state his case, but a second later he dipped his chin and settled back in the rocker.

"I've never put myself in your shoes. Oh, I said I understood, but I always followed it up with, 'but I lost a mother, too.' And while true, it didn't—doesn't—negate or diminish your pain, your grief. Cole said something. He was talking about loving another child after losing his, but it still struck me when I thought of you. He said he didn't want to love another baby because it felt like a betrayal to the ones he'd lost. And that he refused to get attached again because the pain had almost broken him the first time."

Noah stared at her, not speaking, and she took that as an indication to continue, that he was listening.

"If you substituted joy for love in that sentence, I realized it could describe you. Maybe you didn't feel like you deserved happiness because it would feel like a betrayal to feel joy without the one who brought it to you. And maybe…" She pushed past the tightness in her chest to finish, because it was this thought that gave her the most pain. For him and herself. "Maybe it would've been easier to let me go than risk losing me like my mother. Because you were barely surviving the first time. Like Cole, you might not have survived if anything happened to me."

Noah closed his eyes, and his shoulders slumped, an audible breath shuddering from between his lips. Or it could've been a sob.

Either way, she inched forward on the rocker and reached out to him for the first time in over twenty years—both emotionally and physically—and laid her hand over his.

The sound that erupted from him was definitely a sob. A loud, jagged thing that had to hurt his throat. It was so wounded that an animal could've released it, and her hand tightened over his, giving him an anchor while lost in a grief that she doubted had eroded in the passing years.

A softer sound caught her notice, and she lifted her head, spying Wolf and her father standing at the bottom of the steps leading to the back porch. Both men, their big frames so similar, stood still and watchful. She suspected they'd been there awhile, overhearing her and Noah's conversation.

Her father's gaze shifted from her to his brother when another terrible cry burst from Noah. He moved forward, about to mount the stairs, but Flo shook her head, stopping him. She needed to be here for Noah. This was their shared sadness, their common loss. And he…needed her. His connection to the wife he'd loved so much.

Ian paused, his foot still set on that bottom step, but after a long moment, he slowly nodded. Then he and Wolf quietly walked away, heading around the side of the house. Something told her, because she knew her father so well, he would be close by just in case she or his brother needed him. Because that was the kind of man he was.

She waited as Noah wept, and she grabbed the small tablecloth off the little table in between the chairs and handed it to him as a makeshift napkin. He wiped his face and nose, and when he lifted his head and looked at her, the crying jag had seemed to leave new creases in his weathered face, but his blue-gray eyes were clear.

"I'm sorry," he rasped.

But she shook her head, assuming he referred to his emotional breakdown.

"There's no need to apologize for mourning her."

"No," he objected. "I'm sorry for leaving you. I don't know if I've ever said that to you before. And until now…" He swallowed and fell silent for a second. But he cleared his throat and repeated, "Until now, I haven't even admitted to myself that I did it for me more so than for you. I was protecting myself, my heart. You said you've been angry. And I guess so have I. Angry at the world, at God for losing the love of my life. But also at myself for losing you. Your mother… You were her everything. And I failed her by not being there in the way she would've wanted, the way I promised to be when I married her. And I couldn't forgive myself for that. I wrapped it up in excuses like I was doing the best for you, or you were with a family and parents who adored you. But the truth was I couldn't look at my own failings—or was afraid to. So it became easier to stay away, to convince myself that I'd done right. When I wronged you, Flo. I wronged you and your mother. And I'm so sorry. So very, very sorry."

"Noah." She gripped his hand with both of hers now, and he turned his over, clinging to her. "I forgive you. I forgave you before I came over here, which is why I wanted to talk to you. Now we both have to find a way to forgive ourselves and let go. Not of Aisha, but of the regret, the pain, the guilt. Earlier, I decided to stop focusing on the negative things when I think of her, like how I missed the opportunity to know her. And instead, I'm choosing to take joy in what she gave me. A new start. A new home. Family. You." She squeezed his hands. "You were part of the gifts, the legacy she left me. And I've decided to embrace it all."

He bowed his head, and his chest rose and fell with rapid, hoarse breaths. She thought he might be crying again, but then he raised his chin, and his eyes were still clear. But his expression… She held back her own sudden sob. His expression held a heartbreaking mixture of sadness, agony and hope.

And love.

"Thank you, Flo," he whispered. "Thank you for that."

"We're going to try—no. No, we won't try. We're going to *do* it. We're going to forgive and move forward. Both of us. Together."

"Yes." He nodded, and for the first time since he returned to Rose Bend—for the first time in decades—they shared a real smile with each other.

"Noah, I…"

He shook his head. "No hesitation, Flo. Just say it. Like I said, don't be afraid to hurt my feelings or to be honest. I think we've come too far today for that."

"You're right," she agreed. "I would really like to have you in my life again. I hope we can build a relationship but as…friends. I already have a dad, and no one could ever replace him. But I would love to have a really good friend."

Noah smiled again, and she couldn't pretend not to see the sadness that lingered. But the lines in his face had eased, and if she wasn't mistaken, peace had settled there.

"I could always use a friend. Especially a really good one."

They sat out on the porch a little while longer, talking. A little stilted at first, but with each passing minute, with more comfort, and soon, even with a bit of laughter. It was a beginning.

And when she glanced up, she glimpsed a big shadow in the mudroom's doorway. Love and joy swelled inside her.

Her father.

Because he was never far away.

As any good dad wouldn't be.

CHAPTER SEVENTEEN

ADAM CLIMBED THE outside steps to Flo's apartment, feeling both silly and worried.

Should he be here at eight o'clock at night? Probably not. He'd left Justine at his house with Jennifer, and God, he still hadn't fully grasped that his ex-wife was here. But when he'd spoken to Flo a few hours earlier, her voice had sounded a little off. Not particularly upset, but maybe subdued? Or… Hell, he didn't know, but it had planted a seed of concern and he hadn't been able to root it out since. So here he was, his ex-wife in his home with their daughter while he stood outside Flo's front door. Feeling a little foolish, but still…worried.

Resigning himself to possibly looking like an overprotective idiot, he raised his fist and knocked on the door. Within seconds it opened, and Flo was there, a surprised but welcoming smile curving her pretty mouth.

And yep, he felt even more foolish because she was obviously okay. And the relief coursing through him didn't come anywhere near to capsizing the pleasure at looking down at her lovely face. He visually devoured her as if it'd been days since he'd seen her instead of hours. This pleasure, it was more than physical. He just…

Yeah, he couldn't go there. Not now.

"Hey, Adam." She smiled wider and stepped back, inviting him inside her apartment. "This is a nice surprise. I wasn't expecting you."

"I know, and I'm sorry for just dropping by without calling."

"No problem. I said it was a nice surprise," she teased, closing the door behind him. "Is everything okay? Is Justine all right?"

A burst of warmth filled him that her very next question was about his daughter.

"Yes, she's fine. When I left her, she and Jennifer were arguing over which movie to watch. If I'm not mistaken, Jussy was winning."

Flo laughed, and he struggled not to touch her. Not to brush his fingertips over that smile. Struggled...and lost. But instead of her mouth, he traced her cheekbone, the arch of her eyebrow. She—touching her, being near her—had become a compulsion he couldn't deny himself.

Jesus, he was in so deep.

"I have a confession," he said, knowing it wasn't exactly wise to admit the truth to her, but hell. It wasn't wise to feel this, this encompassing need for her, either. "I was worried about you, and I couldn't shake it. Something didn't seem right earlier, and I had to...come see if you were okay."

Her grin softened, as did her face, and her pretty eyes brightened. She moved closer to him, not stopping until her breasts brushed his abdomen and her thighs pressed to his. Without his permission and completely out of his control, his cock hardened. A natural occurrence around her, it seemed. Her hands slid over his waist to his back, her fingers denting the taut muscles.

Tilting her head, she said, "Not that I'm not happy you're here, but you know you could've called and asked me if I was all right."

Yes, he'd considered that very thing as he walked out of the house. As he started his car. And as he drove through the quiet, pretty streets of Rose Bend. Definitely as he approached the building that housed her studio and apartment.

And even now.

All he said in response to her observation, though, was, "Yes."

Her mouth stretched with the return of her grin, and her fingers dug harder into his spine, sending curls of heat from there straight to his cock. He couldn't stop himself from pressing closer to her, from cupping the nape of her neck.

"You're not wrong," she said, but her smile didn't dim. And the knot that had tightened his stomach at her words eased as he studied her face. "Something happened today. But not bad. Not bad at all. Come on."

She stepped back, releasing him, and he immediately missed her hands on him. But she led him toward the living room, scooping up a stack of mail off a small table by the door with the other.

"You have good timing, actually," she said, sinking down to the couch and tossing the envelopes onto the coffee table. Curling a leg under her, she turned to face him as he followed her down onto the cushion. "I just got home about five minutes before you arrived. It's been..." She sighed, but it wasn't weary. Quite the opposite. It sounded light. "A day."

Leaning a shoulder against the back of the sofa, she started telling him about her conversation with her brother, and then going to her family's inn to see Noah. Astonishment winged through him as she talked. Astonishment and pride. In her courage and vulnerable, forgiving heart. Regret coalesced in his belly. God, he would've loved to have been there for her, even if only for support. Or maybe just to witness that act of bravery. She'd faced her fear, confronted her past and forged a new path for the future. That took guts and a beauty that momentarily stole his breath.

"We ended up having a family dinner, a complete family dinner, for the first time in years. And it was great. Dad with his brother, and seeing them laugh and cut up together? It was..." Her voice thickened. "It was really amazing. For the first time I could see how much Dad had missed him. I think he might've hidden that in the past because of me."

"No," Adam gently corrected. "Because of his love for you. There's a difference."

"Yes." She nodded, her eyebrows wrinkling in a tiny frown before clearing. "Yes, there is a difference. But it was good to see that he didn't have to hide it anymore."

"I'm glad for you. For all of you," he said, then huffed out a small laugh. "Look at you. Today you're two for two. First, you did...whatever you did with Jennifer. I'm still not exactly sure what happened there." She chuckled, and he shook his head. "My mind's still reeling from the *great father* compliment. And then this with Noah. I wasn't kidding when I called you a miracle worker."

Flo buffed her nails and blew on them, smiling. He laughed and shifted forward, cradling her cheek, and she leaned into his palm, rubbing against it. And because he couldn't resist, he leaned in and took her mouth. She melted into the kiss, parting her lips for him and he took full advantage, indulging in the feel and taste of her.

"I know you can't stay," she murmured against his mouth. "You need to get home to Jussy. But have you eaten? I brought home tons of leftovers. Moe made sure I didn't leave without enough for at least a week."

Adam squinted, and his stomach rumbled at the mention of food. Jennifer had just brought Jussy home when he'd asked her to stay while he left to check on Flo. He'd been too worried to concern himself with dinner.

"I'll take that as a yes." Flo snickered and started to rise from the couch. "I'll go get a plate together for you."

"No," he said, setting a hand on her slim thigh. "I have it. You just got home. Relax."

"I'm not going to argue," she joked, sinking back down. "Take whatever you want. I haven't put the food in the refrigerator yet, so everything should still be warm."

"Got it."

He headed for the kitchen. Like she said, the food was still warm. He made a plate and threw it into the microwave to give it more heat. By the time he returned to the living room, Flo had opened her mail. Head bent over an unfolded sheet of paper, she didn't look up as he lowered to the couch, completely engrossed in what she was reading.

Frowning, he set his plate on the table. Her grip tightened on the letter to the point where it crinkled in the silence.

"Hey," Adam murmured, cupping her bended knee. "You good? Is everything okay?"

Finally, she lifted her head with a look of such awe that it took him aback. His grip on her tightened. "Flo?"

She blinked. Then her face broke out in a delighted grin; it lit her up like one of the flashes on her cameras.

"I can't believe this," she whispered. "Oh my God, I can't believe this."

"Baby, what?" He shifted closer, his hand moving to her thigh. "What's going on?"

"A job. I've been offered a job." She laughed, her head falling back, and she murmured something he didn't catch. When her gaze met his again, excitement gleamed there. "I can't believe this," she repeated for the third time, shaking her head and holding up the paper. "I didn't think I would…"

"Flo," he said her name again, firmer. "Tell me what's going on."

"I'm sorry. God." She laughed once more. "I'm not making sense. You remember when we met, and I told you about the terrible trip to Thailand? About my former professor and mentor?"

"Of course."

"Well, I knew Paul would start some kind of whisper campaign against me. He was so petulant, so angry, that I recorded the video and threatened him. I had zero doubts he would try and sabotage me. But he didn't. Or rather, he couldn't. This—" she held the paper up higher "—is from the new dean of the College of Fine Arts, a position formerly held by Paul Coolidge. Apparently, a student came forward and complained about inappropriate behavior, and this revealed that it hadn't been the first time. Which led to one of my colleagues on the Thailand trip—a colleague who had remained silent—coming forward several weeks ago and relating everything that happened with me."

"Flo. God." He exhaled, and it ended on a stunned laugh. "That's amazing. I wish that person would've had your back sooner, but it still took courage to speak out. I'm happy for you."

She nodded, still appearing a little dazed with the turn of events.

"It did take courage. And I'm thankful. But that's not all the new dean wanted. She reviewed my portfolio and admired it. She has contacted a friend of hers who is looking for a photographer to accompany her on a trip to Kenya. The woman is an author and she's writing a book about her family, tracing it back to the Nilote ethnic group, specifically the Turkana tribe. It'll take about three weeks, but the author is paying well, and the dean thinks I would be perfect for the assignment." Flo fell back against the arm of the couch. "I can't... Who would've thought the day would end like *this*?"

Her delight permeated the room, and ice threaded through his veins, covering his chest in a frozen sheet. Not shock.

Fear.

And resignation.

Flo, oblivious, threw her hands up, the letter with the job offer still clutched in her fist.

"I'd kind of given up on having another opportunity at a dream job like Thailand. At least not anytime soon. But this... I get a redo. And *Kenya*," she breathed. "This is more than I dreamed."

"Congratulations," Adam said. It sounded flat, dull, even to his own ears. And he hated it. Hated the numbness that coated him from the inside out instead of feeling the excitement and happiness that radiated off her. "I'm happy for you. This is a wonderful opportunity."

Flo slowly lowered the paper, her gaze sharpening on him even as a small frown creased her brow. "You don't sound happy." She tilted her head. "What's wrong?"

"There's nothing wrong," he lied. "This is an amazing career opportunity, and I'm thrilled you have this chance."

He'd known this would happen. Had predicted it. But at some point during the past few weeks, he'd gotten caught up in this...thing with Flo. Had let himself forget that history could, and probably would, repeat itself. Even with Jennifer sitting in his house as a reminder, he'd allowed himself to get comfortable, to...believe.

Flo continued to study him, and he caught the moment awareness dawned in her eyes. The moment those eyes shuttered.

"Oh," she said, her tone now as flat as his had been. "We're back here. I was hoping we'd gotten past this, that you'd learned who I am and let this go. But apparently not, because here we are."

Adam dragged a hand over his face and beard, turning from her and propping his elbows on his knees. He stared down at his clasped hands, and the silence that fell between them weighed down his shoulders, his back.

"What do you say to me? Look at me," she ordered, a hard note entering her voice. "Look at me and tell me again there's nothing wrong. That when you walk out of here tonight you don't plan on distancing yourself from me? Haven't already started relegating me to coworker and nothing more in your mind."

She could never be just a coworker to him. They'd come much too far for that. But the rest of it? Yeah, he couldn't admit it. But she was right.

"Flo," he murmured.

"Don't *Flo* me," she said, and a moment later she moved from the couch to the coffee table, shoving his untouched plate aside and sitting down directly in front of him. "If you're going to do this, *to us*, you're going to look at me and tell me the truth."

To us.

Panic clawed at him, and he recoiled. Both from the panic and the *longing* attacking him. Something in him stretched toward her, toward that *us*, and it scared the shit out of him.

"Flo, I've never lied to you," he murmured, meeting her gaze. "I've always been honest about where I'm at, about my priorities and yours. There hasn't been an—"

Yeah, he couldn't even utter that lie. Couldn't push it

past his throat. But she jumped on his unspoken word, her spine snapping straight, her eyes narrowing.

"There's no us," she said. "That's what you were about to say, right? There's never been an us?" She loosed a sharp, humorless laugh. "Liar," she accused, then shook her head, her locs flying over her shoulder. "No, coward. You're a coward if you sit here and say that to me knowing it's a lie."

He surged to his feet, stalked around her and over to the window. Staring sightlessly down at the dark and quiet Main Street, he tried to get his thoughts together. But that proved an impossible feat. Not with the betrayal and pain saturating Flo's voice, and her anger beating at him like small fists.

He needed to go.

He wanted to stay.

Lifting a fist to the window, he pressed hard against the cool glass. This was his fault. He'd known. *He'd known.* And he hadn't cared. Now, not only was Flo hurt, but Justine would be, too. He had no one to blame for their pain but himself.

"Flo, I'm sorry," he said, turning around to face her. "I didn't mean to hurt you, but I am. I—"

"Cop-out," she snapped, rising from the table. She took several steps toward him before she drew up short. "That's nothing but a cop-out." She sliced a hand through the air as if cutting off his apology. "I'm not asking you to stay. I'm not even asking you to commit to me. I've never demanded either from you. But I won't allow you to stand there and pretend like what we've shared is one-sided or in my imagination. Give me that, at least."

"I do care for you. I won't ever deny that."

Her mouth curved into a humorless, jaded smile, and the sight so contradicted the joyous one she'd worn just minutes ago that it struck him in the chest like a wildly swung fist.

"Gee, thanks," she drawled, sarcasm dripping from the words. "From almost the first, you've accused me of being too young, too driven, too inexperienced, too ambitious. You've marked me with this scarlet J for Jennifer. When I'm. Not. Her. But it's safer for you to paint me with her brush because it's easier than taking a risk. It's easier than you trusting that I won't hurt you, walk away from you. It's easier than you believing that you can love me like I deserve and sustain a relationship. You live your life afraid and closed off because it's just *easier*."

Adam reeled from her accusation, but he didn't move. Couldn't move. He wanted to deny her words, tell her he wasn't just looking out for his daughter, but for her, too. Protecting her, but not stifling her creativity or career aspirations. But the explanation lodged in his throat. Not that Flo seemed like she wanted to hear his reasons.

No.

His excuses.

That was what she would call them. No matter how valid they were.

"I've lived in fear for so long," she said, quieter now, that edge of anger softening. But the intensity in her eyes remained. She moved toward him again, but again, she stopped. As if she wanted to be near him, but wouldn't allow herself. Or maybe he was just projecting. "For more than half of my life, I've had this wall built around myself where I don't let people too close, only permit them to get so far before I shut the door, closing them out, shutting myself in. And I preferred it that way. Because if I didn't let myself depend on them…love them…then when they left, when they fucked up, I couldn't be hurt. I'm tired of that, Adam. So damn tired."

She held up her hands and stared at them as if all her fears weighed them down. And when she dropped her hands to her sides, she released those fears, letting them litter the floor around her feet.

A stab of envy shook him.

"I refuse to live in fear one more day. Fear you'll leave. Fear you'll decide I'm not worthy of you and Justine. Fear of…loving and eventually losing. Fear that rejection of that love will destroy me. All of it has consumed me, and I won't do it any longer. It robs me of happiness, peace and possibilities. You and Jussy, you're a part of those possibilities. I didn't know it when I walked into that bar weeks ago, that you would end up being a part of my hopes and dreams for the future. I didn't know that I would love so strongly, so completely, that I question how I didn't feel like something was missing inside me before then. I don't question whether I can have my passion and you and Justine. I don't have to choose." Her eyes narrowed while her voice remained soft yet filled with the passion she just mentioned. "And if you make me choose between them, then you aren't the man I need."

I didn't know it when I walked into that bar weeks ago, that you would end up being a part of my hopes and dreams for the future.

I didn't know that I would love so strongly, so completely that I question how I didn't feel like something was missing inside me before then.

Jesus. Had she just admitted she loved him, was in love with him? He couldn't move, shock seizing him. Something primal demanded he trek across the space separating them and yank her into his arms. Take her. Claim her. That same something nearly demanded she repeat her words, mark him as hers, too.

But the panic crackled through him more powerful

than ever, fisting his lungs, his heart, polluting his blood.
Refusing to let him accept what a part of him so desperately yearned for.

"Flo, I..." A frustrated growl because he couldn't find
the words. Couldn't find the courage that she deserved.
"I never meant to hurt you."

It was all he could say. All that he had.

And he could tell by the flattening of her mouth and
the pain glistening in her eyes that it wasn't enough. It
gutted him.

"You've said that, and you know what, Adam? I believe you. But it's not enough for me," she whispered,
echoing the thoughts in his mind. She inhaled a deep
breath, her shoulders straightening, her expression blanking. "Thank you for coming over to check on me. If you
don't mind, I'd like you to leave now."

"Flo," he called her name, even held his hand out toward her, but she took a step back from him.

"Good night, Adam."

She turned and walked away from him, leaving him
alone.

No, not alone.

He had his resolve and his fear to keep him company.
Like always.

CHAPTER EIGHTEEN

"YOU, ADAM REED, are an ass."

Adam glanced up from the stove where he stirred tomato sauce for the spaghetti he prepared for dinner and met his ex-wife's narrowed glare. She stood on the other side of the breakfast bar, palms flattened on the surface. Sighing, he tossed a look toward the hallway that led to Justine's room.

"She's in her room," Jennifer said, catching where his attention had shifted. "And I closed the door. I wouldn't want her overhearing that her father is an ass."

"Why, thank you for that consideration," he drawled, tapping the spoon against the saucepan and laying it down on the saucer next to the stove. "And just think, it wasn't too long ago when I was a great dad."

"Oh, you are a wonderful father. But being an ass isn't mutually exclusive."

"Jennifer," he said, switching the fire to a low simmer and then turning to face her. "What's the problem?"

She straightened, crossing her arms and scowling at him.

"What's the problem? You can really stand there with a straight face and ask me that?" She scoffed. "You're screwing up a perfectly good chance to be happy with a woman who loves you, but hey, there's no problem. Nothing to see here."

His chest pulled tight at her mention of Flo's loving

him. *How do you know? Did she tell you that?* The questions bombarded him, but he couldn't bring himself to ask them.

Didn't think he had the right to. Not that Jennifer would answer. Not with her looking at him like she'd really enjoy slapping him with the serving spoon.

"Sarcasm duly noted," he murmured.

Hell, he didn't need this. It'd been hard enough seeing Flo nearly every day on the renovation set for the past eight days and not talking to her outside of anything related to the job. Being so close yet, emotionally, hundreds of miles away. She was beyond him, and he only had to look into the mirror to find out why. His reasons might be real and solid, but the image of her face as she turned from him followed him into sleep. It wouldn't leave him alone.

"Jennifer," he said, the weariness that had been dogging him for the past week seeping into his voice. "I don't want to talk about this. Let it go."

"Too bad." She slapped her hand on the bar top then rounded it, stepping into the kitchen. "What're you doing, Adam? Flo is hurt, and Justine already notices that she's not coming around your house. She misses seeing Flo every day. And though you work with her, I'm betting you miss her, too."

"How do you know Flo is hurt?" he demanded, pushing off the stove. "Has she said something to you?"

Jennifer's scowl deepened. "Of course not. She wouldn't. But her refusal to admit anything at all about you—or what happened between you two—says it all. That, and I recognize pain when I see it. And Flo is covered in it. Same as you."

"Since when did you become such good friends with her?" he questioned, avoiding the last part of her statement like someone sidestepping a pile of dog shit on a sidewalk.

"Now you're just sounding petty." She crossed to the refrigerator and opened it like she lived there. She pulled out a bottle of water and twisted off the cap, lifting the bottle to her mouth and eyeing him while she gulped. "And nice try with that little transference trick. But to answer your question, just because you've fucked up doesn't mean Flo should be removed from Justine's life. I've taken her over to Flo's studio several times, and Justine has seen her at the inn."

"I don't want to remove her from Justine's life," he murmured, turning away from Jennifer on the pretense of grabbing a colander from the cabinet and placing it in the sink. As his ex, she knew him too well, saw much more than he was comfortable with. "Justine loves Flo and vice versa."

"That's right." Jennifer paused. "But she isn't the only one, is she?" Moments later, she appeared at his side, the pot of spaghetti in her oven-mittened hands. "Move," she ordered, and poured the water and pasta into the colander.

While he shook the strainer, his ex-wife moved the empty pot back to the stove.

"She isn't the only one, is she, Adam?" Jennifer pressed.

He turned, scrubbing his hand over his head, staring at the corner where the ceiling met the wall instead of meeting Jennifer's gaze.

"I never lied to Flo," he quietly said, repeating the same answer he'd given Flo over a week ago. "I never led her on. I was always clear about why there couldn't be anything between us. Not to mention I'm here for a job, and when that job ends, Justine and I will be returning to Chicago."

"I didn't ask what you told Flo or whether or not you intend to stay here in Rose Bend. I asked, do you love her?"

"Jennifer, this is ridicu—"

"The fact that you won't answer my question is answer enough." Jennifer pointed a finger at him. "Adam, I was with you for years. And yes, we didn't make it, but that doesn't mean I'm not one of the few people who knows you better than anyone. I'd like to think I was your friend as well as your wife. At least until we weren't." She tilted her head, and her gaze softened, filled with a sympathy that dug under his skin, made him itch with discomfort. "Adam, you're not your father."

Her gently spoken words slapped at him, and his head jerked back from the verbal blow.

"You're going too far, Jennifer," he snapped. "I'm not talking about that with you."

"Then who?" she challenged, striding forward until only inches separated them. She punched her fists onto her hips, thrusting out her chin. "Who else are you going to talk to about it? Because let's be clear—you don't. You don't ever talk about the fact that your self-image is wrapped up in your father."

"I don't—" he growled, but she shook her head, holding up a palm.

"Stop it. Stop lying to yourself. While other sons might strive to emulate their fathers, your sole goal has been to be the complete opposite of him. Calm to the point of being so guarded you can be emotionally shut down. To be so self-reliant you refuse to lean on anyone, depend on anyone. And so driven to prove you're not toxic, you're incredibly hard on yourself. Unforgiving of yourself." She sighed, lowering her arm to her side. "You have never given yourself grace, and for such a confident and self-assured person, you don't believe in yourself."

"Jennifer, please," he rasped, desperate for her to stop this line of conversation.

Desperate for her to convince him of her convictions. He squeezed his eyes closed. But he couldn't block her out. Maybe…he didn't want to.

"What you don't realize is that you were never your father. A great dad like you? One who has always been there for our daughter? Who loves her unconditionally and makes her feel like everything kind, beautiful and smart in this world? No, you could never be him. And Adam—" she closed the distance between them and settled a hand over his chest "—this heart is good. It's so big and incredibly vulnerable. You were a great husband, a great partner. We just weren't meant for each other. The end of any marriage isn't all one person's fault, so you shouldn't shoulder all the blame. And I…" She dipped her head and when she lifted it, remorse darkened her brown gaze. "I wasn't ready for you. Honestly, I wasn't ready to be anyone's other half because I wasn't whole. I'm working on that. Starting to work hard, and I'm beginning with myself and Justine. I want to be the parent I once was, the one I know I can be again. And you're that role model." She dropped her hand and stepped back, smiling at him. "Don't cheat yourself out of the love you deserve. Who you came from doesn't determine the man you've worked so hard to become. Let the past go and grab on to the future right in front of you, if you just have the courage to hold on to it."

She patted him on the chest one last time then turned and left the kitchen.

He sucked in a breath and held it until his lungs burned. Only then did he release it.

Was he cheating himself out of love?

Yes.

The answer didn't whisper across his mind; it roared in his head. In the space of minutes, with one conversation with his ex-wife, he could see so clearly what he had been in denial about. Did she undo years of negative self-talk? No. But she'd planted seeds, and he could—if he made the choice to—water them, nurture them. He had to, and not just for his sake. But for Justine's.

And Flo's.

Because though he hadn't responded directly to Jennifer's question, she'd been correct.

He loved her. Fear had stilled his tongue the last night they'd been together in her apartment, but he couldn't deny it any longer. All those reasons he'd given her for why they could never be were just the excuses Flo had called them. Convenient excuses to protect himself from the terror of failing. Somewhere in these past few weeks, he'd fallen so in love, Flo terrified him, threatening every conception he held about himself, about the life he wanted, the life he saw for him and his daughter.

Now that view had changed. Mostly because he couldn't see that future without Flo in it.

Oh God.

He loved her. Yes, fear still tiptoed through him, but it didn't rule him any longer. For once, his hope for himself, for his family and for love overpowered everything else.

And he'd only needed his ex-wife to show him the way. He loosed a bark of laughter. How ironic. Shaking his head, he smiled, and for the first time in, hell, years, he felt lighter. Not burdened. Hopeful.

But he wouldn't be complete until he convinced Flo that they belonged to each other.

Damn, after the damage he'd inflicted, he had his work cut out for him.

But for the first time in a long time, he wasn't running away.

He was running toward something. His happiness.
His future.

Love.

And he had everything to lose.

Good thing he had zero plans on losing.

CHAPTER NINETEEN

FLO STOOD ON the sidewalk alongside Main Street, surveying the… Well, the only thing she could really call it was a block party. She grinned.

Take that, Jasper Landon.

What had started out as a book rally in front of the library to protest the banning of books had turned into a town-wide rally down Main Street to protest the banning of books. The business owners had volunteered to do much more than post flyers in their storefront windows and donate funds. From Elegant Occasions, Patricia Collins's boutique, to Six Ways to Sundae, Flo's former employer, down to Get Booked, the local bookstore, they all offered to host giveaways with prizes from their stores, get a counterpetition against banning books signed and hand out the potential banned books listed on the original petition. And as far as the eye could see people were decked out in We Read the Banned T-shirts. Paid for and donated courtesy of their resident *New York Times* bestselling authors Beck Dansing, aka Jenna Landon, and I.M. Kelly aka Israel Ford. Who, coincidentally, were parked out in front of the library signing complimentary copies of their books—books also included on the original petition's list.

Smirking, Flo smoothed a hand down the front of her own We Read the Banned T-shirt. She hadn't seen Jasper Landon today, but rumor was he'd been down at City

Hall throwing a hissy fit and trying to get the rally/party shut down. Yeah, good luck with that. Remi Donovan had covered all her bases *and* permits.

Damn. She just loved when evil was thwarted for another day.

"Hey, babe!" Leo approached, waving with the hand not curled around her son, Bono. "This is crazy, isn't it?" She grinned, and Flo swore she glimpsed every last one of her teeth.

"Crazy beautiful," Flo said, taking Bono, who stretched his arms out toward her. Smacking a loud kiss on his cheek and making him giggle, she settled him on her hip. He started playing with her locs. And it was one of the very few times it was quite all right for someone, other than who she permitted, to touch a Black woman's hair. "I can't believe the turnout. I swear, everyone in town must be here."

"Not everyone." Leo snickered. "Helene closed down her store and hightailed it out of here along with her shady as—" she abruptly cut off, glancing at Bono "—asinine husband."

"Of course she did," Flo drawled and cackled along with her sister.

"I saw your people from *Vintage Renovation* around here, too. The producer? Mira's her name, right? She was down at the library with one of the television crews. Can I stress *one of*? I saw at least three, and one was from New York."

Flo nodded, absently removing Bono's fingers from the hoop earring he tugged on.

"That would be Mira's friend. She offered to let them know about the rally. I wasn't sure if they would come since we're a small town in Massachusetts. But apparently having two famous authors—one of them formerly reclusive—in the midst of a book-banning protest brought them out."

"Good, whatever it takes." Leo rubbed her hands together. "With this much coverage and most of the town's participation, just let Jasper try to railroad something like this again. Jacka—" Once more she glanced at her son. "Apple."

"That looked so painful," Flo said with a crack of laughter.

Leo sighed. "You have no idea. He's at that age where he's repeating everything he hears, and I'll be...doggone if I'm blamed for his agitated adjectives before Owen."

"You and Owen actually turned childrearing into a competition of who can curse less?"

Leo's look clearly said *duh.* "Uh, yeah. He's an athlete. He shouldn't be afraid of a little competition." Holding her arms out to Bono, who eagerly went back to his mom, Leo cuddled him close then smiled, poking his stomach and eliciting a giggle. "I'm going to take this little guy down to the bookstore to buy our copy of *Worm Loves Worm.*"

"Go ahead and have fun, my little anarchist."

"Love you!" With a grin, Leo walked off, disappearing in the thick crowds gathered on the sidewalks.

For the next hour Flo strolled up and down Main Street snapping pictures of the event. Mostly of the people and their different reactions to the protest that had pretty much turned into a celebration of literature—*all* literature. She caught people laughing as they talked with one another. Eating hot dogs, cupcakes and drinking beverages. Signing the petitions wearing determined expressions. Reading the books they'd received or bought. Or just sitting on the benches dotting the sidewalk, quietly people-watching, wearing their banned books T-shirts.

She smiled, leaning against the brick wall outside Mimi's Café, scrolling through the pictures. They were great shots. Most of them she would post on Rose Bend's social media pages as well as her own. One of the convenient parts of living in a small town? She knew mostly everyone, so hunting them down to sign releases would be easy.

"Flo!" Justine slammed into her legs only a couple of seconds after she yelled her name.

Laughing, Flo sank to a knee and gathered the little girl in her arms. She hadn't seen Justine in the past three days, and that hurt. Flo missed her. Missed her voice that never dropped below an eight in volume. Missed her mispronunciation of words and funny, brutally honest observations. Just missed *her*. Yet, even knowing everything with Adam would end up as it had, Flo could never regret getting to know and fall in love with his daughter.

"Hey, Jussie." Flo tugged on one of the twists Jennifer had continued for her daughter. "I'm so glad to see you. Are you enjoying yourself?"

"Uh-huh." She nodded her head so hard her twists swung around her face. "I got hot chocolate and books!" Then she switched subjects with lightning speed, throwing her arms around Flo's neck and squeezing. "I miss you, Flo."

"I miss you, too, sweetie," she murmured, voice suddenly husky with emotion.

Shit. She refused to cry on Main Street in front of God and Rose Bend. She just refused to cry, period. Not only would it probably upset Justine, but she'd done more than her fair share in the past two weeks.

"I miss you, too."

She stiffened at that voice. At that beloved voice of whiskey and sin that had haunted her waking and sleeping hours. Her heart throbbed against her rib cage, and she forced herself to look up from Justine to meet the golden gaze of her father.

Adam.

She'd seen him almost every day at the renovation site, but they might as well have been hundreds of miles apart. She'd ached for him these past two weeks and being near him only increased that hurt. She loved him, but she didn't regret her choice. She couldn't fight for the two of them unless they were both willing to go to battle. She couldn't be in this alone. And Adam hadn't even armored up for it. Moe was fond of saying never be someone's backup plan when they're your only plan.

Well, she wasn't even Adam's Plan B.

But now he was here, standing in the middle of a packed sidewalk, declaring he missed her.

It struck her as cruel. And anger rose swift and hot inside her. But with Justine there, she couldn't unleash it on him.

Slowly rising, she cupped Justine's shoulder and said, "Hi, Adam," not addressing his declaration.

"Flo! Flo, guess what?" Justine bounced on her toes, doing her adorable, twisty dance and twirling. She didn't wait for Flo to reply, but blurted out, "We live here! We live in Ross End!"

Flo frowned, interpreting "Ross End" into Rose Bend, but still not grasping the rest of what Justine had just said. *We live here.* Well, she and her father had been in town for weeks now. Maybe Justine thought they did live here. For a five-year-old, that had to seem like a long time.

"That's nice, sweetie," Flo said, hesitant. It wasn't her place to correct her. That was Adam's job.

"Jussy," Adam said, raising an eyebrow.

"Oops." Justine comically clapped both hands over her

mouth and mumbled from behind them, "Sorry, Daddy." Dropping her arms, she peered up at Flo and whispered loudly, "It's a secret."

Now *really* confused, she glanced at Adam, frown deepening.

The corner of his mouth quirked, most likely at his daughter's antics. But his eyes, bright and somber, were fixed on her.

"She's right. We live here now."

Her breath snagged in her lungs, and if not for the brick wall at her spine, she might've staggered back. But she stared at him, frozen with bewilderment, residual traces of anger and…hope. Stupid, relentless hope that hadn't learned its lesson yet.

"What?" she asked.

Adam nodded, his gaze roaming over her face, lingering on her mouth before rising to her eyes again.

"As of this morning, we have a contract with Isaac Hunter to buy the house we've been staying in. Rose Bend is our new home."

"I don't…" Her voice trailed off, stuttering to stunned silence.

"We love you!" Justine crowed, throwing her arms wide.

Several people smiled as they passed by, and others laughed. Their little trio had become a sidewalk show, and all they needed was a hat for change.

"I love you, too, sweetie," she whispered, but that *we*… It had stopped the thudding of her heart for a couple of seconds, and now it raced like an escapee.

"Justine," Adam said dryly. "I'm going to take it from here, okay, baby girl?"

"Okay, Daddy!"

He neared Flo, and again, she was thankful for the

building behind her. It held her up when her legs had the consistency of water.

"Flo, Jussy's not wrong. We love you. I love you," he murmured.

She was projecting. She'd finally cracked under the pain and sadness and was now imagining things because she could've sworn Adam said he loved her.

"Told you so!" Justine boasted.

"Jussy."

"Sorry, Daddy!"

Shifting his attention back to Flo, he lifted an arm, his cupped hand hovering near her cheek. But he dropped it, rubbing his palm over his thigh.

"I'm sorry, Flo," he said, and for a bemused moment, she thought he referred to nearly touching her without her permission. But then he dispelled that by continuing. "I was the coward you called me. But it didn't have anything to do with you. It was all me. I used your age and career as an excuse not to face my own fears and insecurities. I didn't want to hear that you loved me because I didn't think I was lovable or able to be the person you needed. Someone who wouldn't hurt you, wreck a relationship. A part of me believed I couldn't be a healthy partner because I didn't see that growing up. I believed I was my father's son."

He inhaled a breath, dragging his hand over his hair, a tell she'd come to recognize when he was uncomfortable or nervous. That she knew that detail about him only emphasized how much she noticed everything about this man. Loved everything about him. And hearing him confess these negative things he'd come to accept about himself had pain and anger sweeping through her. But not *at* him. *For* him.

"I don't know your father," she said hotly, eyes narrowed. "But from what you've told me, you are nothing like him. You are your own person, not a carbon copy of him. And there's nothing unlovable about you."

His lips twitched again, but then he sobered. "I'm starting to believe that. And you're the reason why. You're the reason why I'm choosing to stop allowing fear to rule every decision I make. I'm choosing you. And Rose Bend. I'm choosing to give my daughter my very best, and that's you, Flo. So even if you decide I'm not who you want anymore and a future with me is not in *your* future, I'm still staying here. I'm still giving Jussy you, and you, her. And when you return from Kenya, we'll be here, waiting for you, trusting you'll return to us."

"And what if I decide I don't want you in my future anymore? You're going to respect that? Give up?" she pressed, her heart creeping up to her throat.

"I'll respect it. I'll even accept it. But give up? Never. I'll just try harder to convince you of the truth. That you are meant for me, and I'm meant for you. I didn't fight for you once. I won't do that again, queen. You're worth waging a war over."

His words nearly echoing her earlier thoughts stung her eyes, and she squeezed them closed. Gentle fingers traced the arch of her eyebrow, the tender skin beneath her lashes, the bridge of her nose.

"Look at me," he softly ordered, and when she acquiesced—she couldn't do anything less—love filled his hazel eyes. So much love she almost disobeyed him and lowered her lashes again. Almost. "Please forgive me for running. No more and never again, Flo. Jussy and I, we're staying still and letting you find your way home to us."

The tangled knot of emotion around her throat wouldn't allow her to speak, but he didn't seem to have that problem.

Cupping her cheek, he lowered his head and pressed his forehead to hers. "You have no choice but to stay with me. Jennifer has decided Rose Bend will now be her home base between her travels. Oh, and she's also decided to become an author now that she's met Beck Dansing. You invited her to a girls' night and gave her friends, so she's your responsibility now. You have to be responsible for saving me from her."

"Do I get hazard pay?" she breathed, choking on a thick laugh.

"A salary, queen. You get me, Jussy, my meddlesome ex-wife and apparently your new buddy. All you have to do is take us. Accept us."

"I love you," she whispered. Then stronger, louder, "I love you.".

"We love you, too!" Justine tossed her arms around her and Adam's legs. "I'm not running, too, Flo!"

Love, joy and hope surged within her, and she couldn't contain it all. So she loosed it. Leaning her head back, she laughed aloud, and it was long, loud and so free.

And as Adam kissed her, swallowing her laughter and giving her his own, she knew her running days were over.

She'd finally come home.

* * * * *

*Look for the next Rose Bend novel
coming soon!*

THE HUSBAND SITUATION

CHAPTER ONE

ALL BROOKLYN HAYES wanted for Christmas was a calm, unexciting, even downright boring, holiday. Oh and maybe some of her gran's homemade peanut brittle in her stocking.

She didn't foresee also wanting, above all, Elvis Presley's *Blue Christmas* to shut. The. Fuck. Up.

"Make it stop." She groaned, rolling over in her bed, wrapping her arms around her pillow and dragging it over her head.

But the thick down couldn't drown out Elvis, and what the hell? Her family was more Jackson 5, *Give Love on Christmas Day* than the King of Rock 'n' Roll. Who'd decided to go rogue? And why were they in her house doing it?

"Oh my God, enough," she muttered, shoving the pillow aside and jackknifing to a sitting position when it started playing over again.

And she immediately regretted the abrupt action.

Holy shit.

She groaned again, her hands shooting up to clutch her head. Pain pounded against her skull. What the...? Who had unleashed the flying monkeys inside her head, and why in the *hell* was that music still playing? And so loudly? Christmas cheer, her ass. Did no one around here respect the dead and dying?

Another groan ripped free of her, and she ground the

heels of her palms tighter to her temples as if that would somehow crush the steady drilling inside her head. Slowly lying back down, she curled onto her side, her foot brushing against a… Oh God! *A what?*

Not giving a damn about her aching head, she threw the covers back and scrambled from the bed. Her heart tried to fight its way out of her chest, scrambling for her throat.

"Oh God," she rasped. Even without her glasses she could see the human-shaped lump under the white hotel blankets. "Oh God. There's someone… There's someone in my bed," she apparently explained to the sleeping *someone*.

Not that he or she was paying attention because, y'know, *sleeping.*

Hand circling her throat, she gaped—until the recycled air of the room's AC brushed over her skin like cool trailing fingertips.

Her very naked skin.

I repeat, holy shit!

Gasping, Brooklyn jerked her head down, staring at *all* of her.

Oh God. Oh *God*. OhGodOhGodOhGod.

What had she done?

Nonono. What had she done and *who* had she done it *with*?

With her fuzzy, nearsighted vision, all she could tell from the figure shrouded by the covers was he or she seemed tall. And a very deep sleeper. Or maybe—she groaned again, one hand pressed to her forehead and the other to her roiling stomach—as hungover as she was.

Hungover. Vegas. Corporate bonding trip for her marketing company, Media Mavens. Casino. Drinks.

Oh Lawd, sooo many drinks.

Slowly dropping her gaze to the floor because damn, even her eyeballs hurt, for the first time she noticed all the clothes scattered around like breadcrumbs. At least, she assumed they were clothes. That could possibly be a dark pair of pants there. Her black skinny jeans there. A blue dress shirt thrown over the back of the chair. Her green cropped sweater at the feet of the same chair. And... She squeezed her eyes shut. Were those her lilac lace panties hanging for dear life to the lampshade?

Oh sweet Lamb of Life, what *happened* last night?

She ground her thumb and finger against her forehead. First things first. Carefully, pushing off the wall, she edged toward the bathroom. Nature and her modesty called, and it was a toss-up on who she answered first. But considering she'd woken up as naked as the day she'd come into this earth, the whole modesty thing might be a case of locking the barn door after the horse got its freak on.

Twenty minutes later she emerged from the bathroom, freshly showered, wrapped in the hotel-provided robe and with a headache downgraded from *Oh God, Why Have Thou Forsaken Me* to *Jesus Wept*. In other words, she might just live. Might. Immediately, she glanced to the bed, and the figure there hadn't moved.

A flash of panic stabbed her in the chest, momentarily overtaking the tiny hammers in her temples. Oh hell. Were they dead? Had she fucked him to death? She didn't know whether to be proud or scared over the possibility...

Locating her glasses had become priority number one now that she was clean, and her mouth didn't taste like the place roadkill went to die. Moments later, and after much patting and skimming with her hands, she found her blue-rimmed glasses on the small table and slid them on. She sighed as her world came into focus. Nothing made her feel more vulnerable than not being able to clearly see past a few feet in front of her.

Swallowing a groan, she shuffled closer to the bed, rounding it, hand outstretched as if approaching a dangerous animal set on snapping off her fingers. She'd never been one to back down from a challenge or a dare. No, she'd always been the one to charge forward. Showing fear meant exposing your throat and making you vulnerable. And there she went with more animal analogies. Still, it fit. Being weak in her family, in her job, had never been an option. Not for her anyway.

Yet, here she stood, only inches from the person she, in all likelihood, smashed genitals with, and she hesitated, fingers trembling.

It's a cover, woman. A simple cover. You've wrestled three fingers of scotch from your mother after Kayla broke off her engagement. You can handle a stranger in your bed. Besides, the person underneath has probably seen you naked, and maybe even twisted you like a pretzel in all kinds of positions you might've enjoyed. A glimpse at his or her face shouldn't be an issue.

As far as pep talks went, it was one of her better ones. And it must've worked because she gritted her teeth, marched the few steps separating her from the bed, snagged the corner of the cover and yanked it back.

Horror slammed into her, and her racing pulse added another cacophonous note in her head.

"No," she whispered, fisting the lapels of her robe together. "It… We… *No.*"

She couldn't force anything else out past her constricted throat. Not words and barely breath.

That face. Half of it might be pressed into the pillow but she knew that face.

The closely cut dark blond hair. The sharp, angular

cheekbones. The thick fringe of long lashes. The narrow, patrician nose. The dusting of hair along his jaw and surrounding his mouth. And yeah, that mouth...

Her belly flipped like a gold-medal gymnast as she forcefully dragged her gaze from those damn near obscenely full lips to the closed eyes. She knew they were a startling shade of turquoise, and a person could imagine themselves swimming in the warm, gorgeous waters of the Maldives when staring into them.

Okay, fine. It was her. She was *a person*.

But noticing their beauty and peering into them while she orgasmed were two totally different things.

One, he was her friend and employee.

Two, he was her sister's ex-boyfriend.

Oh no. This had Brooklyn's Biggest Mistake Evah scrawled all over it. In neon graffiti.

"Patrick," she called his name. When he didn't stir, she cleared her throat and tried again, louder this time. "Patrick."

Nothing.

His back rose and fell, so he wasn't dead. Imagine explaining *that* to Kat Owens, her business partner and best friend. *I took our employees to Vegas for a pre-Christmas retreat and apparently fucked one of them to death.* Thank God for small favors she could now avoid that particular conversation.

"Patrick." She shifted closer and nudged his shoulder—his bare shoulder.

Wow, did the man house a furnace in that big body? His skin burned hot to the touch. Deliberately, she kept her gaze on his shoulder and above. Because if she'd woken up naked... *Oh boy*. Was it a blessing or a curse that she couldn't remember what all lay stretched out beneath those blankets that seemed an even starker white against all that golden, taut skin...?

Don't even go there, sister.

"Patrick, wake up," she ordered, shoving him a little harder.

A low moan emanated from him, a small frown wrinkling his forehead. One second passed. Then two. And another. Finally, those ridiculously long, dense lashes fluttered and lifted. And a sliver of blurry turquoise appeared. His lids lowered again, and she swallowed an impatient sigh, moving closer to shove him again. But instead, he flipped over onto his back, exposing a wide expanse of mouthwatering muscles, skin and...nipples.

Girl, stop staring at that man's nipples!

So her scrutiny dipped to a corrugated ladder of muscles lining either side of his torso and a flat belly that, once upon a time, she would've traded her younger sister for. Well, to be fair, she would've given Kayla away for free as long as they signed an NDA and a No Return disclosure, but that was neither here nor there.

And she was staring. Hard. But god*damn*. Patrick had been hiding *that* under his clothes all this time?

Jerking her attention back to his face, where it was safe, she met his hooded but sharpened gaze.

"Finally." She crossed her arms, wrestling down the rising panic and increasing sense of powerlessness that scrabbled for a foothold in her chest.

He squinted at her. "What're you doing in my room?" he asked, his voice all grit and gravel as he stretched.

And no, a shiver did not work its way down her spine.

"Your room?" She scoffed, tightening her arms across her chest. "Sorry to break it to you, guy, but last time I checked, this room is reg—*holy shit!* What is that, that *thing* on your hand?"

Brooklyn stabbed a finger toward the bright pink plastic ring on his finger. Shaped like a diamond so large it would've given the Crown Jewels an inferiority complex, the ring claimed all her attention. Why in the world was that toy gumball thing on Patrick's finger?

Even as she asked the question, the awful, inconceivable truth yawned wide inside her.

Only it was all too conceivable.

Vegas. Waking up hungover. And naked. A plastic diamond on his left ring finger.

Nope. No way. She refused to accept what stared her right in the face—literally. Things like this only happened in Harlequin books and rom-coms starring Drew Barrymore. Not in real life.

Not to *her*.

She didn't do impulsive. Didn't do foolish.

Methodical, circumspect—that was her.

Yet, here she stood in her hotel room, naked under a robe, staring at her sister's ex who wore a bubblegum toy on his ring finger.

And god*damn*, Elvis still hadn't shut up.

Though the truth loomed over her like a dawning zombie apocalypse, she still scowled and stabbed a finger at him.

"Patrick," she ground out. "What is that on your hand? And why is it there?"

He lowered his arms and silently stared at his finger. Long seconds passed, and the air in the room seemed to throb with the tension that slowly stiffened his body until he could've passed for one of the marble statues in the hotel lobby.

Finally, he shifted his scrutiny from the ring to her, and it struck her hard, like all the drinks she'd undoubtedly imbibed the night before. If not for her leg braced against the edge of the mattress, she would've swayed from the impact of that pretty and powerful gaze.

"You want to explain why I'm in your bed wearing nothing but a Blow Pop ring?"

"I wish I could. Actually, I was hoping you remembered more about the last eight hours than I do."

He lifted his hand again, peered at it as if the plastic jewelry would evaporate if he stared long enough. But yeah, that wasn't happening.

"Are you kidding me?" he breathed, scrubbing his bejeweled hand over his head. "Brooklyn…"

A train of emotions raced over his face, too fast and way too enigmatic for her to properly decipher. And God, she wished she could. What she would give to know what tracked through his mind right now. Horror? Shock? Anger? Confusion?

Because all of those emotions stomped through her.

Horror over being in this situation with her friend, her employee, *her sister's ex*.

Shock… Well, see horror.

Anger at herself for being so foolish and irresponsible that she'd not only jeopardized a valued relationship, but also a comfortable and safe work environment. Hell, if anyone else witnessed their actions, she could've threatened the reputation of the company she and Kat had sacrificed so much for these past seven years.

Confusion over how she'd allowed herself to end up in this predicament.

Confusion over why she couldn't tear her damn gaze from all that bare golden skin and taut muscles.

A new ache announced itself in that moment. Now that the headache had abated a little, the soreness between her thighs decided to make itself known. A sensual, delicious soreness that assured her it didn't matter if she couldn't remember Patrick being deep inside her; he had been. And yes, the alcohol-clouded blank space in her head didn't allow her to recall if the sex had been as amazing as that beautiful, big body promised. But the deep ache informed her she'd been well and truly stretched and branded by a cock that was probably as gorgeous as the rest of him.

Only with Patrick could she ever assume that a dick was pretty. It would be a damn shame if it wasn't, given that perfect bone structure, stunning eyes and the sculptor's work of art that was his body. God, if she could only remember how he'd worked that...

No, no and hell *no*. She refused to go there. Well, technically, she'd already been *there*. And neither her mind nor her body were taking a return trip.

"The last thing I remember is that fourth round of Patrón shots and someone suggested walking the strip," he said, sitting up. "And..." He frowned. "David Copperfield?"

The covers dipped to his waist, exposing more of him, and she pinched the bridge of her nose, squeezing her eyes shut. But nothing could erase the sight of him from her mind. It only flickered across the backs of her lids like a slideshow on repeat. Dammit.

Swinging his legs over the edge of the mattress, he muttered, "I don't remember anything about the strip or a magic show, but there's not enough tequila in the world to make me forget...oh. Shit."

He snatched something up off the bedside table and stared down at it for several long seconds. When he lifted his head and looked at her again, he wore an impassive mask that only sent more nerves squirming in her belly. Funny how right now, she so sympathized with that worm on a hook, about to stare death in the face.

"Patrick, what?" she whispered, hating that her voice lacked the strength that had also decided to abandon her. "Tell me. What is it?"

Instead of answering, he stretched his arm toward her, offering her whatever he held in his hand. She resented her moment of hesitation—but the fact that she did hesitate propelled her forward. She didn't shy away from anything. Not a slightly crazypants family. Not from the challenge of two Black women starting a social media management and marketing business with ten thousand dollars and a million dreams.

Not from the bare-assed, tattooed Adonis in her bed. God, how hadn't she known that ink curved around his ribs?

Oh right.

She'd never seen him unclothed before.

Now that she had, she couldn't seem to drag her gaze from the wooden cross wrapped in a pair of large, delicate wings. She also couldn't help but follow the floating trail of feathers that disappeared under his arm and around his torso…

Shaking her head, she moved closer and grabbed the object out of his hand, careful not to brush her fingers against his.

A picture. It was a picture.

"Oh God."

It came out as more of a wheeze than a whisper, and her grip tightened until the glossy print crackled under her fingers. But even if she crumpled it up in a ball and pitched it across the room in an impressive curveball, that image would be branded on her mind.

Her, in the black jeans and green sweater from last night accompanied by a long white veil propped over her head. Arms raised, she clutched a bouquet of pink roses in her hand, and a wide grin stretched her mouth. Though his huge, solid body bent over hers and his face was buried in her neck, his mouth opened wide over the skin there, she could clearly see it was Patrick. Unbidden, she lifted her free hand to her throat, trailing her fingers over the same spot he kissed in the picture. And yes, it was impossible, but she could feel the hot press of his mouth, the wet lash of his tongue. She couldn't remember the moment captured in time by a camera, but it didn't matter. Heat swirled in her veins, swelling her breasts and pinching her nipples tight. And lower, between her thighs? Said thighs clenched around the deep, sweet and painful ache blooming there.

Snatching her hand away, she dropped her arm to her side and deliberately switched her attention away from Patrick—and his mouth. Instead, she focused on the bright pink plastic diamond on his hand.

And the huge, neon green one nestled on the finger of the hand grasping the bouquet.

She blew out a shuddering breath and lifted her gaze. But it didn't meet Patrick's.

Because he stared at the spot she'd been touching just moments earlier. And something she refused to define flashed in those narrow eyes.

Well, she might've decided not to define it, but her vagina cheerfully spoke up and volunteered an answer.

Desire.

Desire darkened that aquamarine gaze to nearly a denim blue.

Her breath snagged directly under the place he scrutinized, and the soft catch echoed in the room like an ear-piercing shriek.

Patrick blinked...blinked again, then his gaze locked with hers.

Breathing didn't become any easier. But it was due to the inescapable evidence in her hand of what they'd done the night before. Definitely not because of the embers of heat that still flickered in his eyes. And *most definitely not* because of the answering flames of need that licked at the underside of her skin.

Denial.

That was new. Must be a side effect of her alcohol-instigated nuptials. She'd rather have the toaster.

"We're married," she announced in a surprisingly steady voice, stating the obvious.

"Apparently."

Patrick huffed out a sharp chuckle, scrubbing his hand over his head, the scratch of his palm over his short hair another almost discordant noise in the room. Dropping his arm, he rose from the bed, tugging the top cover and wrapping the voluminous white comforter around his hips.

She didn't gape at him. She *didn't*.

"Hey." Fingers snapped in front of her. "Up here."

Dragging her attention from the flex and play of taut muscles under gorgeous golden skin, she met his too-amused gaze and smirk.

"Whatever. It's not like it's something I haven't seen before." Not a lie. She'd seen those broad shoulders and wide chest—and probably had her tongue all over them—last night. She just couldn't remember any of it. Still... Flicking a hand, she continued, "Can you stop preening and get dressed? We're in deep shit here, and have—" she lifted the slim, gold Cartier watch from the night-stand, the one that had been a gift from her father on the first anniversary of Media Mavens's opening "—an hour to figure out who knows about this and what we're going to do."

She'd scheduled an escape room outing followed by a lunch at the Peppermill for their last day in Vegas. God, she ground the heel of her palm over her right eyebrow where the headache began to throb again. And she doubted the cause could be attributed to the ungodly amount of liquor she'd drunk last night. No, it had much more to do with the possibility that her employees had been witnesses to, at best, her extreme unprofessionalism. At worst, her lack of control that ended up in this, this...husband situation.

"Oh God, I can't believe this is happening to me." She groaned, dropped her hand away from her face. "What the hell could I possibly have been thinking? Well, that's just it, right? I obviously wasn't thinking. If I was, I wouldn't have made the biggest and most *ridiculous* mistake of my damn life," she rambled more to herself than Patrick.

But when she glanced up and caught his face that could've been carved from stone, she quietly cursed.

"Patrick, I didn't mean—"

"That I was a mistake?" A tight smile pulled at the corners of his sensual lips. It was full of mocking derision and completely void of humor. "We're not just husband and wife, Brooklyn, we're friends. There's no need to pull your punches for me. This is a shitshow, but it's a shitshow of our own making."

"You think I don't know that?" she snapped, sweeping a hand over the bun she'd corralled her hair into before her shower. "It's bad enough we might have..." The words to describe exactly what they might've done in that bed stuck on her tongue like super glue. Instead, she settled for waving a hand back and forth between them. "But married? This was not on my bingo card for the year." Inhaling a deep breath through her nose, she held it for several seconds then slowly released it. Nope. That coping mechanism was a total fail. Panic still clawed at her like a sadistic beast that wouldn't be satisfied until she cracked under the anxiety and pressure. "How can I face everyone after my behavior last night? They'll never look at me the same way again. Shit, forget that. How am I going to explain all of this to my *parents*? Not only did I go ahead and do the most cliché thing possible in Vegas, but I did it with my sister's ex?" Her grated burst of laughter scraped her throat. "Obviously, my motto when it comes to fucking up is go big or go home. And I for damn sure can't go home married to you. No offense."

"None taken," he drawled, a note of humor warming his voice.

But that amusement hadn't thawed the ice in his eyes. A pang thumped in her chest, and she resisted the urge to rub the spot directly between her breasts. Still... He lied. He had taken offense, and she regretted being the cause of it. At the end of the day—or honeymoon, or...whatever—he was more than her employee. Patrick was her friend. Aside from Kat, her best friend. Tragedy tended to bring people closer.

The tragedy in question being his relationship with her sister.

"Patrick, I'm sorry." She rubbed her forehead. "I keep putting my foot in my mouth when it comes to you. It's not like there's anything wrong with you. You're my friend, you're great. But this situation—"

"Stop." The quiet order laced with an undertone of steel cut off her flow of words, sending a frisson of shock through her. She blinked. He'd never used that tone with her before. And she didn't like it. Right? "I know what you're saying, so either stop trying to explain or hand over the shovel so I can stop you from digging that hole deeper."

Striding past her, he rounded the bed and spotting his pants, bent down and reached for them. The hand clutching the white bedcovers opened and the fluffy material fell...

"Shit!" She slammed her eyes shut. Even going so far as to slap a hand over her eyes.

But nothing could erase the image burned into her brain like the scar left behind by a branding iron. The deep vee just under his ridged abs and above his hips. A flash of the firm, muscular curve of his ass. A glimpse of the dark blond, nearly brown, thicket of hair just above his...

Spinning around, she gave him her back and blindly stared at the opposite wall and down the hall that led to the hotel room door. She deliberately kept her gaze from straying to the stripped-down bed and its tangled sheets.

"You could've given me some warning, dammit."

Irritation, mortification and...*nononono*...lust swirled through her veins, heating her up like the bright red sign welcoming every tourist to Sin City. In an instant she'd become a freaking beacon of need, and it terrified her. She couldn't want Patrick. She could randomly stop a car on Fremont Street and find someone less...burdensome than Patrick.

Not prettier. Not with a hotter body. Not funnier. Not...Patrick-ier.

But definitely less burdensome.

"You just told me it's nothing you haven't seen before, so what's the problem?" he asked, lobbing her words back at her. "You can turn around now. I'm decent."

"That's up for debate." she muttered, cautiously turning back around. Decent? He now wore pants, but they

remained unbuttoned as did the shirt left open, granting
her an unhindered view of his chest. They obviously had
different definitions of *decent*. "Patrick," she murmured,
sinking to the bed and keeping her focus firmly on his
face. "What're we going to do? We can't go home—" she
dropped her gaze to the plastic ring still adorning his finger, and her mouth went dry "—together."

She'd already said *married* once; she couldn't do it
again.

That panic started to rise again, scratching at her, steal-
ing the air from her lungs. Her breath rushed in her head
like a wind tunnel, deafening her to everything but the
soundtrack of her own anxiety.

"Hey." Two big hands cupped her face, tilting it down.
"Look at me, Brooklyn. Look me in my eyes."

His touch penetrated the storm whipping inside her
head. It burned through the fog like sun through an early-
morning mist. His words reached her next, and though the
panic still grasped and tore at her, she obeyed him, lifting
her lids and meeting his beautiful gaze. She tumbled into
it, grabbing on to the calm, reassuring raft he tossed her.

These episodes didn't occur often; she hadn't experienced one since her father had a health scare nearly two
years ago. Another instance where the situation had been
completely out of her control. When she couldn't make
things better.

"Brooklyn."

The pads of his fingers pressed harder against her
cheeks, and she battled against closing her eyes once more.
This time to float in the strength and steadiness of his
touch, of him. She prided herself on standing on her own,
on being the rock everyone leaned on. But in this instant,
she wanted to be the one taking that support, depending

on it. And that sharp need had her lifting her head, angling away from his hands.

"You good?" he asked, lowering his hands and settling them on her thighs. "What do you need?"

With his fingers only centimeters from her sore sex, that was a dangerously loaded question. She shook her head as if that would dislodge her inappropriate thoughts. Even if they were for her husband.

Stop that, dammit.

She sighed. "I need you to be my friend right now. I need…" She groaned.

"Help," he supplied. "You need help. It's so hard for you to admit that." He shook his head, a half smile riding the corner of his mouth. "Last I checked you weren't in this by yourself. Look…" He rose, sitting beside her on the mattress. "First thing we do after we return home is go see a lawyer. See if this marriage is even legal. Because of the circumstances, it might not be."

Hope trickled through her, and she straightened. "Of course. Why didn't I think of that? We were both drunk and can't even remember the wedding much less exchanging vows. That has to illegitimatize this whole thing."

He nodded and stood, crossing the room to the table. Pulling the chair out, he dropped onto it and grabbed his shoes.

Head bent, he said, "As far as today, we do what most adults do when they've been caught doing wrong—we pretend shit didn't happen."

"Oh so we pulling a Shaggy. Wasn't me. Got it." She nodded and rose, too, clutching the lapels of her robe together.

Staring down at her magenta-painted toes that peeked out from under the robe's hem, she hesitated. And because Patrick was who he was, his socked feet appeared in her line of vision.

"Brooklyn."

He didn't need to tell her to look at him this time. She lifted her head, obeying the silent command.

"Tell me what you're thinking, sweetheart." He slid a hand in the pocket of her robe and covered hers, gently squeezing.

That *sweetheart* shivered through her, and she felt its reverberations *everywhere*. Had he called her that last night? While he kissed her? While he was inside her?

Best not to dwell on that.

Best not to dwell on the dark coil that unfurled low in her belly at the thought of whether or not he'd called Kayla that, too.

Not your business.

"I'm thinking you need to go back to your room so I can get dressed and downstairs to meet everyone else," she said.

Deliberately, she stepped back, making his hands fall away from her. And she told herself that her skin didn't tingle from the lost connection. That her body didn't whine for him to put them right back on her.

She took another step back. And another until her thighs hit the edge of the mattress.

And from the slight narrowing of Patrick's eyes, he didn't miss her maneuver. Any other time, she would've bluffed her way out of this tension-filled moment with a slick comment. But she was desperate for air that wasn't infused with *him*.

"Okay." He studied her for another long moment. "I'll see you down there."

He returned to the table, grabbed his shoes and headed for the door.

"Wait!" she called after him. Patrick stopped, turned around. "Your—" she cleared her throat "—ring. Can you please take that thing off?"

Patrick blinked then glanced down at his hand as if he'd forgotten the gaudy plastic jewelry still adorned his hand. When he lifted his head and met her gaze, he shook his head.

"Sorry, sweetheart. I'm not one of those husbands who refuses to wear their ring. I'm proud of being your man."

"Patrick," she growled his name like a warning. No, a threat.

But the corner of his mouth quirked in a slight smirk, then he turned and continued down the hall and out of her room. She didn't move, but stared at the space he used to occupy.

I'm proud of being your man.

Dueling emotions of fear and, God help her, pleasure, twisted together, snarling until she couldn't separate one from the other. As his words echoed in her head, the two emotions became synonymous.

"Oh damn," she whispered. "I'm in trouble." Heaving a louder sigh, she sank to the bed.

Though she had to get dressed, down about two gallons of coffee and meet her employees downstairs in the hotel lobby, she didn't move. Didn't do anything but stare at the window and the sprawling view of Las Vegas. She beat back the edges of panic that tried to tackle her again and drag her under.

She hated being out of control.

She hated being a prisoner to her own bad decisions.

She hated being uncertain of the future.

Most of all, she *hated Blue Christmas*.

CHAPTER TWO

COLE DENNISON, ATTORNEY-AT-LAW and Rose Bend's mayor, stared at Patrick and Brooklyn across his desk as if they were two strangers—two aliens—instead of people he'd known for several years. In Patrick's case, almost two decades.

And maybe because of that long friendship, Cole's gaze remained on Patrick the longest. With a "Huh," the attorney fell back against his office chair and continued to scrutinize them, his fingers steepled under his chin.

Hell.

"That's all we get is *huh*?" Patrick asked, drumming his fingers on the arm of his chair. "Is that a legal opinion?"

Cole shook his head, a smile slowly curving his mouth.

"It's the best one I have at the moment." His smile deepened, broadened, lighting up his brown eyes. "I have to admit," he said, leaning forward and propping his forearms on the desktop, "I've been a lawyer for years, and over those years, people have come to me with some pretty out-there things. But I can honestly say this is my first Vegas elopement." When Brooklyn's lips parted, Cole held up a hand, forestalling what would undoubtedly be an objection to *elopement*. "Sorry, not an elopement. A drunken night of revelry that ended up in a marriage. Still, this is my first. And though I've heard and litigated weirder cases, I'm still a little stunned."

"Try waking up married with no memory of how you got that way," Brooklyn muttered.

Waking up married, no memory and naked. Can't forget that. There was no way he could ever forget that, Patrick silently added. Even if he had no memory of getting her in that state. *Dammit*. But since she wouldn't appreciate the reminder, he kept it to himself.

"Is the wedding or marriage legal?" Patrick asked, gripping the chair arms.

Realizing just how tight his fingers clutched the wood, he deliberately relaxed his hold. And shut down the foolish, ill-advised slivers of hope that slipped between his ribs, refusing to be plucked free.

Hope that Cole would say yes, their marriage was legal and binding. That yes, they had no way out of this situation they'd created and had to make the best of it. Oh yeah, he hoped that he could keep Brooklyn Hayes as his wife. Keep her as his.

But he couldn't voice any of those thoughts. Because that would mean betraying his longest and most closely held secret.

That he was in love with his ex-girlfriend's older sister.

And had been for three years.

He and Kayla had broken up two and a half years ago. Yes, he'd started wanting Brooklyn before he'd broken up with her sister.

That made him an asshole. Especially in Brooklyn and her family's eyes, if they ever found out. But no one had, and no one would. This was his burden, and even before he'd ended things with Kayla, Patrick had accepted he could never have Brooklyn.

But then fate, God, tequila… One or all three had thrown him a bone, and at Christmas, too.

Fuck if he would look a Christmas gift in the mouth.

Even if he could only have that perfect present for the amount of time it took Brooklyn to end them. And she had every intention of doing so. She'd made no bones about that from the moment he'd woken up in her hotel room. In her bed. Tangled up in sheets that carried her jasmine-and-vanilla scent.

Shit.

He was here in Cole's office to nullify his marriage, not think about consummating it.

Goddamn, he wished he could remember that. Remember how it felt to slowly push into her undoubtedly silken, tight-as-a-fist heat. Remember the erotic sounds she made as she pulsed around him, milking him. Remember how her curves aligned perfectly to his as he held her tight afterward.

He didn't need his memories to know he'd held her. Not when he couldn't be within her presence for mere seconds and not damn near hum with the need to touch her.

"I'm sorry," Cole said, interrupting his thoughts. *Thank God.* "But your marriage is perfectly legal and recognized outside Las Vegas and the state of Nevada. You two are husband and wife in the eyes of the law."

Brooklyn released an audible, tired sigh beside him. He glanced over in time to catch her pinching the bridge of her nose.

"I had a feeling you were going to say that," she murmured.

Glimpsing the disappointment and weariness etched into her lovely features, Patrick smothered the urge to lift her out of that chair, take her place, set her on his lap and cuddle her close. Assure her everything would be okay. That they could and would get through this together.

But she didn't want that from him.

And years of hiding in plain sight had ingrained a self-protective instinct that had been finely honed by the fear of rejection from this woman who owned him.

Owned him and had no clue.

Just going by her reaction in the hotel that morning three days ago and now here, in the office, she still didn't. That was his only saving grace in this whole mess. He might never be with the woman he loved, but at least he had his pride.

That and his annual binge of *A Christmas Story* would have to be enough.

"What's our next step?" he asked Cole, his voice even, calm. Even though inside he wanted to growl, *Fuck next steps*. "What do you need from us?"

"Well, we have two options. You can file for divorce, or I can file an annulment."

"What's the difference? I mean, obviously, I know the difference," Brooklyn said, waving a hand, "but what does that mean in the eyes of the court?"

"Simply put, a divorce declares the marriage legally over. A divorce acknowledges a valid union while an annulment regards the marriage null and void. Under the law, it never happened."

"An annulment." Brooklyn leaned forward. "That's what we need. Do you agree?" She turned to Patrick, her gaze expectant behind her blue-framed glasses. And filled with hope.

A hope that cut him to the quick.

"Yes, that would probably be best," he said, dipping his chin.

He really should've majored in theater instead of graphic design. Apparently, he was one hell of an actor.

"Let me give you all the information before making your decision. A divorce is much more commonplace than an annulment and easier to obtain. Your reasons can be as simple as irreconcilable differences. An annulment, on the other hand, requires specific conditions and criteria are met, and it can be harder to get the courts to grant one." He rubbed a hand across his chin. "The court-acknowledged circumstances that are grounds for annulments are fake pretenses, mental incompetence, bigamy, underage marriage, incest, concealment and failure to consummate the marriage. I'm going to assume you weren't tricked into marriage, neither of you already has a spouse, you're not related and well…" He cleared his throat and winced. "What happened in that Vegas hotel room is your business."

Brooklyn groaned, tilting her head back to stare at the ceiling.

"Answer enough." A smile jerked at Cole's mouth before he continued, "But we can definitely make a case for mental incompetence since you were both under the influence of alcohol. If you're certain this is how you want to move forward, I can get started tomorrow."

"How…public will this all be?" Brooklyn whispered.

Cole cocked his head, and the sympathy in his eyes reflected in his voice.

"Court filings are public records and available to anyone who goes looking for them."

"Shit," she muttered.

He shouldn't take her frustration and distress personally. She was disgusted with the situation, not him. He got that. Still…

"Someone would have to go looking for the information to find it, Brooklyn. And we haven't exactly been going around announcing our big sin. Let Cole get started on undoing this thing, and we'll keep our dirty little secret between us for as long as possible," he drawled.

Cole's gaze narrowed on him, and Patrick tried not to stiffen at the knowing gleam in the other man's eyes. Hell, he'd sounded bitter even to himself.

But of course, Brooklyn didn't notice. She never... noticed.

"Easy for you to say," she muttered. "You won't have the wrath of your family raining down on your head if they— *Shit*. Patrick..." She turned to him, remorse and horror darkening her eyes. "I didn't mean it like that. I'm sorry."

She appeared stricken and reached for him, covering his hand with hers, slipping her fingers between his and squeezing. Despite the deep cut her inadvertently careless words inflicted and the bloom of old pain in his sternum, he shook his head and flipped his hand over, holding hers tighter.

"It's fine."

That sharp stab of pain was already fading, but the reminder of being alone in this world didn't. A year later, and sometimes the loss of his father remained as sharp as the day he was taken from him.

"It's not," Brooklyn argued on a low murmur.

He gently squeezed her fingers.

"Let it go, Brook," he quietly ordered.

She studied him, those dark eyes roaming over his face. Finally, she nodded and shifted her attention back to Cole.

"Fine," she muttered. "But you're no one's dirty secret. Don't say that again or I might reconsider my stance on pacifism."

Surprise momentarily struck him in the chest, pilfering his breath and any response he had. Not that he did have one. He could only stare at her deceptively delicate profile. What did she mean by him not being a dirty secret? Did she…?

Mentally, he shook his head. *Stop projecting*, he silently ordered himself. She hadn't even said *her* secret but *no one's*. Small difference, but so huge. Because one claimed him as hers, and the other… Well, the other meant he belonged to no one, just as she'd said.

Jerking his gaze from her, he murmured, "I wasn't aware you had a position on nonviolence. All those true-crime shows you watch are terribly misleading, then."

She turned back to him, her eyes narrowed behind her stylish blue frames.

"I'll have you know they're very educational as well as entertaining," she snapped.

Patrick slowly nodded. "Good to know," he said, then glanced at a silent Cole. "Cole, she finds shows about offing your spouse educational. You heard it right there. So if I disappear before this annulment goes through, don't believe that I left town for a job no one's ever heard of. Nor did I leave her for another woman. You're my witness."

Her growl echoed through the room, and despite the reason they sat here in an attorney's office, he smirked.

And because he couldn't help himself—and that little growl she gave was both cute and arousing—he added with a cocked eyebrow, "I think I should have my will drawn up while we're here. She gets nothing in the case of my untimely death. Especially if there's a home invasion and she makes it out alive while I'm murdered."

"We don't even live together, numbskull," she sniped.

"Semantics."

"Uh." Cole coughed into his fist, but he couldn't completely hide the smile tugging at his mouth. "I'll make a note of that, Patrick. As enjoyable—and maybe a tiny bit disturbing—as this has been, I need to end our meeting. Yulefest starts tonight, and I have to head over to the town hall to handle a few last-minute things. Is there anything else you need to discuss with me?"

"No, I think that's it," Brooklyn said.

Patrick shook his head and rose along with Brooklyn and Cole. The attorney rounded his desk, hand outstretched. Brooklyn, then Patrick, shook it, thanking Cole for his help. Moments later they left the office and stood outside the brick building with its white scrolled sign. Cole's office stood on a corner lot off Main Street. But this road, like the rest of Rose Bend, proudly wore all the holiday decorations as did most of the town. White and multicolored lights, poinsettias and garland wrapped around every iron lamppost, over most of the awnings, and were strung across the street from building to building. Huge wreaths and red bows hung over the streets, forming multiple decorative arches. Not even the telephone poles missed out, adorned with garland, tiny toys and more lights.

At this time of year, Rose Bend transformed into a cross between a winter wonderland and Santa's workshop.

He loved it.

Christmas in his hometown was downright magical. And yes, he did feel slightly foolish even thinking that at his big age of thirty-three, but given the cheer of Rose Bend's annual, monthlong holiday festival, and the way the entire town threw itself into celebrating this time of year, he could be forgiven his temporary flight of fancy.

"That wasn't so bad," Brooklyn said, her breath a cloudy puff on the cold December air.

She slipped her hands into her gloves and settled earmuffs over her head. The sight of them never failed to drag a spurt of humor out of her. The overtly feminine headwear with its purple band and puffs of white fur so contrasted her no-nonsense personality. He loved the contrast.

Shit, he just loved her.

He smothered a sigh and tried to let the air that practically crackled with anticipation and the festivity of the season replace the tiny kernel of resentment that burrowed under his ribs.

Not resentment of her. He couldn't blame her for not loving him, for not even seeing him as anything but her friend and employee. Just as he couldn't help loving her, being bitter at her would be hypocritical.

No, all his resentment was self-directed. Because if his father had taught him anything it was the futility of wanting someone who didn't want you back. Patrick had believed he'd learned that lesson as an unwilling pupil. But apparently, he'd failed. And epically.

"No," he replied to her statement. "Not too—*whoa*." He just managed to brace himself as Brooklyn's body collided with his own. On pure reflex and instinct, his arms rose and wrapped around her even as she gripped the back of his coat and held him close. "Sweetheart, what's this? What's wrong?"

He lowered his head, her thick, dark brown curls tickling his chin and mouth. His eyes closed, but a second later he opened them, staring at the Christmas tree in the window of Dyson Realtors. He *had* to focus on that six-foot tree decorated with ornaments shaped like houses and keys. Otherwise, he might concentrate too closely on the feel of Brooklyn's petite frame pressed to his taller one. Give too much attention to her abundant, sexy-as-fuck curves and how her soft lushness cushioned his bigger, harder body.

Jesus.

He wasn't a saint. *Don't even fucking think about it*, he snarled to his unruly dick. He struggled to control his body's response. Fought not to let it betray the lust swarming through his blood like a thousand enraged bees let loose from their hive. But the longer those small, firm breasts, softly rounded stomach and thick, gorgeous thighs pressed against him, the more difficult it became to hide just how beautiful and hot he found her.

A Christmas miracle. Where was a damn Christmas miracle when he needed one?

"Sweetheart," he said again, voice rough with need. "What's going on?"

"I'm sorry, Patrick," came her muffled answer.

"For what?"

She tipped her head back away from his chest. "For being a thoughtless asshole back there." Her eyes appeared rounder, softer, behind her glasses as she studied his face. "This time of year must be hard for you," she whispered. "And I didn't mean to hurt you with my careless words."

Realization that she was referring to her comment about family dawned on him, and he vacillated between removing her arms and stepping back, as if emotional distance would emulate physical distance, and drawing her impossibly closer, stamping her skin, her scent, her fucking *being*, on him.

Instead, he landed somewhere in the middle.

He didn't release her; he wasn't that honorable. But he did shift backward just a little, placing air between their bodies. It did nothing to calm the hungry roar inside him demanding he claim that carnal mouth, mark that elegant neck. Grind his aching cock against her belly.

Inhaling a deep breath, he stroked a hand up her spine

under the guise of comforting her when he was taking shameless advantage of just being able to touch her without revealing his secret.

Cupping the nape of her neck, he said, "It's fine, Brooklyn. You didn't—"

She shook her head, a small frown creasing her forehead. "No," she interrupted. "Don't tell me I didn't hurt you. I've known you too long and too well. You were hurt. I hurt you."

She didn't know him *that* well. If Brooklyn did, she wouldn't be standing here, arms around him. No, she would be lecturing him on why they wouldn't work. All while slowly backing away from him as if he'd sprouted horns and cloven feet.

"Stop."

He squeezed the back of her neck. Her lips snapped shut, trapping whatever point she'd probably been about to make next. She slightly stiffened against him—the action so small that if he hadn't been fine tuned into her exact frequency, he would've missed it. Her eyes dipped to his mouth, and just as his gut clenched hard, she lifted her gaze to his.

Was it his imagination or… No. Couldn't be.

Even as his mind told him he was reading too much into her reaction, he once more flexed his fingers around her neck.

Fuck. Him.

Desire. Surprise and desire glinted in her dark gaze. Her lashes lowered, almost immediately concealing her eyes, but no, he hadn't imagined it. He *hadn't*. Lust whipped through him like the winds of a destructive storm, threatening to tear him to shreds.

"Brooklyn…"

"It's a good thing we're not staying married," she said,

stepping back and stuffing her hands into the pockets of her red bubble coat. "I'd have to smother you in your sleep if you tried to order me around."

He smirked, concealing the confusion and arousal eddying inside him.

"Believe me, Brookie, if I were giving you orders, you'd know it." He shifted forward, reclaiming the space she'd placed between them. Bending his head over hers, he murmured, "And like it."

Her soft gasp whispered over his lips, and it was the closest thing to a kiss. It set him on fire.

He was pushing it—pushing her. And he couldn't even say why. Maybe if he hadn't glimpsed that desire in her eyes, he wouldn't have allowed those words to slip out of his mouth. But he couldn't unsee it. Didn't want to.

"Have you met me?" She snorted, arching an eyebrow. "That's extremely doubtful."

But her shadowed eyes and the slight tremble of her lips didn't match up with her sardonic tone.

Back up. Give her room. Let her breathe.

But why should she get to breathe when he couldn't?

"Is that a challenge?" he softly asked.

Uncertainty shimmered in her eyes as she silently studied him, and he bit off a curse, lifting his hand to cup her cheek. Fuck what she would think about her *friend* touching her in a way he wasn't supposed to. That doubt constricted his chest, and he couldn't bear seeing it on her.

"Brooklyn? Patrick?"

The familiar feminine voice doused him in freezing-cold reality. He stiffened, and Brooklyn leaped away from him like a cat desperate to save its ninth life. *Shit.* What was he thinking? They stood on the sidewalk in full view of anyone driving or walking by. And in Rose Bend someone was *always* driving or walking by. So caught up in the silken web of her, Patrick had inadvertently made them a possible target for gossip. He wasn't protecting her. And now the very last person Brooklyn wanted to encounter stood several feet away from them, her dark, curious gaze shifting to Brooklyn, then to Patrick.

"Hey, Mom." Brooklyn greeted her mother, her wide smile taut at the corners. "What are you doing here?"

"Your father said he wanted my fried steak for dinner, so I had to go to the meat market and pick up some cube steaks," Lily Hayes explained, waving a hand toward the small supermarket across the street from Cole's law office. "What are you two doing here? Shouldn't you be at work?" Before Brooklyn could answer, her mother frowned, glancing behind them. "Are you coming from Cole Dennison's office?"

"Um, yes," Brooklyn said, and maybe her mother didn't hear the threads of panic in her voice, but Patrick did. "We were just…"

She glanced at Patrick, her lips parted and eyes wide.

"We were just there to discuss some matters regarding Media Mavens. Since Kat had a meeting she couldn't reschedule, I offered to come with Brooklyn," he smoothly finished for her.

"Oh, okay." Lily shook her head, tsking. "Honey, you work too much. I keep telling you that. But you never listen to me. I'm just your mother."

"Oh God." Brooklyn groaned.

Lily's eyes narrowed on her daughter, and Patrick wisely choked back a laugh. He'd been around the Hayes family enough to predict what was to come.

"Excuse me, Brooklyn Regina Hayes?"

"Oh damn. She's using my government name," Brooklyn muttered.

This time Patrick couldn't contain his snicker. She shot

him a glare, and he shrugged. He'd helped her out with the excuse to throw her mother off the scent of why they were at Cole's office. And once Lily Hayes caught whiff of something off, she transformed into a bloodhound. She didn't let go until she uncovered the truth.

He cocked an eyebrow at Brooklyn.

A little gratitude would be nice, he silently relayed.

"Excuse me?" Lily asked, her narrowed gaze fixed on her daughter. "Care to repeat that?"

Brooklyn immediately shook her head. "No. Repeat what? What did I say? I don't even remember speaking."

Her mother sniffed, squinting at her. "Humph. That's what I thought." She shifted her attention to Patrick, and he wiped all amusement from his face. Lily Hayes had that effect on people. She carried that "Straighten up and do right" energy. "I'm actually glad to see you, Patrick. It saves me a phone call. We're having a family dinner tonight before the tree lighting. You're invited."

"Oh wow, uh…" In his peripheral vision, he caught the almost infinitesimal shake of Brooklyn's head. Even if he didn't catch that, though, the mouthed "hell no" would've been a clear indication she didn't want him to accept. "Thank you for the invite, Mrs. Hayes, but—"

"No buts," she interrupted with a wave of her hand. "You're coming to dinner and that's it. You don't just work for my daughter. You're family. And we don't leave family behind."

A fist of emotion shoved into his throat, and he swallowed, working to clear the blockage. But he couldn't. She could've been referring to his breakup with Kayla, but Lily wasn't—or at least not only that.

He'd lost his father this time last year. A sudden heart attack had taken his only parent, as his mother had left both of them before Patrick had turned two. Brooklyn and her family had been there for him. Lily had made sure his refrigerator stayed stocked. Several times a week, Milo Hayes, Brooklyn's father, had dropped by the house he'd inherited from his father on the pretense of catching the game of whatever sport happened to be playing on television that night. And Brooklyn...

Brooklyn had been his rock. Being his ear when he needed to talk, or his shoulder when he just sat there in silence. All of them had helped him go through his father's belongings, and it'd been Brooklyn who'd spent the night in his spare bedroom because she refused to leave him alone afterward.

Patrick didn't know how he would've made it through the most difficult time of his life. And this would be his first Christmas without the parent who had molded, shaped and loved him into who he was today. The thought of decorating the house without Lionel King there to give him shit about where he was putting the tree, or how many lights he hung outside—never enough, according to his father—it sat on his chest like a hundred-pound weight. And he'd been avoiding dwelling on it.

But he should've known Lily would come for him.

We don't leave family behind.

No, she didn't. They didn't.

"You stole that from the marines," Brooklyn muttered.

"Excuse me?" Lily asked, sliding her daughter an arch look. "Did you say something, honey?"

"Nope. Not a word."

"Uh-huh." She returned her gaze to Patrick. "So tonight, five o'clock sharp. Then we can head over to the tree lighting together. Okay?"

"Okay," he agreed with a smile. "I'll see you tonight."

"Good." She nodded and pulled him close for a hug. When she stepped back, she nailed her daughter with another narrowed glance. "I know I'll see you there. Don't be late."

"Yes, Mom."

Grumbling, Lily moved to her and, cupping Brooklyn's face and tilting it down, smacked a kiss on her forehead. Brooklyn had inherited her five-foot-two-inch height from her mother, and they appeared more like sisters than mother and daughter. They also shared the delicate bone structure, curvy frame and thick, tightly spiraled, shoulder-length curls. Although Lily's contained a sprinkling of gray.

"Bye, you two," Lily called, and with a wiggle of her fingers, strode off down the sidewalk.

They stared after her for several silent seconds. Then Brooklyn sighed.

"I'm the most selfish bitch walking," she murmured to herself, but he caught it, and he frowned down at her.

"What the hell?" he asked.

"I am." She tilted her head, and her solemn gaze took him aback. "I was so concerned with us not being around my family together to avoid any kind of slipups or stir their suspicion. All I thought about was me and our current situation. And I completely didn't consider that this is your first Christmas without your dad. Of course I want you there with us. You *belong* with us."

Shaking his head, he couldn't *not* reach out to her. Not touch her. Sliding his hand over her shoulder, he cupped her nape.

"I've never said that about you, and I don't want to hear you say that about yourself, either. Brooklyn, you are the most selfless person I know. This situation isn't… simple and it's not like either of us have ever experienced anything like it." He paused, cocking his head. "Unless there's something you want to tell me." She snorted, rolling her eyes, and he chuckled, squeezing her. "Don't apologize for your feelings. They're valid and—" he edged closer, staring down into her eyes "—thank you for trusting me with your feelings and yourself."

Her teeth sank into her bottom lip and his fingers itched with the need to tug it free, stroke a caress over the tender flesh.

"So you've never called me a bitch? Not even in your head?" she asked.

"That's what you got out of everything I just said?" He scoffed, giving her a wry smile. "But no. Never."

She studied him for a moment. "What about crazy?"

"Oh hell yeah."

A grin slowly widened her mouth, lighting her face. Then she tipped her head back, and a bark of loud laughter escaped her. He chuckled and drew her close, hugging her. Torturing himself with the feel of her. Punishing himself with the crisp and sultry scent of her.

"It just so happens I adore your crazy, Mrs. King," he teased, though his pulse sped up at the thought of being able to give her his name.

No. At the thought of her accepting his name.

"See?" Leaning back, she scowled, jabbing a finger at him. "That right there. No more of that Mrs. shit. I just know you're going to slip up tonight. You can't hold water."

His chin jerked back, and he widened his eyes in exaggerated offense.

"Me? I beg your pardon." He splayed his fingers wide over his chest. "Name one time I didn't keep a secret."

She tapped her chin, eyes squinted.

"You mean like when you spilled to Jeremy about the surprise party we planned for him at the office?"

"He knew about it anyway." Patrick scoffed.

"Or about the time you told Kat about the new car Sam bought her?" Brooklyn continued, poking him in the chest. "Or when you let it slip to Katherine what the sex of her baby was and pretty much ruined the gender reveal party her husband had planned."

"You dug deep for that one. That was three years ago," he muttered.

"John still gives you side-eye when he comes to the office," she pointed out.

"Fine." He threw up his hands. "So a few times I've *accidentally* divulged some information." He ignored her snort. "How about a bet?"

She crossed her arms over her chest. "What kind of bet?"

"If you tell about the—" he dramatically lowered his voice "—situation, then you have to declare February second Patrick King Day, and it comes with a cake and speech extolling all of my virtues. Don't worry. I'll write it for you."

"And if I win," she said, leaning forward, "you have to walk down Main Street carrying a sign that says Brooklyn Hayes Rocks. Deal?" She thrust out her hand toward him.

"Deal."

They shook on it. And grinned at one another.

"You're going down, King."

"Bring it, Mrs. King."

CHAPTER THREE

"Ten... Nine... Eight... Seven..."

Brooklyn shouted along with the rest of Rose Bend's citizens, counting down the seconds until...

"One!"

The lights on the enormous Christmas tree in the middle of The Glen, a huge meadow at the end of Main Street, flared to life. Though this was her umpteenth Christmas tree lighting, the event that kicked off Yulefest, it never failed to fill her with a sense of awe. The towering tree in the middle of the field with its homemade ornaments and beautiful glass balls was the perfect emblem for the holiday and the festival that drew visitors from neighboring cities and states.

The beauty of the tree and the holiday cheer that seemed to permeate the air almost wiped away the memories and anxiety of the disastrous family dinner earlier that evening.

Almost.

A vise grip tightened around her chest, and she inhaled a breath, attempting to release the hold that very recent memory had on her.

"This never gets old," Patrick murmured from beside her, nearly echoing her thoughts from moments ago.

"It really doesn't." She smiled and pretended not to notice how the red, blue and green lights highlighted his chiseled cheekbones, the sharp line of his jaw and that full bottom lip. Nope. She didn't notice at all. "It's no wonder why this is my favorite time of year."

"Mine, too." He glanced down at her, the corner of his mouth quirked. "And it has nothing to do with the bonus you give us at work."

"Of course not." She smirked. Shifting her gaze back to the tree, she sighed. "You know, it's ironic." She huffed out a soft chuckle, shaking her head. "When I was younger, I would dream about my wedding day. And I pictured getting married right in front of this tree. I'd carry a bouquet of poinsettias and have them in my hair. And I'd wear a white fur shawl over my dress. And *I Saw Mommy Kissing Santa Claus* by the Jackson 5 would be playing as I walked down the aisle." At Patrick's snicker, she held up a gloved hand. "Listen, I was eleven." But her quiet laughter joined his. "God, I haven't thought of that in a long time."

"I'm sorry you didn't get the wedding you imagined," Patrick murmured.

"That was a girl's dream," she said, waving away his words with a flick of her hand. But she couldn't dismiss the twinge in her chest at the long-forgotten memory. Silly. The regret in her heart was silly. "And I'm far from being that little girl. Life isn't a thirty-minute sitcom or a romance movie. More like women's fiction with horror elements."

She expected him to laugh, but he didn't. Instead, Patrick cocked his head and his bright gaze roamed over her face. As if searching out the truth behind her words. As if he didn't believe her.

"You deserve the dream and a romantic movie ending," he softly said.

That twinge in her chest pulled taut, vibrating through her. When a person looked at Patrick, they would see the proud, nearly stark bone structure, the sharp gaze and lush mouth. They'd also take in the tall, wide-shouldered big build and might be intimidated or believe him to be aloof, reserved. And that wasn't altogether false. He could come across as standoffish. But most people didn't realize that Patrick was almost shy around those he didn't know well. Only when he was comfortable did he lower his guard and allow a person to see the funny, sensitive and unerringly kind man he was.

Pride swelled inside her that he counted her among those precious few he called friends.

Friends? Friends don't notice each other's thighs and ass.

They did if they got married and ended up naked in the bed together.

She silently sighed. This same back and forth had been warring in her head since her return from Vegas.

"And you're sweet," she murmured, replying to Patrick. Averting her gaze—afraid if she met his eyes, he would glimpse the confusion and the darker, twistier emotion she refused to name—she tugged her hat farther down over her curls. "Now, come treat me to some hot chocolate."

They crossed the field, winding their way through the festive assortment of booths offering everything from steaming hot beverages and food to Christmas ornaments and ugly sweaters. Made sense the latter booth had a line gathered in front of it given the holiday ugly sweater competition was slated for next week.

Minutes later a large hot chocolate cupped in her hands with the warmth seeping through her gloves, Brooklyn forged a path toward the funnel cake fryer located under the huge tent on the far right side of The Glen. As they moved through the line to all that golden, fried, powdered-sugar goodness, she chatted with friends and townspeople she'd known one way or another her entire life.

And right at her elbow stood the quiet pillar of strength she'd come to depend on not just as an employee, but as her friend.

Don't forget husband.

How could she? And boy, had she tried.

She slid a sidelong glance at him as Tricia Martin shook powdered sugar over her funnel cake. He'd been her employee for four years, and her friend for almost as long. And other than objective appreciation for his loveliness, Patrick had only been just that—her employee and friend. And oh yes, her sister's ex. Couldn't forget that fact.

But since she'd woken up in that hotel room with him, she couldn't look at the marble-like line of his jaw and not wonder if she'd trailed her lips along it. Couldn't peek at the breadth of his chest and not speculate if she'd nuzzled it, rested her ear against his heartbeat.

Couldn't glance at that mouth and hope she'd devoured it…and pray it had returned the favor.

No, since that morning, he'd become so much more. Her every desire.

And goddamn, it was *so wrong.*

"Brooklyn, Patrick."

She stiffened, a charge of unease and shock tripping down her spine.

Damn. It.

Turning around with a piece of funnel cake lifted to her mouth, she forced her lips into a smile she prayed didn't appear as strained as it felt.

"Hey, Kayla," she greeted her sister. Then, spotting her parents behind her. "Mom, Dad."

And with those words—and her family standing in front of her—the calamitous dinner popped back into her head. Well, not that it'd been very far from her memories. But the lighting, the hot chocolate, funnel cake and Patrick had aided in sublimating it.

And with the reemergence of just how *cringe* the earlier part of this night had been, she shifted away from Patrick, inserting the smallest amount of space between them. But when she glanced at him, and her gaze collided with that turquoise hooded stare, it felt like an ocean could fit into that space.

But what could she do? There wasn't a handbook on how to react when your baby sister showed up for dinner, surprising you and the man she almost married. The man who you *did* marry. Didn't help that all through the awkward meal and small talk afterward, she could've sworn *Married in Vegas* blinked on her forehead like a neon vacancy sign on a cheap hotel.

Guilt and fear comingled in the nastiest of cocktails, guaranteed to leave her with a worse hangover than the one that had gotten her in this predicament in the first place.

"How'd you enjoy the tree lighting?" Brooklyn asked Kayla and her parents, desperately searching for something, *anything*, to say. Okay, to deflect.

"It's the same as ever," Kayla said, her shrug as dismissive as her tone. "I mean, once you've seen the one on Boston Common, this one kind of pales in comparison. They bring that tree in all the way from Nova Scotia, not just some Christmas tree farm."

Brooklyn gritted her teeth, trapping her instinctive, "Bitch, please." It was the holidays after all, and her present to Kayla could be not calling her out on her bullshit. Better than the sweater from Kohl's she planned on purchasing.

Her relationship with her sister was…complicated.

Something that smacked of sibling rivalry but dug just a bit deeper. Kayla had always been in competition with Brooklyn, trying to one-up her in academics, sports and now, in careers. And Brooklyn...

Well, for the past twenty-seven years—ever since Kayla had been born when Brooklyn had been three—she'd been competing in the match for their parents' love and attention. More often than not, she came in second. And there were only two of them.

"Well, I'm biased. Nothing compares to a good ol' Rose Bend tree lighting. No offense to Boston," her father added with a warm smile. He wrapped his arm around her mother's shoulder and planted a kiss on her thick curls. "Especially when I have the love of my life by my side. This will be our thirty-second lighting together. It was—"

"Our first date," Brooklyn and Kayla finished his sentence together.

Patrick chuckled beside her, and her father grinned.

"And our first kiss. Right, sweetie?" he asked, and when her mother tipped her head back, they shared a kiss right in front of God, country and their daughters.

Kayla groaned, and Brooklyn grimaced.

It was sweet...and ew.

She might be thirty, but when her parents went into PDA mode, she reverted to a twelve-year-old. No one wanted to see all...that. Primarily her. Shit, she still denied they'd actually had sex.

Still, with the story of their first date hammered into her head since she was little, she couldn't be blamed for imagining her wedding happening in the same place. But as she'd told Patrick, that was a girl's dream.

"Right, baby." Her mother preened under his obvious affection and devotion, and Brooklyn would be a liar if she didn't admit to a pang of envy...of loneliness.

While her parents might be a wee bit nauseating with their open displays—she'd caught him copping a feel of her mother's breast in the kitchen last Thanksgiving— she couldn't deny she'd wanted what they had once upon a time. Back before she realized any man she pledged her fidelity and future to would have to pass the gauntlet of her sister. More specifically, not spying her younger, skinnier, more fun, conventionally beautiful sister and falling in lust and love with her on sight. It'd occurred with her first and second boyfriends in high school. Happened with the man she'd been dating for six months in college. Transpired again four years ago when she met the man she'd been talking to online for five months in person for the first time. All had one thing in common. They'd taken one look at Kayla and decided they'd all dated the wrong Hayes sister.

And then there was her husband.

God. She broke off another piece of funnel cake and ate it, swallowing her unwanted resentment along with it. *I definitely seem to have a type.*

"You might want to slow down on that, Brooklyn," Kayla said, frowning as her lips turned up. "As they say, a moment on the lips, a lifetime on the hips." Her gaze scanned down Brooklyn's body, settling on the offending area—at least in her opinion, it seemed.

Instead of verbally replying to that unsubtle dig about her weight, Brooklyn popped another piece of the fried dough into her mouth, chewing slowly and deliberately. Screw her. She loved her wide hips. And her small breasts and big ass. And don't get her started on her thick thighs. It'd taken years for her to appreciate all the curves she possessed, as well as refuse to allow other people's ideals of beauty to define hers. It'd been a hard-won battle, but she adored every curve, dip and dimple of her size sixteen.

"A lifetime on the hips?" Patrick spoke for the first time since her parents and Kayla approached them. "Eat up, then."

He reached over and broke off a piece of the treat and held it to her lips. And with shock shimmering through her, she parted them and allowed him to slip the dough inside. Only when a faint smirk rode his mouth did she break free of her paralysis and horror swelled inside her.

Horror and heat.

They tussled and tangled with one another, each vying for dominance.

Holy shit.

She blinked, jerking her too-enraptured regard away from him and back to her family, who stared at them with varying degrees of surprise and annoyance.

"It seems like you two have become...friendly—" Kayla bit off the word, sounding decidedly *un*friendly, her narrowed stare shifting from Brooklyn to Patrick, and then back to her "—in the time I've been gone."

"Don't be silly," her mother scoffed. "They're just friends, and don't forget Patrick works for your sister. Although," she continued, "I wish Brooklyn would listen to me and put as much effort into finding someone as she does into that business. A company can't love her back or give her a family."

"I'm standing right here," Brooklyn said dryly.

Did her mother's criticism sting? Yes. All her accomplishments with building a highly successful company that literally started in an efficiency apartment and now employed eleven people and operated out of a suite of offices right there on Main Street didn't matter. Not when compared to a husband and children. None of those things she claimed to want, by the way. At least, not aloud. Her mother, God love her, dismissed Brooklyn's achievements, her success, and reduced her to a womb.

"I have to respectfully beg to differ." Patrick lifted his cup of hot chocolate for a sip, his quiet objection drawing three pairs of eyes his way. "A company isn't comprised of brick and mortar. It's the people who show up for work every day, nurturing a vision, and who are dedicated to its survival. In that way, it can love you in return. And those same people become a family of choice not blood."

Silence seemed to throb in their small circle, temporarily dulling the laughter and chatter surrounding them under the tent.

Pressure shoved against Brooklyn's ribs, and for a moment she couldn't identify that immense, nearly suffocating, feeling. But the longer she stared at Patrick, the clearer it became, like a fog being swept out to sea by a mild but insistent wind.

Awe. Pure and simple.

He was defending her, having her back.

How...novel.

And hot. Damn, was it hot.

She wanted her husband.

Oh, she was so fucked.

"I can't say I've ever looked at it that way before," her father said into the deepening silence. "But I suppose you're correct. Hell, Lily's always calling my squad down at the firehouse my 'other family.'" He smiled, and her mother rolled her eyes. Dad had left a career as a teacher to become a firefighter, and now, twenty-three years later, he was the proud chief of Rose Bend's fire department. And yes, he did consider the men and women under him his family. "If you have that, honey, then I'm happy for you."

Kayla blew out a loud breath and moved forward, slipping between Brooklyn and Patrick, and threading her arm through his.

"Pat, it's been a long time since we've talked. Too long. Buy me a cup of apple cider and catch me up on what's been going on with you?" Kayla murmured, tipping her head to the side, her long ponytail sliding over her shoulder.

Jealousy splintered inside Brooklyn, and she didn't try and pretend the sharp thorns embedded in her chest were anything else.

They looked good together—no, they looked like they belonged together. Kayla—tall, slim, with her delicate bone structure and almond-shaped eyes—was the perfect foil to Patrick's big, wiry frame. They made sense in a way Brooklyn—short, fluffy and surly—did not. Yes, she loved all her curves, but most men who looked like Patrick didn't appreciate a woman of her stature and size. Shame on them, not her.

Still...

Maybe a tiny part of her would like to know what he preferred. At least when he wasn't drunk off his ass.

"Sure," Patrick said. Then jerking his chin up, he asked, "Brooklyn? Are you coming with us?"

"Why? She already has hot chocolate and—" Kayla dropped her gaze "—cake. Besides, she gets to see you every day. She can do without you for a little while."

Kayla moved forward, but Patrick didn't budge, his attention remaining on her. "Brooklyn?"

Curving her lips in a smile that she didn't feel, she lifted her plate. "No, you two go ahead. I'm going to finish up here then head out for the night. See you tomorrow."

For a long moment he didn't move, and she held his

stare. Yes, part of her wanted to rip Kayla's hands off him. But as quick as the thought entered her head, she dropkicked it down. A certificate didn't make them husband and wife.

Deliberately turning away from him, she smiled at her parents.

"One of my coworkers is over there. I'm going to say hi real quick. I'll talk to you guys later."

Crossing the few feet separating them, she kissed her mom's cheek, then her dad's. Then she left, not turning to watch her husband walk away.

With her sister.

CHAPTER FOUR

PATRICK LOWERED HIS cell phone from his ear, staring down at its home screen. He'd been expecting the call he just ended, but now that it'd arrived...

"Shit," he murmured, rubbing his hand over his head.

Pushing back from his desk, he stood and slid his phone into his front pants pocket. A glance around the open area revealed only empty cubicles. At a little after six o'clock on a Friday evening, he wasn't surprised. The Reindeer Games started in a half hour, and most of the town would be at The Glen for tonight's Yulefest activities.

Most of the town didn't include him and Brooklyn.

He glanced down the length of the room toward the closed office door. Light filtered through the blinds, and he could just glimpse Brooklyn behind her desk. Normally, she worked until six or a little after. But for the past week, she'd extended that time, not leaving until almost seven.

There could be a variety of reasons for that. An uptick in the workload because of the holidays, for one. Preparing for the week after Christmas when Media Mavens would be closed, for another. All legit. But Patrick didn't believe they were the only reasons. Something told him her late nights had something to do with him.

More specifically him and Kayla.

Firming his lips, he bent over, shut down his computer,

grabbed his car keys and, instead of heading for the exit, strode past the empty cubicles toward the closed door.

Enough of this, he growled to himself.

He briefly knocked on the door, and once her, "Come in," filtered through the wood, he turned the knob and entered Brooklyn's office.

Brooklyn glanced up from her computer, and surprise didn't flash through her eyes. As a matter of fact, he couldn't decipher anything from her gaze or expression. That bothered him. In the years they'd known each other, he'd always been able to read her. But now she'd shut him out.

Unease crept through him, and he had to force himself to stay on this side of the office and not round that desk, cup her chin, tilt her head back and demand she talk to him. Order her to let him in.

He thrust his hands into his pockets, fisting them.

"Hey, Patrick. What're you still doing here?" she said, voice pleasant, nice.

He detested it.

Snap at me. Argue with me. Show me you feel something...for me.

"I could ask you the same thing. You've been pulling longer nights lately," he said instead.

She leaned back in her chair, setting the pen clutched in her hand on the desktop.

"With City Hall hiring us to promote Yulefest, there's more to do than usual. But nothing I can't handle." She tilted her head. "Everything okay?"

He considered leaving her to it and walking away, saying nothing. But he couldn't. He wouldn't.

"Cole just called," he informed her. "He has the annulment papers ready for us to sign. Once we do, he can file them with the court. And we'll be done. The marriage will be over."

His gut tightened to the point of pain just uttering the words.

She slowly nodded and exhaled a low, long breath.

"Okay. For some reason I thought it would take longer," she murmured, as if talking to herself. Shaking her head, she met his gaze. "That's good. When are you going over to sign them?"

He shrugged, a flare of anger igniting inside him at her seeming eagerness to end them.

There's no us. There never has been, he thought, and mentally scrabbled away from the resentment in his own head.

It wasn't her fault she couldn't really *see* him.

It wasn't her fault she didn't love him.

"Probably tomorrow during lunch," he said with a shrug of a shoulder. "Did you want to head over together?"

"No, that's okay." She picked up her pen again, fiddling with it, and he focused on the tell before lifting his gaze to hers again. She avoided his eyes by shifting her attention to her computer monitor. "I plan on working through lunch, so I'll call Cole and arrange a time for me to go."

"Why are you avoiding me?" he bluntly asked. "And don't lie to me and say you're not."

"How can I avoid you when we work together?" she tossed back.

He chuckled. "This is how you want to play it? Okay, I'm in." Approaching her desk, he quietly laughed again, and to his own ears, it sounded hard, sharp-edged. "For the last week, you haven't talked to me unless it's work related, and you make damn sure you're not alone with me. When I call, you don't answer and reply by texts.

You've been working late nearly every night and, though Yulefest is one of your favorite festivals, you haven't been to one activity since the lighting." A frown marred her forehead and her lips parted, but he shook his head. Hard. "Don't bother with an excuse. It would only be bullshit, and we both know it."

"I don't know what you want me to say," she said, rising from her office chair.

Pride and a bolt of lust lit him up like a lightning strike. This was the woman he'd come to know and secretly love with a need and passion that, at times, scared him. She didn't back down from anything or anyone, and that stubbornness, that strength, that fierceness, was hot as hell. It stirred a lust in him that had only grown over time, and damn if he didn't think it would drive him out of his mind.

"The truth. Be honest," he snapped, purposefully goading her. Wanting her to unleash her fury on him. Mark him with it. "Tell me why you suddenly find it too hard to talk to me, to be with me."

Be with me.

The words seemed to echo in the taut silence that fell between them. He should've tried to mitigate them, explain that he meant *be with him* as her friend.

But there was enough lying, enough hiding, between them. And in this moment in her office as they stared at one another across her desk like gunslingers intent on taking one another down, he stood on the edge of a precipice. Yes, it sounded dramatic, but he couldn't shake it. This moment would determine how they moved forward with one another.

It would change their lives.

"I don't," she said, that dark brown gaze shifting away, and both frustration and anticipation surged inside him, shoving against his chest. "You're either imagining this or making too much out of it. I'm fine. We're fine."

"No, sweetheart. We're not. And if you don't want to be honest with me, I'll do it." He paused, studying her until she looked at him again. Did she even know how those formerly shuttered eyes now revealed her uncertainty? She'd deny it if she did. Would hate it even more. "Ever since the tree lighting you've been distant. Ever since you left me alone with Kayla—"

"I didn't leave you alone with her," she hotly contested, her eyes narrowing. "You voluntarily left with her, and I don't recall you putting up a fight to stay with me."

Once more a silence descended on the office, and he slowly smiled. For the first time in days—hell, in three years, hope swelled inside him. Hope that maybe, just fucking maybe, this…this thing inside him that craved her wasn't exactly one-sided.

"I asked you to come with us," he softly reminded her, a part of him afraid she would run even now. Not physically, but emotionally. Shut him out.

Brooklyn barked out a dry laugh. "Right. Because I've always enjoyed being the third wheel. It's one of my favorite pastimes," she drawled.

"You wouldn't have been the third wheel," he said. And when she snorted, flicking a dismissive hand at him, he planted his palms on her ruthlessly organized desk and leaned forward so she had no choice but to meet his gaze. Lowering his voice, he reiterated, "Understand what I'm saying, Brooklyn. *You* wouldn't have been the third, unwanted party there."

She stared at him, her chest rapidly rising and falling. The shadows in her eyes deepened, and he immediately knew the moment she'd drawn away from him. Saw the instant her gaze became shuttered again. And he could've roared in defeat, in frustration.

No. Hell no.

For years, he'd backed down. Choosing not to rock the boat. Opting to have a friendship with her rather than no relationship at all if he ever confessed his true feelings for her. Not anymore. For once, he was ready to burn it all to the ground for honesty. To be free from this secret.

To risk it all.

"I don't know what you mean," she whispered. "That doesn't make sense. Kayla's your—"

He sliced a hand through the space between them.

"Kayla hasn't been my anything for a long time," he growled. "You were there. You remember when she broke up with me and ended our relationship. So don't use that to avoid understanding and accepting what I'm telling you."

"You just said it," she said, a glint sparking in her eyes as she jabbed a finger in his direction. "*She* broke up with *you*. And yes, I was there. I also remember how hurt you were when it happened. Those feelings don't just go away. And you weren't exactly fighting her off at the lighting."

He huffed out a low chuckle, true surprise sweeping through him.

"You saw what you wanted to see. What was comfortable and safe for you to see." He straightened, pinning her with an unflinching stare. She tried to glance away from him again, but he wasn't having it. "Look at me, Brooklyn," he quietly demanded, and a shot of pure lust hit him when she obeyed. "Do you know why Kayla and I broke up?"

"Because she left Rose Bend and you didn't want to follow her," she murmured.

"Yes, that's what I allowed her to believe because it was kinder. True, she wanted to leave Rose Bend, and I had no intentions of moving. But in the end, I was more guilty for the end of us than she was."

Brooklyn frowned, her chin jerking back at his cryptic statement. Cryptic to her anyway.

"What are you talking about? What could you possibly have to feel guilty about?"

"If I truly loved Kayla—like she needed and deserved to be loved—nothing would've kept me from being by her side. For the woman I truly, desperately loved, I would follow her across the state, across the country. Hell, across the globe. Job, love for my hometown, be damned. Nothing could keep me from being by her side." He took in her thick curls gathered in a bun on top of her head. The pretty brown eyes wide behind her glasses. The thrust of her firm breasts and the sensual flare of her rounded hips under her purple sweater dress. Desire crackled over his skin, sizzled in his veins, hardening his cock to painful fullness. And his heart... His heart pounded, the beat throbbing in his temples, echoing in his head. Fear, and yes, excitement, hummed inside him, but they were here now. There was no going back. And he didn't want to even if he could.

"Ask me who I would go to the ends of this earth for. Ask me who I would chase down just to be close to her, just breathe her in. Ask me who that person is, Brooklyn."

She swallowed, and he caught the shiver that slightly shook her petite frame. Her eyes closed for a long moment before those thick, dark lashes lifted and she looked at him again. Indecision, and maybe hints of trepidation, flickered across her face. His gut hollowed out.

Fuck.

Maybe he'd pushed too far. Maybe he was so consumed with what he was feeling, what he wanted from her—had wanted for three years now—that he was infringing on her rights, her comfort. No, that wasn't what he—

"Who are they?" Brooklyn's soft question dropped between them like a bomb set on detonation.

And his answer would be the explosion, leaving them forever altered. Either leaving them in pieces, resembling nothing like who they were…or leaving them different but stronger, closer, better.

Again, he flattened his hands on the desk and leaned forward until their faces were only inches apart.

"You. You're the one I'd say fuck it all and follow. You're the one I'd burn my world down for. You're *the one*, Brooklyn."

Slowly, she shook her head, and stumbled back a step. Away from him.

Pain splintered in his stomach, his chest, embedding in his skin, his fucking soul.

He'd taken the risk.

And he'd failed.

He straightened, already preparing to retreat, to withdraw. Of course, he'd known there was a possibility this could happen, had convinced himself he could handle it. And he would. He had to give himself some time, but he would accept her rejection. He loved her enough that he would never punish her for not wanting what he did. Not wanting *him*.

But damn.

None of that meant he didn't feel like he'd drunk a glass full of nails and bled from the inside out.

"You don't want me," Brooklyn whispered, and he froze, unable to leave, to move forward. Unable to breathe. "I know you," she continued in that low, almost pained voice. "You don't want me. You can't…"

"Can't what?" he pressed when she trailed off. An

urgency took residence in him, and he shifted forward until, once more, he neared the desk. "Can't want to take that pretty, sexy mouth and work it over like I want to do to your body? Can't want to drag my name out of that same mouth while I put my hands to those curves that have teased and haunted me for years? Can't want to lose myself in you, watch those gorgeous brown eyes darken as I sink my cock into you?"

He moved even closer until the edge of her desk pressed into his thighs.

"Can't want to protect you though you're strong enough to fight the world? Can't love you beyond reason?" He laughed, and the humorless sound abraded his throat. "Do you know the one regret I have in all of this? Not that I married you. Because even drunk off my ass I would do it again in a heartbeat if it meant I could call you mine. No," he rasped, "my one regret is that I finally got to touch you, kiss you, be deep inside you, and I can't remember one fucking moment of it. I would give anything for those memories. Anything."

He laid it all out there—his truth, his heart, his soul. And his harsh breaths punctuated the room like physical blows.

He stood there, emotionally naked, stripped bare, and he didn't try to cover himself. Slowly, he rounded the desk, giving Brooklyn plenty of time to order him to stop, to move, to retreat again.

But she didn't.

And when he sank to his knees in front of her, his hands cupping her hips, he still paused, offering her the chance to reject him.

But she didn't.

With a half growl, half moan, he pressed his mouth to her gently rounded belly, kissing and nipping at the flesh through her dress. She shuddered, and he absorbed it into his body. But when her hands slid over his head, her nails grazing his scalp to hold him close, he sank into her.

And lost the last of his control.

He shot to his feet and on a low, damn near animalistic growl, he captured her lips, not waiting for her to part for him, but thrusting his tongue inside her mouth. *Fuck.* The taste of her. He licked, stroked, devoured, giving in to and mimicking every dirty fantasy he'd ever dreamed. Burrowing his fingers under her bun, he tugged, and his other hand cupped and squeezed her jaw, commanding without words for her to open wider, give him more. With a moan, she did.

And he gave her mouth a good fucking.

Over and over, he plunged his tongue in and out, back and forth, consuming her. It was everything carnal, wild. And she wasn't a passenger on this roller coaster of a kiss. No, she gave as good as she got. And he—he shuddered in response.

Not content with the kiss, not after imagining this moment for years, he bunched her sweater dress in his fists, yanking it up her thighs, hips, breasts, and finally, over her head. She stood before him, all that gorgeous brown skin gleaming against the white lace bra. God, she was sex and purity. Sin and innocence. Every sweet dream and nasty fantasy all rolled into one lush, sexy package.

He hooked his fingers in the band of her black leggings and dragged them down and off, pausing only to remove her boots. Then, with her startled yelp in his ears, he lifted her in his arms and deposited her on top of the desk.

"Oh my God," she breathed, sitting before him, naked except for her bra.

He took her in, savored the sensual sight that could

grace a classical painting in an Italian gallery...and be depicted in vivid color on the pages of a magazine's centerfold. Exposed, vulnerable yet strong, and so lovely he wanted to bow down before her and worship her.

So he did.

He palmed her thighs, pushing them apart and giving him an unobstructed view of the swollen, glistening folds of her sex. The air in the room vibrated with lust and tension, and her scent, that vanilla-and-jasmine scent, seemed to thicken, adding a decadent perfume to the office.

If he expected her to be shy or modest, she torpedoed that notion immediately when she slid back on her desk and opened her legs wider, fully offering herself to him. Goddamn. Did she crave this as much as he did? That didn't seem possible. But the glistening wetness on her flesh declared otherwise.

"Patrick," she whispered, propping one hand on the desk for support and skating the other over his head, cradling the back of it. Pushing him closer to the hot, soaked center of her.

Right where he wanted to be.

He parted those pretty lower lips with a swipe of his tongue, and added a long, greedy swirl and suckle to her clit. She cried out, her back bowing in a deep arch. Her hips twisted, writhed, and he splayed the fingers of one hand across her belly and thrust his fingers inside her tight, hot sex with the other. Dipping his head, he licked the entrance even as his fingers plied her stroke after stroke.

"Goddamn, sweetheart. You're tight. And wet."

For him. All for him.

He worked another digit inside her, stretching her, and shifted his mouth back to her clit. The taste of her—so tart and fresh on his tongue—had lust threatening to burn him to ashes. His cock throbbed behind his zipper, demanding a sample of what his fingers and mouth enjoyed. Damn, he just needed to fist himself—just one quick tug to ease the ache. But that would require removing his hands from Brooklyn. And that, he wasn't willing to do just yet.

He kept up a steady pump, twisting his wrist to corkscrew his fingers deeper, higher inside her core. Her soft mewls fell around him as she writhed and ground her flesh, meeting every plunge of his fingers.

"That's it, sweetheart," he muttered against her, the sound of his fist bumping against her folds punctuating the air. Her slick walls fluttered around his fingers, signaling her impending orgasm. "Let go. Come for me."

And in the next instant, she stiffened, a low, muted wail escaping her. He continued to thrust into her flesh, making sure she rode the wave of every aftershock. When the last shudder rippled through her body, he rose and recaptured her mouth, giving her the taste of herself. And she didn't shy away from it. Instead, she moaned and licked at his lips, his chin. Then she claimed him in a wild, raw kiss that snapped the last ragged remnants of his control.

With trembling fingers, he tore his shirt off, and his pants and shoes followed. Her hands skated over his shoulders, his chest and belly. And as he ripped open the condom he grabbed from his wallet before tossing it to the floor, too, she fisted his dick and pumped, stroked.

Fire raced up his spine and sped back down, concentrating in his cock and balls. *Holy fuck.* He almost fumbled the condom as he pulled it free and tossed the foiled package in the direction of the wastebasket. He wasn't going to make it. If she continued to jerk him off with her delicate fist and nearly brutal grip, he wouldn't make it inside her.

Gently knocking her hand to the side, he rolled the protection down his length, and because he believed in multitasking, he leaned forward and bent his head, latching on to her nipple over the white lace.

"Oh God. Patrick." She panted, grabbing his head with both hands, and cradling him to her.

He swirled his tongue around her nipple and sucked, and then switched breasts, giving it the same treatment. It wasn't enough. Nothing would ever be enough until he was buried deep inside her.

He glanced down between their bodies, and fuck. His cock appeared damn near brutish pressed against her silken, soft, beautiful folds. So goddamn beautiful, he briefly closed his eyes to block out the sight. To try and gather his fractured control.

Grinding his teeth, he slid his cock between her slick cleft, coating himself in her moisture. The head bumped her clit, and their twin moans permeated the room. His flesh jumped of its own volition, and he couldn't wait any longer.

"Are you with me?" he asked, lodging the head of his dick at her opening.

As much as he just wanted to thrust home and end this torture for both of them, he hesitated. Because after this… There would be no turning back to who and what they'd been to each other. This changed everything. Before he irrevocably altered them, he needed her agreement. Her assurance.

"Sweetheart?" he urged, his voice rough, ragged from the agonized pleasure that had him in a clawed, inescapable grip. "Tell me if you're here with me."

She nodded, gripping his upper arms.

"I'm here." Leaning forward, she brushed a gentle, barely there kiss over his lips. "Fuck me, Patrick."

He thrust forward.

Sheathed all of his cock in the impossibly tight and perfect clasp of her sex.

A cry wrenched free of her, and she buried her face against his chest, her nails digging into his skin. Her muscles quivered around his cock, working to accept and accommodate him. Somehow, he held still, letting her become used to him. It just might cost him his sanity, but he waited. In the meantime, a desperate and ravenous desire twisted his belly, sizzled in the base of his back, tugged at his balls. He was going up in flames, and he wanted to burn in this fire.

"On you, sweetheart," he gritted out between clenched teeth. "Goddamn, you feel so good…"

Her harsh puffs of air battered the bare skin of his chest, but she nodded. And it was all the permission he needed.

He slowly withdrew, and she cried out. Hell, he almost did, too, as his dick dragged over the slick walls of her sex. When only the tip remaining notched inside her, he plunged back in.

Sex shouldn't be this—fuck, *good* didn't cover it. Couldn't begin to describe the heaven and hell of pushing into her and feeling her sex give way for his penetration. His possession. With every stroke, every thrust, he claimed her as his. And with every ripple of her sex over him, whether she acknowledged it or not, she branded him as hers.

On that thought, he gripped her hip and the back of her neck and set a steady, hard ride. He rocked inside her, and the sexual melody of skin smacking skin, the suction of wet flesh releasing and accepting a thrusting cock, his grunts and her whimpers filled the room.

He angled her hips, slamming his to hers, taking her over and over. He wanted to—needed to—lose himself in her. But the crackle and snap of electrical pulses tripping down his spine and burning the soles of his feet relayed he wouldn't last much longer. But he refused to go over into that sweet oblivion without her. Reaching between them, he circled his thumb over her clit, ruthlessly teasing and circling the bundle of nerves.

"Give it to me, Brooklyn. Come for me," he demanded, and as if she'd been waiting on those words, she stiffened, throwing her head back, and erupted with a soundless scream.

And after two, then three pounding strokes, he followed. Just as he would willingly follow her anywhere.

So this was peace. This was contentment.

He hadn't believed he'd ever experience it again. Especially after his father's death.

But this…calm that sank into his bones exceeded anything he'd experienced before. He hadn't known what it was to be truly whole until now. Until he had Brooklyn's scent on him, her body pressed to his, her breath whispering across his skin.

Patrick sighed, nuzzling Brooklyn's curls.

"Are you okay?" he murmured, stroking his hand up and down her spine.

"Yes."

She didn't say more, but her formerly pliant, relaxed body gradually went rigid until she felt like a marble statue on his lap. The peace that had filled him slowly became a thing of the past as dread pressed down on his lungs, infiltrated his veins and spread the unease to every part of his body.

"Sweetheart?" He leaned back, pinched her chin and titled her head up. He needed to peer into her eyes and prayed that he would only glimpse remnants of the pleasure they'd just shared instead of remorse. "What's wrong?"

He would hate to be her regret.

"I..." She turned her head, dislodging his hand. "I should get up. I need to get dressed."

Her usually fluid movements jerky, she scooted off his thighs and bent down, hurriedly grabbing her clothes off the floor. For a moment all he could do was watch her dress, numb with shock and confusion. Finally, as she tugged the sweater material down over her legs, he jolted out of his paralysis and rose from the chair. Their nudity hadn't bothered him just seconds ago, but now he felt exposed, raw.

Following suit, he dragged his clothes on and buttoning his shirt, he studied Brooklyn. Noted her trembling hands as she smoothed them over her hair, then down her hips. In the space of seconds, they'd gone from lovers to awkward strangers.

And he hated it.

"Brooklyn," he murmured, abandoning his shirt and moving toward her, hand outstretched. "Sweetheart, what's wrong?"

She shifted backward, away from him, and he jerked to a stop, dropping his arm to his side. Pain bloomed behind his sternum, red hot and searing.

"Patrick." She stroked her palm over her hair again, the gesture nervous, agitated. "I don't..."

"Nothing's changed," he finished flatly.

"I don't want to hurt you," she whispered. "God, I don't want to hurt you. But this..." Her lips flattened, and she briefly closed her eyes. "This was a mistake. We shouldn't have—"

"Why? Give me your reasons why," he demanded, voice a harsh rasp.

Give me your reasons why you're throwing us away before we truly begin.

"Patrick, there are several reasons, and we can't ignore any of them as if they'll just disappear because we will them to. I'm your employer," she said, ticking them off on her fingers. "You're still my sister's ex. We wouldn't just be hurting her, but my whole family. Kayla and I might not be close, but I can't do this—" she waved a hand back and forth between them "—to her."

"So what's changed? You were my boss when you moaned into my mouth. I was your sister's ex when you welcomed me inside you. You were—"

"Please. Stop," she rasped, holding up a hand, palm out.

But he didn't stop. Not now when it seemed as if he was fighting for them. Not when he was losing. He moved forward until that palm pressed against his chest, and he covered her hand with his.

"I won't. Not when you're determined to place everyone's opinions about who you are and what you do above your own. What do you want? What about your happiness? Isn't yours as important—if not more—than anyone else's? Don't you deserve a life that doesn't just include work but love? You should be a priority in your own life."

"Are you kidding me?" She snatched her hand out from under his. "Are you really saying this to me? Sex doesn't suddenly make you an expert on me or what I should want or deserve."

"Maybe not. But years of friendship does. Sweetheart." He spread his hands wide, staring down at them. Imagining them stroking over her skin. Hurting at the thought of never doing it again. He fisted them and looked up, meeting her angry gaze. "You've spent so many years fighting for your parents' approval, their attention, that you don't know what it looks like to be unconditionally accepted and loved. You don't recognize it when it's standing here right before you, offering itself to you. No strings. No conditions."

He ached to touch her, draw her close, hold her. But he couldn't—no, he wouldn't. And not just because he respected her space and obvious desire to place emotional and physical distance between them.

No, he refused because he'd fought for them. It was her turn now.

"I love you," he murmured. "I've loved you for longer than I had any business doing. Yet, I've never regretted the space you've carved out for yourself inside me. I've chosen you—I did years go. But this time, it's your turn to choose me...choose us."

"Patrick." Her voice broke on his name, and he stepped back, fixing his clothes.

As brave as he wanted to be in this moment, he couldn't look at her any longer. If he did, he might fall to his knees and beg her to take him as hers.

And he couldn't do that. Not to her. And not to himself.

Both of them deserved more.

"I'll see you Monday."

He rounded the desk, pausing only to grab his keys from where he'd dropped them on the floor and left the office, quietly closing the door shut behind him.

Shutting the door on what could've been.

CHAPTER FIVE

THERE WERE *SO* many Santas.

Brooklyn stood in front of Sunnyside Grille, scanning Main Street and the crowds of people dressed in Santa Claus costumes. They congregated in the cordoned-off street and on either side of it, filling the sidewalks to capacity.

The annual Santa Run was set to commence, and everyone's excitement practically danced on the air. This time last year her own eagerness and delight would've joined theirs. This Yuletide event had always been one of her favorites. Seriously, what wasn't to enjoy about people partnering up and running an obstacle course down the length of Main Steet, and all the while dressed up as Santa? Absolutely nothing. And that money earned from the run went to charity only sweetened an already fun occasion.

But this year was different from last year and all the ones before it. Then, she'd been blind to so many things. Then, her happiness didn't hang in the balance.

You've spent so many years fighting for your parents' approval, their attention, that you don't know what it looks like to be unconditionally accepted and loved. You don't recognize it when it's standing here right before you, offering itself to you.

Patrick's words rang in her head as they had been for the past two nights. They haunted her, pursued her even into sleep. She couldn't escape them. And after not hearing from him for the past couple of days, she realized she didn't want to outrun them. On the contrary, she longed to embrace and hold them close like a treasured heirloom, guarding them in her heart.

Maybe because he'd made love to her with such passion and emotion that she'd been irrevocably changed afterward... Maybe because he'd been so damn brave and laid himself bare before her... Maybe because she'd never felt so desired, so needed, so vital to someone else's existence in her life... It could be all three or none of them, but whatever the reason, she'd felt a yawning void inside her, and it'd only grown wider and deeper with each passing moment that she didn't hear his voice, or see his beautiful face or touch that strong, sheltering body.

When confronted with the emptiness that had nearly swallowed her whole, fear had no place to hide or seek cover. She'd rather face the rejection and anger of her family than not be with the man courageous enough to love her.

So she had a decision to make.

"Brooklyn, we've been looking everywhere for you," a very familiar and oh yes, grating, voice called.

Showtime.

She turned to face Kayla, who stood behind her with their parents. Brooklyn's heart hammered at her chest as if it were trying to make a hole to the other side. Fear tasted metallic on her tongue, but she didn't allow that to stop her from approaching her family.

"You asked us to find you down here, and that it was urgent," Kayla griped, crossing her arms. "Although I don't see what could possibly be so important if we're discussing it during a Santa Run."

Patience. She's your sister. You cannot air her out in

the middle of Main Street. No matter how much you're dying to.

"Is something wrong, honey?" Her mother tilted her head, her gaze roaming up and down Brooklyn as if searching out any possible injuries.

"No, I'm fine. It's just that I have to do something this evening, but I needed to talk to all of you first before I did it." God, that sounded cryptic as hell. And confusing. "I know I'm not making much sense at the moment."

Kayla arched an eyebrow, but before she could respond, her father shifted closer and said, "What is it, honey? We're listening."

Giving him a grateful look, Brooklyn inhaled a deep breath and took a moment to meet the gaze of each of her family members. How to broach this? Ease into it with some background about her and Patrick's friendship? Apologize and then—

"Patrick and I are married."

Well, damn.

That announcement leaped out of her mouth before she even registered what she'd been about to say. And now, despite the racket going on around them, the words seemed to reverberate and gain volume with each passing second.

But it was out there now, and she couldn't take it back. And she wouldn't even if she could. A huge weight lifted from her shoulders and chest, and for the first time since she'd woken up in Vegas, she could breathe deep, easy. It was cleansing. And she felt almost…free.

"I'm sorry," her mother slowly said. "Did you just say you and Patrick are married?"

"My Patrick?" Kayla repeated, staring without blinking. She shook her head. "What the hell are you talking about? That's not possible."

"Language in front of your mother, Kayla," her father said to her, but not moving his gaze from Brooklyn.

"Not your Patrick," Brooklyn said, gently but firmly correcting Kayla. "Mine. Because yes, it's not only possible but fact. He's my husband."

Kayla's mouth went slack with shock and her arms dropped to her sides. Before she could reply, though, her mother held up a hand, silencing her.

"Brooklyn Regina Hayes. Explain. Everything," she ordered in a flinty voice that brooked no argument.

And so she did, relaying their drunken marriage in Las Vegas—but withholding that part about waking up naked next to each other—seeking an annulment from Cole, and finally Patrick's declaration of his feelings for her. Again, leaving out having sex in her office.

"I know this is shocking to you guys. Honestly, it still is to me, too. This is so new that I'm still wrapping my head around it. But..." She shook her head. "I don't want the annulment any longer. I love Patrick. And if he'll forgive me, I'm going to ask him not to sign the papers and remain married to me."

"Forgive you?" her father asked. "For what?"

"For being afraid." She glanced to the left, suddenly aware that they stood in the middle of a festival while she came clean to her parents, her sister. Which was silly since she'd asked for this meetup here. Shrugging, she forged ahead. "I was too afraid of what you would say, how you would react, to accept his love for me. I let him walk away and I'm not sure if he will forgive that."

The corner of her father's mouth twitched. "Oh, I'm betting he will. You Hayes women have a way with your men. We'll give you anything, including grace."

"Milo," her mother snapped. "Now is not the time."

"I'm giving our daughter advice. How isn't it?"

"Daddy, are you serious right now?" Kayla turned and pinned their dad with an incredulous look. "How can you be so calm? And so…" Her hands flapped in front of her before she whipped back around to glare at Brooklyn. "You stole my man. God, will it ever stop with you? It isn't enough that you've always tried to one-up me our entire lives. Yet, this one man in all of Rose Bend, hell, the state of Massachusetts, and you want him? You marry him? Have you ever heard of loyalty? Or doesn't it bother you even a little bit that he chose me first and you're my sloppy seconds?"

"Kayla Ryan Hayes!" Their mother jerked toward Kayla, shock widening her eyes. "We don't talk like that to each other in this family."

"No, Mom, that's okay," Brooklyn said, and then focused her attention on her sister. "For some reason, you've always thought I was in competition with you or vice versa. When I've only ever wanted to celebrate you, not undermine you in any way. You may not believe this, Kayla, but I did none of this to hurt you. As a matter of fact, you were one of the reasons I demanded an annulment and turned Patrick away. I didn't intend to fall in love with him, but I also can't deny that I did, and I do. Love him, that is. And as much as I love you and regret hurting you, I won't give him up."

"You're selfish, and no, I don't believe you didn't do this to deliberately hurt me," Kayla snarled, and Brooklyn sighed.

She wouldn't get through to her sister now—if ever. Here and now, no matter what Brooklyn said, Kayla wouldn't hear it. And if their roles were reversed, Brooklyn might feel the same way. Still, she couldn't pack everything back inside. And she had no desire to.

"I'm sorry you think that," Brooklyn murmured. Shifting her gaze back to her parents, she continued, "I'm sorry if I've disappointed you or let you down. I tried to avoid this. I really did. But as much as I love you both, he's my happiness, my future."

Her father frowned. "You've never disappointed us, Brooklyn. I would be lying if I said this didn't come as a shock, but you should never question my love for you. Or your mother's."

"What your father said. We're going to have a conversation about this disappointment thing," her mother warned, eyes narrowed. "But we love you and Patrick. And well, you're already married…"

"Mom, Dad." Kayla gaped at her parents, then shot an ugly look at Brooklyn before turning back to her parents. "You can't be supporting this. What—"

"Kayla, I love you, but this isn't about you." Her mother patted her sister's arm. "Go get your man, honey," she said to Brooklyn. "And bring him to me later so I can rip him a new one for lying to me about this marriage."

"What your mother said," her father added with a wide smile.

Love for her parents swelled in her, and the last sharp edges of her fear crumbled away. They didn't reject her. And possibly…they never had. Maybe she'd had their approval and affirmation all along, and her own insecurities had prevented her from seeing it or accepting it. Maybe…

She'd analyze it all later. Right now she held tight to her parents' love and needed to go claim her own.

"I'll be back," she promised, then turned and strode forward into the crowd.

Finding him among the Santas wouldn't be easy, but giving up wasn't an option. Patrick wouldn't skip this event; he was out here somewhere, and she would find him.

She pushed through the people, scanning her side of the sidewalk, the street and across it. As she neared her office building, she pulled her cell free from her coat pocket. Maybe he would answer although they'd left things—

"Patrick," she whispered his name but somehow he seemed to hear her or perhaps sense her.

He leaned against the doorway of their building, a red-and-white Santa coat over his sweater and jeans, a hat loosely held in front of him. As he lifted his head and caught sight of her approaching, he slowly straightened, pushing away from the brick doorway.

All the things she wanted to say rolled through her mind on a whirlwind. But she didn't say any of them.

No, she strode up to him and didn't stop. Didn't stop until she reached him and threw her body against his, depending on him to catch her. And he did. His big, strong hands gripped her hips, and she cupped his face, tipping it down as she rose on her toes.

She kissed him.

In front of the whole town, right there on Main Street, she kissed him and claimed him as hers.

At first, he didn't react, remained frozen.

And as her heart throbbed painfully in her chest, his grip tightened on her. He parted his lips and wrenched control of the kiss, taking her mouth in a furious, fierce kiss that set her ablaze. Winding her arms around his neck, she clung to him, surrendering to the passion that wrapped around them in a fiery embrace.

When he finally lifted his head, it was only far enough to stare down into her eyes, their breath still comingling.

"Tell me," he ordered, raising one hand to her cheek. "I need to hear it."

She didn't need for him to clarify. She simply knew.

"I love you. And I'm so sorry for not taking that leap with you on Friday. For letting you leave. Please forgi—"

"Shh." He shook his head, placing a softer but no less passionate kiss on her lips. "There's nothing to forgive or apologize for. You just had to get here, and I'm just thankful you didn't take too long."

She smiled, and not even the Christmas lights strung above them could rival the brightness inside her.

"Me, too—oh wait." She loosened her arms from around him and dug a hand into her coat pocket. A moment later she pulled free the large plastic ring and held it up. "Patrick King, will you marry me...again?"

A grin slowly spread across his face, and she blinked at the beauty of it. He lifted his left hand, and she slid the plastic jewelry on his ring finger.

"On one condition." He threaded his fingers through hers, kissing the backs. "You meet me in front of the Christmas tree, and we make both of our dreams come true."

She blinked back the sudden sting of tears, and briefly closed her eyes before reopening them and meeting his beautiful turquoise eyes.

"Deal."

He sealed his promise—and their future—with a kiss.

* * * * *

Do you love romance books?

JOIN

on Facebook by scanning the code below:

A group dedicated to book recommendations, author exclusives, SWOONING and all things romance! A community made for romance readers by romance readers.

Facebook.com/groups/readloverepeat